THE HUMMING BLADE

CHRISTOPHER CLARK

ISBN: 978-1-4834-4715-5 (sc)
ISBN: 978-1-4834-4717-9 (hc)
ISBN: 978-1-4834-4716-2 (e)

Library of Congress Control Number: 2016903034

Lulu Publishing Services rev. date: 02/25/2016

For my father, who taught me three important things: courage in the face of adversity, calm during the strongest of storms, and the proper way to attach jumper cables without electrocuting myself.

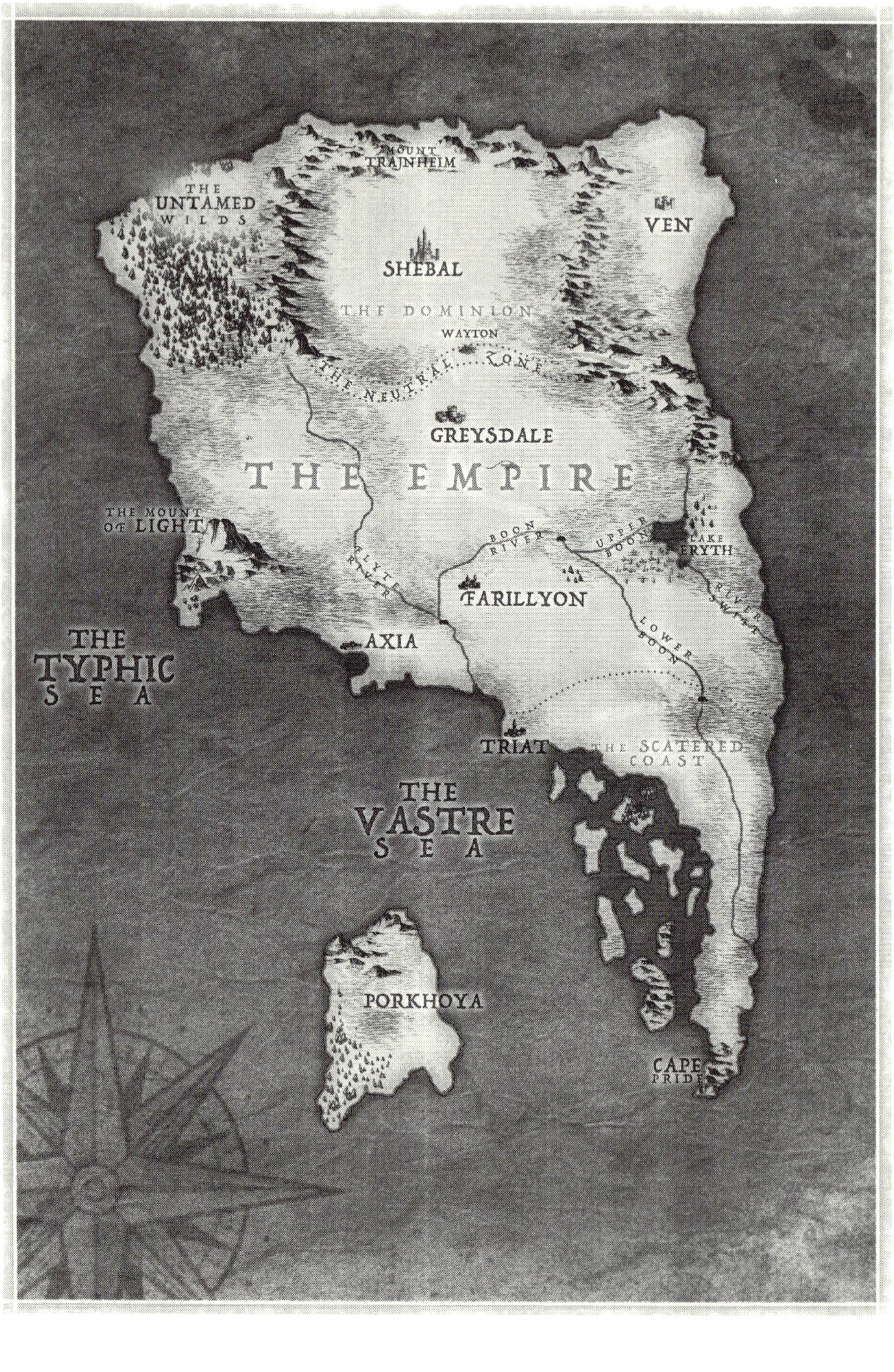

MOUNT TRAJNHEIM
THE UNTAMED WILDS
VEN
SHEBAL
THE DOMINION
WAYTON
THE NEUTRAL ZONE
GREYSDALE
THE EMPIRE
THE MOUNT OF LIGHT
BOON RIVER
UPPER BOON
LAKE ERYTH
FLYTE RIVER
FARILLYON
RIVER SWIFT
LOWER BOON
AXIA
THE TYPHIC SEA
TRIAT
THE SCATERED COAST
THE VASTRE SEA
PORKHOYA
CAPE PRIDE

CHAPTER ONE

Lub-dub. Lub-dub. Lub-dub.

Someone was beating a drum. The deep, rhythmic pounding resonated in Wyatt's ears, making it very difficult to sleep. The more he tried to ignore it, the louder it seemed to get, which deeply annoyed him. Why was someone playing a drum while he was trying to sleep?

Suddenly, the world slammed back into place with alarming, painful quickness. Wyatt gasped in pain as he shifted underneath a pile of sharp, heavy debris. Everything sounded muffled and distorted, as if his head were underwater. He could still hear his heart thrumming in his ears, bringing a fresh surge of pain with every beat. He tried to take a deep breath, but the acrid taste of smoke caught in his throat and he choked and coughed, his lungs burning in his chest.

Gritting his teeth, he steeled himself for a moment before giving a mighty pull, wrenching his leg from underneath something heavy. He desperately thrashed his arms and, when he felt a small pocket of open space, crawled out from beneath the pile of debris. He rolled out onto the cobbled stones of a street, blinking furiously as he stared out into the flickering light of a fire that lit the otherwise-black night.

Or many fires, he realized, as he took in his surroundings, trying to get his bearings. He was in the flaming ruins of a city, having just wrenched his way free of the demolished wreckage of a small building. All around him the city burned, producing a haze of black smoke and stifling heat that made him briefly reconsider his decision to climb free.

1

However, he could see that the street continued to his left, toward the heart of the burning city. To his right, it appeared that another large building had collapsed, blocking the street with a mountain of stone and wood.

Wyatt clambered to his feet, checking himself over quickly. He was covered in scrapes and bruises, but nothing important seemed to be damaged. His clothes were tattered and torn, appearing to have taken most of the abuse caused by whatever it was that had happened to him.

He looked around again, trying to fight the panic that was rising within him like a hot, bubbling acid. He didn't remember being in a city. He didn't remember ever being in a city at any time in his life. He'd only ever seen paintings and read descriptions of the magnificent cities of the Empire. His home city of Ven was about the furthest thing from a city it could possibly get. How had he gotten here?

He slowly walked down the street, keeping his eyes open for anyone who might be able to tell him exactly what was going on. After a few moments, he stumbled, nearly landing face-first on the hard stones beneath him as something caught between his feet. He twisted, landing awkwardly on his back and looking down at his feet in alarm. Somehow, they had gotten caught on a leather baldric that he had managed to completely miss as he was walking. He adjusted himself and sat up, grabbing the scabbard attached to the baldric and pulling it close to inspect it carefully.

The leather was in pristine condition, expertly tooled with intricate, elegant designs. The scabbard itself was equally beautiful. It wasn't gaudy or flashy; rather, the designs on the leather were so subtle and well designed that only the closest of inspections would show just how expertly the whole thing was crafted. From the end of the scabbard jutted the handle of a blade. Wyatt could see a simple curving crossguard that capped off a black, leather-wrapped grip. The pommel was perhaps the most strange of all; it flared out at the end in the shape of a flat hexagon. Wyatt peered at it closely, and saw that the points on the edges were all connected in the center by carefully etched lines.

He took the grip in his hand, and suddenly the throbbing in his body and the fear inside of him eased as his mind focused. As he touched the sword, the whole thing seemed to hum in response, a hum that permeated his whole being. It moved within him, settling his nerves with a soothing strength. It reminded him of being a scared child, comforted by his mother during a storm. He breathed deep, for the first time not noticing the smoke or ash as his lungs tasted cool, sweet air.

Instinctively, he gripped the scabbard in his left hand and drew the sword in his right, seeing his bright blue eyes reflected in the gleaming, polished surface of the blade. It was not unlike the arming swords that Imperial soldiers carried. The blade was slightly broader at the base than it was at the tip. However, it was longer than those Wyatt had seen carried by the soldiers, as was the handle. It was light, perfectly balanced, and expertly crafted, the perfect match to the scabbard that had held it. And like that scabbard, the blade was not flamboyant, but commanded a different kind of power and respect in its simplicity.

Wyatt slid the blade back into the sheath, and before he knew it he was lifting the leather baldric over his head and strapping it around his chest. It fit him perfectly. The sword rested comfortably at his hip, and even without his hand on the grip Wyatt could still feel it humming softly. He felt that same presence, radiating strength and focus through his entire being.

Climbing to his feet, Wyatt set off down the road again, resting one hand on the pommel of the sword. He walked with a quicker, more determined pace now; although he had no idea what was going on, he at least had one good thing that had come out of this strange series of events. More importantly, he didn't feel as terrified. The sword was like a friend at his side; although they were both lost in the dark, Wyatt knew that somehow, he was at least not alone.

Wyatt made his way through the city, unable to stop himself from being amazed at the architecture and grandeur that spread around him. But as amazing as the great city was, just as amazing was the level of destruction that had come down upon it. He looked down side streets and alleys and saw entire sections of the city in ruin. Towers had toppled. Cathedrals had been wrecked. And nearly everything was on fire.

Alarm was steadily growing within him. He had been wandering through the sacked and broken place for what felt like ages, and yet he hadn't seen a single soul. Not even a body or any other sign of life. He couldn't find anybody trying to escape, nor did he encounter looters making use of the chaos and destruction. After a long time of unsuccessful searching, he was starting to get paranoid.

Where was everybody?

Finally, after several more fruitless minutes of walking around and peeking into wreckage after wreckage, the long street Wyatt had been wandering opened up into a magnificent square. The center was barely illuminated by the burning buildings around it, but Wyatt could just make out a large shape at the center, likely a fountain or obelisk of some sort. The thought of water in his dry mouth was more than enough motivation for him to investigate, so he pressed forward at a faster pace, deeply hoping that it was a fountain, and that it still worked. ·

As he drew closer, he nearly yelped in joy as he saw that it was, in fact, a large fountain. He couldn't yet tell if there was still water pouring out of it, but before he could draw close enough to find out, he saw something else at the base of it. A single human form was lying there, looking like it had been trying to climb up the base and into the water. Its arms reached pitifully upward, but they moved no longer, frozen in death.

Wyatt took a deep breath and gripped the hilt of his sword, steeling himself for the worst as he slowly, cautiously walked toward the body. He got within a few feet of it when, to his shock, it stirred.

Wyatt leapt backward, landing in a crouch and watching it with narrowed eyes as it slowly, awkwardly got to its feet. Wyatt tried to calm himself; he realized that whoever it was must not have been dead, and had probably just fallen before he saw them and just now come to. Likely, they were wounded in the disaster and would need his help.

"Hello," said Wyatt cautiously, calling out to it and standing up straight again. "Are you okay?"

The form's head cocked, and after a moment it turned to look at him with a slow, jerky motion that was incredibly off-putting. Wyatt looked at the face for a moment before shock and fear hit him like a fist to the gut. Panic danced at the edges of his mind as he backed up.

The eyes of the figure were black and lifeless. Its skin, bloody and rotting, hung off in flaps, revealing patches of bone and muscle beneath it. It opened its mouth as it slowly staggered forward, letting out a sound like a hiss and a roar at the same time as black, stinking fluid leaked out from the gaps left by its missing teeth. The scent of decay assailed Wyatt's senses as the horrible monster staggered toward him, hands raised.

Wyatt went for the sword, but the hilt that his hand had been gripping moments before was suddenly gone. He blinked in confusion and looked down, staring at the spot where the sword had hung from the baldric. But the baldric was gone too, and gone with it was the feeling of strength and calm that the sword had sent resonating through his entire being. Fear and panic rose inside him, and he was struggling to keep them from taking him over.

His eyes flicked up again. The corpse was closer, its rotting dead fingers mere feet from his face. He skipped backward again, unable to suppress a shout as it swiped at him. He turned to run from it, fear taking him over as hope was banished from his mind. But he stopped short, recoiling again as more ragged, rotting forms staggered out from the shadows around him. They came from all directions, and Wyatt could see the burning city reflected on their dead, soulless eyes.

He turned, looking in every direction for some kind of escape, some avenue that he could use to flee. But they drew in from every direction, and he realized soon that they were closing in all around him like a horde of bloodthirsty animals. They hissed and roared and snarled as they drew in on him, the horrible sounds ringing in his ears as the stink of them grew stronger, almost overpoweringly so.

He bumped into something, and felt a hand grip his shoulder. He shouted and lashed out at it. His fist connected with a sickly crunch as he smacked the thing aside. He danced away from it, but he bumped into another one. He was flailing and kicking at them, but they surged in all around him, hissing as they drew near to their prey.

Wyatt fell, landing harshly on his wrist. Pain seared through his arm as he rolled awkwardly, trying to get to his feet. But he realized that it didn't matter. He had nowhere to go.

Dead hands reached for him. Wyatt closed his eyes, sending a frantic prayer to anyone that might be listening as doom closed in all around him.

Deep beneath the earth, something stirred in the very dark. It wasn't a new something, and up until that moment, it had forgotten that it was even a something at all. But the circumstances had been predetermined, and in that moment, it began to be again.

The ground rumbled, a sympathetic reaction to the force that stirred within it. The earth itself seemed to yawn and stretch, shrugging off centuries of sleep.

At that very moment, in that very cave, a small, tan cat faded into view, his luminous golden eyes peering around the cave with distaste. He didn't remember going to sleep in a cave. In fact, he didn't remember much of anything. But, considering the situation, it was entirely likely that he had been put there with the hope that he would never get out.

They had always underestimated him.

The cat curled up on the stone, licking his left paw pleasantly. It felt good to be awake again, he realized. Now if he could just remember why he was supposed to wake up…

Wyatt,

It feels like ages since I left home, even though it's only been six months. Soon I get to leave this smelly training academy and venture out into the front lines. No doubt those will be smelly, too, but at least I won't have to do pushups out there. It's definitely nice to be looking at the end of training. It's been hard, but I will say I learned a lot.

It sounds like I'm going to be sent to the northwest, where the Empire's having problems with wildlings. I heard they've been knocking over little farming towns for supplies, kidnapping the women and children, that kind of thing. I had hoped they'd send me south to the Scattered Coast. I've always wanted to see Cape Pride, and I definitely like the idea of riding on a boat battling pirates, but I think they want to save that stuff for more experienced soldiers and sailors. I've never sailed a day in my life, so that probably didn't do me any favors.

The captain of my unit took a liking to me, though. First in class with an arming sword and a longbow. He wants me to try my hand at mounted combat – says my parents are wealthy enough that someday, I'll be able to make it as a Knight if I study and pay attention to what he does. I never even considered being a commander, but it seems that's the way things are going.

You'll be here with me soon, though. Don't worry. Once you make it through the harvest, your mom said she'd give you her blessing and let you enlist. You'll be a bit behind, but I can probably swing getting you assigned to my unit. You've always been a great fighter, and I know you're an even better shot with a bow than I am, even if you are out of practice. It'll be great, Wyatt. That's what we trained so hard for growing up, right?

I'll be back in Ven soon, but I only have a day to be there. Let's meet up in the usual spot. I'm not sure what day I'll be back, but I'll get the message to you when I am. Be ready.

I'll see you soon, Arden.
Des

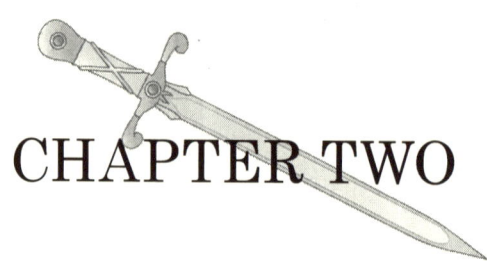

CHAPTER TWO

Wyatt twisted, landing awkwardly on the floor with a painful thud. He groaned, trying to roll over, but he only half-managed it. He realized foggily that something was holding his legs. He lay there for a moment, his heart pounding in his chest. He could feel sweat soaking his clothes. Finally, he let one eye peek open and winced at the harsh light of the day. He looked down at himself, utterly bewildered.

His blanket had wrapped around his legs like a snake, binding them in a wholly awkward position. He looked around, trying to get a handle on whatever was going on. But he wasn't in that strange city anymore, nor was he being devoured by walking corpses. He was in his bedroom, lying on the floor and feeling exceptionally foolish.

"It was a dream," he whispered, trying to slow his heart, which felt like it was trying to break out of his chest.

He twisted himself again, removing the blanket from around him and throwing it irritably back up to the bed. Climbing to his feet, Wyatt moved to the corner of his bedroom, where there stood a tall mirror. He steadied himself in front of it, took a deep breath, and peered into his own very blue eyes.

Stormy blue, his mom had always called them. She said they changed color with his mood, like the sky during a thunderstorm.

But aside from being a little shaken and sweaty, he looked fine. His messy brown hair, ever the object of his mother's ire, hung down into his eyes, damp with sweat. A patchy beard was beginning to show on his strong jaw. He scratched the stubble, annoyed at the thought of having to shave it yet again. It was one of the less-great things about getting older. His mother always seemed to complain about that, too. He had to be presentable, after all.

The rest of him was exactly the same. Tall and thin, he had put on a bit of muscle in the last few years, resulting in a lean, tough frame. Tan lines framed his arms and neck, a result of many hours spent working in the fields. A pale, splotchy scar highlighted the right side of his chest from an accident in the blacksmith's shop when he was a child. He traced it idly with one finger for a moment, his memory flashing back.

Shaking himself, Wyatt focused, trying to remove the last lingering effects of the dream. It had really felt like he had been there. He was finding it difficult to get those images out of his mind: the smell of smoke, the heat, the feel of those rough hands on him... All of it was still fresh in his mind, making it hard to focus on the day ahead.

Finally, Wyatt tore his gaze away from the mirror, looking out the window. The dim morning light confirmed his fear; it was just before sunup, hours before he had intended on waking up. He looked longingly at his bed for a moment, but decided it wouldn't be worth the little extra sleep he may get. The way he was feeling, he'd probably just end up lying there, staring at the wall. The dream had shaken him too much, and he knew that if he did get back to sleep, it would be just in time for him to wake up and get moving. He decided that it was best just to get an early start and try to ignore the fatigue.

He glanced at the open letter on his desk. It was a big day. Today was the last opportunity he'd have to see his friend Desmond before he marched off to the Imperial Army, fighting wildlings on the other side of the continent. Today was Wyatt's last chance to wish his best friend good luck, and his last chance to relive the memories of his childhood that seemed to grow more distant every day. Desmond and Wyatt had always dreamed of joining the Army together, but when the time came to enlist, Wyatt decided that he was needed in Ven, on the farm, with his mom. Desmond had no such restrictions.

Wyatt grabbed a towel out of his dresser, along with a cake of soap. A quick wash in the river would help him clear his mind, he decided.

He quickly made his bed, setting everything back in its place, erasing the chaotic state it had been in when he woke up. He'd never hear the end of it if he left the bed so unkempt. That done, he headed out of his room and down the stairs into the main floor of his house.

His mother was sitting in the kitchen, eating a small breakfast before she started her work for the day. Her graying blonde hair was tied back where it always seemed to be, in a messy bun. As Wyatt grew older, he seemed to notice more and more lines on her face, but she was beautiful nonetheless. Most of all, she was quite happy; a cheery smile always seemed to grace her lips. Whenever she saw him, that smile broke into a grin, a look she reserved for her son alone.

As he walked into the kitchen, Nora did just that. She looked up from the table, her eyes shining with pride and love and a lot of other things Wyatt couldn't quite understand. Having grown up with only one parent, Wyatt was incredibly close to his mother. He was also incredibly protective of her. A few years ago, one of her business partners had gotten angry with her over some crops that were lost due to a freak storm. He had raised his hand, but before the man had been able to strike her, Wyatt was there. When Nora told the story, she said that it took everything she had to pry Wyatt off of the man. By the time she managed it, he'd already received a sound beating at the hands of a fourteen year old.

She later had proclaimed it one of the proudest moments of her life.

"What's got you up so early?" asked Nora softly, sipping from a steaming cup of coffee. Wyatt had no idea how she could drink the stuff.

"Had a bad dream," mumbled Wyatt. "You know how I get those sometimes."

She set down her coffee, frowning. "Yeah, but I don't really like it. Want to talk about it?"

Wyatt shook his head. "I'm gonna go for a wash in the river… clear my head. I'm fine. I'll be back in a little bit."

His mother watched him for a few moments, her soft brown eyes studying him. After a bit, she nodded. "Sure. Don't forget that I need you to run into town and fetch some things from Kelsar. The weather seems favorable, so I imagine it's a good day to get it done."

Kelsar was the town blacksmith, and also a very close family friend.

Old, grizzled, and huge, Wyatt had known few men to cut as imposing a figure as Kelsar. He'd been around as long as Wyatt could remember, always helping Nora when she needed it. He'd often wondered if there was a history there, but Nora had always treated him with a bit of detachment, so Wyatt had eventually decided that they were simply colleagues and friends. Wyatt had never had a father, but he did have Kelsar, who did his best to teach Wyatt whenever Nora wasn't around. The old man would never admit it, but he was very fond of the both of them. He was always there when they needed him.

"Yeah," said Wyatt with a nod. "I'll have plenty of time. I want to see Des too, you know... before he leaves again."

She smiled at him warmly, setting down her coffee. "Take your time, honey. There's no hurry."

He nodded again, waving at her as he ducked out the door. In all honesty, his dream and his best friend leaving weren't exactly things he wanted to talk about. He was close to his mother, sure, but he'd never been good at getting things out, getting things off of his chest. Their bond was a quiet, unspoken thing. They didn't need words to understand each other.

Wyatt could smell the springtime as he stepped out into the crisp morning air. Wearing only his bedclothes, he was a little bit chilly, but he knew that the river would warm him up. That river was one of the attractions of Ven; even in wintertime, the waters ran warm and clean. A traveling merchant had once told him that there was a spirit of fire living under the ground that heated the water with its anger, but Wyatt didn't believe it. That kind of stuff never happened so far away from civilization. Ven wasn't interesting enough for a fire spirit to settle there, if there was such a thing.

The river was only a few hundred feet behind the house, at the bottom of the hill on which the house sat. Trees sparsely lined the edge, giving it a decent amount of shelter from view, and also providing a good shelter from the chilly wind. The location of this particular bend in the river was one of the things he'd always loved about living here; it was convenient, and a good place to relax and wind down when he didn't want to be around anyone else.

Shedding his clothes, Wyatt set his things aside on the shore and slipped into the warm waters. The current tugged lazily at his feet, but it wasn't nearly strong enough to actually pull him anywhere. He'd been to this spot numerous times, and knew that it was the perfect place to bathe. He grabbed the soap and began to scrub himself intently, his mind wandering far from that little river.

Thoughts of his dream slowly crept back into his head. He'd never had one like that before. He'd had bad dreams before, sure. It was sort of a recurring condition, something his mother had always worried about. But he'd never experienced anything like that. And he couldn't help but feel that this one really was different. It had been so vivid, and he could still place all the sensations. He could still smell the smoke, feel it burning in his lungs.

But the sword… well, he would have to ask Kelsar about that. If anyone knew about famous, possibly magical swords, it would be the blacksmith. Wyatt was pretty sure Kelsar knew everything about everything. The old man had never failed to answer one of Wyatt's many questions. Hopefully the two of them could figure it out. Wyatt wasn't likely to forget what it looked like, and knew he could probably draw it if necessary. Maybe it really was real, and had belonged to some famous Knight or hero.

"Stop being stupid," he told himself. "You've never seen a weapon like that. There's no way it could be real if you've never seen it before. It was just a dream, Wyatt."

Sighing, he finished washing himself and floated in the water for a time, in no real hurry to go back to the house and start running errands. Even worse, he was getting closer and closer to having to see Desmond off. Thinking about it made his insides twist and squirm. He was happy that his best friend had found a calling in life, but he also couldn't help but be jealous. His mother needed him here, and he wasn't going to be able to join the Army like Desmond until after the harvest. And Desmond had already gone through training, something they were supposed to do together. The Army was the only real way out of a town like Ven, and Wyatt couldn't quite suppress the creeping feeling that he wouldn't ever get out.

After a few more minutes of thinking and floating, Wyatt sighed again and climbed out of the water. After drying off, he threw his clothes back on and started back up the hill, toward the house. He always hated the walk back up that hill, as the cool morning air became quite cold on his damp, warm skin. By the time he got back to his house, his teeth were chattering.

Wyatt walked back into the kitchen, peering around. It looked like Nora had already gone out to start working with everyone else. After a bit more investigation, however, he found a note from her on the table, pinned to a list of items he recognized as blacksmith's products. He picked it up, reading it over quickly.

> *Wyatt,*
> *Here's the list of things I need you to get from Kelsar. He already has a copy of the list, but he does like to forget things. He'll probably have it all ready for you, but please check it over before you go into town. Once you get that done with, you have the rest of the day to yourself. I don't want to see you anywhere near the fields.*
> *Love,*
> *Mom*

Wyatt smiled, setting the note down. She was too nice for her own good, some days. He knew she needed as much help in the fields as she could get, but he also knew that she would physically throw him out if he did come try to help today. She was freakishly strong for being so wiry. In her eyes, spending the day with his best friend was much more important than helping her work. Despite how badly he wanted to help her, deep down in his chest, he agreed.

Wyatt went up to his room, changing into real clothes and finding his good walking shoes. Ven proper was a good hour-long walk from the house, so having a good set of shoes for that walk was a must. Once he had started working full-time with his mother, she had given them to him as a reward. They, like many other things, reminded him of her.

He tucked the note into his pants pocket before heading out the door and locking it behind him. He had considered bringing a traveling cloak, but already he could feel the warmth of the sun heating the air and the ground, and knew that he would have just gotten hot. So he set out on the road, hands in his pockets, whistling lightly as he walked toward Ven. His dream was already beginning to fade into the background of his mind.

The walk into town was uneventful, save for the colorful folk that could almost always be found on the main road during this time of year. A major artery for the province, the main road connected many of the outlying farms to Ven, and was also the central route through the mountains and toward the heart of the country. Wyatt had always loved strolling along the road and meeting people from all over who had some business in Ven. Now, with the harvest upon them, the area was absolutely overrun by scrambling farmers and eccentric foreign merchants, eager to sell their goods in the market square of Ven.

In truth, Ven was only a busy city for two weeks out of the year: during the harvest. In those two weeks, Ven hosted merchants from all over the world who ran shops in the market square. They, in turn, bought crops from the farmers in the area and took those goods back to the mainland with them, spreading Ven's famous products all over the continent. It was an odd balance, but it was necessary for the very-secluded Ven to stay afloat.

The harvest would begin in a few days, and Wyatt would assist his mother in gathering their crops and selling them in the market. It was a stressful time, but Wyatt loved the exposure to foreign people and goods. Being so secluded, Ven rarely saw any real kind of excitement, but the harvest was the one exception. Not only did it attract merchants, it also brought entertainers of all kinds, ranging from bizarre circus performers to magicians to beast handlers. Wyatt had once seen a man who traveled on an enormous bird.

Finally, the small collection of buildings and streets that was Ven came into view. Wyatt moved through the city gates, instantly spotting the carts and wagons that had begun to gather in the market square. These large carriages usually were modified to fold out into pod-like shops, where the traveling merchants could sleep as well as work. Many were already hard at it, trying to hawk their goods to anybody that came near them. Criers touted the wares of the men that employed them. Colorful signs promised cure-alls, crop growth potions, insect repellent, and other miraculous products.

None of these things worked, of course. At least not that Wyatt had ever seen. These were the fringe members of the merchant community. By the time the harvest actually started, they'd be lucky if the others didn't force them to set up outside of the city, having "real business" to attend to. Wyatt's mother had scoffed at the thought of using strange concoctions to assist with her farming, saying that it would make things too easy and ruin the experience. Having seen an entire field of corn ruined by a dose of growth potion, Wyatt was inclined to agree. But the merchants, undaunted by the jeers from local farmers, always seemed to find someone to sucker into a sale. The harvest made a lot of folks crazy.

Wyatt made his way quickly across the square, ignoring a particularly boisterous merchant who was assuring Wyatt that he had a tea that could make him not need to sleep. Why wouldn't he want to sleep? He loved sleeping. He slipped down a side road toward the small portion of Ven that housed its few citizens. Kelsar lived here, above his blacksmithing shop. When the time came, Kelsar would also have a small shop set up in the market square. He was a world-renowned blacksmith, and nobles from far-away lands requested his work every year.

Wyatt had never gotten Kelsar to say why he lived in Ven. Wyatt had always assumed that the old man had just wanted his solitude, but Kelsar seemed completely in his element every year during the harvest, when he hawked his goods to everyone he could find. He haggled with the most expert hagglers, and almost seemed to enjoy himself. Plus, Wyatt had never seen metalwork as fine as Kelsar's, and had always wondered why the old man wasn't in a great city like Axia or Farillyon, where he could sell these products year-round.

The shop itself was one of the larger buildings in the area, with a large amount of space on either side of it in case of fire. There had only ever been one fire at Kelsar's shop, but it was enough to fully justify why the old man had the shop built the way he did. He might be old and gruff, but he had a mind to safety and an uncanny knack for predicting the inevitable.

Wyatt knocked on the door, but received only silence as an answer. He knocked again, but once more he heard no answer. He shrugged and pushed the door open, slipping into the interior of the shop.

He knew that a bell over the door would normally signal to anyone in the shop that someone had entered. But it was drowned out as the telltale sound of metal on metal rang from the back room, along with the sound of roaring flames and steaming water. Wyatt knew that Kelsar was hard at work on some project and hadn't heard the knock. Wyatt didn't bother calling out to him just yet, instead peering around the shop and looking for things that his mother had requested.

The walls were covered with shelves and pegs, where a seemingly random assortment of tools, weapons, and other metal goods could be found. Wyatt had never understood Kelsar's so-called "organization system," but he hadn't really ever tried to learn it, either. The blacksmith was the only person who could ever find anything in here, so either he had a very sharp memory, or there was some underlying pattern that only a crazy old blacksmith could grasp.

"Oye!" yelled Wyatt, stepping up to the counter at the back of the room and ringing the little bell several times. He knew Kelsar hated that. "Customer in the shop!"

The sounds of Kelsar's work abruptly stopped, followed by a jarring crash and a litany of curses. Wyatt snickered. The haggard old man limped out of the back, glaring at Wyatt in his usual fashion. Wyatt flashed him a cheerful grin in response.

"Ain't no damn customer in the shop," growled the smith, eyeing Wyatt with distaste. "Yer not a customer, yer jus' an errand boy!"

Standing well over six feet tall, Kelsar cut an imposing figure, even with a gut and wrinkled skin. Gruff, muscular, and hardened, the old man was a mountain of grit, carrying scars from flame and blade alike. He had a bushy beard and a mop of messy gray hair. He had never said anything to suggest it, but Wyatt had always secretly imagined that Kelsar was a soldier or a famous adventuring warrior in his younger years. His dark eyes scanned the room before settling in on Wyatt again, scrutinizing him with fierce intensity.

Wyatt rolled his eyes. "Yeah, yeah, I've heard all about it. Mom ordered a bunch of stuff. I'm here to pick it up."

Kelsar nodded, turning away toward one of the walls where he had hung a large burlap sack. He trotted around the room, tossing various things from the walls into the sack, nodding and grunting occasionally as he did so. Kelsar often acted like he was having a conversation with himself. Wyatt found the whole thing to be very amusing.

"If yeh weren't such a damn terrible apprentice, yeh might've done this for yerself," growled the smith, handing the bag to Wyatt in one hand. Wyatt took it from him, not initially realizing how heavy it was until Kelsar let go of it. It dropped quickly before Wyatt strained and hoisted it up over his shoulders, ignoring Kelsar's smirk. He realized that walking back into town with a sack full of horseshoes and tools wasn't going to be very fun.

"I told you," protested Wyatt idly as he hefted the bag, "that whole thing wasn't nearly as bad as it could've been. And it was Des's fault, anyway. He was the one who came up with the idea and he stole the bellows from you!"

Kelsar chuckled, patting him on the shoulder. "He's jus' as bad as yerself, Wyatt. He got the lecture earlier. Yer gonna go see him before he leaves, yeah? He was askin' 'bout you."

"Of course," said Wyatt, doing his best to not think about it. "He's my best friend, how could I pass it up?" He was still dreading it, but he wasn't going to miss the opportunity to say goodbye to Desmond either.

"Jus' checkin'," said Kelsar, giving him a rare, lopsided smile. "You get that stuff back to yer mom, boy. She's sorely needin' it, even if she don' wanna admit it. I wish she'd let me help more."

Wyatt shook his head. "You know her. She barely lets me help." He adjusted the sack and held out his hand toward Kelsar's, who gave him a firm, vicelike shake. "Thanks, Kelsar. It means a lot to the both of us."

Kelsar waved him off. "Get movin', kid. Yer wastin' time already."

Wyatt nodded, heading back out into the morning air and smiling slightly. Kelsar was rock-solid, but he harbored a soft spot for Wyatt and his mother. Wyatt never really knew why, but he was grateful for the blacksmith and all the help he had given the two of them over the years.

Wyatt waved at the blacksmith, heading back out the door into the sunshine. With the sack of goods slung over his shoulder, he headed back onto the main road out of Ven. He still had plenty of daylight left, and would have plenty of time to spend with Desmond before tomorrow came, before the change that he had been dreading would finally settle down into his life.

On his way out of town, Wyatt noted the presence of military recruiters that he hadn't seen on the way in. Several young men from the area stood listening to the speech given by one of the Knights, a weathered old soldier who looked like he had seen many battles. Wyatt was tempted to listen in, too, but he knew it would be a bad idea. It would make him want to enlist even more than he already did, but because he couldn't, it would be a waste of time as well.

He had been with Desmond when the two of them had met their first recruiter, when they had decided on their dream of joining the Army together. He sorely wanted to go with his friend, to travel the world and fight wildlings and savages from the Dominion. He wanted to experience all the glorious things that the recruiters promised. Desmond would get to do all of that, but Wyatt had made the hard choice to stay home and help his mother. She couldn't afford to lose him just yet.

Desmond had no such obligations. His family was wealthy, and Desmond rarely worked with them. In fact, the older he had gotten, the less time he had spent around them. He had spent most of his time with Wyatt, helping him on the farm or exploring the landscape. Nora loved Des, too, and had always treated him like another son. But now he could go wherever he wanted, and Wyatt couldn't help but be a little jealous. He loved his mother, and the farm and the house meant a lot to him, but… it was hard seeing his friend getting to move on and live while he was left behind.

Shaking himself, Wyatt put those thoughts behind him for the moment, shutting the door on all his negative feelings and looking forward. Today was Desmond's last day in Ven, and Wyatt wasn't about to screw it up by being moody. He picked up his pace, setting out toward the house at a jog, trying to ignore the heavy weight of the sack on his back. He put his eyes ahead, intent on having as much time as possible with his friend and the last dying days of his youth.

After dropping the stupidly heavy sack of tools off at home, Wyatt got back onto the road. But this time, he headed away from Ven, away from any farms or houses or any other people. His new destination was in the hills to the west, hills that stretched all the way to the mountains that separated the peninsula from the rest of the continent.

After twenty minutes or so, Wyatt began to climb the hills. They were rolling and uneven, making the trip slow and difficult. But it wasn't far, and he had made the trip so many times that he no longer had to think very hard about where he was going. He recognized the landscape quite clearly. His destination was a rocky outcrop a few hundred yards off of the road, where he and Desmond had discovered a hidden tunnel as children, buried beneath a thin layer of rocks and dirt. They had dug it out with their bare hands, bathing secretly in the river before returning home so that their parents would not catch on.

Wyatt surveyed the rocks, peering into the tunnel below. He had always felt a little nervous about being underground, away from the sky. It bothered him in a weird way, but he would never admit that to Desmond. This cave had become the place where they went to get away, to hide from chores, angry parents, and bad days. Neither of them had ever shown the cave to anyone else. It was their place, a place where the rest of the world didn't exist.

The tunnel wound downward for several hundred feet, into the dark underground. In previous years, Wyatt had needed a torch or lantern, much to Desmond's chagrin, but he knew the route now, so the brief period of darkness didn't bother him as much anymore. After more walking and squeezing through narrow spaces, the tunnel leveled out, opening into a decently well-lit cave, where Wyatt was fairly confident that Desmond would be waiting for him.

The cave was a grotto, completely covered in crystalline structures. Some of these structures gave off a weird bluish light, reflecting off of the others and giving the room a fairly bright yet oddly shadowless glow. Wyatt had always loved that glow, reflected around the room by the beautiful geological formations. It was a strange place, but Wyatt had never really stopped to consider the oddness of glowing rocks like these. He'd always just assumed that it was a natural, if maybe exceptional, place.

Wyatt stepped quietly into the cave, peering around and detecting no sign of his friend. That was odd. Desmond was supposed to be here waiting for him.

The hair on the back of his neck stood up, and Wyatt turned, instinctively stepping away as he heard a familiar popping sound behind him. He dodged a kick, dancing backward and crouching, guarded.

Desmond grinned at him, a charming thing that usually gave Desmond great luck with the girls. "Almost had you, Arden. Eyes in the back of your head, just like always."

Wyatt laughed, relaxing as he inwardly chastised himself. Desmond wasn't going to leave without one more fight, one more battle between them.

"You always give yourself away, Des. You breathe too hard, and your knee always pops."

Desmond bolted forward, intending to tackle Wyatt, who dodged out of the way again with another laugh.

It was their ritual; in that cave, Wyatt and Desmond had sparred hundreds of times. When they were young, they had trouble with bullies from other farms picking on them. After finding the cave, however, they had a place where they could practice fighting, where their parents couldn't see. They used that time and place to teach each other how to fight. That gave them the edge they needed against the bigger kids. The bullies hadn't bothered either of them for a long time.

Desmond had always been just a bit better than Wyatt, of course.

Wyatt was fast and had a knack for avoiding things, but Desmond was strong and sure-footed. He was more muscular, built much more like a soldier than Wyatt. He almost always came out ahead in the end, which he never let Wyatt forget. Now, after six months of hard military training, Wyatt probably didn't stand a chance.

Wyatt leapt over Desmond's attempted grip, lashing out with a kick of his own. Desmond caught his leg and twisted, sending Wyatt tumbling over his shoulder and crashing into the ground. He landed hard on his back, letting out an audible "oof" and rolling away, but Desmond had already taken the advantage. He pounced, landing on Wyatt and pinning him down. After a few seconds of struggling, both of them relaxed, and Desmond patted Wyatt's head before helping him up.

"You're good, you know," said Desmond, sitting on a low rock near the wall, his usual spot. "Fast, faster than me, and you react well. You just don't take chances, Wyatt."

Wyatt sat down on his own spot, an angled, fallen stalagmite. He reclined back, trying not to notice the bruise that was forming on his back.

"Yeah, well, you hit hard, Des," remarked Wyatt with a smirk. "And you've got those unbreakable knuckles. Not a chance I really want to take most of the time."

Desmond smirked back at him. "Yeah, well, they won't do me much good in a real fight, will they?" he remarked, cracking those knuckles menacingly. "I'd take armor over knuckles any day. Still, though, you have a point. But I have training. You do really well, and you don't have any."

Wyatt shrugged. "I've seen you practice, and we fought with training swords whenever Kelsar wasn't looking. You're just as good with a sword as you are with your hands, Des. You'll be a pretty good Knight, I'm betting. And you haven't even gotten into the real fights yet. That's where you really learn."

"I hope you're right," said Desmond with a sigh, looking up at the glowing stones above him. "Training seems to be all I ever do anymore. I've never really seen my old man get excited about the things I'm doing, but… toward the end here, he's taken an interest, which of course means I have to practice even more."

"It's what you're meant to do," responded Wyatt firmly, a little surprised by his friend's concerns. "You said it yourself. Besides, your dad should take an interest. His son's gonna be a famous knight and bring glory and honor to his household."

Desmond laughed, his expression just a little bit sour. "He's already got plenty of glory and honor, Wyatt. It's called gold. But you're right. I'll make him proud, and show him that I'm not the lazy slouch he likes to tell me I am."

Wyatt shook his head. "It doesn't really matter what he thinks, Des, or your mom or anyone else. If you like what you're doing, if you like where you're going, then the rest doesn't matter. Live by your terms. Not his."

Desmond laughed, shaking his head. "Not the best in a fight, but damn good at inspirational speeches. You're right, of course. Always are. It's gonna be a hard road, I think, but I'll definitely make it. And I don't care if I make them proud, but I do care if I make you proud. If you never make it out of this place, I'll come back and tell you all about the world and everything else, Wyatt. You'll see."

Wyatt smiled at his friend. "You never know, Des. I might go find adventures of my own."

The two of them shared a laugh, and for a few moments, forgot about their impending separations, forgot about the futures looming before them. It was easy to get lost in those moments, especially as adulthood crept closer and closer toward them. Wyatt savored it, and part of him didn't want it to end.

For the next few hours, the two of them talked, laughed, and fought. For a while, they got to just be ten again, their worries traded in for dirty hands and faces. It wasn't often that Wyatt got to act like this, and he soon realized just how badly he had needed it. He felt like he was slowly beginning to shrug off whatever weight was hanging around his neck, finally beginning to come to terms with the future.

"I can't see the sky, but I've got a feeling that I need to go back soon," said Desmond, holding up a hand to signal the end of their fight. He was panting slightly, giving Wyatt a small amount of satisfaction in knowing that he had pushed his friend to the limit.

"Yeah… mom is probably expecting me back too," agreed Wyatt, although he wasn't very happy about it. "I'll be there tomorrow, though, to see you ride off. Mom, too. We wouldn't miss it, not for anything."

Desmond nodded at him with a grin. "I'll be back, you know. I promise I will. And I'll bring you a shrunken head or something equally cool."

Wyatt laughed, smiling in spite of the deep, horrible sadness that was spreading in his chest. "I can't wait. Good luck out there, Des. Stay safe."

The two of them clasped wrists and hugged, their tradition. Separating again, they watched each other for a moment in silence. Finally, Desmond grinned and saluted.

"Keep busy, Wyatt. Your time will come. I'll be seeing you soon, sooner than you know," said Desmond. Wyatt smiled and waved at his friend as Desmond disappeared out the rear entrance of the cave, leaving Wyatt alone with his thoughts.

He sat back down on his usual rock, reclining comfortably. He didn't really have any desire to go home and face his mom just yet. She'd want him to talk about it, and he wasn't good at that. He was best left alone, to process things and mull them over. He would talk when he was ready, but that wasn't going to be today.

Adulthood was creeping up on him with inescapable celerity, and he had very mixed feelings about it. Seeing Desmond getting ready to leave Ven, to join the Army and do something with his life… it was scary. And Des was so… ready. He had been ready for ages, not really realizing what his attitude did to Wyatt. For Wyatt, the thought of being held back, even if it was for a good reason, was a hard thing to face. Wyatt desperately wanted to join Desmond, but his obligation to his mother and her farm, their farm, was something he could never ignore.

With a resigned sigh, Wyatt closed his eyes, enjoying the complete silence that was afforded by being so deep underground. Sometimes, he still found himself feeling nervous about being so far underground, but those thoughts were far away at the moment. Right now, solitude was what he needed, providing a kind of comfort that was impossible for him to get anywhere else. He needed that time with himself to breathe and think and release.

Soon, however, the fatigue that he'd been ignoring all day caught up with him. He'd forgotten that he had slept so poorly, but before he realized it, he was already drifting off to sleep. It didn't occur to him that falling asleep in the dark underground wasn't the greatest idea, especially when his mother would be waiting up for him. In fact, sleep seemed like the greatest idea in the world at that moment. He adjusted himself comfortably on his rock, and after a short time, Wyatt was fast asleep.

CHAPTER THREE

Unbeknownst to Wyatt or Desmond, their cave was not the only cave tucked beneath Ven. In fact, their cave was one of many; an entire system of interconnected, mazelike caverns designed to appear as natural as possible. Designed to deter anyone from walking to the end of that maze. To keep prying eyes away.

But someone had walked to the end. The final cave was a large, circular room, expertly crafted. Its shape was perfect, and not at all natural. All over the walls, crisscrossing veins of a mysterious glowing stone cast a fuzzy blue light over the room. The floor was etched with a masterful hexagonal rune, etches that dug shallow channels in the floor. The rune likewise glowed, a glow reflecting the power within it, the power that held something at bay. Near the entrance of the room, a skeletal old man crouched, jabbering quietly to himself as he worked a pestle, creating a mixture for the next step of the plan.

Apep the Snake was very busy. He had been busy for decades now, busy working and maneuvering toward a goal that he had first believed impossible. But his goal was taking shape, and he actually had begun to believe he would reach it. His hands shook with excitement. Soon, his master would rise, and together they would take back their land, their rule, and their rightful place in the order of things.

Setting the pestle aside, he wiped a finger through the dark purple paste in the bowl. He peered closely at his fingertip for a moment before plugging it into his mouth, tasting the mixture and nodding in approval to nobody in particular. Gathering the necessary herbs for this had taken a long time, and he was glad to see that he had done things right and it would work. It had been a long, long time since he had last attempted this, and he wouldn't want to experience failure. He reached down, gripping the hilt of a ceremonial dagger. With careful precision, he scooped up a handful of purple paste and began smearing it onto the obsidian knife.

Finished coating the blade, Apep turned away from his small workstation and limped over to the large altar that had been erected against the far wall of the chamber. The wall behind the altar was quite unique; it was the only stone surface in the entire cave system where flecks of obsidian were mixed in with the bedrock. The obsidian was the sign that he had sought for years. It betrayed the binding, telling any careful observer what might lie beyond that wall.

Atop the altar, a bound form struggled. Dressed in a long white gown, she was certainly a beautiful woman; long brown hair tumbled down behind her, complimenting her warm brown eyes and soft feminine features. She was a special girl, and Apep had gone to great lengths to abduct her. The ordeal had cost him dearly, but his master had made it quite clear that the girl was necessary for their plans. Her wrists and ankles were tied to the rock, leaving her little room to move. But move she did. She whimpered and tugged at the ropes that bound her, ropes that glowed with strange, blood-red runes.

Apep slapped her forehead, looking into her deep brown eyes with a wicked grin. She whimpered, her noises muffled by the dirty rag that he had stuffed into her mouth, tied in place by another rope. He liked her whimpers. In another time in his life, he'd have loved to spend an extended amount of time with her before he killed her. He'd have savored those whimpers. Eventually, he'd have liked to remove her gag, and savor her screams. But he didn't have time for that, and he needed her vessel to be unharmed.

He stared into her eyes for a long moment before her whimpering subsided and she relaxed. He nodded with satisfaction, walking away from her and back toward his small worktable. He gathered up his materials, preparing for the final steps in the ritual.

He carried everything back over to the girl, setting the various tools around her as she watched him with fear. Reaching under his robes, Apep retrieved the inky black book that he always kept at his waist. He flipped it open, skimming over the pages cautiously.

The book was a necessary tool for any true Necromancer, and Apep was just that. It contained the writings of the master himself, offering priceless insight to his children if they could get their hands on one of the few copies that still existed. But the writing was dangerous; those who weren't fully trained or were weak-minded could be consumed by the words, driven into a deep, incurable insanity. The various copies of the book had claimed many souls throughout the ages. Those souls had been consumed by the books and offered up to the few who were strong enough to use them.

After finding the passage he was looking for, he set the book aside, taking up his ceremonial dagger. The flawless obsidian blade had been crafted long ago in homage to his master, passed down through Apep's family. The paste he had created covered the dagger, giving it a sickly purple sheen. It quivered with unnatural power.

The woman caught sight of the dagger, and her struggling resumed. Apep could see tears streaming from her eyes as she attempted in vain to get away from him, to get anywhere else. But she had nowhere to go. Normally, he would expect a lot more trouble from one such as herself. But the special ropes that bound her hands, feet, and mouth kept any danger at bay. Tonight, her powers were useless.

Apep smiled at her again, patting her cheek as she tried to scream at him. He leaned in close, his face inches from her own. He could smell her hair, a pleasant smell that would've given him pause in his younger years. But he was too old to care. He stared into her eyes once more, eyes from which tears streamed. They pooled on her cheeks as she silently begged him to reconsider, begged him to let her go and let her go back to her normal life.

He shook his head, his smile vicious and cruel. "No, my sweet. We need you. We need you just like this. We need you to die."

She let out a low, muffled cry in response, a cry that only served to make his joy grow. Apep leaned in closer, close enough to lick a tear from her soft, pale face. She flinched and strained to get away, but she could feel his dried, blackened tongue slide across her cheek. He smiled again, savoring the salty taste.

He patted her cheek and took up the dagger. He leaned in, carefully cutting a slit into her face, right where he had licked her. He pressed the stone into her skin, letting the blood run down the blade and mingle with the purple mixture that was coating it. She tried to cry out in pain, but she could only manage to make a bit of noise through the gag.

As the blood mingled with the mixture on the dagger, the entire thing began to shimmer with eerie red light. Apep looked over at the book, reciting the forbidden words of the Gods that had been passed down in secret through his people. As the words flowed from his mouth, his throat burned, and he could taste coppery blood. The words carried power, and that power wasn't meant for a body like this. It wasn't meant for any mortal.

The cave around him rumbled, reacting to the power of the words leaving his mouth. His whole body shook, threatening fall to pieces. But Apep didn't care. If it did come apart, he'd make another. He hadn't expected his current shell to make it through the evening, but the price of making another would be more than worthwhile. Apep had long ago lost the need for his own body, opting instead to inhabit them only when necessary. Sometimes, subtlety required it.

Apep's hands shook as he flipped the dagger over, gripping the hilt in both hands as he raised it over the woman's breast. The wall behind her began shifting strangely, the obsidian stirring and blending with the bedrock as the entire thing darkened. Strange symbols swam across the surface, glowing with unnatural purple light. The symbols of his master.

Gripping the dagger tight, Apep practically shouted the final word in the tongue of the Gods as he plunged the knife down, slamming it into her heart. The power was roaring through him now, roaring through the cavern and the girl. They were all united in this. Her eyes went wide with pain and fear as her whole body tensed, trying to break away at the last second. Shapes moved in the wall, reaching out toward her, beckoning. Finally, her form went limp as blood spread over the whiteness of her gown.

Apep's senses branched outward, and he could feel her soul begin to peel away from her body. It was already searching for Adala, searching for the Light and the hope and the great beyond. But he would not let her escape into the Light. He needed her. He grabbed onto her soul firmly, directing it into the writhing black mass that was the wall looming over her body. He fed her into it, into the symbols on the wall and what rested beyond them. His glee surged as he felt the thing beyond the wall reached out, taking grip of her for itself. Apep felt like his body was fraying at the edges.

The ground rumbled again, stronger this time. There was a concussive blast of air in his face, and Apep's thin, ragged form was cast across the chamber. He tumbled end over end, breaking several bones in the process, before slamming into the far wall and landing in a heap. He looked up hazily toward the reddish light, but he could make nothing out, his vision blurry and his mind fuzzy.

He reached out, shaky and nearly blind. Through the haze, he thought he saw something move, thought he saw a shadow step across his vision. But he couldn't be sure. The air felt thick and hot, and a pressure was growing in his ears. His arm fell to the ground, suddenly refusing to work. Blackness closed in all around him.

For the second time that day, Wyatt fell out of bed. An intense rumble startled him, causing him to twist and roll. He rolled right off of the stone slab he had been sleeping on, experiencing a brief drop before landing with a harsh thud on the stone floor. He groaned, groping around in the suddenly dark cave, completely off guard, completely bewildered.

The ground rumbled again, causing little bits of dust and flecks of stone to fall on his head. Strangely, the crystals that had once lit the cave perfectly now seemed to have lost nearly all of their light. Wyatt could just see them, glowing weakly as they framed the cavern. He wasn't sure that they even cast enough light for him to be able to find an exit without hugging one of the walls. He could feel the panic inside him start to rise, and he did his best to ignore it, trying to ignore his thoughts about being away from the open sky, buried far under the earth. What was going on?

He clambered to his feet, slamming the lid on his fear and taking hold of his determination. He'd get out, it just might take him awhile. He'd made the trip in and out of this cave dozens of times in his life. He'd never tried it, but he was fairly confident that he could make the trip in the dark.

Fairly.

After groping around in the almost complete blackness for a moment, Wyatt found what he hoped was his exit. He proceeded cautiously, still very unsure, but paused when the ground rumbled again.

Ahead of him, a thunderous crash echoed throughout the cavern, and Wyatt leapt backward. He landed on his back, his head smacking the stone painfully. He rolled, trying his best to cover his neck and ears at the same time as bits of debris rained down onto him. It sounded and felt as if the cave itself were coming down around him. After a few moments of lying on the ground, Wyatt could tell that he was coated in a thick layer of dust and dirt.

Finally, the noise subsided as everything seemed to calm down. Wyatt stood again, doing his best to dust himself off. His head was pounding now, a result of the combined efforts of the loud crashing and his head slamming into the floor. He stepped forward again, slower this time. But after a few steps, he met a wall of stone debris that completely blocked his passage into the tunnel. He groped around it for a moment, trying to find some kind of way through it, but the path was completely blocked. His panic began to grow again, and he had to sit back down for a moment to rethink his plan.

Clearly, he wouldn't be getting out that way. There was another exit, of course. Desmond's usual one. But he'd only ever taken it a few times, and surely hadn't committed it to memory like the other. He turned around, squinting into the near-darkness. He could just make out the other end of the cavern, which appeared to not have been affected by the cave-in. Wyatt climbed to his feet, moving forward at a quickened pace, now slightly desperate just to get outside.

Suddenly, two odd spheres of light appeared low to the ground in the far tunnel, stopping him in place. They were tiny, glowing with a gold light that certainly stood out in the barely perceptible blue of everything else. He watched them for a moment, completely at a loss.

The lights went out, and then came back on, several feet further into the tunnel. There they sat, unmoving. Then one of them went out, and then came back on. Wyatt blinked, staring at them. Were they...

"Eyes?" Wyatt whispered, staring at the strange golden orbs. They disappeared again, reappearing even further away, and suddenly Wyatt realized that he should probably follow them. They seemed to be leading him down the tunnel. Whatever was going on, he'd take the opportunity to get out of the cave.

He set off at a quick pace, following blindly through the dark cavern. As long as he was oriented straight at the orbs, he figured he wouldn't have to worry about running into something. His intention was to catch up to them, but every time he drew near, they moved further away. They would always wait for him, though, never going out of eyesight. His heart was racing and something inside of him was practically screaming about unknown danger. As much as he agreed with that voice, he knew that this was his best chance.

Wyatt followed the orbs for a long time. How long, he wasn't really sure, as he was concentrating on keeping pace and not clipping the walls with his arms and shoulders. He tripped several times, but he had good reflexes and managed to roll through when he did, coming out with little more than scrapes and bruises. Eventually, Wyatt saw light ahead, light that was not a pair of strange glowing eyes. Excitement rose within him. That had to be the exit. He raced ahead, and caught a glimpse of something tan disappearing through the lit corridor, into the light beyond.

Wyatt rounded the corner, arriving in a small, well-lit chamber that appeared to have no other exits. Where the light was coming from, Wyatt had no idea; it seemed to emanate from everything, as well as nothing in particular. He cast no shadow. He backed up cautiously, scanning the room for whatever had led him here, led him to what he now feared was deeper into the caves.

At the base of the far wall, there sat a tan housecat, licking its paw. It had short, tan fur and luminous golden eyes. Wyatt was no expert in feline expression, but he was pretty sure that if a cat could look bored, this one was certainly doing that. It paid him no mind for some time, intent on its paw. Wyatt sighed, dropping his guard entirely and plopping onto the ground.

"Of course you're a cat," he said softly, equal parts annoyed and dismayed. "Of all the things to find down here…"

"What, were you expecting a fish?" replied the cat, eyeing Wyatt for the first time with extreme disinterest. Its voice was deep, strong, and masculine, not at all what he would expect from a tiny little housecat. It seemed to echo from the cat, but also from far beyond it, ringing through the air around Wyatt and even through his mind.

Wyatt stared at the little beast for a long time, utterly dumbfounded. Either he was still dreaming, or he had knocked his head a lot harder than he had thought. The cat… was talking to him. He slowly scooted backward, trying to keep his calm.

"Did you, um… just talk to me?" he asked stupidly, scratching his head with confusion as he tried to look behind the cat, or maybe even beneath it.

The cat stretched at yawned. "Quite the sleuth, aren't we? Yes. Now come over here and pet me."

Wyatt scooted forward, reaching out dumbly to obey the cat. He patted it on the head awkwardly, scratching it behind the ears. He was rewarded with a light purr. As near as Wyatt could tell, it was a perfectly normal cat, aside from the glowing eyes and the talking.

"Good, good," said the cat smartly, walking in a catlike circle around him. "I am… well, a lot of things. But for the time, you may call me Shem. I am to be your guide."

"My… guide?" Wyatt replied warily, very confused. Guide for what?

The cat nodded seriously. "Yes, yes. Unless you want to stay down here, of course. I could certainly just let you try to wander out on your own, but I'd like to point out that in following me this far, you made your way even deeper underground."

Wyatt cursed himself inwardly. Whatever the cat was, it had lured him here for some reason, and that idea wasn't sitting well with him. Much worse, the cat had him over a barrel. He had no choice.

"Calm yourself, Wyatt Arden," instructed Shem the cat, staring at Wyatt unblinkingly with his eerie golden eyes. "I am not here to hurt you. I truly am here to guide you. The first order of business is to help you out of your current predicament, but there's more to it, too."

Wyatt leaned back, sighing. "I don't really have a choice, do I? Alright, fine. How do I make it out of here, Shem?"

The cat stood and stretched. "First, you'll want to collect your reward for making it this far."

"My reward?" replied Wyatt, blinking and looking around. The wall above them seemed to shimmer slightly, the rock becoming translucent, like glass. Slowly it grew clearer, and eventually, he could just make out a gleaming band of metal in the now crystalline wall. Wyatt stood up, staring at it as his question seemed to answer itself.

He stepped forward, looking closer as the crystal slowly became more translucent. Wyatt's nose was nearly touching the stone, but finally, the thing inside of the wall became clear enough to see. It was a gleaming sword with a mirror-like blade that reflected his dumbfounded expression right back at him.

It was the sword from his dream.

Every detail was just as he had remembered. The ebony handle was capped off with a polished metal pommel in the shape of a hexagon. Wyatt couldn't see it, but he was sure the same image he had seen in his dream would be etched into the bottom. It was masterful and flawless, just as he had remembered it. The length, the size of the crossguard... everything about it was perfect.

Wyatt pressed his hands to the crystal, and he could almost feel the humming of the blade, beckoning him to it. He leaned in close, as if he thought he could press his hands through the crystal and grab it. But the cold translucent barrier persisted, keeping the blade locked safely inside of the stone.

Wyatt turned to the cat, who was watching him with interest. "How do I get it out?" he asked, sounding more excited than he had wanted to. The sword... it was so different, and he felt so strangely connected to it.

It felt like it was his, and it seemed to open up so many possibilities in his head, dreams that he had always tried to ignore in favor of the dull life of a farmer. It was hard for him not to be excited.

The cat cocked his head. "Hmm... Well, first, you should let me see your hand."

Wyatt leaned down, presenting his right hand to the cat. Shem sniffed his palm for a moment, as if he were trying to determine its flavor. Then, before Wyatt could even react, the cat slashed a claw across it, the sharp point cutting a single line on the edge of Wyatt's hand. His hand seared with pain as blood streamed from the wound.

Wyatt yelled out, instinctively kicking out at the cat as he drew his hand close to his chest. Shem yowled and leapt away, glaring at Wyatt from the rock upon which he was now perched.

"You dimwit, I was helping you," admonished Shem, sounding highly annoyed. "You need to present your blood to the blade, so it can decide whether or not you are worthy. And you're not making a very good impression."

Wyatt looked at his bloodied palm sourly. "And I suppose telling me that beforehand would've been too difficult for you? I do have a knife, you know."

The cat shrugged, settling down on the stone perch. "No, but I wanted to test you. You react well. I suppose you'll do."

Wyatt sighed. He turned back to the wall, pointedly placing the cat firmly behind him as he reached out with his bloody hand. He thought he heard a snicker as he pressed his sore palm against the crystal, directly over the location of the sword.

Wyatt felt a mighty tug at his navel, as if something were being drawn out of him. He let out a small gasp as fatigue washed over him. As he leaned on the crystal wall for support, a glowing symbol appeared under his hand, casting a fiery golden light around the room. He stumbled backward, taking his hand away and looking at the wall from further back, trying to get a better view.

There was no blood on the wall, but the same symbol that Wyatt had seen etched on the bottom of the sword could be seen where his hand had been, lines of fire that flickered intensely on the wall. Wyatt looked at his hand, only to find that the bleeding had stopped and the cut had closed, leaving nothing but a thin pink scar. Even the blood that had leaked all over his hand and dripped from his fingertips had disappeared.

The surface of the wall began to shift, dragging Wyatt's attention back to it. The stone rippled, resembling the surface of a pool of water that had just been disturbed by a falling branch. Wyatt looked over at the little cat again, who had returned to licking his paws, ignoring Wyatt completely. Wyatt hoped the cat could feel his annoyance.

Wyatt turned back to the sword, stepping closer. The stone wall rippled again, and an idea popped into Wyatt's head. Without really realizing what he was doing, he reached out and slid his hand into the now liquid crystal. He winced slightly as an odd sensation crept up his arm. It felt like he was sticking his arm into a vat of cold honey.

He reached toward the sword, his hand pressing slowly forward as he went deeper into the wall. By the time his fingers touched the handle, he was nearly shoulder-deep, doing his best to keep his balance. By the time he had managed to get a firm grip on it, he was trying very hard not to stick his face in. He squeezed the handle and drew back, bringing the sword slowly, painfully toward him and out of the wall.

Wyatt gave a mighty pull, staggering backward as the sword came out of the glowing wall with him. He had been sure that the viscous substance would leave a sticky, gooey residue all over his arm and side, but no such reside was left. The glowing symbol on the wall faded, and the surface of the wall stopped moving. Within moments, it faded back to its previous stony form, completely normal. It bore no hint that it had ever been anything other than a simple stone wall.

The sword in his hand gave a merry hum and, suddenly, Wyatt didn't feel so fatigued. He looked over the sword closely, making sure it was exactly how he had remembered it. Everything was right, just as he had seen in his dream. It was perfect, and the same strength and confidence that had wrapped around him in his dream was rolling over him now. His headache faded into the background, along with his lingering claustrophobia. Excitement was burning in him like a wildfire. He wanted nothing more than to get out of this cave so he could ask

Kelsar about the sword. He wanted so badly to figure out what it was and where it had come from.

"Are you done gawking?" asked Shem, his deep voice betraying a hint of annoyance. "If so, could we please leave? I haven't seen the sky in a very long time."

Wyatt looked over at the cat, ignoring the question. "Um, what just happened?"

Shem hopped off of the rock, sitting down at the exit to the room. "We'll talk about that later. Getting out of the cave is more important right now. We shouldn't stay down here any longer than we have to. Other things may wake up."

Wyatt blinked at the cat. Other things? He wanted to ask what the cat meant by that, but he got the distinct impression just looking at the little beast that now wasn't the time. He sighed and nodded, conceding defeat. He still felt a little uneasy down so far underground, even with the sword in his hand. He didn't relish the thought of being stuck.

"Good," said Shem, walking in circles impatiently in the doorway. "Now put that thing away before you hurt yourself. It's sharp."

Wyatt looked down at the gleaming weapon in his hand, frowning. "Put it away? Um... Shem, I don't have anywhere to put it. It didn't come with a scabbard."

The cat paused his walking, looking over his shoulder toward Wyatt. "Think about a scabbard. Picture it in your mind, and hold the sword tight in your grip. Focus, and the sword will help you."

Wyatt looked down at the blade again, his brow furrowed. He still remembered every detail of the expertly tooled leather baldric from his dream. As if it had been his for years, he could recount every seam, every curve, every single inch of it. He concentrated on that image, drank it in and focused on it and only it. Soon, that image became the only thing in the world. He didn't notice the sword in his hand begin to hum vigorously, too lost in his concentration.

He felt another pull at his navel, but it wasn't as bad as the last, and managed to stay on his feet. His eyes closed momentarily as he felt the energy surge out of him, from somewhere deep within his chest, a repository he had not known to exist. When he opened them again, he saw that the sword in his hand was now wrapped in the same exquisite leather scabbard that he had seen in his dream. It had become real, just as the sword had.

Wyatt took a moment to stare in amazement at it, but he felt Shem's hot, impatient gaze descend upon him and did his best to act nonchalant. He calmly lifted the baldric over his head, adjusting the straps so that the leather was tight and the sword hung at his hip. Even there, he could still feel that same reassuring warmth radiating from the weapon, taking the edge off the chill of the cave and helping to suppress his fears about being so far underground. His confidence seemed to grow every moment that it was in his possession.

"Do try to keep up," called Shem, and without another look back, the cat bounded out of the cave. Wyatt blinked, and a second later he took off at a hasty run after the bizarre, difficult cat.

As he ran along, Wyatt began to realize just how much his life had changed since he had that dream. Before, he'd been worried that he'd end up spending his entire life in Ven. That he would live and die as a farmer, and the extent of his excitement in life would be limited to bad winters and rampaging cows. But now... even though he didn't understand why he had it or why it had appeared, he felt as if the sword gave him purpose. Even though he had no idea where it would take him, he could nevertheless feel the sword taking him somewhere. Taking him forward.

Things were looking up.

"Finally," groaned Wyatt as he pulled himself out of a narrow hole in the ground, the exit from the cave that he had nearly found himself trapped inside of. The hole was rocky and awkward, and he had to be careful not to cut himself or fall back down into the cave. He had chased after Shem for what felt like hours, and his optimism and excitement had both been replaced by sweat and scraped knees.

"You're a little out of shape," remarked Shem as Wyatt struggled to climb. He sat a few feet in front of Wyatt, not at all appearing bothered by the long run the two of them had just had through the cave. In fact, he looked amused by the entire situation. "Maybe you should exercise more."

Wyatt clambered to his feet, glaring icily at the cat. "I am in shape," he growled, annoyed. "Just not used to running blindly through a cave. I don't have the benefit of being a magical… cat thing."

Shem licked his paw. "Pick me up. I'm tired."

Wyatt stared back at Shem, trying to sputter out a response and failing miserably under the stern, unblinking gaze of the cat. He sighed, holding up his hands in defeat before scooping up the insufferable little monster and placing him on his shoulders.

Looking around, Wyatt realized that he had been away from home for much longer than he'd anticipated. The only light in the fields was provided by the stars and the moon. Thankfully, it was a clear night, but it was still well past sundown. With a jolt, he knew that his mother would be up late waiting for him, sick with worry. She always worried whenever he came home late, especially if it was after dark.

Wyatt swore loudly, taking off at a run and ignoring Shem's cries of protest. He had a vague idea of where he was after looking around the hills, and hopefully he could make it back to the house before too much time had passed. He seemed to have forgotten his fatigue entirely, now too worried about making it home and not being unceremoniously murdered with his new sword by his mother.

"Hey!" yelled Shem, digging his sharp little claws into Wyatt's shoulders. "Be careful! You're going to drop me!"

Wyatt snorted, ignoring the cat. His mind was elsewhere. His mom was probably worked into a worried frenzy, and Wyatt hated doing that to her. She didn't like it when he went out into the hills alone. Despite her worries, she had always tried very hard not to limit what he wanted to do. She realized that he had to spend a lot of time on the farm, and whatever freedom he could get would be necessary for him to grow. She was a very fair parent in that regard, and that made it harder on him when she worried about him. He felt even worse.

She might've even felt the earthquake, he realized. That was even better. If she felt the ground shaking and knew he was in the hills, and if she found out that he'd been in a mysterious underground cavern when it occurred, her heart might give out. It wasn't going to help anything when he showed up hours late, covered in dirt and scrapes.

He was dead. She'd kill him, probably flog him with Kelsar's bag of tools and bury him on the farm or feed him to the cows.

"You're an idiot," said the cat, no longer protesting. "She's already asleep. But she is worried about you, and she is going to be quite mad."

Wyatt glanced over his shoulder, baffled. "What, you can read my mind too?"

The cat stared off into the distance. "To a degree. I'm connected to the sword, and the sword is connected to you. It's not like I hear your inner monologue, but I get a general idea, especially when there are heavy thoughts on your mind. And right now, you're so busy fretting and imagining your own gruesome death that anyone with the talent within about a mile could pick up on it. Control yourself. Trust me, you'll be fine. Slow down before you get hurt."

Wyatt slowed his running to a jog.

"You're going to be answering a lot of questions, cat," he said dully, trying his best to not be creeped out.

He couldn't be sure, but he had the strange suspicion that the cat was smirking. "Naturally. You wouldn't be the right person if you weren't asking questions, Wyatt. I expect it, and look forward to it."

The more the cat said, the more confused Wyatt was becoming. Whatever was going on, it was certainly not what he had expected to happen today.

After thirty minutes or so, the house came into view. By the time he reached it and slowed down to a walk, Wyatt was exhausted and soaked in sweat. He hadn't run that hard, for that long, in a very long time. Making a long and painful trek through an underground maze beforehand hadn't helped him, either. He wanted nothing more than to go to bed and sleep for about a week.

Wyatt crept slowly along the side of the house, crouching low and peering into a side window as he passed by. He wanted to know what he was getting into, but the house was mostly dark, save for a bit of flickering light coming from the kitchen. He cursed his stupidity once more and headed around the building toward the front door, now fully aware of what he'd find inside.

The third floorboard always creaked when he stepped on it, something he had learned and ingrained into his mind at a young age. Normally, he made an effort to avoid it. Old habits. But now, his mind elsewhere, he completely forgot. As he moved into the main hall, he pressed his full weight into that floorboard, receiving a loud, drawn-out groan from beneath for his efforts. He nearly smacked his forehead, cursing himself again, but the damage had already been done. He heard Nora's groggy voice calling his name from the kitchen.

Shem leapt off of Wyatt's shoulders, bounding across the hall and up the stairs at the far end without making a sound. No doubt the cat had already figured out where Wyatt's bedroom was located and would be fast asleep on Wyatt's pillow when he got upstairs. Wyatt briefly considered the image of throwing both cat and pillow across the room before sighing, shaking his head, and stepping into the dim light of the kitchen, hanging his head and awaiting his fate.

"Hi, Mom," he said meekly, staring at his feet. He really did feel terrible, and he knew that he looked terrible, too. He could feel her staring at him for a moment, as if he weren't actually real. That moment seemed to drag on and on, and Wyatt wondered if time had stopped. But finally, she moved quickly across the kitchen and gripped him by the shoulders.

"Wyatt!" she scolded, her grip as sure as iron. "Where have you been? What happened to you?"

He looked up at her. "The caves, where Des and I always used to play as kids," he said, not bothering to try to lie. Honesty would be the easiest in the long run, the cleanest break. "We agreed to meet there one last time, away from everyone else. We talked and wrestled for a long time. Eventually he left to go wrap everything up, and I stayed behind to think about things. I guess... I guess I fell asleep."

She gaped at him, her hair disheveled, her eyes betraying her fatigue and her stress. "You guess you fell asleep? Wyatt, how many times do I have to tell you that those caves are dangerous? There was an earthquake earlier, and by the look of you, I'd say you found that out first hand! You could've been killed, Wyatt! What were you thinking?"

She was trying to slip that guilt-noose around his neck, and it was working.

"I know," he replied dully, looking down at his feet once more. "It was stupid of me, I know. But it was the only place that Des and I could meet and be away from Ven and the farms and everything else. We've both got a lot of good memories there. It's our place."

And memories were all that was left, he realized. At least one entrance to that cave had been destroyed in the earthquake, and he honestly had no idea how to find his way back to that chamber through the maze of tunnels he had used to exit it. There was very little chance that he'd ever have the opportunity to go back there, much less with Desmond. By now, the rest of it might've already caved in.

His mother sighed, loosening her grip and drawing him into a hug. "I know, honey. I'm sorry I yelled, but you really worried me. The earthquake was just a little rumble here, but I've heard stories about cave-ins and... well, I guess I just thought the worst."

He gave her his best, most sorrowful look. "I know. I'm really sorry, Mom." And he was. He felt awful.

She nodded, releasing him from the hug and sitting back down at the kitchen table, where she had evidently fallen asleep. Wyatt saw her cup, which had probably been filled with several servings of coffee. She wouldn't sleep well tonight.

"You should get to bed," she said, tidying up the table a bit. "Desmond is marching out early in the morning, and it's already very late. If you want to go see him leave, you'll need to get some rest."

He nodded, wondering how exactly he ended up with a mom who was so understanding in times like these. "Yeah, I'm pretty worn out. When I got out of the cave and realized it was dark, I, er, ran all the way here."

She didn't say anything, putting her cup away and busying herself with the kitchen. Wyatt fidgeted.

"Thanks for not killing me, Mom," he said meekly. "I'm sorry again."

She turned to face him, a light smile on her face. She seemed to have shrugged off some of her worry, much to his delight.

"Thanks for not getting yourself killed, Wyatt. Now go to bed."

He smirked at her and turned back into the hallway, making his way upstairs. His door was cracked open, a sure sign that Shem had somehow managed to not only operate the door handle, but open the door and get into the room. He slipped inside, looking around warily as he did, trying not to picture the cat with two fully human hands, fumbling around at the door.

Shem sat idly on his pillow, exactly where Wyatt had expected to find him. He was licking his paw with a look of pure boredom on his face. Closing the door behind him, Wyatt kicked off his shoes and sat down on the bed, looking at the cat that sat next to him.

"I told you she wasn't going to murder you," remarked Shem, his gaze flicking to Wyatt briefly before returning back to the paw.

"Yes, you're very clever," responded Wyatt, equal parts exasperated and exhausted while he glumly kicked off his boots. "Do you have any other insight to offer, oh wise one?"

"Of course," remarked the cat smartly, watching Wyatt unblinkingly. "But before we get to all of that, you should take those filthy clothes off. You'll get your sheets dirty."

"Yes, Mother," muttered Wyatt, stripping off his clothes with disinterest and tossing them haphazardly into the corner. He wasn't really in the mood to be tidy at the moment. Shem's attitude was making him a little combative. He pulled the baldric off and set it on the floor beside the bed, the only thing he took time and care to place. Finally, he sat back down and faced the cat, unsure of where to start.

"We've got a lot to discuss, Wyatt," said Shem before Wyatt could begin unloading with his questions. "You've got a lot of questions, most of which I probably can't answer. But before we get to all of that, you need to rest and recuperate. Your body underwent a lot of strain today, and if you aren't careful, it could do permanent harm to you."

Wyatt stared at the cat, suddenly realizing how fatigued he was feeling. It was a different kind of fatigue, something he felt at his core, in his bones. It was almost like a chill he couldn't quite get rid of.

"You're talking about finding the sword, aren't you?" he asked suddenly, remembering that feeling of something tugging at his navel. "And those weird feelings, like something being pulled out of my chest. That's what you mean."

The cat nodded slowly, staring at him with unblinking luminous eyes. "You have taken the first steps toward your destiny, Wyatt Arden. It is prudent to ensure that you do not screw it up this early on. It took a lot of energy to get that sword out of the wall. Even more to summon the scabbard. If you don't rest, it might hurt you. So before you begin bombarding me with questions, get some sleep."

Wyatt wanted to protest, wanted to put his foot down and remind the cat that he was the one wielding the sword. He wanted to get firm and tell the cat how things would be, but that seemed like a profoundly bad idea. He had the fleeting suspicion that the cat would just laugh at him, anyway.

Deep down, he knew that Shem was right. He was exhausted to his core, and he might not even make it through all of his questions before passing out. It would be better to ask them when he had a clear head and a clear mind, rather than miss things or not fully understand while he was tired. So he sighed again and nodded.

"You're on my pillow, you know," muttered Wyatt, shifting to get underneath his blankets. Shem yowled petulantly at him and hopped down, padding across the room to find something soft to sleep on. He settled for an extra blanket that was folded up in the corner of the room, which Wyatt used only during the winter. Wyatt settled in, fatigue closing in on him before he could even begin to ponder the cat, the sword, or the earthquake. Within minutes he was fast asleep, his doubts and worries put to rest, for the time.

The little tan cat watched Wyatt from across the room, his eerie eyes unblinking. Things were finally starting to get interesting again. About time.

CHAPTER FOUR

everal hours later, Wyatt awoke to Shem gently batting has nose like a dead mouse that he had decided to toy with. He rubbed his eyes and looked up, finding the oddly luminescent golden orbs of his strange companion staring down at him. He sighed, pushing the cat off of him as he sat up groggily. Trying to get any more sleep was, evidently, out of the question.

"What time is it?" he asked wearily, looking out the window. The morning light shone into his room, making his eyes sore. He certainly felt better than he had the previous night, but he still longed to sleep for a few more hours.

"Noonish," replied the cat, his voice coming in a bored yawn. "I've been trying to wake you for an hour or so now, but you are quite dedicated to your uselessness."

Wyatt blinked, clearing his eyes again. Something felt amiss, but he couldn't quite place what it was. He scratched his head and turned, swinging his legs out and putting his feet on the ground. He was momentarily surprised to feel cool metal underneath his right foot, but the cold quickly grew warm. A gentle, reassuring hum followed, filling his entire body with calm, focus, and clarity. The lingering effects of sleep were quickly flushed from his mind.

Desmond. He had forgotten Desmond.

It hit him like a fist to the gut, making him feel suddenly shaky and sick. Noonish, Shem had said. Desmond would already be several hours out of Ven, long gone with the rest of the recruits from the area. He had missed his chance to say goodbye to his best friend.

Wyatt looked over at Shem, stricken. "I missed it. Shem, you should've woken me up earlier!"

Shem gave him an even, almost annoyed look. "I am not your mother, Wyatt Arden. As I said, I have been trying. And speaking of your mother, she left shortly after you fell asleep. I believe there was a commotion of some sort in town."

Wyatt sprang off of the bed, gathering up clean clothes and quickly throwing them on. He had his foot in one shoe when Shem called out his name with stern, even force.

"Wyatt," called the cat again after Wyatt ignored the first, "she's on her way back already. Calm down, we have things to talk about before you go running around."

Wyatt threw his shoe down and ran a hand through his hair out of sheer nervous anger. "Mom wouldn't leave without saying something unless whatever went on in town was really bad. And to let me forget Desmond… yeah, something bad happened, Shem."

The cat hopped onto his bedpost, letting out a light purr. "Perhaps. But as I said, she's on her way back already, so clearly the situation has been resolved. As far as your friend goes… I apologize. I didn't know about his departure this morning, or else I would have put more effort into waking you. I endeavor to not read all of your thoughts, Wyatt. I daresay that invading your privacy isn't my goal. You must have kept your thoughts of him deep for me to not have picked up on them."

Wyatt sighed, closing his eyes and pinching the bridge of his nose. Sincerity. That was a new trick.

"It's not your responsibility, Shem. Don't worry about it. I'll calm down and wait. I have things I want to ask you, anyway."

Shem somehow managed to remain perched on the small bedpost. In fact, he looked quite comfortable, his eyes unblinking as he watched Wyatt. Finally, he gave a slow nod. "Ask away."

"What are you?"

The cat cocked his head. "I am Shem, the cat that lives in your sword. Beyond that, I am forbidden to say."

Wyatt stared at him, his annoyance and curiosity bubbling up in equal measures. "Forbidden...? So you're not living inside of the sword by choice, then?"

"Oh no," replied the cat. "I was put there, a long time ago, by people who wished me ill. Due to their meddling, I'm unable to discuss my nature, and a sizeable list of other things that they deemed too sensitive for me to pass on to future minds."

Wyatt made a face. "So you tell me to calm down so we can talk, only to tell me you aren't going to be able to answer any of my questions?"

Shem blinked, his head cocking to the side. "When did I say that? I said that I couldn't discuss my nature, and a number of other things having to do with the past. If they come up, I'll gladly refuse you. But you're entitled to ask me anything you would like. If I am able to, I will answer."

With a sigh, Wyatt rubbed his face and nodded. "Okay then. Why were you down in that cave, inside a magical wall of crystal?"

"Hard to say," replied the cat thoughtfully. "Perhaps to keep me in a safe place. Perhaps to guard me from prying eyes. Perhaps to prevent me from being found. If I had to hazard a guess, I'd assume some combination of the three."

"Why did you appear to me?" asked Wyatt, sounding slightly more nervous than he wanted to admit.

There was a large part of him that was afraid that he was simply a means to an end, and that once Shem used Wyatt to get wherever he wanted to go, Wyatt would lose his connection to both the cat and the sword. He didn't like the idea of facing his normal, boring life again.

Shem watched his face for a moment, apparently thinking. Finally, he answered, his words slow and careful. "Many reasons, I think. Normally, I lie dormant within the blade, but I do occasionally wake up. Usually it's when something of significance happens in the world. When something makes waves, even in deep slumber I can feel them. When I woke up, I realized that I was deep underground, and surprised to feel your presence nearby. I decided that it couldn't be coincidence that a young Adept would be so near me when I happen to wake up."

"And... you're planning on staying with me, then?" asked Wyatt, again sounding a bit more nervous than he'd have liked. But he couldn't help it. "You aren't waiting for some Great Warrior to pick you up and bring glory and honor to your sword?"

Shem chuckled, a first for him. The sound was deep and carried around the room, carried around Wyatt's mind. Wyatt found it off-putting.

"I don't care much about glory and honor, Wyatt. I care only about making sure that this world stays in one piece, and the people that live in it remain happy and whole. You are the right person to wield the blade."

"You called me an Adept," Wyatt suddenly realized with a blink, reeling slightly from the feeling of an electric jolt going through him. "You don't mean... an Adept, do you? Like, wizards?"

Shem let out a noise somewhere between a hiss and a gag, looking at Wyatt, startled. "Wizards? You mean to tell me that, at your age, nobody has told you what you are?"

Wyatt stared at the cat. "What I am? Are you trying to say...?"

Shem leapt from the bedpost, slinking back toward Wyatt. "You are an Adept, Wyatt Arden. Not a wizard, or magician, or any of those other street alley performers. You are one of the bearers of the spark of Adala, the Life-Giver. You hold within you a piece of her divinity, and carry with you the distinction of thousands of years of history. Your blood is rich with power, Wyatt." The cat scoffed again. "Wizards."

Wyatt continued staring at the cat, not even realizing that his mouth was hanging open a bit. He was reeling, trying to grasp what the cat was telling him. But he couldn't quite manage it. His blood... had power?

"You mean..." began Wyatt, finally finding a few words, "you mean, like in the history books? Necromancers and Pyromancers and the lot?"

Shem nodded, and his nod was almost enthusiastic. "I can't be sure, but you smell like an Aeromancer. Hard to say without seeing you actually try to use your power, but it's my best guess."

The possibilities were already racing through Wyatt's head. If Shem were right, he would command one of the six Aspects of Adala, the goddess who had created mankind. If that were true, he'd have to go to the imperial city of Farillyon to receive training from the Adept Council. From there, he'd be able to travel the world. Explore distant, uncharted shores. Fight evil Adepts who abused their powers. His future… it was limitless.

"You're sure about this?" he asked, wanting to remove any doubt. "Please don't lie to me about something like this, Shem. Please."

The cat gave him another even look. "I don't lie, Wyatt. And I'm never wrong about things like this. Not only can I smell it all over you, but ever since you touched that sword, ever since you pulled it out of the wall, your power has awakened. I can see your connection to the world around you. It begs to bend to your will."

Wyatt wanted to jump and scream. He hadn't been this pleased about anything in ages, not since his thirteenth birthday when he had gotten a set of wooden training swords from Kelsar. Those had been broken shortly thereafter, and were promptly replaced with padded steel.

"So that means that I have to go to Farillyon, right? To be taught?"

Shem thought about it for a moment. Wyatt imagined him trying to scratch his chin, and decided that while it would look odd, it was a distinct possibility.

"That is the general course, yes. Especially difficult to get around these days, what with the close ties between the Adept Council and Imperial law. Although… I don't foresee you doing things the normal way, Wyatt. You aren't exactly… typical. Don't worry about your training for right now. These things have a way of working themselves out."

He nodded, now on his feet and pacing around the room excitedly. It was hard to sit still, now that he knew all of this. An Adept. An Aeromancer, Shem had said. Which meant that he could control storms and sky, could cause weather patterns to change on a whim.

Seemingly out of nowhere, thunder boomed outside, shaking the house and rattling the windowpanes. Wyatt jumped, startled. He dashed to the only window in his bedroom, crouching down and peeking out at the sky. The clouds were gray and swirling angrily, a change from their position a few minutes ago.

Behind him, he could hear Shem laughing, a genuine sound that was much less creepy than his earlier chuckle. His deep, merry voice rang out in the room, making Wyatt turn to peer at him suspiciously.

"Definitely an Aeromancer," remarked Shem, appearing to be enjoying himself immensely. "That's a good sign, Wyatt. Your power is waking up fully now. You didn't even realize it when you called that storm. And you didn't even feel it."

Wyatt grinned sheepishly, trying to control his excitement. He didn't want to accidentally blast anybody with lightning the next time he got too giddy about something. With a bit of effort, he slowed his breathing down and focused on calming himself.

"So what about the earthquake?" asked Wyatt, remembering what happened in the cave, a near-death experience that he could still recall all too vividly. "What do you think caused that?"

Shem shrugged. "Whatever woke me up, I'd guess. Hard to say for sure without further investigation, but I imagine that whatever it was will not stay quiet for long."

Wyatt blinked. "You think it's something bad, then?"

Shem bobbed his head up and down. "Oh yes, certainly. If it weren't, I doubt it would've been important enough to wake me up."

Wyatt scratched his chin. "So what am I supposed to do with you? There's got to be some reason that you woke up, some reason that I was the one who found you."

Shem shrugged yet again, appearing utterly unconcerned. "Not sure. Time will tell, I'd imagine. For now we enjoy brief peace and rousing conversation."

Noises came from downstairs before Wyatt could continue his questions. Wyatt pushed the window open, craning his head outside. He managed to see the corner of a carriage that had pulled up in front of his house. It looked like his mother was home.

Wyatt finished putting his clothes on, setting the sword on his bed. He wasn't sure how to talk to his mom about this just yet, so he decided it would be best to just leave the blade up here. He wasn't even sure if she'd be able to see Shem. There was quite a bit about the unusual little cat that he still didn't know.

"I'll be back in a while," he called to Shem, whose response was to curl up in a ball on his bed and ignore him. Wyatt smirked, shaking his head.

He made his way hastily downstairs, flinging open the front door and stepping out into the warm morning sun. Evidently, he had succeeded in calming his emotions, as there were now no clouds in sight. A large carriage was parked outside his house, pulled by two huge horses, the kind that Wyatt knew Kelsar preferred when he had to travel. Wyatt recognized the carriage as Kelsar's. The driver stepped into view, pulling the door open and ignoring Wyatt.

"Kelsar?" he called, now slightly concerned. The blacksmith rarely came by their house, and he never came with a carriage. This was certainly unusual.

Kelsar slowly backed out of the carriage, clutching a woman in his arms. She could barely stand; her skin was coated in a sheen of sweat and marred with bizarre purple blotches.

His mother.

She looked at Wyatt instantly, her eyes oddly distant. She lurched out Kelsar's grip, staggering toward her baffled, shocked son. His heart was pounding, threatening to leap out of his chest.

Nora grabbed the collar of his shirt, putting her weight on him and looking him full in the face. Her eyes were bloodshot and hollow. "Stay with your grandfather," she rasped, her voice broken. "Only he can put you on the path."

Wyatt blinked at her, dumbfounded. He didn't quite know what to do or how to react. Before he could respond, she collapsed into his arms, her energy finally failing.

Kelsar stepped up behind her, grabbing her under the arm and lifting her up. He had an easy time of it, his huge arms more than strong enough from years of hard work. He scooped her up in both arms and brushed past Wyatt without another word as he carried Nora into the house.

"Grandfather?" whispered Wyatt, suddenly very confused. "What in the world happened, Kelsar? What's going on?" His calling fell on deaf ears.

He followed Kelsar into the house, who headed straight for Nora's bedroom. Wyatt didn't even think Kelsar knew where it was, but the weathered old man found it with little trouble. After a bit of struggling, he got her comfortably situated in the bed, and he knelt at her side.

"Earthquake," grunted Kelsar, holding Nora's small hand in both of his. His thick, calloused hands were huge by comparison. "It's complicated, Wyatt."

Wyatt walked up to the bed. "She said something about my grandfather. Was... was she talking about you?"

Kelsar paused for a moment, still looking at Nora. But he finally seemed to come to a decision and nodded.

"Yes, Wyatt," he said quietly, his gravelly voice coming slow and low, "I'm yer granddad."

"Why didn't anyone tell me?" asked Wyatt, anger flooding through his voice even as he tried to keep it back. He couldn't help it. "After all these years, why didn't you tell me? Why didn't SHE tell me?"

Kelsar sighed, finally turning to face him. The blacksmith looked older and more tired than Wyatt had ever seen him. "It's complicated, Wyatt. Go inter the kitchen, pour me a cuppa coffee, and we'll talk."

Wyatt stared at his mother for a moment, suddenly realizing just how bad the situation was. He'd never even seen her sick before, much less looking like this. He swallowed and nodded, trying to keep his anger at bay. Slipping out of his mother's room, he stepped into the kitchen and headed for the fire. He busied himself filling a kettle with water and beans, setting it over the fire. His mind was still racing.

After a few minutes, Kelsar limped into the room. Wyatt hadn't noticed him limping earlier, but he could tell now that Kelsar was hurt in some way. Kelsar lowered himself into a seat at the kitchen table. Wyatt wordlessly set two cups of coffee on the table and sat down, facing his grandfather.

Kelsar took his cup and stared into its murky contents. He didn't even seem to care that it was hot. After a time, he sipped from it. Wyatt was still blowing on his. Wyatt didn't even like coffee, but it seemed appropriate, the kind of thing that his mother would do in this situation.

"Yer not a normal boy," began Kelsar, his voice uncharacteristically quiet. "Not normal like Desmond or any o' yer other friends. Yer an Adept, Wyatt."

Yesterday, this news would've come as a shock. But, of course, Wyatt already knew this, having learned it not even an hour prior to this. He tried to act surprised.

"You mean... like the ones that live in the capital? The great wizards who've been fighting each other for centuries?"

"We're not wizards," growled Kelsar, exasperated. "Yer a chosen one, Wyatt. One o' Adala's gifts was passed down to you, through yer blood. Yeh might say it runs in the family."

Wyatt stared at him, taking a sip of his coffee. He tried his best to keep a straight face, even though the stuff tasted absolutely horrid.

"Why didn't you ever tell me that you are my grandfather? Why didn't mom?"

Kelsar sighed. "Yer mother is in hiding. She's... a fugitive, wanted by the Empire fer treason. She managed teh disappear, with my help. I'm still involved with them, an' I couldn't let on my relation teh her, otherwise they would've found the both of yeh."

"She's a fugitive?" asked Wyatt, leaning back in his chair as the implications washed over him. "What... why is she wanted by the Empire? Why is she in hiding?"

"I never knew," replied Kelsar, with more than a hint of bitterness in his voice. "She an' I were estranged fer a long time. She never told me what happened. Hiding the two of yeh was how she an' I patched up."

Wyatt ran his hands through his hair. He was beginning to feel a little overloaded by everything that was happening. It was all so much to be dumped on him in such a short time.

"What happened to her?" he asked, leaning forward again and clutching his cup tightly as the murky coffee swirled within it. "Is she going to be okay?"

Kelsar looked out the window. "I'm Ven's guardian. I was assigned here teh keep watch over the town an' keep it safe from monsters an' the like. I had a few of 'em locked up in the shop, ones that I didn' have the power teh kill. The earthquake... made somethin' happen, woke one of 'em up and let 'im loose. It caught me by surprise. Yer mother... she saved my life, Wyatt. Helped me beat 'im."

The old man, always bulky and muscular, looked very small at the moment. "I got hurt in the fight," he said bitterly. "Poisoned. Strong stuff. Yer mother, she's a Vitamancer… life magic. Healing. She did 'er best, but ter heal it completely she had ter take the poison inter 'erself and let 'er power purge it."

"Kelsar," said Wyatt, his voice more stern than he had ever thought it capable of being, "is she going to be okay or not?"

The blacksmith sighed again, fidgeting with his coffee cup. "I don' know, Wyatt. She's strong, even as Vitamancers go, but… I've never heard of somethin' like this. But… I think so. I think the fact that it hasn' killed 'er yet is a good sign."

Wyatt stood, pacing around the kitchen nervously. His chair clattered to the floor, but he didn't seem to notice it. He was itching to ask if Shem knew anything about the situation, or if he could offer any insight. Maybe Shem would know about the thing that attacked his mom. Maybe he knew a cure for the poison.

"We've got things teh do, Wyatt," continued his grandfather. "I need yeh to go inter town and fetch some books from my shop. I've got teh stay here and look after yer mother."

"Books?" asked Wyatt, raising an eyebrow. "I didn't know you had any books in that shop, Kelsar."

Kelsar nodded, taking a gulp of coffee. "I grabbed some stuff from the Imperial Library before I came here. The books in there, they'll help yeh learn about yer gift, Wyatt. They should help train yeh."

"Alright, where are they?" Wyatt knew Kelsar's shop pretty well, but he'd never been down to the lower level. It would be interesting, to say the least.

"Downstairs, in my office," said the smith. "Yeh need ter be careful, Wyatt. The earthquake damaged the building, and there's some dangerous stuff down there. Stuff that'll kill yeh if yeh look at it wrong. Don' touch anything, except the books."

So he got to wander around in a damaged, death-filled basement that he didn't know his way around. Looking for books. Wonderful.

"Wyatt, I wouldn't ask yeh to do somethin' like this if it weren't important," added his grandfather, looking a little worried. "Yer growin' up now, and as an Adept, yer life is gonna be filled with risks and danger. Yeh've got to accept yer destiny. If you don't, it'll eat yeh alive."

"Yeah, I know, Kelsar," replied Wyatt, something he'd learned earlier than the smith knew. "I don't know that I like it all that much, but I do believe you when you say it's important. I'll get going right away." He stood and headed for the stairway, for his walking shoes and pack. And for his sword.

"Yer a good boy, Wyatt," grunted Kelsar quietly. "I'm sorry I didn't tell yeh about... all o' this sooner. I wanted ter let you in on it, I did. But it wasn' my place."

Wyatt paused in the doorway, looking toward the stairs. "I'll wait until I talk to Mom before I get mad about anything. Let's not worry about it right now."

The truth was that Wyatt was mad about it, but Kelsar wasn't the object of that anger. He had spent his entire life believing that his mother never kept everything from him. It was hard to accept that she had so many secrets, and that so many of them directly affected him. She should have told him sooner. She knew him well enough to know that he'd find out someday if she didn't.

"Yer right," agreed Kelsar gruffly. "And yer definitely Nora's son. Get movin', we've got a lot of work teh do."

"I do have one question," he asked, looking back over his shoulder at the old man. "Who is my father?"

Kelsar didn't respond for a moment. "If yer mother isn't awake when yeh come back..." he began slowly, his voice distant, "we'll talk about yer father. I don' feel right talkin' 'bout him unless there ain't any other option."

Unless he had to. So if Nora didn't come out of this, he would, but otherwise it wasn't his place. That alone told Wyatt a lot about the situation. He closed his mind down, pushing those thoughts away as he stepped into the hallway, leaving his grandfather behind him.

Wyatt made his way upstairs first. There was no way he'd be leaving Shem and the sword behind. He was also hoping that once he got back, he'd be able to ask Kelsar about the sword and try to figure some of this mess out. If anyone knew something about a magical, ancient sword with a mysterious beast living inside of it, it had to be Kelsar.

Shem sat waiting for him on his bed when he entered the room. The cat looked up, ears perked, eyes twinkling.

"I was wrong again," he said, his voice low and subdued. "It was bad."

Wyatt hastily began to throw on his traveling clothes, flashing the cat a scathing glare. "You're not setting a great pattern for yourself, cat."

There was silence between them for a few moments, the only sounds in the room coming from Wyatt's clothes as he scrambled to get them on. He took a small satisfaction in knowing that the cat was so taken aback.

"It's been awhile since I've had to see the world through the eyes of humanity," replied the cat after a time. "I am sorry, Wyatt. I will try to do better."

Wyatt studied the cat's eyes for a few moments. He truly did sound it, too. Wyatt hadn't yet heard this quality in his voice; it was a deep sadness that seemed to stretch out of the house and beyond Wyatt and his family. It seemed to be much bigger and deeper than Wyatt could know.

Finally, Wyatt nodded as he stuffed his feet into his good boots. "It's fine, Shem. I wouldn't have been able to do anything anyway, and I'd just be more tired and less alert. But I do need your help, so you're coming with me."

Shem cocked his head. "Where are we going?"

"Into town," replied Wyatt, although he suspected the cat probably already knew. "To get some books from Kelsar's shop, and to make sure that nobody else in town is hurt or in need of our help." Stepping over to the bed, Wyatt picked up the leather baldric that held the sword and strapped it over his shoulder. Securing the blade at his hip, he took a quick glance at himself in the mirror.

He already looked different. He looked older. He looked like an Adept.

Looking around, Wyatt was pleased to note that the interior of the shop wasn't as deadly as the smith had suggested. It was, however, disgusting. Nearly everything inside was coated with some kind of gray, gloopy resin that smelled an awful lot like rotting plants. Wyatt was doing his best to avoid touching it, afraid of whatever strange properties it possessed and what it might do to his skin. Shem was clinging to his back, staring at the walls with apprehension.

Worse yet, Wyatt realized with closer inspection that the resin appeared to be dissolving everything it touched. There were pits in the floor and holes in the walls. Tools were missing pieces, swimming around in the resin in broken disarray.

"Any idea?" he asked the cat, peering at the coating on the walls. It was everywhere.

"Your grandfather had some nasty things locked up in here," replied the cat quietly, his head right next to Wyatt's ear. "This… residue is left by an Atumen, a spirit of decay. I had thought that most of them were bound or broken long, long ago, but by the look of it your grandfather had one here, probably locked within a frozen flame. Perhaps it hid, escaping destruction by the first Adepts. I cannot say."

"An Atumen," muttered Wyatt, processing the word as he glanced around the shop. "Is that what got Mom sick?"

"Most likely," answered the cat. "A Vitamancer heals others with her purity. It takes a strong one to be able to withdraw disease into their body. It is very rare. But the taint of the Atumen is likewise powerful, and not an easily defeated foe. I'm sorry, Wyatt, but your mother has a hard fight ahead of her."

Wyatt already knew that, but it wasn't really comforting to have his thoughts confirmed. His insides twisted as he tried to ignore his worries. The worst part was not being able to do anything. He wanted to help, not sit by and run errands.

"She is strong," added the cat quietly. "I believe she can make it, Wyatt. Have faith."

Wyatt muttered a thank you, but didn't speak beyond that. He took a moment to gather his focus and cast aside his worries. Taking a deep breath, he focused on the humming warmth that came from the sword. He let it roll over him and calm his nerves. Then, with his mind clear once again, he delved further into the wreckage of the blacksmith's shop.

He slipped behind the counter, ducking into the back area where he had not been allowed since he was a boy. The forge was red with heat, showing that Kelsar never had the time to quench it. But Wyatt had no idea how to do that, so he moved on, silently hoping that it wouldn't burn the shop to the ground if he left it unattended. He peered around the back area, finally locating the stairs and ducking through the doorway.

The smell from the resin was absolutely putrid. It was worse the deeper he went into the shop, as more and more of the gloopy fluid coated the walls and floor. He found it difficult to make it down the stairs, having to leap from safe spot to safe spot to avoid landing in a puddle of goop. But finally, perilously, he made it to the bottom and peered around.

The end of the stairs branched off in two directions. To his left, Wyatt could see a small room where Kelsar likely slept. He saw a small cot and a desk, but the room was very sparse and didn't appear to hold anything else. So he turned to his right instead, down a short hall. At the end of that hall, he found a door on the ground, broken and discarded. He saw large claw marks in the back of it. It, like the rest of the shop, was mostly coated in gray resin.

Through the doorway, Wyatt found what he was looking for. The room itself was mostly destroyed; piles of wood and tools were scattered around haphazardly. But at the back of the room, a tiny shelf sat against the wall, miraculously resin-free. Wyatt cautiously made his way through the room, stepping over the piles of junk to reach the bookshelf.

The books looked correct. Some of the titles were too faded to read, but they looked ancient and mystical, just how he imagined tomes of untold power and secrets would look. He glanced over his shoulder at Shem, who nodded at him. Fair enough. He began scooping the books into the burlap sack he had brought with him. No time for any ceremony now.

The last book in the shelf drew his eye. It was the only book on the bottom shelf, the plain gray cover bearing no title or markings. Wyatt picked it up and flipped through it with interest, but he found he couldn't read the text inside.

His brow furrowed as he stared at the pages. He could tell that there was writing in the book, but it swam before his eyes, jumbling up and making no sense to him. It was as if the letters were alive and were constantly shifting, trying to conceal their secrets from him or anyone else that might happen upon the volume and try to read through it.

"A good read," mused Shem, looking over Wyatt's shoulder. "Though I doubt you can right now."

"What is it?" asked Wyatt, his curiosity piqued.

"The kind of book you need," replied the cat, seeming to enjoy his own mysteriousness. "A book of knowledge and instruction of the magical kind. Magic was invested in the writing, ensuring that no person of insufficient power or experience can see it. Bring it with you."

Wyatt nodded, dropping the book in his sack. After securing the sack, he stuffed it into his pack, straining a bit to buckle it closed with the large cargo inside of it. But he managed to get it closed. Setting Shem aside, he slung the pack over his shoulder, suddenly dreading the long walk home. Shem climbed back up, adding to the weight on Wyatt's shoulders. Wyatt idly wondered if the cat even really had to weigh anything, or if he just liked to.

"As I recall," began Wyatt hotly, "you do have legs of your own."

He heard Shem snicker. "Yes, but if I don't need to use them, why bother?" asked the cat innocently. "Besides, it's good for you."

"Yeah, but you aren't even a real cat, are you? Why not just sit in the sword until you have something... I don't know, useful, to do?"

The cat snorted. "Have you ever lived inside of a sword, Wyatt? It's boring. I've been stuck in there for a long time. I'm enjoying the scenery, the birds, the breeze."

Wyatt sighed, conceding his point. Shem had spent a long time stuck in a cave. He would probably want to be out, too. But he wasn't so sure that the cat would be riding along on his back for the entire trip.

After taking one last look around the area to make sure he hadn't missed anything, Wyatt began climbing back up the broken stairs into the main level of the building. He did his best to avoid the piles of resin on the floor, fearing that it would destroy his good boots if he stepped in it.

"Dodge!" hissed Shem suddenly, and Wyatt dove to the side, toward a hopefully resin-free spot in the shop. Just as he did, a large glob of fluid fell from the ceiling, landing with a plop exactly where he had been standing. It was large enough that it would've covered his head and shoulders easily. He stared at it for a few moments, his heart pounding.

"See?" said Shem quietly in his ear. "I'm very useful."

Wyatt nodded dumbly, wiping some sweat from his forehead. It suddenly felt very hot inside the shop.

"Let's go," he said finally, shaking himself out of his brief shock. He cautiously moved forward, keeping his eyes on the ceiling as well as the floor. More of the resin seemed to have appeared in the short time he was downstairs. Had he dawdled any longer, he might've ended up trapped, forced to step through it to get free.

"Strong Atumen," muttered the cat, looking around at the resin. "That's not a good sign, Wyatt. It takes a strong binding to keep an Atumen down. It takes an even stronger thing to break that binding. One that would leave this much resin behind… it does not bode well at all."

"Mom's made of tougher stuff than you know," replied Wyatt hotly, making no effort to hide his irritation. "She's going to be fine."

The cat stayed silent, which Wyatt was thankful for. He didn't need Shem's pessimism weighing him down. He already had the cat on his back.

He ducked through the doorway, glad to be out in the open air of Ven. Pausing for a moment in the street, he checked himself over, just to be sure there wasn't any sticky gunk anywhere on him eating through his clothing. He'd hate to find it later after it'd destroyed his cloak. He didn't need any more nasty surprises.

Satisfied that he was resin-free, he made toward the alley, away from the shop. As he did so, he heard a loud groaning from behind him that came rolling out of the open doorway. He looked back just in time to see the roof buckle, sending a plume of dust and debris into the sky, along with several globs of sticky resin. He just stood there for a moment, gaping at the collapsed wreckage as he realized just how close he had come to being inside of it.

"Good timing," remarked Shem, clearly amused.

"You're not helping," said Wyatt dully, shaking his head. It was hard to get worked up over surviving, but it was certainly a sobering experience. His life had been defined by the boredom of farm life, but this last day had been a rush of new experiences. His life was rapidly changing, and watching a building that he had exited only moments earlier collapse was certainly a good reminder to be careful.

Wyatt focused his thoughts and set back on the road toward home. He felt a pang of worry about the shop. Wyatt hoped that there wasn't anything else important inside. He also hoped even more that there weren't any more dangerous creatures inside. Wyatt didn't need another horrible monster springing from the wreckage to eat him alive.

"Ven is quiet today," observed Shem pensively. "The merchants have cleared out, and there is barely anyone wandering the streets."

Wyatt peered around, looking down the side streets and the alleyways as he walked through the town. The cat was right; few people could be seen, and those that could were walking quickly, intent on their destinations.

"The earthquake must've spooked everyone," he offered, shrugging it off. "People in Ven tend to be a little superstitious. An earthquake coming during the harvest... that's a bad omen. Everyone is probably praying, fasting, and sprinkling holy oil on their fields, or whatever the fanatics do in situations like this."

"Not the religious type, then?" asked the cat, genuinely interested. "Most Adepts view Adala with great reverence."

Wyatt shrugged. "I'm still getting used to being an Adept, as I've only known about it for about a day. But no gods have ever come down from the sky and brought rain or good weather, even when we did pray. I guess I just never saw the point. There are too many things for me to do."

"Wise words," remarked his feline stowaway. "Perhaps you are not as one-dimensional as I had once believed."

"Shut up," replied Wyatt hotly. He was getting tired of the cat's constant double-talk. Shem didn't ever seem to say anything with just one meaning.

"As you wish, master," replied the cat slyly. The image of him punching the cat squarely in the face briefly crossed through Wyatt's mind. He heard Shem snicker.

After a few more minutes of walking, Wyatt found his way onto the main road out of Ven and began the long trek home. He hadn't seen very many people out and about in town, and it was still bothering him a little bit. The merchants had disappeared, the people were gone… it was as if the harvest had just been canceled halfway through.

To further punctuate the lovely day he was having, rain began to fall as Wyatt walked home. Shem let out a sharp yowl and wormed his way into Wyatt's pack, which Wyatt tried not to think too hard about. There had barely been any room left in there as is, with all of the books. But Shem wasn't a normal cat, either.

Cold rain continued to fall as Wyatt walked home. He glared up at the sky, hoping to shoo the clouds away with his newfound power. But the clouds remained, seeming unimpressed by his mental flexing. In fact, it seemed like the rain intensified, almost as if the sky was just trying to spite him. He had no control over his power right now, which meant he was going to continue to be wet and cold.

"Can't you do something about that?" came Shem's muffled voice as Wyatt trudged through the mud, rubbing his arms for warmth. "I really don't like being wet."

Wyatt ignored him. Shem knew better, but Wyatt suspected he just enjoyed being able to whine about something. Wyatt did his best to stay warm, stuffing his hands into his armpits as he continued on the road ahead.

After an excruciatingly long and cold walk, the house finally came into view. Wyatt walked up the hill, panting with the effort of pulling his feet through the mud for so long. The rain continued to pour unforgivingly, only making things harder for him.

He stepped up to the front walk, peering in through the windows. He didn't see any light, but being that Kelsar had been up all night fighting the Atumen, it was possible that the old man had turned in for a nap. Wyatt paused at the front door to scrape the mud off the bottom of his boots and dry off just a little bit. Unconscious or not, his mother would find a way to scold him if he got the house dirty. Finally satisfied that he was clean enough, he stepped quietly inside, setting his pack down beside him.

He made it three steps into the front hall when the hairs on his neck stood up.

"Wyatt! RUN!" boomed Shem's voice in his ears, rattling the walls with its sudden power. Everything seemed to slow down as Wyatt turned and stepped in one motion, running back out the door as fast as he could. He had the sense to grab one of the straps of his pack with his left hand as he did, and could feel it swinging wildly behind him. He made it one step out the door when he felt a concussive thump on his back. Noise roared in his ears, and suddenly, Wyatt was no longer running; he was flying.

Pain seared through his back and arms as he soared down the hill toward the creek. He landed hard, his forward momentum causing him to tumble and roll like a child's wooden doll. His entire body flopped and thumped awkwardly, and although he was doing his best to pull his arms into his chest, he couldn't seem to work them properly.

With one final "oof," Wyatt landed hard on the bank of the creek, sinking into the muddy ground with force. His legs splashed into the water, sending a cold sensation up his back that clashed with the heat of the pain. He tried to lift his head, but was so dizzy and dazed that nothing seemed to be working properly.

He couldn't lift his head, so he glanced down at his arm, which was the only part of his body he could see. Pain blossomed through the entire limb as he noticed a spike of bright white sticking out of a ragged patch of red flesh. Nausea filled him as he tried to scream, but everything was going white around the edges.

He kept trying to scream, but he only seemed to be able to manage moans and gurgles. He tried to move, but only managed to send another wave of agony and nausea through his body. Everything felt heavy, and he lost his grip on the world. Everything faded into white, and Wyatt drifted into unconsciousness.

Sometime later, Wyatt's left eye slid open, glancing around. He felt confused, and his entire body was throbbing with pain.

He looked around him, but it was hard to make out what was going on. He was either moving, or very dizzy. He tried to lift his head, but only managed to instead let out a weak cry of pain.

"Easy," came a soft voice from above him. He looked over, trying to focus. A shadow crouched over him, pressing a hand to his chest. He winced, expecting pain, but a slow warmth moved through him. It was not unlike the warmth that the sword gave him, but somehow... more focused.

"I'm trying to heal you, but if you keep struggling and wiggling, you'll only make this harder on us," said the voice again. Wyatt decided it was a female voice, though he wasn't really sure. He was finding it hard to concentrate on anything. He did his best to relax, but the pain made that so hard.

"There you go," she cooed, another hand touching his shoulder. The warmth filled him, dulling the pain a bit and helping to calm him down significantly.

"Water," he croaked, his lips cracking with the effort. He felt like he could drink an entire river. The shadow shifted, drawing out a skin of some sort and pouring cool water into his mouth. He drank clumsily, the water spilling down his front, but he didn't care. It might've been the most delicious thing he had ever tasted.

"You're going to make it," said the woman as she stowed the water away. "You're in really good hands, trust me. Just rest now, rest easy." Her hands moved to other parts of his body, sending warmth and peace radiating through him. He looked up at the form, focusing for one brief moment on eyes of soft, deep green. He held onto that color, locked it in his mind. He had never seen green like that before.

Whatever he was riding on hit a bump in the road, sending a fresh wave of rocking pain coursing through him. He cried out, the calm slipping from his mind as the pain resurfaced. He tried as hard as he could to focus on those green eyes, but the whiteness overtook him. Everything drifted away again, pulling him back into unconsciousness.

Wyatt,

I left this letter with your mom knowing you wouldn't get it till after I was gone. That's what I wanted and she promised not to give it to you until after I left, so don't get mad at her for it.

Listen, I know you're upset that you couldn't join the army with me. I know you feel like you're stuck there, without anywhere to go or any excitement in your life. But the truth is that you're really lucky, Wyatt. I didn't have any kind of attachment to Ven because I never had the family connection that you have. My parents love me, sure, but they're wealthy farm moguls. They don't work the land anymore, just the books. There's no heart in that and I didn't want any part in it.

You and your mom have it right. You're doing something real, something that your blood and soul is put into. I honestly envy that. I'm going to travel the world, but I'll never really have that connection to one place like you have to Ven. Even when the time comes and you do make it out of there, you'll always have Ven to go back to. I'd rather come to see you and Nora than go back to my own house.

I'm going to make sure that I write you letters as much as I can. You're going to see the world through my eyes. You're going to fight the wildlings with my arms. And you gotta write me back, kid, because I'll pull my eyes out if I don't hear back from you. This is all strange enough, so I need some normalcy in my life.

Plus, Annie Staghorn is single and she's staying home at her farm, too. You two should, you know, keep each other company.

We're still best friends, no matter how far away we are. I'll be back before you know it with all kinds of gifts from far off places. You just wait there for me, Wyatt. Everything will work out in the end.

Des

CHAPTER FIVE

unlight crept over the hill, scattering beams of light throughout a small, quickly assembled campsite. Birds chirped merrily in the distance. Red coals glowed from within the heart of a shallow pit dug at the center, a remnant of the fire from the night before. Two horses were tied off at the edge of the camp, grazing lazily from the forest brush. There were two bedrolls around the fire: one empty, the other containing a still, sleeping figure.

A beam of light slowly made its way across the small clearing, ominously headed on a linear path toward the face of the slumbering form. His stillness would defeat him as, eventually, that little beam of light began to drift directly across his face. Wyatt didn't notice the light at first, but after a few moments, he shifted stiffly and swatted his face. He stretched within the bedroll, feeling sore and sluggish.

Two low voices echoed from the other side of the camp, and Wyatt's sense of danger flared. He scrambled out of his bedroll, falling back in a crouch as adrenaline shot through him, briefly letting him forget about his stiff joints and sore limbs. Without even a conscious thought from Wyatt, the sword sprang across the clearing. He gripped the hilt and unsheathed the blade in one clean motion. He held the sword up as he stared across the clearing at the other two that were with him. How had he gotten here?

"Easy!" yelled a voice, and Wyatt heard the telltale sound of steel being drawn, a ringing that cut through the morning air. He stared at the source; a muscular man in his mid-twenties with close-cropped hair and steel-blue eyes stood with sword drawn, just in front of a younger, redheaded woman. Both of them wore simple leather armor, and the man had a small buckler in his off-hand to complement his sword.

Wyatt's heart was pounding in his ears, and he could feel Shem's caution as well, pushing into his mind from the sword. Even the cat wasn't sure what was going on, which wasn't a good sign. Suddenly, the wind kicked up, swirling around them and sending the girl's hair dancing into a fiery frenzy.

"We're not the enemy, kid," said the man across the fire. His voice was low and deadly. "We pulled you out of that creek and healed you."

Wyatt looked at him for a moment, but didn't react. His only experience with swordplay was his years fighting with Desmond. He'd never learned any real combat styles or methods. But he was pretty sure the other guy knew a thing or two about it. His tall, lean frame and hard eyes left Wyatt with little doubt as to what the man was: a soldier.

As his mind raced, Wyatt could feel the pain slowly creeping back into him. His entire body ached, and he could feel warm blood in a few places, from freshly opened wounds.

"He's not lying to you," called the girl from behind the man, her voice soft, yet somehow just as firm as his.

Wyatt looked past him, into her eyes. She also looked like a warrior, but her green eyes stirred Wyatt's memory. She was the one who had been taking care of him, he realized. He remembered her hair, her voice. He remembered her eyes. He relaxed a little, letting the blade down but not letting go of it.

"I… what… what happened?" he asked, looking at the both of them, his voice displaying equal parts confusion and desperation.

The other two shared a brief look, and the man dropped his sword as well. "We were hoping you could tell us that," he answered wearily. "We were traveling through the area when we heard the explosion. We found you half dead in the creek, about to drown. Rubble was everywhere. Wood, stone, and virtually everything else, but we couldn't figure out where the explosion started. We put you on a pallet and dragged you away from the area."

Wyatt looked down at the sword in his hand, which shimmered

and returned to his scabbard. Evidently, Shem had passed judgment on the situation.

"Sorry. I don't really know why I did that. Instinct, I guess."

The man nodded and sheathed his sword. "It's okay, kid. It seems like you've been through a lot. I expected you to be a little on edge." He walked around the fire pit slowly, stopping just short of Wyatt and extending a hand. "I'm Jag Mercer. This is my sister, Grace."

Wyatt took the gesture, clasping wrists with the man. Mercer was the name of an unclaimed child, he recalled; those with no parents to give them a surname. Only those of no parentage had that name.

"Wyatt Arden," he responded, giving them both a sheepish, apologetic smile. "Again, sorry about all the... er, hostility. You both saved my life. I'm really grateful."

"You need to sit down, Wyatt," said Grace, walking over to him and nudging him back down onto the bedroll. "It looks like all that motion might've opened a few of your wounds. Sit, so I can look you over."

He went without complaint, realizing just how much pain he was in. It was getting hard to breathe.

She touched his temples with two fingers on each hand, closing her eyes. The same warmth he had experienced while riding on the pallet flowed into him, and his pain lessened considerably. He had to stop himself from letting out a relieved groan, instead looking at Jag questioningly as he tried to keep his eyes from crossing.

"She's a Vitamancer," he said, eyeing Wyatt with a wary, cautious look. "One of the few left in the world. She doesn't know much about the art, but she managed to pull you away from death, so I'd say she's doing great."

Wyatt's heart skipped a beat. A Vitamancer? Another Adept!

Grace opened her eyes, giving him an even look as the healing energy slowly subsided. "You're going to need to take it easy for a while," she said quietly, lowering her hands. "You could still do a lot of damage if you move around too much, so nothing strenuous for a week or so." With that, she walked back over to the other side of the camp, crouching down to pack up the other bedroll. Jag watched her for a moment, quiet.

"How did you do that?" he asked suddenly, looking back to Wyatt. "With the sword. Is it spelled?"

Wyatt looked down at the sword in his hand, his mind racing. "I... yeah. It's a family heirloom."

Jag eyed him again for a moment. Wyatt had the distinct impression that he was being studied like a book, but finally, Jag nodded and looked away.

An awkward silence settled over the camp as Jag moved to help his sister. It was clear to Wyatt that they were both suspicious of him, and his little stunt with the sword probably hadn't helped matters any.

He turned to the bedroll he had been sleeping in, crouching down to wrap it up. His entire body still ached, and he had odd, random itches all over. Nevertheless, he was alive, and he could tell that whatever Grace had done to help him had helped him a whole lot.

Wyatt paused. He could feel eyes on him, from somewhere in the trees. He slowly looked up, only to find Shem sitting on a nearby stump. The cat was staring back at him, his luminous golden eyes twinkling. Wyatt glanced over his shoulder, but Grace and Jag were busy packing up their gear. He figured he had a few moments.

"Be careful, Wyatt," hissed Shem. "The boy is a very accomplished soldier, and the girl is very strong. Not very trained, but very strong."

"She's a Vitamancer," replied Wyatt, his voice a low whisper. He pretended to be busy with his packing. "Doesn't that make her good?"

Shem visibly scoffed. "Nothing is ever so black and white. Especially with magic. People are good or bad. Magic is magic."

"What happened?" asked Wyatt, looking up at the cat searchingly. He felt utterly lost. He had missed several hours, if not days, and needed to know what was going on.

"Something bad," offered Shem quietly. "A lot of power was waiting for you in that house. I didn't realize it until it was too late. I'm sorry, Wyatt." He actually sounded it, too.

Wyatt shook his head. "What about Mom, and Kelsar?"

Shem sighed. "I don't know. I didn't feel any other life in the house when we got there, but I also wasn't really looking. Once I felt the spell that you triggered, I was more worried about warning you."

Wyatt felt a pang of fear in his chest, and he had to pause his packing momentarily. Mom and Kelsar weren't even there… they could've been killed by whatever came into the house. Or, maybe they had been there, unnoticed by Shem and killed by the explosion. His heart felt heavy in his chest as the scenarios ran through his head, pulling his focus away. He didn't notice Jag walking up behind him, peering down at him.

"Kid?" called Jag with a frown. "Who are you talking to?"

Wyatt blinked, looking up toward the stump quickly. Shem was gone.

"Just thinking out loud, I guess," he lied after a short pause. "I'm still a little rattled. Just trying to make sense of everything."

Jag inclined his head. "Understandable. Well, we're about all packed up, and you're probably fine if you want to go off on your own. But Grace wants to keep an eye on you, so you're welcome to come with us if you want. Your choice."

Wyatt turned, glancing over at Grace. She was still across the camp packing the last of their things, but seemed to hear what her brother had said. She glanced up at Wyatt for a moment. Her green eyes looked at him for just a heartbeat before drifting back down to their packs.

"I'd like to come with you," said Wyatt suddenly, although he wasn't really what sure made him say it. But the more he thought, the more sense it seemed to make. "I don't really… know where to go from here. But I need to get some answers. I need to find out what happened to me."

Before Jag could even respond, Grace looked up again. "We can take you wherever you need to go, Wyatt. We can help you get answers."

Jag turned to face her, and the two of them shared a look. Something unspoken seemed to happen between them, but Wyatt couldn't follow it.

Jag let out an exasperated sigh and turned back to Wyatt. "Yeah, we can help you out, kid. Where do you want to go?"

Wyatt wasn't even sure how to answer that question. If his mom and Kelsar were alive, he had no idea where to start looking for them. Ven was the only place that made sense, but that was back toward whatever had blown up his house.

"I know we're running away from there, but… Ven," he replied quietly. "I can't think of anywhere else to find the answers I need."

His companions were silent for a few seconds. It was Jag who spoke first.

"Well, we're not that far," he said, scratching his head. "We had to drag you on that pallet, so we weren't exactly making good time. I think we can work that out. But there's no telling what we're going to find. It might be dangerous, kid. You prepared for that?"

"Did you not see what was left of my house?" asked Wyatt quickly, looking at Jag in near-defiance. "I think I've covered dangerous already."

The two of them exchanged looks again. It was Grace who answered, this time. "Wyatt, we grabbed you and got away pretty quickly, but… there wasn't any house left. The top of the hill was completely blown away. There was a lot of rubble, but nothing else."

Wyatt looked toward the rising sun, swallowing and nodding. That didn't bode well for Kelsar or his mother. It didn't bode well for a lot of things.

"We should get going," said Jag quietly. "We'll get back on the road to Ven. While we're traveling, you can tell me who you are, and why someone would try to blow you up."

Wyatt strapped the baldric around his shoulder and assisted them in gathering up the rest of the camp. Wyatt realized that not only had these two saved his life, they had also shared their bedroll with him, fed him, and offered him safe travel. They wanted to help him. Normal people didn't do something like that. It was becoming clear to him that these two, whoever they were, were something special.

They got back on the road after a few more minutes; Wyatt rode one horse while Jag and Grace shared the other. They moved at a slower pace, with Jag asking many questions about Wyatt's life: his parents, his upbringing, his friends. Wyatt was mostly honest, but he avoided bringing up Shem and the sword. When he talked about the earthquake and the Atumen, Jag nearly fell off the horse.

"You mean to tell me that some crazy old blacksmith was keeping an Atumen locked up in his basement?" he sputtered, stunned with disbelief. "Was he trying to get Ven destroyed?"

Wyatt shrugged, nudging his horse onward. "He said that he was the Guardian of Ven, appointed by the Crown to watch over everyone in the area. He fought the Atumen a long time ago and couldn't kill it, so he bound it and kept it close by."

"Wyatt, I've met most of the Guardians," responded Jag slowly. "I've never heard of Ven having one. Last I knew, it was too much of a fringe territory for the Crown to appoint one. They had to pull their power inward and strengthen their core defenses when the war ended."

"I don't know what to tell you," sighed Wyatt, shaking his head. "I barely know anything about him, apparently. He was a really, really good blacksmith, and his works were sought by men all over the continent, but other than that... I didn't even know he was a Pyromancer until after the earthquake."

"Jag... what about the great smith, from the war?" offered Grace, leaning ahead a little so that they could hear her. "They say he retired after the war and took a Guardianship. But he kind of dropped off the planet after that. You wouldn't have met him if he never came back to the capital."

Jag glanced back at her. "Honestly, sis, I didn't think he was still alive. That war was a long time ago, and he wasn't exactly young then. But it could be, I guess. Some people say he never even existed."

"I don't know much about him, but I do know him," said Wyatt firmly as he watched the road. "Kelsar would never endanger the lives of the townspeople if he wasn't sure of himself. He was always the first to help anyone in a crisis, first to offer anything he could to help his people."

Jag sighed and shook his head, obviously at a loss. "You're probably right. I don't know what to make of it, kid. I don't know why anyone would blow your house up. Maybe they wanted that sword of yours?"

It hit Wyatt like a hammer. The sword. Shem said that something in the world had happened, waking him up. Whatever it was had to be tied to this. There was no other explanation. Whoever or whatever had attacked his home was either after him or after the sword. Maybe even both. They had gotten there while he was in Ven, and had lain in wait until he returned.

Things just kept looking worse and worse. His only hope was that Kelsar had been strong enough to get them away from the house, to run instead of fight whatever it was that had come looking for Wyatt.

"Uh, kid?" asked Jag, and Wyatt snapped back to reality. Jag and Grace were staring at him.

"Sorry," he replied quickly, shaking his head. "I don't really know much about the sword, honestly. Just that it's a family heirloom, and it's meant to be mine. It has some kind of special qualities, but it was never explained to me."

"There have been inscribed swords that've popped up here and there over the years," said Jag, frowning and scratching his stubbly chin. "That could certainly be one of them. I've never heard of one that could just... jump into someone's hand like that, though. It must've been in your family for a long time."

Wyatt shrugged, looking back to the road. "Again, I don't really know much about it. I never knew my dad, and he's probably the one that would know more about it. Mom didn't tell me anything about our family."

He felt guilty for lying to them, after they had already done him so many favors. But Wyatt still felt uneasy about the entire situation, and he couldn't shake the feeling that there was more to both of them than he knew. He was pretty sure they felt the same way about him, but he didn't want to dwell on it.

"Sorry," said Jag, giving him a sympathetic look. "I know what it's like to not have a lot of family. I'll back off. Let's pick up the pace here, and we can hopefully get to Ven by day's end."

Wyatt was glad for the reprieve. He wasn't sure how much longer he'd be able to lie about the sword, and he knew that every lie made it that much more likely that he'd slip up and make a mistake. He was mostly just anxious to get to Ven and see what had happened.

He and his strange new companions nudged their horses onward, increasing their speed and preparing for the worst.

"Yeah..." muttered Jag as he peeked over the edge of the low hill that looked over Ven, "something definitely happened here. It's too still. And there's nobody here." Jag and Wyatt laid low on the hill, their heads just poking up as they tried to get a clear view of what was going on. From their current vantage point, they had a pretty good view of the main street through Ven, as well as the market square that sat in the center.

Wyatt poked his head a little further over the edge, peering out over the town. Jag was right: the shop booths and wagons were gone, as if the square had been completely abandoned overnight. Debris littered the area, a clear product of a hasty exit by many merchants at once. Signs, tarps, and, in some cases, goods had all been left behind. Worse than that, however, was that Ven appeared to have been abandoned by more than just the merchants. Wyatt couldn't see anyone milling about in the street. He saw no silhouettes moving across windows. He couldn't hear horses or voices or any other signs of activity. It was as if Ven had been completely deserted.

"I don't like it," muttered Grace from behind them. She sat up and scooted back, looking at them both with a frown. "Why here? Why would anyone attack a little place like Ven?"

Jag sighed, twisting around to face her. "I don't get it either. Even during the harvest, Ven doesn't see enough merchant activity to justify something like this. Though, considering the Atumen... maybe it was another rogue beast of some kind. Maybe your blacksmith had other things locked up in his shop?"

Wyatt looked out over the still, silent town. It looked dead. There were no plumes of smoke from the chimneys, no birds chirping merrily from rooftops. His heart felt hard and heavy, like he were watching the only place he had ever known die right in front of him.

"I don't know guys," he said quietly, running a hand through his hair. "I'm no expert, but I've never heard any horror stories about monsters blowing up houses. Eating people, ransacking villages, sure. But blowing up a house? Isn't that... well, more like Adept territory?"

Jag rubbed his eyes, sighing. "Yeah. Grace, if that is the case... we need to go in there. We need to see what's going on."

Wyatt looked over at him. "What do you mean? Why do you need to go investigate?"

Grace looked at her brother for a moment before answering for him. "It's why we're out here," she explained slowly, as if trying to choose her words carefully. "We work to keep rogue Adepts down, to make sure that magic is used properly, and, most of all, to prevent another war."

"We don't have time for a lengthy explanation," added Jag, before Wyatt could spout out more questions. "We need to get into the town and see if we can find anyone to question. By the look of it, that's going to be hard to do, but we need to start somewhere. It's going to be dangerous, Wyatt. You don't have to come with if you don't want to."

Wyatt gave him an incredulous look. "Are you kidding? Jag, my house just blew up. I want to know what happened."

Jag gave him a wry smile and nodded. "I figured you'd say something like that. Grace, I think you should stay here. The horses are on edge, and someone needs to keep them from spooking. Wyatt and I will sneak in, poke around, and get out quickly once we've figured something out."

Another unspoken something happened between the two of them as Grace gave her brother a fiery, defiant look. But after a moment, she sighed and nodded.

"Just be careful," she said, obviously annoyed at her brother's protectiveness. "I'm still really tired from healing Wyatt the first time. If either of you gets hurt, I don't know how much I'll be able to help. So don't."

Jag waved at her dismissively, a sly smile on his face. "We can take care of ourselves. The kid has a magic sword, Grace. A magic sword! We'll be fine."

She eyed Wyatt for a moment, her expression flat. "Yeah," she said finally, standing and turning away from them. She walked to their nearby horses. "Just hurry up."

Jag and Wyatt left her behind, slipping down the hill quickly and dashing behind the nearest building on their way into Ven. Jag motioned for Wyatt to follow before darting down the nearest alleyway, straight for the heart of the small town.

Wyatt quickly followed, finding it slightly difficult to keep up with his wounds still fresh. His skin felt tight in places, and his bones and muscles ached. But he didn't want to slow Jag down, so he swallowed the pain and pushed onward.

Suddenly, Jag held out a closed fist and froze, crouching low. Wyatt slowly crept up just behind him, taking a knee and looking at him questioningly. Jag pointed into the market square, and Wyatt followed the finger.

A lone form stood near the center of the square, swaying slightly but otherwise standing still. Wyatt couldn't see his face, but he could tell that it was a man. He didn't appear to notice either Jag or Wyatt, and seemed very busy with staring off into the town. He continued to sway slightly, and the motion stirred something in Wyatt's memory. But he couldn't quite place it.

"What do you make of that?" asked Jag in a hushed whisper, glancing at Wyatt.

"Dunno," murmured Wyatt, shaking his head. "I can't see his face from here, so I have no idea who he is. Or if I even know him. Maybe we should go talk to him. He might've seen something."

Jag frowned, looking back to the strange, swaying man. "There's something... no, you're right. I'll get his attention. Stay close."

Wyatt nodded, and Jag stepped out from behind the wagon. "Sir?" he called questioningly, keeping his stance neutral and his voice pleasant as he stepped slowly into the square, Wyatt close behind him.

The man stopped swaying and turned, the motion slow and awkward. He fixed a glassy, vacant stare on Jag and let out a low moan, jerking forward. He lurched toward Jag slowly, his gait uneven and clumsy.

Wyatt blinked, and suddenly, he remembered where he'd seen that motion before. His dream. This was one of the horrible things from that dream, the one he'd had right before all this chaos had happened.

Wyatt gripped Jag's shoulder, pulling him to a halt. "Jag," he hissed, his other hand clutching the hilt of his sword. "That's some kind of monster. Be careful."

Jag glanced over his shoulder at Wyatt, nodding. "Dammit," he cursed, staring at the thing with disgust. "I knew there was something off about this. Dammit twice. I could smell it, but I couldn't place it. That's a drone, a... dead body, reanimated by a Necromancer."

Icy fingers caressed Wyatt's spine. "A Necromancer? Jag, you don't mean..."

Jag nodded slowly, his iron gaze on the lurching form that was slowly drawing closer to them. He drew his sword, glancing back again at Wyatt. "There's a Necromancer in Ven, and he's likely the one responsible for all of this. This is… a lot worse than I expected, Wyatt. If you want to go back and wait with Grace, I understand perfectly. This could get ugly."

Wyatt walked up beside him and took the most battle-ready stance he could think of. He, too, drew his sword, feeling the warmth flood over him as he did so. He knew he didn't have anywhere near Jag's training level with a blade, but he was determined to hold his ground.

"I'm not going anywhere, Jag," said Wyatt, his voice low and determined. "This is my home."

Jag eyed him for a moment, his expression only a little surprised. Finally, he nodded, and before Wyatt could even react, he was moving toward the shambling corpse. It was over in a flash. Jag raised his sword in both hands and brought it straight across the monster's neck. There was a sickening thud as the blade bit into flesh, and the body's head soared through the air before landing several feet away. It rolled awkwardly for a few more feet as the rest of the body fell in a heap at Jag's feet.

Wyatt blinked. "Well, uh, that works I guess."

Jag smirked at him, cleaning his sword off on the fallen corpse's clothes before sheathing it. "Haven't been in many fights, have you?"

Wyatt shook his head, returning his own sword to its scabbard. "No. I mean, I used to wrestle a lot with my best friend, and I scrapped a few times with some other kids when they were trying to bully me. We've practiced with training swords our whole lives. But never anything serious. Never… anything real."

Jag scanned the rest of the square. "I get the feeling that you're going to get your fair share in," he mumbled, peering down a side alley. "Are you ready for that?"

"I guess I hadn't really thought about it," Wyatt replied, trying to be as alert as Jag as he glanced around the square. "I don't really want to worry about what's going to happen. I haven't even figured out what has already happened."

Jag motioned for him to follow and darted down an alleyway. Wyatt sped after him, feeling more energized and less sore after getting a little bit of adrenaline flowing.

"That's a good attitude," murmured Jag as he slowed down, crouching behind a crate and peering further into the alley. "Just be sure that you're ready for it. Don't let it sneak up on you and shock you, kid."

Wyatt nodded, looking over Jag's shoulder. Just ahead of them, he could see a group of several drones trying to dig through the wreckage of the shop. He watched in silent amazement as one of them stuck its arm into the heap of debris. It pulled back, drawing a large piece of wood out with it. But the wood and the thing's entire arm were coated in the sticky resin of the Atumen. The beast seemed to realize that its arm was losing strength and gripped the huge beam with both arms, covering it in more resin. It tripped backward, crushed by the beam. The others moved to take its place, clumsily removing more from the heap. There was a large hole in the center. They were making progress.

"What do you think?" asked Wyatt slowly, doing his best to keep out of sight. The last thing they needed was the entire horde realizing they were close and moving their way.

"I think that something important is inside of that building," Jag replied quietly. "Do you have any idea what that might be?"

Wyatt shook his head. "That's Kelsar's shop, but I don't know what they'd be looking for. I was in there earlier, and the entire inside of the building was coated in a weird gray gunk, from the Atumen."

Jag glanced over his shoulder. "How did you know that a matured Atumen leaves behind that residue?"

Wyatt blinked, realizing his mistake. "Er," he mumbled, cursing himself inwardly, "I guess I just assumed. Dunno what else it could've been, really."

Jag eyed him for a painfully long moment before continuing. "Looks like he had some other important stuff in there, too. No sign of the Necromancer, though. I wonder—"

All at once, the whole wreckage shifted as the hole collapsed, crushing the drones that were nearby. More debris rolled out, peppering the entire group. Wyatt and Jag backpedaled immediately, dashing back toward the square before the group found the two of them.

Suddenly, Jag reeled, throwing his arm out and stopping Wyatt short. The two of them stood panting, staring ahead into the square, where a lone figure stood over the fallen drone that the two of them had left behind. Tall and skeletally thin, the form was hooded and wrapped in black robes. He looked up, showing a white half-mask that covered his eyes and nose, a mask which seemed to shine from within the darkness of the hood.

The figure straightened, looking up at the new arrivals. His mouth split into a grin, revealing brown, uneven teeth. His lips and jaw were wrinkled and scarred.

"So you're the ones who destroyed my pet," he said, his voice dry and rough, like a cascade of stones. "That will cost you both greatly."

Jag cocked his head, and Wyatt saw a look of defiance flash across his face. He stepped forward, drawing his sword. Wyatt followed suit, but glanced behind him, making sure that nothing was coming after them out of the alley.

The robed man paused, his mouth twitching. But he was looking past Jag. In fact, he didn't even seem to notice the young warrior; he was staring at Wyatt through the slits of his bone-white mask.

"My, my," he hissed as he began to slowly and soundlessly walk toward them. "Where in the world did you find that? Well, I thank you for delivering such an interesting item to me. I'll be taking it now."

"Necromancer," Jag hissed, stepping out in front of Wyatt and adopting a battle pose. He gave the strange man a cocky, lopsided smirk. "Yeah, well, you've got a long way to go before you get it, old man."

The robed man laughed, a cold and heartless sound that made Wyatt feel incredibly uncomfortable. He continued his advance, his grin wide and unnerving.

"Yes," he began with a hiss, "Your soul is full of fire and life. I can smell it, boy. I will have it, and I will break it."

Jag surged forward, his movement faster than Wyatt would've believed possible. He aimed a hard, two-handed swing toward the robed man, and Wyatt could hear the point whistling through the air.

The man raised his arm lazily, catching the blade directly on the middle of his forearm. There was a soft thud as the blade stopped, much to Jag's surprise. It didn't even seem to faze the robed man.

A wrinkled hand shot out from under the robe, grabbing Jag by the throat before he could react. He lifted Jag into the air with one arm, his strength inexplicable. The eyeholes in his mask glowed with an eerie red light as he narrowed his gaze on Jag.

Wyatt stood, paralyzed, as Jag's sword clattered to the ground. The young warrior clawed and scratched at the hand around his throat, but he didn't appear to be having an effect. He gripped the man's wrist and began kicking his torso repeatedly, but that didn't seem to do anything, either. The smile beneath the skull-like mask was wide and unmoved by Jag's struggling.

"Stupid boy," hissed the man, pulling Jag a little closer so that his voice could be heard. "No weapon like that can harm me. I am beyond the weaknesses of man. You are beneath me."

The old man stepped to the left, tossing Jag across the square like he weighed nothing. Jag tumbled and skidded across the smooth stones, shouting in pain as his body smashed against stone. He came to a stop against one of the nearby buildings, slamming into it and bouncing back onto the ground. He let out a low, desperate moan, but didn't move.

Wyatt's heart was pounding as the Necromancer turned back to him with that same sadistic grin. He took another step forward, and Wyatt took one backward as fear surged through him, gripping him in indecision.

Wyatt. Shem's voice echoed in his mind like a church bell through the midnight fog. *I can help you. There are two seals on this sword that lock me within it. If you release the first, I can assist you.*

Wyatt's mind raced as he continued to backpedal, staring at the advancing, hungry form before him. "Okay," he said, doing his best to keep calm. "Okay. How in the world do I do that?"

You must offer your blood and your power to the sword and command that the seal be released, replied the cat. Wyatt could feel the urgency behind his words, and could likewise feel the cat's desire to have a real fight. The sword was practically twisting in his hand, aching to be used.

The robed man increased the pace of his advance, his smile souring, becoming an annoyed scowl. He cast a hand out, sending a sphere of dark energy roaring through the air at Wyatt, the gesture almost lazy.

Wyatt yelped and leapt aside, narrowly dodging as the dark orb streaked past him to strike a nearby building. The dark energy seemed to meld into the structure, and the wood where it had struck suddenly dried and cracked. The withering spread through the wall for a ways before the entire front wall collapsed in a rush.

Wyatt was running now, trying to reach Jag. He dodged more orbs of darkness, running and tumbling wildly. Dead and rotting forms began to stumble out of every alley and road, closing off every avenue of escape. Shem's voice once again roared through his mind.

WYATT! RELEASE THE SEAL!

"Right!" shouted Wyatt to nobody in particular. He ducked behind one of the leftover carts and quickly sliced his palm open along the blade, wincing in pain as the steel bit into him. Streams of red ran down the length of it, dripping onto the ground. He raised the sword up and stared into it, his pulse pounding in his ears.

"Release!" yelled Wyatt, putting every ounce of focus, pain, and fear into that word as he squeezed the handle, ignoring the pain in his palm. He could feel it trying to twist and jerk in his hand as the being inside of it ached to be free, ached to do its master's bidding.

The blade shimmered with light for a moment, and suddenly, the twisting stopped. The blade ceased its typical humming, and for the first time, it felt like just another sword in Wyatt's hands. He stared at it, dumbfounded.

The cart he was hiding behind exploded, shaking him back to the present. He dashed out from behind the cloud before a second orb of darkness could follow the first, running for any kind of shelter. But he could see nothing else. The square was in ruin around him.

He stopped and turned, realizing that he had nowhere to run. He looked to the advancing form of the Necromancer, to the dead that now drew together in a line on both of his sides. He gripped the bloody sword and held it out, his expression defiant and firm. He had no choice. He had to fight.

And then he heard it. A horribly loud, bestial roar echoed through the square behind him. Wyatt turned, craning his neck to see what was happening.

A great ring of golden fire had blossomed in the air, perhaps five feet above his head. The fire danced and shone as the roar grew louder. Wyatt watched in awe, completely forgetting about the threat that was now behind him.

An enormous golden lion appeared inside of the ring, leaping out of it and over Wyatt's head to land between him and the robed figure. It roared again, its entire figure rippling with power. But instead of a mane of fur, this lion had a mane of golden fire that surged with intensity as the beast roared. The very air around the beast seemed to hum and crackle, reacting to the heavy presence of the great magical beast. It crouched, growling with menace, its luminous golden eyes fixed on the dark form ahead of it.

The man stopped, eyes narrowed. His small army of dead likewise stopped; even the mindless dead seemed to understand that oblivion stood in front of them, hungry and waiting.

"You... shouldn't have been able to do that," said the man quietly, staring at the lion. Wyatt couldn't be sure, but he thought for a moment that the man might actually be scared.

The lion roared again, sending a wave of heat blasting outward that made Wyatt's eyes water. The drones around the man crumbled to dust, crushed by the pressure of the lion's presence. His hungry, blazing eyes never left the robed form ahead of him.

The Necromancer hissed, throwing his hands out, sending a massive blast of dark energy screaming toward the lion. But the lion roared again, running toward it, and Wyatt watched in awe as he met the sphere head-on, destroying it without a flinch. It bounded toward the robed man like a streaking comet.

"Not today!" shouted the man, twisting in place as the cat leapt toward him. Just as the lion's hungry claws would've sunk into the man's flesh, his form broke into hundreds of little motes of darkness. The lion passed straight through it, the little orbs of darkness scattering around it and raising into the sky. They connected back together far above the cat. The great shadowy shape coalesced in the sky before speeding through the air, away from Ven.

The cat looked up, watching the thing go with great distaste. After glancing around to be sure that they were safe, the lion trotted back over to Wyatt, the flames on his mane shrinking to a simmer.

"You are safe, Wyatt," came Shem's voice from the great beast as it knelt before him. The cat began to glow, shining like a brilliant star. Wyatt was forced to avert his eyes, covering them with his forearm. The sword in his other hand gave a great jump, and the light finally faded away.

Wyatt looked back toward it, his eyes focusing again on not an enormous, glowing lion, but a tiny, tan cat that was busily licking its paw. He sat down in a heap, losing whatever it was that was keeping him up. He stared dumbly at Shem for a moment, groping for words that he couldn't quite find.

"I… you… what… are you?" stammered Wyatt, glancing at the sword in his hand, which once again vibrated and hummed with a pleasant warmth. The cat looked up at him, cocking its head to the side slightly, eyes glowing faintly with a golden light.

"I am Shem," responded the little feline, his voice devoid of its usual sarcasm. Instead, he seemed subdued, almost subservient. He slowly walked to Wyatt, pressing his little pink nose onto Wyatt's bleeding palm. There was a flash of light, and the wound closed. The blood coating the sword and Wyatt's hand vanished.

"You are safe," continued the cat, sitting back down, looking up into Wyatt's eyes. "That is what matters. But your friend is going to need some attention from his sister, I think. His wounds are beyond my help." He inclined his head across the courtyard, to Jag's crumpled form.

Wyatt leapt to his feet, hurrying over to his fallen friend. He crouched, rolling Jag onto his back and checking him over. After a moment of careful prodding, he found Jag's pulse. That was a good sign. But he was covered in scrapes and bruises, and Wyatt knew that after a tumble like the one he had taken, he probably had broken several bones. He might even have internal injuries that nobody could see. Nobody but a Vitamancer.

"Shem," said Wyatt quietly, noticing that the cat had followed him over. "I need to go get help. Can you… I don't know. Stay here and watch him, or something?"

The cat snorted. "Unlikely. You stay here. I'll go and get the girl," he declared, peering off toward the hills. "Provided she hasn't moved."

Wyatt blinked. "What are you going to do? They don't even know you exist. You can't really just plod over to her and tell her to follow you into town."

"I have my ways," replied the cat with a sly air of mystery. "Don't worry about that. Just keep him from dying, would you? There might still be some drones wandering about the town. Keep your eyes open."

Without another word, Shem padded away from them, disappearing from view. Wyatt wasn't sure what the little cat had planned, but he realized that he didn't need to worry about it. He scanned the square, gripping his sword tightly and waiting for the worst to come.

Grace was pacing. She was trying not to fret, of course, but how easy was that when your only brother ran off with some stranger into the heart of almost certain danger? She was pacing a lot, lately. Every time Jag decided to go off on his own on some grand adventure, he got hurt and she had to put him back together. This felt like that again, and now they had the wildcard of Wyatt to worry about.

In truth, bringing Wyatt with them hadn't been the greatest idea. She was certain that Tythas would chastise her for the decision, but she couldn't help but feel like she had done the right thing. There was just something about him, something she couldn't quite pin down. And he had that sword…

She paced near the horses, which grazed happily on the brush. She hated being left behind. But Jag had always told her that she was too valuable to risk getting caught in one of his fights. She'd fought against that notion before, but it had never quite worked out the way she wanted.

She set her mind on tending to the horses. They had been nervous and jumpy ever since they got near Ven, and waiting like this in the eerie silence wasn't helping them. It wasn't helping her, either. She walked over to the nearest, rubbing his neck and cooing reassurance in his ear.

The horse seemed to be responding well, for a few moments. But before she could make much progress, he started, letting out a startled breath and stamping his hooves angrily. He was staring at something behind her, pulling against the rope that tied him to a nearby tree.

She turned slowly, the hairs on her neck prickling. She didn't immediately see what had spooked the horse so badly. But then she looked down.

A tiny housecat stared back up at her, its head cocked to the side. It was a plain tan color, with strangely luminous golden eyes. She stared at it for a few moments before crouching down, holding out a hand. The cat watched her with interest.

When she was a mere fingertip away from the cat, it took a few wary steps back. She made a face, scooting forward to try to pet it again. But once more, it backed up, and their game continued until she had scooted to the very edge of the hill.

"Grace!" came Jag's voice from down the hill, seeming strangely loud in her ears. She blinked, looking down into Ven. But she didn't see anything. She'd heard noises from the town, but no voices.

"Grace! Get down here!" came Jag's loud voice again, urgent and pleading. She glanced back, checking to make sure that the horses were secured. They both looked restless and nervous, but they'd have to survive without her. Without another glance back, she ran down the hill, leaving the strange cat and the horses behind.

"I heard your call," panted Grace as she skidded to a stop in front of Wyatt and Jag. She looked down at Jag, her brow furrowing in puzzlement as she realized that her brother was quite incapable of calling out to her. "Or at least... his. But... he's unconscious. How did he call out to me? He... sounded so close..."

"That was me," lied Wyatt quickly, glancing at the sword and mentally cursing the cat. "We got attacked by a Necromancer and a bunch of, uh, Drones. We managed to fight them off, but Jag got messed up pretty badly."

Grace knelt down over her brother, checking his pulse as Wyatt had. She glanced back up at Wyatt. "I was certain that I heard his voice," she said quietly, before closing her eyes and sending a bit of magic into Jag. He groaned and shifted, the first sign of life he had shown since he'd been tossed across the square like a ragdoll.

"It was me," said Wyatt again, holding her gaze. He needed her to believe him right now, and that somehow made lying to her a little easier. He didn't have time for a debate. "Jag's been knocked out this whole time. He couldn't have called to you, Grace. Maybe the distance warped the sound a bit. I don't know. But it was me."

She stared at Wyatt for a moment before turning back to Jag, concentrating on healing him. He let out a groan and opened his eyes, looking around in confusion. He was awake, but it was pretty obvious that he wasn't alert just yet.

"He's pretty banged up," said Grace, her voice strained. "I'm not going to be able to heal him all the way, not when I'm already weak."

"Just do what you can," replied Wyatt warily, peering around the square. "Now that you're here, I'm going to scout the rest of the town to see if there are any... survivors."

Grace bit her lip, nodding softly. "Alright. Just be careful, Wyatt. You're on your own now."

Wyatt sped off down the alley that he and Jag had explored earlier, heading straight for Kelsar's shop. The drones had been waiting there, as if the Necromancer had expected someone to show up. That didn't bode well, and it also suggested that the Necromancer had believed there was something in the shop of value. He had wanted Wyatt's sword, but there could still be something else there, buried in the rubble.

Wyatt reached the end of the alleyway, pleased to see that there were no drones waiting there for him. Live ones, anyway; the drones that had been waiting at the end of the alley had all collapsed in a heap, unmoving. Wyatt guessed that the Necromancer's flight had released whatever power kept them moving. Wyatt gave them a wide berth anyway, just in case there were any lingering surprises, and approached the pile of rubble that had been Kelsar's shop.

He knew that he'd need a whole crew to search through the

wreckage. Even now, he could see the sticky gray substance left behind by the Atumen consuming everything. It seemed to be spreading, reaching out in tendrils to the surrounding buildings, hungry fingers of destruction. Wyatt didn't know what he could do to stop it.

He sighed, suddenly remembering all the things that the shop had meant to him. He had a lot of good memories in that building, and suddenly, he was faced with very real proof that his life was changing, and his past was about to be left behind.

Almost without thinking, Wyatt reached into his pack, drawing out some flint. He drew his belt knife as well, kicking some of the rubble around. After a bit of searching, he found a few dry pieces of wood that weren't coated in purple-gray gunk. He shaved them into tinder, something that would spark up easily, and stuffed them into a pocket of larger wooden pieces. He crouched down, arranging them on the rubble, and struck the flint. Sparks rained down on his little makeshift firepit, and after a bit of coaxing, he managed to start it on fire. He stepped back and watched as a slow flame built, preparing to consume the shop. He didn't want anything else getting inside, in case anything else was left inside. And he didn't want that gray gunk spreading any further. He wasn't sure why, but this seemed like the only way.

He watched it burn for a few minutes, staring into the flames as if they might tell him what to do. But they had no answers for him. He felt exceptionally lost without his mother and Kelsar to guide him. He'd never been in a position like this before, alone at the helm of his life.

Suddenly, a black shadow flickered around the alley, moving over him and heading toward the square. Wyatt turned and looked up into the sky to see a strange black shape flying soundlessly toward the market square. Wyatt stared at it for a moment before it hit him. It looked like the shape the Necromancer had taken when he fled, like a gigantic bird made of pure shadow. Endlessly black, it seemed to absorb all the light that shone down on it. The hairs on Wyatt's neck prickled.

He drew his sword and set off at a dead run down the alley, leaving the flaming wreckage behind him.

CHAPTER SIX

Wyatt nearly tumbled back into the main square as he tried to turn at a flat run, but he caught his balance at the last second. He skidded around the corner, scrambling to reach Jag and Grace before the huge black shadow. He saw the form touching down near them, like a great black bird settling into the nest. Grace stood nearby, staring up at it. But to Wyatt's surprise, she wasn't doing anything to defend herself. She hadn't seen the Necromancer leave. She didn't know!

He drew his sword as he ran, blood pounding in his ears. He pushed down the pain that was flaring along his body as he pushed it further than his freshly-healed wounds should've been pushed. He didn't care if he hurt himself. He had to do something.

The shape seemed to melt, shrinking in size. Grace watched it warily, but she didn't look overly concerned as the dark shape changed into the form of a man.

Wyatt slid in between them just in time, panting as he pointed his sword at the face of the man in front of him. It hummed with a renewed hunger. But to his surprise, the man standing before him was not the Necromancer. Emerald green robes hung from the frame of an older man who was certainly not as unkempt or, well, evil looking as the Necromancer had been.

Short gray hair and a perfectly trimmed goatee adorned his sharp features. He was tanned and wrinkled, but he didn't look old; rather, he almost looked young in spite of his body. An eyebrow arched above his deep brown eyes as the elder man regarded Wyatt's swordpoint with a wry, amused smile. He didn't appear at all concerned with it. If anything, he looked... curious.

"Uh, kid, you should probably put that away," muttered a voice from behind Wyatt. He blinked, turning. Jag was lying in his sister's lap, but his eyes were open and he looked like he had come through the worst of his injuries.

Wyatt blinked again, giving the man a dumbfounded look for far longer than he should have. At the other end of his sword, the man gave a cheery wave, smiling with amusement. His eyes drifted to the sword that was pointed at him, and his mouth twitched.

"Vance Tythas, I'd like you to meet... well, I guess you could call him the newest addition to the team. Wyatt Arden, farm kid and, apparently, fearsome warrior. Kid, seriously, put that thing away before you put your eye out."

Wyatt nodded, hastily sheathing the sword. He scratched his head sheepishly, looking up at the man. "Yeah, sorry. I saw you, uh, fly up, and I got a little paranoid, I guess. You looked like... he did, when he left. Sorry."

The emerald-robed man scratched his goatee, but his eyes didn't leave Wyatt. "Perfectly understandable, I quite think. Defending your allies is the height of honor. No harm done."

"Wyatt, this is Vance Tythas," said Grace softly. She sounded exhausted. "I guess you could say he's our boss."

Tythas gave her a sideways look. "After all these years, that is how you introduce me? Your boss? I had no idea that you had such strong feelings about our relationship, Grace."

Grace rolled her eyes and started to speak, but Jag cut her off. "Not now, you two. We've got bigger problems. Tythas, it's good that you finally showed up. We're going to need all the help we can get."

Tythas looked around the square, his eyes seeming to see more than the rest of them could. "Yes, you certainly are," he mused quietly, scratching his goatee again before looking back to Jag. "I can tell you already that most of the people got out before the worst of it. I scouted the area before I arrived; the main roads toward the pass are all quite clogged. Only so many can go through the pass at once, so many people are camped out, waiting for their turn."

Wyatt sighed with relief, sitting down on the ground as some of his worry flooded out of him. "That's a relief. Then he didn't... kill that many of them."

Grace shook her head. "Wyatt... it's still pretty bad. I can... I can feel it. The doors of Death are hanging open in this place. Ven has become a grave."

Tythas motioned behind them, in the direction of Kelsar's shop. "Soon to be a pyre, I think. Your curious young friend here set fire to one of the shops in town. We should probably get moving," he added dryly.

Grace and Jag both gave Wyatt startled looks. "What..." sputtered Grace, staring at him in astonishment. "Why... Wyatt, what did you do that for?"

"The Atumen," said Wyatt quickly, trying to push back the sinking feeling that burning the old shop had given him. "It left behind this... residue. Sticky gray stuff that was almost... eating the building. And it was spreading, to the nearby shops. I didn't want it to do any permanent damage to the area. I figured that a fire would take care of it and prevent it from spreading any further. It seemed like... a good idea at the time. I didn't really have a lot of options."

"An Atumen?" said Tythas sharply, looking to Grace for confirmation. She nodded in response. He looked back to Wyatt. "Then you did the right thing. An Atumen is a spirit of decay. The only way to prevent the spread of its taint is to purify the area. In a perfect world, Grace would have been able to do it for you. But she is far too tired, and I doubt she's ever even attempted something on that level. Purification by fire... is another method, a much easier and similarly effective one."

Jag reached out a hand toward Wyatt. "You hear that, kid?" grunted Jag as Wyatt pulled him to his feet, helping to shoulder some of the man's weight. "You made the right call. Good job. I'm more curious about how exactly you beat that Necromancer."

Wyatt gave a shrug. "Just got lucky, I guess," he said quietly. "I think you hurt him more than you realized."

Grace made her way over and took Jag's other side, helping Wyatt take some of his weight. "We don't have time to talk about that right now," she said, draping his long arm over her shoulders. "Jag, you really need to spend more time resting. But we don't really have the luxury of that, I guess. Vance, what do you think? Where do we go from here?"

"Wayton, I think," said Tythas after a brief pause. "Getting Jag some bedrest is our first priority right now."

"We've got two horses and four people," noted Wyatt, silently thanking Grace for diverting Jag from the topic of his inexplicable victory. "One of us is barely fit to walk a horse, much less ride one."

"I could perhaps carry one of you," said Tythas, looking them over, "but not all of you. It may be better if you allow Jag to come with me, Grace. You can travel with Wyatt on horseback across the Tritoch Pass. It's at least a three day ride, but trying to make that trip with Jag would stall us even longer."

It was Jag who spoke first. "I don't like that idea," he said, his voice the most commanding that Wyatt had heard it since he had regained consciousness. "The kid barely knows anything about using that sword, and there still could be danger in the area. Grace is… she needs to be protected, Tythas."

Wyatt wanted to disagree. He wanted to puff out his chest and claim his superior knowledge of the blade, wanted to claim that he could protect Grace just fine. But he couldn't. He knew that Jag was right: he had no formal training with a sword, and there was still the enormous question mark that was Shem the cat.

"Your young friend here is much more equipped to protect your sister than you currently are," replied Tythas sagely, nodding at Wyatt. Wyatt felt a small swell of pride. "In case you forgot, he was the one who scared the Necromancer away. He's stronger than he looks, Jag. And she's stronger than you've ever given her credit for. They'll be fine, Jag."

"He's right, Jag," said Grace wearily, giving her brother's shoulder a squeeze. "You're too injured to travel on horseback, and he can take you to a real healer much more safely and quickly than we can. You need to go with him, and you need to not complain about it."

Jag sighed, the defiance leaving him. "Alright," he said with a resigned nod. He looked over at Wyatt. "Keep her safe, kid. I wasn't sure what you were about before all of this, but I trust you now."

Wyatt gave him an even look. "I will, Jag. I promise."

"Wyatt..." began Tythas, scratching his chin. "I'd like a quick word. Let these two say their goodbyes while we talk." He motioned for Wyatt to follow him, walking through the square.

Wyatt handed Jag's weight back to Grace, who helped him walk to a nearby crate and sit down. Wyatt followed Tythas in the opposite direction, several feet away from the others. Ahead of him, he could just make out smoke rising in the distance, a sure sign that the fire Wyatt had started was beginning to do its work.

"You know, I assume, what it is that you carry with you?" said Tythas after a time, his voice low and casual. The two of them walked slowly around the square, surveying the damage.

Wyatt glanced down at the hilt jutting out from his hip. "Honestly... no, not really," he said, idly tracing the etching in the pommel with a finger. "I know a bit, but... certainly not enough. Do you know what it is?"

Tythas shook his head. "Not at all. I recognize an immensely powerful magical relic when I see one, but I've never heard of a sword of this particular... quality ever mentioned before. That itself is slightly concerning, but not completely unusual. Does it have any... unique qualities?"

Wyatt almost laughed, but caught himself. "One or two," he said, shaking his head in spite of himself. "Let's just say it's been a handful. But it... I don't know. Helps me focus."

Tythas nodded thoughtfully. "Quite. What sort of Adept are you?" It was both a question and a statement.

"I'm an Aeromancer," replied Wyatt, not even taking the time to be surprised that Tythas knew. "But I don't know anything about my power. I didn't even know about this until I found the sword."

Tythas nodded again. "I thought so. We'll work on that. I understand that there's probably much more to the story than I currently know, but Jag can fill me in. I'm glad to have you on the team, Wyatt. If Jag trusts you, I certainly do."

Wyatt didn't know why, but he felt an overwhelming sense of

respect and trust for Tythas. It felt good to have someone with a little more experience around, someone who could take some of the burden of responsibility from him.

Tythas clapped a hand on his shoulder. "Take care of Grace, Wyatt. We'll get to the rest later. For now, just be strong. There's a small village called Wayton, just on the other side of the pass. It's primarily a traveler's rest stop, but it exists outside of the Empire's authority. We'll meet you there. Oh, and Wyatt?"

Wyatt glanced over at him. "Yeah?"

"Be wary of that sword. Old things seldom reveal themselves fully. Maintain your solidarity."

Wyatt mulled over their conversation as the two of them walked back over to Jag and Grace. Tythas stooped, helping Jag to his feet and motioning to the sky. "It's going to be a bit of a trip, Jag. I need you to hang on and stay with me."

Jag nodded. "I know. I'll be fine. Just get us there soon." He gave his sister one last glance before walking with Tythas to stand a little bit away from the group.

Tythas raised his hand to the sky, pointing one finger at the clouds and making a circular motion, almost as if he were trying to stir them. The wind kicked up around them, tossing dirt and debris into the air as Tythas's robes flared magnificently. Satisfied, he clutched the amulet on his chest, and his form suddenly began to shift. Within moments, he had taken on the shape of a great shadowy bird. Jag slowly climbed onto his back, taking his time. He waved to Wyatt and Grace before the Tythas-bird kicked off and the two disappeared into the sky, guided by the winds at their back.

"Tythas is an Aeromancer, too," muttered Wyatt, more to himself than anything. He suddenly realized that he'd have someone to teach him, if they ever managed to meet up again. That's what Tythas had meant, when he said that they would work on it.

"We should get going," said Grace quietly, motioning toward the hills in the distance where the horses were tied. "We need to get away from here before the fire spreads further. And before anyone else comes to investigate."

Wyatt voiced his agreement and the two of them set off toward the horses. With Grace in a weakened state, Wyatt didn't want to push her, so they took their time. They didn't say much, both of them immersed in the situation, their thoughts distant and deep.

After reaching the spot where the horses were tied, they saddled up and got on the road out of Ven, toward the Wayton pass and the inland area. Ven was closer to the coast; a vast mountain range separated the peninsula from the rest of the continent. It would take them a day or two to reach the pass, and another day to get through it. Wyatt had traveled the area many times throughout his life, and he was fairly confident that he knew the trip well enough.

The road wound through the hills around Ven, making it difficult to travel in a straight line. Adding to that annoyance was Grace's silence, likely from a combination of exhaustion and stress. Wyatt wanted to talk to her, to ask her so many of the questions that he hadn't gotten to ask Kelsar or his mother.

His mother... a wave of fear and worry swept through him as he thought about her. He still didn't know where she was or what had happened, and he had no idea if he was getting any closer to finding her. But he didn't know what else to do. He was trying his best to keep those feelings down, but as the smoking wreck that had been Ven grew smaller in the distance, he couldn't help but think about how quickly everything was changing. He felt like he was lost and alone; his best friend and his only family were gone, replaced by mysterious strangers who probably had as many secrets as he did.

He gripped the hilt of the sword, focusing on the humming warmth. He let that reassuring heat wash over him, pushing those feelings back down and setting his eyes on the road. Things were too hectic right now for him to focus on the negative. He needed to keep his head up, to focus on the solution. He could worry when he was safer.

"I'm sorry you got dragged into all of this," said Grace quietly as they rode, breaking the silence. "We're not supposed to bring outsiders in."

Wyatt shook his head, glancing over at her. "No, it's not your fault. I got attacked, and you saved my life. I'm grateful, to both of you. Without you I wouldn't be able to investigate whatever happened to my family. Had we parted ways back there, I probably would've gone to Ven on my own and gotten myself killed."

"Tythas will know what to do," she replied, looking off into the distance. "He's a remarkable man, and he's never steered us wrong. If anyone knows how to save your family, it'll be him."

"What is it you guys do, exactly?" asked Wyatt curiously. "You said that he's your boss."

Grace gave him a slightly pained look. "We're... well, don't take this the wrong way, but we're officially classified in the Empire as terrorists. We work to liberate the residents of Porkhoya and find them better homes. We smuggle them to areas not incorporated in the Empire, or find ways to hide them within the Empire."

Porhkoya was a large island south of the main continent. Nearly forty years ago, a war had ravaged the Empire—a war between Adepts that lasted for over a decade. The Empire and what remained of the Adept Council had won, and post-war paranoia had resulted in a very harsh decree; anyone even allegedly involved in the other side were exiled to the island and left to fend for themselves. The island, a lush tropical jungle, was uninhabited and not at all suitable for so many people to be dumped there all at once. It was still a pretty hot topic, something Wyatt had studied in school when he was younger.

"So you're apostates, then?" asked Wyatt quietly. He didn't want to sound like he was accusing her of something, but apostasy was a hefty crime in the eyes of the Adept Council. Any Adept acting without the direction of the Council was considered and apostate.

"Yes, Wyatt, I am, and so is Tythas," she replied, her voice a little hard. "But the issue is bigger than that, bigger than anyone knows. If I have to be branded a bad person to accomplish some good, so be it."

"I'm not trying to judge you, Grace," he said quickly, looking over at her and holding up a pacifying hand. "You saved my life; I owe it to you to hear you out. Besides, I know only what they teach in school about the Council and its rules. I'm sure I don't actually know much about it."

She didn't reply. After dwelling on it, he realized that his mother, and quite possibly Kelsar, were apostates as well. He wasn't planning on telling Grace this just yet, but it certainly made it easier to sympathize with her.

In truth, the locals had always painted the Adept Council as one of two things: either as the guiding light of the Empire, or a group of lunatic religious nutjobs. If they were willing to exile thousands of people to an inhospitable scrap of land like Porhkoya, it was difficult to see them as being completely rational.

"Vance used to be the High Chair, you know," she said quietly. "He was in charge of the entire Council, during the war. And he led the Adepts in battle against the Necromancers. But the war disillusioned him, and he kind of... lost the faith for a little while, I guess."

"I knew I had heard his name before," mused Wyatt. Vance Tythas, one of the few Adepts in history to manifest more than one Aspect; he had nearly full control of both Aeromancy and Pyromancy. He was a decorated war hero, and perhaps the most powerful Adept alive. During the war, he became very well known for his philanthropy and his honorable attitude toward combat.

"Yeah," said Grace with a light smile. "He sort of fell out of view, after the war. Took a quiet job teaching at the Academy and stayed away from politics."

"So I get that you guys liberate the oppressed refugees from the war, but what were you doing all the way up here?" asked Wyatt as they continued down the road. Ven was a very long way from Porkhoya, after all. Ven was a very long way from anything.

"We also try to intercept rogue Adepts before they can," she replied after a moment. "Vance has a lot of contacts in the Empire that leak information. We try to get to these Adepts first, to help them see the light before the Council finds them and condemns them."

"So you're working with them, in a way," said Wyatt, scratching his chin.

"Tythas likes to say that the Council and our little group have the same goals, just different methods. Mostly because we're not bogged down by the bureaucracy that they have to deal with all the time."

"What keeps you from being led astray, though?" asked Wyatt, trying not to sound accusatory. "I'm not saying that the Council is always right. I don't really know much about the topic. But that bureaucracy keeps them in check, doesn't it? Isn't that the point of the system?"

She smiled at him, nodding. "I know. I worry about that every day, honestly. That we'll take it too far or make the wrong choice. And then we'll be no better than them. But it's Tythas. He's so... committed. To undoing the Council's mistakes, and to righting the wrongs that, in a weird way, he helped to cause. I think anyone else would just be set on anarchy, but Tythas is working for the entire world."

Wyatt gave a thoughtful nod. They continued talking about the Council and the state of things for a few hours, which made the ride through the countryside go infinitely quicker. Before Wyatt knew it, the light was fading and they needed to find a place to camp. Wyatt pulled them off the road, into a small copse of trees with a clearing at the center. They tied up the horses out of sight and made camp.

Sometime later, Wyatt stared into the crackling fire that he had made, just like his mother had taught him when he was young. Grace was sleeping on the other side of it. It hadn't taken her long to fall asleep, with how exhausted she had been. Wyatt had offered to let her take second watch so that she could get some sleep right away. He was still feeling pretty awake, though, and didn't actually intend to wake her up. She needed rest more than he did.

"This is quite the predicament we're in," came Shem's deep, distant voice from the other side of the camp. Wyatt looked up to see the cat's tiny shape next to the fire, his luminous golden eyes staring into Wyatt intently.

"What's going on, Shem?" asked Wyatt quietly, failing to hold back the torrent of questions that was ready to burst out of him. "Who was that Necromancer, and what was he doing in Ven?"

"I have no idea," replied the cat in a low voice. "As I said, I haven't really been paying close attention to the movements of the world. I can tell you that he's old, perhaps several centuries, and powerful."

"Centuries?" sputtered Wyatt in response, taken aback. "Shem... how is that possible? I mean, he looked old, but..."

"Necromancers have a unique relationship with Death, Wyatt. The most powerful among them can not only raise the dead, but lengthen their own lives with their power. They absorb energy from the souls of the freshly dead and preserve their lifelines. But the more their soul ages, the more they become saturated with Death, the more taxing their essence becomes on their form. True Necromancers know when Death comes for them, and go willingly. Corrupted Necromancers do not."

"He looked like he was falling apart, but he was so strong," muttered Wyatt, picking at a twig and throwing pieces into the fire. "There's no telling what else he can do. He didn't even have to try to beat Jag and I."

"His body looks like it's falling apart because it is," replied Shem, intently staring at beetle that was crawling in the grass near him. "At this point, he has probably eschewed his true body and left it behind, long ago. He resides now in a simulacrum, just a… puppet, essentially, that he has made for himself. It's not something very many Necromancers can do, as the energy required to maintain one's life in purely ethereal form is extraordinary. It certainly doesn't bode well."

"Great," breathed Wyatt, shaking his head. "Just great."

"I think we have more immediate concerns right now, Wyatt," stated the cat, looking back to Wyatt, the beetle having disappeared. "Are you sure that you can trust these people? They smell like secrets."

Wyatt gave Shem a firm, even look and nodded. "Yes. They saved my life. They are apostates, but… I don't really think that means that much anymore. The Council doesn't seem to be what it used to be, what it is supposed to be. And I've got a good feeling about them. It just seems… I don't know. Right."

"Just as long as your good feeling isn't going to get us killed," replied Shem dryly. "Be careful when you're on the road. The Necromancer could still be in the area. I am on the alert, but as we have discovered, I sometimes miss things."

"Yeah, I know. I'm doing my best to keep the both of us out of sight."

Shem licked a paw. "One more thing. Tythas is incredibly powerful, but he is a bit unstable. I know his story. I did not anticipate this path, nor did I foresee the Adept he would become. Be careful when you are dealing with him."

Wyatt nodded softly, tossing the rest of his twig into the crackling fire. "I got the same impression from him, to be honest. At any rate, I'm going to be careful around all of them."

Shem gave a very catlike stretch, his whole body arching and lengthening in strange ways. "I'll watch over the camp if you want to rest, Wyatt. I'll wake you up if something comes too near."

"I'm not tired just yet," said Wyatt in response, waving the cat off. He wasn't tired, but he was… weary; the kind of weary that would prevent him from getting any real rest should he actually fall asleep. "I think I'll just think for a while."

"Well, keep your eyes and ears open, then," said the cat with a shrug. "Don't get caught staring off into the distance."

Wyatt smirked at him and looked back to the fire. This part of the world rarely saw travel, and he wasn't worried about getting found by anyone at random. True, the Necromancer could still be lurking somewhere nearby, but he had Shem. That alone was enough to greatly bolster his confidence.

But Wyatt, intent on the fire, didn't notice the little cat sliding out of his view. He couldn't hear the soft paws on the earth as the cat made his way behind Wyatt. He heard nothing as the cat leapt up onto the log that Wyatt was leaning against. He didn't notice a thing, until he suddenly heard Shem's heavy voice whispering in his ear.

"Go to sleep, Wyatt Arden," came the voice, a voice thick with power. The words filled Wyatt's ears and mind, and after only a moment, seemed to flow through his entire being. He didn't even realize it, couldn't even comprehend what the little cat had said. His whole body felt heavy, and his head slumped down as he drifted off to sleep.

Shem curled up on the log, smiling.

"You let two children scare you off?" boomed a voice, the entire cavern shaking in reaction to the power carried by that voice. "Two children, one of which didn't even bear the Spark?"

Apep the Snake cowered on the ground, prostrating himself before his master. He pressed his sweaty forehead onto the stone, his eyes closed tightly. "M-my lord, it's more complicated than that. The other, he had some kind of relic! He used a sword of immense power to call forth a great lion of fire!"

A swift blow came at Apep, but it wasn't one that he could block. This was a blow to his spirit, sent by a power far greater than any protection he could muster. His very being shuddered in pain as the power of creation itself surged through him.

"A relic," mused the master, its form that of a beautiful, blonde-haired woman. A teardrop of blood fell down from her eye, trailing down her face as if she were crying. "A relic and a lion…"

"What is it?" begged Apep, kissing the woman's feet. Relics from the Old Age popped up now and again through history, but he'd never heard of something like the sword and the lion he'd fought.

His master shrugged. "Nothing of consequence. It stirs my memory, but if it were something important, I am sure I would recognize it."

Apep finally dared to look up at his master. Bloody sores had broken out all over her skin, a sure sign of trouble. The body was already starting to decompose, literally rotting from the inside out.

"This form grows weak, Apep," she said quietly, her unnaturally deep voice a stark contrast to her beautiful, lithe body. "For now, it would be wisest to ignore them and continue on to the next seal, before this body fails completely. I will walk this earth again in my true form."

Apep nearly shouted out with glee. His master wanted his help. No, his master needed his help, and that was a priceless distinction.

"We will bring you back, my lord! You will crush your enemies beneath your feet and this world will be yours, as it always should have been!"

"The next seal lies in the mountains," said the master, closing her red eyes. "The Pyromancers still guard it zealously, as their patron taught them. We must get moving. There is much to be done."

"Yes, master," responded Apep with a bow. "We will ignore the children for now and continue to the mountains. Our horses await."

"They were fools to leave me behind, Apep," murmured the thing that lived inside of the beautiful blonde woman, sending an uncommon tingle down Apep's spine. "They thought their world would be safe from me… No, Apep. Nothing is safe, now. Everything shall be broken."

Apep stared at his master in wonder as she walked out of the cavern, leaving a trail of bloody footprints on the ground behind her.

"My lord… it appears that there has been a disturbance of some sort in the northeastern peninsula, near Ven," muttered the elderly man seated next to the Emperor. "Reports are coming in that their local harvest was disrupted by some strange occurrence, forcing locals and travelers alike to flee into the mainland."

"What sort of disturbance, Mugalo?" replied Emperor Tyvarion Il'Vir, Lord of the Empire. His gravelly voice and iron gaze would shake a normal man, but Mugalo had seen more than one intimidating Emperor throughout his life. In his old age, he found it hard to be shaken by much of anything anymore.

"The reports are not exactly clear, my lord," Mugalo responded smoothly, paging through the paperwork in front of him. As the Emperor's adviser, it was his job to be informed, and to do the informing as well. "We've only begun receiving the reports, and most of the information is coming from frightened commoners who aren't exactly reliable sources. It's hard to say what is real and what is simply the product of too many frightened, uninformed imaginations."

"What do the reports say, Mugalo?" growled the Emperor. He hated it when the old Adept skirted the truth.

"Much," said Mugalo with a shrug, flipping quickly through the pages and reciting snippets of what he saw. "Inexplicable weather patterns. Random geological events. What could be an Atumen, raging through the center of the little town. A Pyromancer doing battle with it. A Vitamancer, arriving late, and saving the Pyromancer's life."

Emperor Il'Vir scratched his stubbly chin, frowning. "An Atumen? That's… certainly odd. We've encountered creatures of old that slipped through the cracks before, but never one of that… magnitude. I don't think anyone alive has ever even seen one."

The old man shrugged dismissively. "As I said, it could be anything. Simple people have a way of turning what they see into extravagant fantasies."

"And a Pyromancer..." muttered the Emperor, staring at the wall of his overly-extravagant office. "Who is assigned to that area? I don't... recall ever picking someone, to be honest."

Mugalo hesitated. "Well, my lord, it appears that you never did. Officially, nobody is assigned there. Rex Kelsar was assigned there during your predecessor's time, although he hasn't sent in a report in... oh, twenty years. His post appears to have been removed, but unfortunately he was never replaced."

Il'Vir raised an eyebrow, giving Mugalo a very harsh look. "And why was I never informed of that?"

Mugalo gave him the best political smile that he could muster. "My lord, I am old and forgetful. Ven rarely sees traffic by normal people, much less by creatures we once believed extinct. In the face of bigger problems, I'm embarrassed to say that I forgot all about it."

Il'Vir didn't believe a word of it. Mugalo, High Chair of the Adept Council, had served as adviser to the Emperor for longer than Il'Vir had been alive. In truth, the Emperor had no idea just how old the wily adviser really was. He had made some pretty loud objections to Il'Vir's rise to the throne, and their relationship had been tense ever since. Mugalo had a way of skirting details he didn't want the Emperor to find out about. Anything to discredit him, he supposed.

"Send a unit," said the Emperor with a sigh, rubbing his eyes. These meetings between the two of them were becoming more stressful every week. "Send them on Glidecraft. An Aeromancer can lead the team, with whomever else you deem fit to go along." With Glidecraft and an accomplished Aeromancer, the team of Adepts could arrive in the area within the day, rather than the span of days it would take on horseback. He didn't want to waste time sending valuable Adepts out on false alarms. They were needed elsewhere, especially now.

"Yes, sir," replied Mugalo slowly, making a note in his stack of papers. "Don't forget that riots keep cropping up along the northern border. Is it really... necessary, to send a full team out on only rumors and conjecture?"

"You brought it up," said the Emperor dryly, making a few notes of his own. "Very few living people have ever even heard of an Atumen, Councilor. If you heard a rumor about something that matches that description, I don't think it's something we can chance. Be sure you send a Vitamancer with the team, as nothing else will save them from the poison should they have some sort of confrontation with the creature."

Mugalo looked up, regarding the Emperor sharply. "Sir, our VItamancers are a dying breed. Do you really think that it's worth risking-"

"Yes, I think it's worth risking," interrupted Emperor Il'Vir, cutting his adviser off harshly. "An Atumen could kill that entire team if they make one mistake. I'd rather risk one Vitamancer than lose an entire team of five Adepts, Mugalo. You may be High Chair of the Council, but I'm still your Emperor. Send a team, Councilor. Lead by an Aeromancer, with a Vitamancer to accompany them."

"Yes, my lord," replied Mugalo sourly, finishing his notes and closing up his little book. "That is all I have. If you have nothing else for me, I will make preparations and go on with my day."

"That's enough for this week, I think," said the Emperor, silently thanking Adala that the meeting was over. "Until next time, Councilor."

Mugalo disappeared from the Emperor's office with a speed completely uncharacteristic of such a stooped old man. Sometimes, Il'Vir wondered if he was privy to some magical form of youth that the rest of them didn't have. He never seemed to tire, not even a little bit.

Il'Vir wished he had that kind of energy. He wasn't old by anyone's standards, but lately, he felt very tired.

Less than an hour later, the Emperor watched as several Glidecraft swooped out of the Imperial Hangar, speeding through the air toward the northeast. With the wind at their backs, they would reach their destination very quickly.

He sighed as he watched them go, disappearing quickly into the clouds. He was beginning to feel like the entire Empire was slipping through his fingers.

CHAPTER SEVEN

oward the end of the third day of their journey, Wyatt and Grace finally reached the Tritoch Pass. The pass, as old as any memory, had always been a particularly rich place for tourism; the path led between a cleft in the mountain, as if it had been sundered by Adala herself. Some claimed that it had. As Wyatt and Grace rounded the bend and everything came into view, they could see that numerous camps had been made around the mouth. The pass was slow-going, and legend had always said that it was unwise to travel the pass at night. A line had formed, and people were slowly but surely making their way off of the peninsula and away from whatever had befallen Ven. But the travel had stopped for the day. It was nearly sundown.

Wyatt slowed his horse down, surveying the scene warily. "There're a lot of people here, Grace," he said quietly, peering out over the huddled masses. "This might not be the best place for us to camp. Maybe we should head back a few miles and find a place off the road a bit. Somewhere more sheltered." If the Necromancer did catch up to them, Wyatt didn't want it to be when so many people were nearby. They would be both fodder and fuel for his dark powers.

"I think we should make our way through tonight," she replied softly, looking up at the towering mountain range before them. "I don't want to waste any more time. I'm fully rested, so let's just push through. We went through the pass on our way here. It wasn't that bad of a ride."

Wyatt rubbed his horse's neck as it shifted restlessly. "The trip itself isn't, but… well, people tend to, er, avoid making the trip at night. It's incredibly dark inside, and there are some places where no light reaches. And there are… stories."

Grace gave him a look that was equal parts amusement and skepticism. "Stories? Wyatt, don't tell me that you buy into the local superstitions."

"They aren't just superstitions," he replied hastily. "Not all of them. There are a lot of stories. A lot. And pretty strong evidence of strange encounters in the pass. Sometimes people go missing. When I was a kid, a group of travelers lost one of their men when riding through the pass at night. They went into one of the dark parts, and when they came out the other side, his horse was riderless."

Grace sighed. "We're running on limited time, Wyatt. We need to talk to Tythas more about what happened in Ven, and we need to find your family."

Wyatt blinked, looking over at her. "You… You're going to help me?"

She looked off toward the pass again. "We saved your life. You risked yours to save Jag. I don't buy into fate and omens and that junk, but it seems to me like those kinds of events mean something. I think, for the time being anyway, that we're stuck together. Besides, there's… something about you. Something about this, that feels right. I want to see it through."

She was sensing the sword, he realized. She probably didn't know it, but Tythas had been able to recognize it just by looking at it. She had felt the power of it, and felt attached to it. Attracted to it.

"Alright then," he said quietly, nudging his horse forward. "We go through the pass tonight. I hope you're not afraid of the dark, Grace. I've never been through at night, but I hear it can get pretty creepy."

"A Vitamancer, afraid of the dark?" she scoffed, looking amused. "I'll forgive you for your ignorance, Wyatt, but I'm going to let you in on something. As a Vitamancer, I am the light in the darkness."

"Fair enough," he said with a chuckle. "Fair enough. Just keep your eyes open, alright?"

They set their horses forward again, moving at an easy pace and pushing ahead, past the groups of travelers and refugees. Many stared at them in disbelief as they rode into the pass, confident and without a shred of doubt on their faces. Wyatt kept his eyes ahead, feeling more awkward than anything, with so many people staring at him. After a few moments, however, they rounded the bend and made their way into the first split in the rock.

Wyatt could probably go through this pass a hundred times and he'd still marvel at the geography. It looked like someone had taken a sword and cleaved the mountain in two, leaving a mostly straight path through the part of the range. The path itself was perhaps fifteen feet wide, leaving just enough space for a dim amount of light to sneak in. The stone walls on either side were impossibly tall, and he could just make out a sliver of sky above him. As they moved further into the pass, those walls would only grow taller, that sliver even thinner.

In truth, this part was the easy part of the journey; the path through this portion of the mountain range was wide and mostly straight. Toward the center of the pass, however, the second half of the path grew jagged and narrow. They'd have to move through single-file. Wyatt had vivid memories of his knees scraping the walls as he rode through. It was an alarmingly tight fit.

Grace looked up at the walls above them, to the orange slash of evening sky above them. "It's amazing. I've seen it before, but… I wish I knew how it was made. It's existed as long as recorded history. It's even played an important role in a number of military conflicts. I studied it a bit when I was younger."

Wyatt nodded softly, reaching out to touch the weathered stone, his fingertips tracing lines in the weathered stone as he rode. "I know what you mean. I always wanted to know that, too. It's not the only place, though. Kelsar told me stories about a hot spring, in the wilds to the far northwest, where the ground actually belches fire. I've always wanted to go there."

Grace smiled softly, nodding. "It's true. I know men who've been there, and I've seen drawings and paintings of it. If your grandfather really was a Pyromancer, it would make sense that he went there. It's an important site for Pyromancers. Even sacred, to some of them."

More that he never knew about. Just how much had Kelsar given up to watch over Wyatt and his mother? Did he leave behind his people and his culture to flee to Ven?

"Pyromancers aren't the only Adepts with sacred places, though," she continued, oblivious to Wyatt's faraway expression. "The Tritoch Pass is very important to Terramancers. Toward the center there's even a shrine that some say was built by their patron. Aquamancers supposedly have a sacred place that was built under the sea, although few people have actually seen it. That one is a bit more of a legend than the rest."

"It sounds like there's a lot of separation between Adepts," commented Wyatt as he looked up at the slit of sky above them. "Almost like they have… different cultures or something."

"They used to," replied Grace, glancing back at him. "Before the Empire, and before the Adept Council, they were separated into six very different and very distant clans. And they constantly fought against one another. It wasn't until the first Great War, about thirteen hundred years ago, that the Empire and the Adept Council were established. But some of those cultures still live on, and many adepts refuse to assist the Council. A lot of Adepts just want to be left alone."

So Aeromancers would have their own sacred site, too. Wyatt wondered where that might be. Maybe Vance Tythas could tell him about it. Maybe someday, he could even go there.

"The Empire has the right idea," continued Grace. Looking at her as she stared ahead, Wyatt wasn't sure that she was speaking to him anymore. She looked distant and conflicted. "They just… go about it wrong. There's too much anti-Necromancer sentiment amongst the Council and the people, and I guess it just… piled up. Became too much."

"So that's why you're working independently," said Wyatt. "You don't want the Empire to back itself into another war."

She inclined her head. "Yeah, ultimately I guess that's the goal. The last war was started by Necromancers, sure, but it was a bizarre and distant sect of them, obsessed with their old and twisted religious ways. Most Necromancers are just like other Adepts, and just want to live in peace and help the world. Unfortunately, their gift is viewed by most as being grotesque and unnatural, and they are shunned just based on their nature."

"Well, it is a little bit creepy," said Wyatt quietly as they rode. He thought of the Drones back in Ven. "But I can see what you mean. They can't be bad people just because of the Aspect they bear."

"Some parts of their power are grotesque, sure," she responded quickly. "But Necromancers have some of the most unique knowledge of life that the rest of us can't even fathom. As a healer, I know where Death begins, where Life ends. But Necromancers... Wyatt, they know what is beyond. They are incredibly fascinating people, and a hundred years ago they commanded just as much respect as any other Adept."

"Why all the fear and hate, then?" he asked, scratching his chin.

"People fear Death," said Grace with a light shrug. "Always have. A handful of bad Necromancers, coupled with that inherent fear... That's where it started. And then during the last war, the Empire threw around a lot of propaganda to get people to oppose the other side. They didn't really bother worrying about the long-term effects of that. That really added a lot to the underlying fear that people already had. It just... became natural, to associate the atrocities committed to all Necromancers."

Wyatt had always hated the simplicity and the boredom of living in Ven, away from the Empire. But now, it seemed like a distant dream, to be back in a world that wasn't so tumultuous and uncertain. He had always viewed the Empire as something great and mighty and strong. But now... it all seemed so broken.

They continued discussing the state of the Empire for a few hours; Wyatt's never-ending questions prompted long, elaborate responses from Grace. He was starting to realize just how intelligent she was, and how equally passionate she was about protecting not just the Empire, but everyone in the world.

Wyatt slowed his horse, looking up into the narrow shaft above them. It was growing harder to see the further in they went, but he was almost certain he had seen movement from above them. The sword at his hip gave a barely-noticeable shiver.

Grace glanced back at him, slowing her horse as well. "What's wrong?"

"You can make light, right?" murmured Wyatt as he continued peering into the open space above them. "It's starting to get a little bit dark in here."

Grace lifted a hand and closed her eyes, her palm upward. After a moment, a hovering ball of light appeared just above it, slightly larger than a grapefruit. It rose through the air to hang several feet above them, clearly illuminating the pass for fifty feet or so in all directions.

"Thanks," said Wyatt, giving her a slight smile. "Just trying to be careful."

Grace smirked at him as they resumed their previous pace. "This place is heavily trafficked, Wyatt. Anything that might've once lurked here is long gone now. Those stories are just stories, Wyatt. The dark and distance do strange things to human perception."

Wyatt shrugged, opting not to say anything. He still felt uneasy, as if he were being watched, or even followed. It was like feeling a spider on his neck, but it was never there when he went to swat it. He couldn't quite figure it out, so he rested a hand on his sword and kept his eyes forward.

I feel it too, echoed Shem's voice in his head, a soft and reassuring rumble. *It's always been here, but… I was under the impression that it had gone to sleep long ago. It's an old creature, from… before. Should it make a move, I believe that you can defeat it. But be wary. Be ready.*

Wyatt almost snorted. No useful information and a not-at-all-reassuring compliment. Typical Shem. Glancing around, Wyatt could almost feel whatever it was, moving just beyond the light range of Grace's orb, impossibly silent. It was watching them.

"We're getting close to the shrine at the center of the pass," said Grace, still unaware of their predicament and Wyatt's hyper-alertness. "Did you want to take a few minutes to see it?"

Wyatt thought about that for half a second before nodding. "Yeah, that would be great. I need to know as much as I can."

Grace gave him a smile and urged her horse to move a bit quicker. Wyatt followed suit. Maybe she was aware that something was amiss, mused Wyatt. She seemed to be in a bit of a hurry to reach the shrine.

A clicking noise broke the silence of the night, sending an icy tingle up and down Wyatt's spine. Grace blinked, looking around uneasily. Wyatt's hand stayed on his sword, but he kept his head level and remained calm.

"Probably just a bird," said Grace quietly, although she looked a little bit more nervous than before. "I think your monster stories are getting to me, Wyatt."

"Maybe, yeah," he replied quietly.

They broke through the first narrow passage, coming out into a gap between the mountains. The cool air had a charge to it, giving a strange life in the otherwise still clearing. To their right, Wyatt could see a place where several great statues had been carved from the rock, standing vigil in a semicircle.

Grace dismounted and motioned for Wyatt to do the same, heading up the hill toward the statues. Wyatt hopped down and directed his horse to the small amount of grass that had managed to grow here, where it happily began to graze. As he and Grace made their way to the shrine, Wyatt couldn't help but be on alert, scanning the area and the mountains above them. He wished he had more visibility. He felt very vulnerable.

Finally, they reached the shrine. The statues were magnificent. Maybe nine feet tall, each was carved in the shape of a cloaked and hooded figure, hands outstretched. Each was carved from a different kind of stone, and each held a different gemstone in their outstretched hands. Time had worn away some of their features, but Wyatt could tell even now that they had been masterfully carved. Some of the intricacy had been worn away, but their beauty was untouched.

Somehow, he'd never noticed this place when he'd come through the pass as a child. In fact, it had never even been mentioned to him, until today. He marveled at that, at how something so beautiful could be unnoticed.

"Five patrons, so the legend goes," said Grace quietly, looking up at the one in the center fondly. It clutched a clear gem in its outstretched hands. "Five children of Adala. Each one is shaped, not carved, from a different stone. It's said that the touch of a Terramancer will reveal their true compounds, and that the rough, common stone we see is simply an illusion."

"Five patrons?" asked Wyatt, blinking in confusion. "Aren't there supposed to be six?"

"For as long as history can remember, there have only ever been five statues here," replied Grace as she stroked the stone in front of her with two outstretched fingers. "It's... part of the argument. If Petra really built this place, well... she wouldn't have mistakenly left out one of her brothers."

Wyatt looked up at the stony, hooded face of one of the statues. It was stoic, but strangely lifelike. It clutched a sparkling blue gem in its hands, a pure sapphire. He felt a strange pull from the statue, as if it were somehow connected to him. Unconsciously, he reached out to touch it, just as Grace had done moments before.

"That's Aeris," said Grace, walking over to him. "Stormshaper, Lady of the Wind and Rain. Aeromancers have her gift."

Wyatt's fingers grazed the stone, and as if the world knew it happened, thunder boomed in the distance. Wyatt blinked, and suddenly, he could feel the power within him stir. He looked around, suddenly aware that Grace was staring at him.

"You're an Adept," she breathed, stepping back, a hand over her mouth. "That's why... that's why I've had this feeling about you. I can sense your power. How in the world could you have hidden from the Council for so long? They usually snatch young Adepts up by the time they're six. I don't understand... I don't understand how that could even happen."

Wyatt stared at the statue, not really listening to her. "I'm an Aeromancer," he said simply, feeling the stone beneath his hand, reveling in the electric power that was coursing through him. He felt awake and alive for the first time in his life. He'd felt his power before, sure, but never like this. It was like it was like a forgotten muscle that he suddenly remembered how to use. He wanted to flex, to let it out. He wanted to call the wind and the rain and shake the world with the glory of it. It was exhilarating.

Wyatt, came Shem's deep, chiding voice in his mind. *Don't lose control. You may not have alerted the Council yet, but if you do that, you surely will.*

Wyatt blinked, sobering immediately. He shoved his power back down, imagining that he were stuffing it into a closet and slamming the door on it before it could escape. He could still feel it inside of him, though, and he knew that whatever connection he had made with the statue had done something within him, unleashed his power in a way that he never even thought possible. There was no turning back, now.

Wyatt let his hand drop, turning to Grace with a slight smile. "I don't really know anything about all that, Grace. I didn't even know about it until Kelsar told me, shortly before he disappeared. I've never been… trained or anything. This is all really new to me."

Grace nodded, smiling wide. "Whatever the reason for it, it's a good thing that we found you when we did. We'll be able to keep you out of the Council's hands, and Tythas will gladly help you learn to control your gift. He hasn't had a new Adept to teach in years. He'll be very excited, I bet."

"I kind of wanted to see the Academy," said Wyatt quietly. "I mean, this is more important, but… I still want to go there. I've heard so many things about all the books and the magnificent classrooms and… I don't know. It just seems so interesting."

"I'm sure you'll get there some day," said Grace happily. "Once all of this calms down. Although it's not really as amazing as you'd think. I didn't study there for more than a few months."

Wyatt cocked his head, puzzled. "I thought all Adepts had to study at the Academy of Farillyon?"

"I was, er, home schooled," she replied quickly, walking back toward the horses. "Sometimes exceptions are made. I was one of them."

She was avoiding his gaze now. Wyatt knew that there was probably more to the story than what she said, but he let it drop. He had his secrets and she was certainly entitled to hers. So instead he sped up, trying to catch up to her.

"Tythas will teach me, then?" he asked, his voice ever so slightly anxious. He still wasn't really sure what to think about Tythas. Grace and Jag had both said such great things about the elder Adept, but there was also something a little… unnerving about him. He just felt strange, in a way that Wyatt couldn't really define.

Grace nodded eagerly at him. "Yes, I'm sure of it. He was a professor at the Academy for a while, after the war. Before all of this madness started. And he was very good, very popular. A little… um, unorthodox, sure, but very good nevertheless. He's got more skill and knowledge than anyone I've ever met."

Unorthodox? Well, that would certainly suit Wyatt, who was becoming more and more unorthodox with every day. The idea of learning from one of the most powerful Adepts alive was certainly tantalizing.

Wyatt grinned in spite of himself. "I think that'll work. But we've got to get out of here first. Let's get back-"

The hairs on Wyatt's neck stood up as both of the horses started, stamping their hooves restlessly. Wyatt gripped the hilt of his sword and grabbed Grace's wrist, holding her back. He could feel the blade humming eagerly. Grace started to ask what was wrong, but he held up his other hand to silence her. He closed his eyes, focusing on the sound of the gentle wind that was moving through the pass around them.

Something stirred, causing the air currents moving invisibly through the pass to change. Wyatt could feel it as well as hear it; whatever it was, it was coming toward them rapidly from the side of the pass that they had already ridden through. Wyatt opened his eyes and stared down the narrow gap in the rock, stepping in front of Grace without even thinking.

Barreling toward them was a massive, gray-skinned beast, at least fifteen feet tall and almost as wide. It had a small head atop broad shoulders, set down and staring ahead with intensely green glowing eyes. It had two massive arms, as thick as trees and as long as the thing was tall. It was using those arms to bound forward, planting them into the stone and swinging the rest of its body ahead, landing on two small legs. Its entire body rippled with muscle, but those huge arms were most concerning. Wyatt could see sharp claws at the end of huge fingers, claws that pierced the stone beneath the monstrous beast without much effort.

"Run!" yelled Wyatt, sprinting the rest of the distance to his horse and leaping up on top of it. Grace did the same, not needing to be told. They kicked and whistled, setting their horses off at a full gallop toward the other side of the pass. Wyatt instinctively drew the sword; the steel sang as he did, ringing out and echoing off of the walls around them.

Glancing over his shoulder, Wyatt saw the colossal monster smashing through the clearing behind them, slowly closing the distance.

Wyatt looked back ahead as they drew nearer to the pass. An idea suddenly sprang into his mind, but he had no idea if it would work. He had no idea how it would even work, but it was all he had. He lifted his sword arm, pointing the tip of the blade toward the gap in the mountain as they dashed toward it. He narrowed his eyes, trying to ignore his pounding heart as he focused instead on the surging power that had stirred within him when he touched the stone.

Power that ached to be released.

They flew into the narrow gap in the stone, their horses moving at a terror-fueled pace that wouldn't have been possible otherwise. The monster's powerful front arms propelled it nearly thirty feet forward with every leap, and it showed no signs of slowing. It was closing the gap at an alarming rate. It would only be a matter of time before the thing caught up to them.

Wyatt's mind went blank as he let loose his grip on his power. Blue light crackled along the length of his sword as he suddenly grasped the intensity of what he was about to do. He felt a familiar tug at his navel, as if something were being pulled out of him. The energy collected in the blade, and with a thunderous, ear-splitting boom, lightning arced out of the sword and slammed into the wall of the pass with ferocious power. Huge shards of rock tumbled down above them, raining down directly onto the monstrous creature. Just as the beast made it all the way into the gap, a huge, jagged boulder slammed down on top of it, pinning it to the ground. More and more rock fell from above, completely blocking the pass with a pile of rubble and finally, obscuring their sight with a cloud of dust.

They slowed their horses, turning to look at the obscured pile of rubble as the last of the rocks fell from above. They could see a huge gap in the narrow slit, where Wyatt had blasted an enormous chunk of rock off of the mountain. The only sound that remained was their labored breathing and the last sounds of settling stone.

"Wyatt..." said Grace in disbelief, staring at the rock pile as the dust settled. "How... you... what in the world did you do?"

"What... worked," he said, panting and clinging to his horse desperately. He felt like he had just sprinted as far as he could go; he was sweating and shaking with the effort of releasing power like that for the first time. He couldn't catch his breath, like the feeling of taking a hard fall and having all the air leave his lungs. His whole body ached, and he could vaguely detect the smell of burnt hair coming from his arm. His hearing was muffled, replaced by an annoying ringing sound.

He understood now why Grace had gotten so tired when she healed him. Being an Adept was not going to be easy.

They watched the pile of rocks wordlessly for a few moments, both still a little numb from what had just happened. Suddenly, the pile shifted, and they both froze, their breath still in their lungs. After a moment, however, the boulders collapsed inward, and the struggle ceased.

Shem's voice rang inside his mind as the sword gave a tug in his hand. *You should get moving. It isn't dead, Wyatt. Just wounded. It's a part of these mountains, and that isn't going to keep it down for very long.*

"We need to get moving," breathed Wyatt as he exhaled slowly, trying to absorb the cat's words. "I don't think I killed it. And I don't really feel like going over there and checking."

"Yeah," responded Grace, her voice equally airy and anxious. She was staring at him. The look on her face was unsettling at best, and it made Wyatt feel like she were peeling him apart with her eyes, trying to inspect the inner parts of him. It was making him more nervous than he already was. Without really actively choosing to, he kicked his horse and they flew ahead of her, out of her intense gaze.

"Wyatt, hold on!" she yelled as her horse gained on his, finally pulling up beside him. The pass here was narrower, and the two of them barely had room to ride side by side. Soon, Wyatt knew that they would barely have room to ride at all.

"I thought you said you haven't been trained," she said, her tone accusatory, although perhaps not intentionally. "That... that is not something that an untrained Adept should be able to do. That isn't something that even an Adept with basic training should be able to do."

"Don't," he said hotly, a result of his aching body and throbbing headache. "Just stop. I don't know how I did it." His vision was a bit blurry, and he was leaning into his horse for support, which the animal probably didn't appreciate. He kept his eyes ahead on the pass, just trying to stay upright.

She appraised him for a moment, her eyes softening. "I... yeah. Sorry," she said quietly, falling in behind him.

He felt bad for snapping at her, but he didn't know what else to do. He had no idea where he had gotten the inspiration for that stunt. He didn't know what he was capable of, and he really wasn't sure that he had even been the one to make the decision. Something else had taken over in him, had made that decision for him. Either his Spark was guiding his hand, or something else was, and he wasn't sure that he liked it.

Well done, rumbled Shem's voice in the back of his mind. *I expected you to win, but... I didn't expect that. Well done, Wyatt. Hopefully you haven't overdone it.*

As the two of them rode in silence down the narrowing pass, Wyatt hoped that he hadn't either.

Vance Tythas was in mid-stride through the streets of Wayton when the hair on his arms prickled. He paused, his head slowly turning toward the mountains to the east, to face the Tritoch Pass and the Shrine of Petra. Something had gone very, very wrong.

Light flickered on the horizon, barely perceptible even in the dark of night. Nobody else would've seen it, but Vance Tythas knew where to look when things were going wrong. He could see things that other people just didn't notice. He could feel things that they couldn't. He reached out, testing the air between his fingers as if it were a fine piece of cloth. He felt the charge of it, smelled the changing wind as it twisted and shifted, flowing toward the east in an entirely unusual way.

"Wyatt Arden," he mused, tasting the air and suddenly understanding.

Tythas had known from the moment he saw Wyatt that the boy was much more than he appeared, but now he was getting an idea of just how much more. Even Tythas had required months of training before he could create lightning of that power, and years of experience to do it without draining his energy completely and passing out. Wyatt Arden, however, seemed to operate under his own set of rules.

Tythas sighed, turning his sights back to the street and heading toward the inn where he and Jag were staying. Having been fast asleep, Jag seemed to have no objections to Tythas running errands around the town. He had found the local herbalist, an old friend, who had just the herbs necessary to speed up Jag's healing process. With those herbs safely in tow, Tythas now made his way back to the inn, smiling cheerfully at the barman as he passed through the main room and ascended the stairs in the back.

Upstairs in their small room, he found Jag awake, leaning up and looking out the window. He was watching the mountains to the east with an anxious expression on his face, the kind he tried very hard to never let his sister see. Although Jag wasn't an Adept, he was certainly perceptive in his own way.

"Any word from them?" asked Jag just as Tythas stepped through the doorway. The older man chuckled silently, setting his package down on the small desk in the room and seating himself in the chair.

"No words, no, but they're alive," replied Tythas simply. "I imagine that they will arrive here soon, perhaps within the next day. Be patient, Jag. Your sister is capable of handling herself."

Jag shifted uneasily, wincing in pain as he resituated himself. "I know better than to question you anymore, Vance. But I hope you're right."

"I have some herbs here for you," said Tythas, gesturing to his bag. "Give me a few moments to prepare you a poultice and some tea, and with any luck you'll be feeling better in a very short time."

"An herbalist too?" said Jag, smirking in spite of his discomfort. "Is there anything you aren't good at?"

"Knitting," replied Tythas with a wistful sigh. "Never got the hang of all the stitches and seams and what have you. But I can make you a poultice that will heal your wound in a third of the time, and I can brew you a tea that will reduce your pain and give you a deep, undisturbed sleep."

Jag nodded, although he looked just a little bit unsure. "I'll be sure never to ask you to knit me anything, I suppose. Where do we go once Wyatt and Grace get here?"

Tythas drew everything out of the bag, setting his herb pouches apart from the mortar and pestle he had also purchased. "I don't know yet. But honestly, I never really do. I will first need to talk to our new ally before we can make that decision, I think."

"You do think he's an ally, then?" asked Jag quietly, watching his mentor closely. "I know I said that I trust him, but I have my doubts. Especially with him surviving that Necromancer... something isn't quite right."

"He saved your life," reminded Tythas, now mixing the herbs into the bowl. "And possibly Grace's, too. Can you really ignore that?"

Jag shifted uncomfortably. "I know. I just... it doesn't feel right. He barely had a scratch on him, Vance."

"He's an Adept," said Tythas simply before tasting some of his herb mash and nodding with approval. "An untrained one, of course. Goddess knows how he evaded the Council's gaze for so many years. He'll have to be trained, and if I can help him control his power, we may have a strong ally on our side. He's a tough boy and a surprisingly powerful Adept. He'll be a valuable asset should we ever have to fight the Council openly. And, thus far, he has proven himself to be a loyal friend."

Jag scratched his chin, nodding. "That... actually relieves me a lot. If he survived that Necromancer, he must know enough about his power to defend himself. Hopefully if the two of them run into trouble, it'll give them a chance of making it out."

"Oh, they have more than a chance, I think," replied Tythas as he prepared the poultice, applying the salve to the bandage. "I have no doubts about their safe arrival here. I just hope that we can continue to hide Wyatt from the Council. It would be bad if they apprehended us, but it would be much worse for him. At this point, I don't think he can make any arguments that would get him out of his apostasy. And I had to break out of that prison once. I don't fancy trying to break someone else out."

Jag began to laugh before wincing, holding his ribs. "Never heard that story," he breathed, fighting back the chuckles. "You'll have to tell it sometime."

Tythas stood up, walking over to the bed. "Remove your bandage," he said, holding the poultice in his hands. "And just to warn you, this is probably going to sting for a minute or two."

Jag grumbled, lifting his shirt to unravel the wrap around his chest. The wrap covered a padded bandage on his left side, just at the bottom of his ribs. He winced as he peeled the padded bandage away, trying very hard not to look down at the wound that it covered. Tossing the bandage aside, he looked up at Tythas and nodded.

"Do try not to hit me," said Tythas cheerfully before applying the bandage with a firm hand. Jag visibly stiffened, looking away and staring at the wall as his facial features tightened. After a few moments of stiffness, he finally relaxed, slowly winding the bandage wrap back around him to hold the poultice in place. Tythas took the wrap from his hands with a gentle chide and finished for him.

"I dunno what you put in this, Vance, but it's some amazing stuff," said Jag slowly as he leaned back, looking out the window. "It barely hurts at all now."

Tythas replied with his most industrious smile. "It's been a helpful mixture more than once in my life. Someday I'll teach it to you and your sister. Sometimes magic just isn't the way to go, my boy. Now, let me get started on that tea."

Jag fidgeted, still watching the mountains. He was probably too protective of Grace, but he couldn't help it. They'd been together for a few years, and she was the most important thing in his life. Protecting his sister had given him a purpose that he had lacked for most of his youth, and not being able to made him feel uneasy. Worse yet, she was in the hands of a stranger. A capable stranger, sure, but a stranger nonetheless.

They had worked together back in Ven, but Jag was still unsure. It had seemed like an easy decision then, but now that he could stop and reflect on it, he had doubts. Tythas seemed to be totally at ease with the situation, which should have been reassuring to Jag. But his baby sister was off with some... boy. A boy they knew nothing about, who could have been lying to them from the start in an effort to get close to them. Tythas said that Wyatt was an Adept. How could they be sure he wasn't just a spy for the Empire?

"Here," said Tythas softly, snapping Jag out of his wandering thoughts. Jag peered at Tythas for a moment and looked down. The old man was stooped over him, holding out a small wooden cup full of a black, steaming liquid.

"It's going to taste terrible, and it'll make your urine blue for a week," said Tythas, seeming pleased by these circumstances. "But it will speed up the healing process considerably, and put you to sleep. You'll sleep for a full day, at the very least. With any luck, your sister and our new ally will have arrived by the time you wake up, and the four of us can plot our next move."

Jag took the cup, sniffing it with a sour expression on his face. It smelled like liquid dirt. He sighed, shaking his head in submission. "Yeah, just be sure you wake me up when you hear something about them. I want to know right away." Without another glance at the cup, Jag plugged his nose and downed the foul beverage in one swift gulp. It was hot and tasted terrible, but in the military he'd had worse. He leaned back and settled into his bed, already amazed at how quickly the world was starting to turn white and fuzzy.

"Well, that's the thing," he heard Tythas say, the words dull and far away in his ears. "You will sleep for at least a day, and virtually nothing will wake you."

Jag stared at the old man hazily as long as he could. No longer able to properly communicate with words, Jag instead focused all of his remaining energy into his best glare, and fixed it on Tythas's smiling face. But eventually, the white consumed everything, and he drifted off to sleep.

Tythas chuckled and walked over to the window, looking out at the mountains. As the wind whistled in the night, the old man could feel the echoes of Wyatt's presence, as if the strong gale were telling tales of the boy's power. He would have to do his best to keep that power hidden, as surely another Aeromancer this close to Wyatt would be able to feel it, too. At least, one with any sense. Wyatt's abilities were both profoundly exciting and profoundly troubling.

Whatever it was that was happening, Tythas had the feeling that these days would be the most important days of his life.

CHAPTER EIGHT

race and Wyatt galloped at full speed through the final narrow stretch of the pass, with Grace in the lead. They both were tucked in tight on their horses, trying to prevent their knees from banging on the walls of the pass that seemed to be closing in on either side of them. The horses were at their limit, and Wyatt was worried that they weren't going to survive the rest of the trip, having been ridden so hard on their journey. They were still miles from Wayton, but both Wyatt and Grace were feeling uneasy and had no desire to stop riding any time soon.

He glanced back. The beast wasn't anywhere in sight, but they had seen it about thirty minutes prior. The rocks hadn't done any visible damage, but it had given them time to get ahead of it. But they had gotten overconfident, and it eventually caught up to them, erupting right out of the wall behind them. It nearly killed the both of them and put the horses into a blind fear. Grace had managed to blast it backward with a beam of light, and the horses took off as fast as they could. Having no other way to go, the horses had been moving at full speed toward the exit of the pass ever since.

Wyatt glanced back again. The walls here were slightly uneven, casting strange shadows all over the pass that made him feel immensely paranoid. He was trying to keep a lookout, but the shadows and the lack of light made it nearly impossible to tell what might be behind them.

The walls around them finally began to widen, signaling to Wyatt that they were entering the final stretch of the pass. As if in response,

Grace's horse slowed underneath her, and Wyatt's followed suit. Both of them were wheezing with the effort of their mad dash. Grace looked back at him, her expression concerned.

"They need to rest," she said, urging her horse to a stop. "If they keep going like this they're going to die." It seemed that their fear had finally abated enough for them to follow commands again. Wyatt stopped his, and the two of them slid off of their horses.

"We can't stop moving," said Wyatt, running a hand through his hair and not even trying to hide his anxiety. "We're nearly there, and if we get out of this pass we'll have a much better chance of fighting that thing. We'll have to walk them the rest of the way. It's only about a mile left, I think."

Luckily, the road ahead of them was relatively straight. It was still dark, so they couldn't see very far down the pass, but Wyatt was almost certain that the end was just ahead of them. They were almost there. They had to be.

"Just be sure you don't walk ahead of it," he added, looking over at Grace, who was leading the horse. "Stay by its side, Grace."

Grace gave him a strange look and did as he asked. "Shouldn't we be leading them?" she asked as she stroked her horse's neck, trying to further ease his tension.

"If that thing finds us again, they'll take off," he said quietly, glancing over his shoulder. "Do you want to be ahead of them when they do?"

"Good point," she said after a brief pause, looking up at the walls of the pass. The path was now wide enough for the beast to find them without hiding in the walls, and they both knew it.

He'd never really liked going through the pass when he was younger, but now that he felt so much more connected to the wind and sky, the whole place just felt wrong to him. He felt so cut off from the world in the silence and darkness in the heart of the mountain. It didn't help that he was so exhausted. The only reassuring thing he had was the sword at his hip, which hummed lightly at his touch. In a strange way, it seemed to be helping him stay on his feet, almost as if that warmth were stabilizing him. Grace looked exhausted and scared. Wyatt probably looked worse.

Something made a snapping noise behind them. Grace and Wyatt both jumped, spinning around and scanning the length of the pass while the horses continued to trot on ahead, tired and oblivious to whatever noise their riders had heard.

Grace glanced at Wyatt. Wyatt returned the look for a moment before looking again down the pass. In the bobbing light from Grace's orb, neither of them could make out any source of the noise. Grace relaxed, shaking her head and letting out an exasperated sigh. She jogged ahead, catching up to the horses. Wyatt watched the path for a moment before walking quickly up behind them. This time, however, he kept further to the rear, his hand on his sword and his mind alert. They were almost out of the pass.

"We're almost there," he murmured, afraid to talk any louder. He had no clue if the beast was following them again, but he couldn't take any chances. "Ten minutes maybe, at this pace."

Grace nodded. "The horses are calming down, but they won't be able to ride any time soon. We need to take a break once we get out of here."

"Yeah, that's probably a good-"

Suddenly, Wyatt cut off, spinning around and drawing his sword as a booming roar cut through the stillness of the pass. In the same motion as the draw, he swung the blade as hard as he could with both hands. The edge connected with a clawed, stony hand that had reached out to strike him. Sparks flew as it bit into the monster's wrist, severing the hand and leaving a stump behind. Sticky black goo erupted from the stump, spraying the wall as the beast howled again, stumbling and slowing. It tripped, crashing down at his feet in a heap.

The horses screamed in terror and took off again at a dead gallop, leaving Wyatt and Grace behind. Wyatt stared at the creature as it struggled. He felt frozen.

"Wyatt!" yelled Grace behind him. "Wyatt, we need to go!" She tugged at his shoulder harshly. Finally, he snapped out of his stupor, and turned to run as fast as his exhausted body would move him. His heart pounded in his ears as he ran, terrified of what might be once again creeping up behind them.

"Just run," he breathed, his voice coming in ragged gasps. Wyatt wasn't concerned about the horses anymore. He wasn't concerned about his mother or the Necromancer or anything else. All he wanted was to get out of this pass, to get under the sky and breathe fresh air once again. All he wanted to do was survive the day. He'd never pushed his body this far before, and he was starting to wonder if it would hold out.

An earsplitting roar echoed through the pass behind them. They could hear it bounding down the pass once more. Its gait was uneven and slower, but it was still moving faster than they could. Wyatt hadn't managed to kill it, but it certainly sounded like he'd made it mad. His heart felt like it was going to give out as he ran, but he kept going, too terrified to care.

"Wyatt!" screamed Grace, her hair whipping behind her as she ran. "It's gaining on us! We're too far!"

Wyatt once again felt that instinct rise within him, and he surrendered himself to it. He let out an uncharacteristic snarl and wildly spun, throwing his arm out as he did. A bolt of lightning burst from his splayed hand with a deafening crack, shredding through the walls behind him and causing huge chunks of rock to rain down on the path below. In the flickering electric light, Wyatt saw that he had missed the monster. But the stones had not, and for the second time that day, huge shards of mountain rained down upon the monster, slowing its already hampered progress even more.

Wyatt focused on the bolt, channeling everything he had into a continuous arc that destroyed more and more stone above the creature. The monster struggled to break free, roaring and pulling with fury. But more rock fell, crashing down on top of it every time it seemed like it would free itself. Wyatt thought it might just overcome the stone, but an enormous slab of rock fell from above, landing with a concussive boom that was nearly as loud as the lightning had been. A wave of dust and pebbles blasted his face as his pace slowed.

Suddenly, he stumbled, his fatigue finally getting the best of his adrenaline. His feet felt like they were made of lead, and he couldn't seem to pick his legs up. He crashed down into the dirt with a cry and a groan. His hand felt burnt.

But Grace was there. She crouched down next to him, catching him under the arm and pulling him back up. She took the weight from his feet and helped him regain his balance. The look in her eyes was fiery and determined as she pulled him down the path, their goal finally in sight. He could only mumble an unintelligible thanks as the two of them dragged each other forward, unwilling to give up when they were so close to their goal.

"Wyatt," she growled, slapping him on the chest with her free hand. "Wake up. I need you to help me a bit. You're too heavy. I know you have some energy left. We're almost there."

As he heard her speak, Wyatt felt a tingling warmth settle over him, like when she had healed him before. She was bolstering him, giving her own energy to stabilize him so that they could make it through the pass together.

Nodding dumbly, his legs screamed in pain as he put more weight on them. But what she had given him was just enough, and he was able to find his legs again. The two of them limped toward the exit, staring ahead at the vertical shaft of light that signaled their freedom.

Finally, with agonizing effort, they broke through the gateway and hobbled into the early morning sunlight. They heard no signs of the beast pursuing them. The only sound they could hear was their own heavy breathing and the chirping of the birds.

Fifty feet or so outside the pass, they finally stopped, turning to look back at what they had conquered. From here, it was just a narrow slit in the mountain, betraying no signs of what they had been through within.

They were silent for a time, just holding each other up and staring wordlessly into the gap. Finally, Grace found some words, glancing over at Wyatt.

"You destroyed the only land route between the mainland and that peninsula," she said, completely deadpan. "Twice."

Wyatt glanced over at her. "Well, it worked, didn't it?"

They both fell into the dirt, laughing as the joy and relief flooded over them. They made it. They were alive.

They stayed like that for a time, too pleased with their survival to care about lying in the dirt. There was no air that smelled sweeter than the air they were breathing in that moment.

Finally, after what could have either been two minutes or two hours, Grace sat up and looked over at him. "We should try to make camp," she said, still grinning. "I think we both need a rest."

"Yeah…" said Wyatt, looking up at the sky, feeling the wind swirl merrily around him, like two old friends reunited after a long time apart. He suddenly felt the exhaustion again, as the adrenaline faded. "I don't know how much help I'm going to be. I… don't know if I can get up again."

Grace turned herself to face him, pressing a hand onto his chest. He felt more of her energy wash over him, easing the aches in his body and giving him a bit more energy. She looked tired, too, but she was much more experienced than Wyatt at using her powers, and probably had a bit more to spare than he did. The feeling of it was intoxicating; a tingling warmth flowed through his entire body, like warm bubbles coursing over his skin. He'd felt it before, but every time he marveled at how amazing the sensation was.

"You need to stay on your feet just a little longer, okay?" she said quietly, looking down at him. "We're not out of danger yet. We need to get off the road and settled in if we're going to rest. That Necromancer is still out there somewhere. He could've been the one that sent that beast after us."

That thought sobered him almost instantly as the warmth faded. "Yeah," he said with a nod. "Though, Wayton isn't really that far… maybe we should just keep going? If we can find the horses we can probably make it today…"

She shook her head, pushing off of his chest and climbing slowly to her feet. "I can still feel them. They aren't far away, but they need rest. They've been pushed too far, and won't be ready to ride again for a while. But never mind the horses. The only thing keeping you on your feet is my healing power, and I'm getting close to passing out, too."

"Good point," said Wyatt with a sigh. "It's hard to tell what condition I'm in, when you do that. It… it's like a confidence boost, and almost makes me forget how bad I feel, at least for a while. It's really nice, but… I could also see it being bad, too."

126

She offered him a hand. "Vitamancers have to be careful about healing. I'm told that the feeling can be addictive, and people who are overexposed can sometimes go through withdrawal when they have to go without it. I've never seen it, but... I wouldn't want to risk it."

Wyatt took her hand, slowly getting to his feet as the aching in his entire body resumed. "Let's find those horses and set up camp. And don't worry, I won't forget the warning."

"Our first reports from the Ven situation have arrived," growled Mugalo as he hobbled into the Emperor's office. He set a packet down on the desk in front of his superior, seating himself in his usual chair. "It isn't good."

Il'Vir opened the packet and laid the pages within on the desk in front of him, scanning them over with the quickest precision he could muster. "This is... Mugalo, it's been burned to the ground. No survivors?"

"My understanding of the supplemental reports is that there is a large collection of people waiting outside the Tritoch Pass, looking to travel back to the mainland," replied the withered old man slowly. "But as you know, the path is very narrow, making the transition very slow. And travel all but halts at night. Something about a monster in the pass, one that comes out at night."

In another situation, the Emperor might've snorted or made a comment. But he was too focused on the reading, too focused on the horror that the pages in front of him were detailing. There hadn't been an event like this since the war.

"Drones..." murmured the Emperor as he read. "Several in the area. The only trace of the people who were in Ven, just wandering the landscape with no purpose. We did have a Vitamancer there, but..."

"They were unable to detect any link to a master, yes," concluded Mugalo, wringing his hands in front of him, a habit he had indulged for as long as Il'Vir could remember. "It is certainly troubling, my liege. It'll take time to move more Adepts up there. The scout cleaned up what they could, but didn't want to attract too much attention to themselves, should whatever or whoever created those Drones still be in the area."

The Emperor rubbed his eyes, as if he could somehow rub years of fatigue from them. "I doubt that will be a problem. Whoever it was, they are very likely long gone. Order the men in the field to scour the area for the remaining Drones. I don't want a trace of that activity remaining, should any of the survivors decide to go back for possessions, or to search for lost loved ones. Order them to stay in the area for a few more days. If it stays quiet, they can return here and give a more detailed report. There isn't much else we can do, I suppose."

"Do you think that we can spare the manpower for that long?" asked Mugalo, his voice low. He didn't sound accusatory, though. It seemed like an honest question.

"I don't think we have a choice, Mugalo," he said quietly. "Whatever happened there is already going to spread through the people once those survivors make it through the pass. We don't have long before the entire Kingdom is whispering about Necromancers again. If we can erase any signs of that before the rumors get out, we may be able to quell their fears."

Mugalo pondered for a moment before nodding. "I will send the message out at the conclusion of our meeting, then."

The Emperor didn't like the situation any more than Mugalo did, but he had a bit more of a practical approach to the commonfolk than the old man. In truth, he wished that he could order his men to stay longer and maintain a presence. But with the continued problems of the southern refugees, and the stirring Dominion to the north, he knew how thinly stretched they already were. They were barely able to keep the peace in the capital; a fringe farming community like Ven was too obscure for him to worry about much longer.

But he couldn't help but feel that Mugalo may use this decision against him someday. The old man had a nasty ability to recall all the hard choices that the Emperor had to make and slant them to suit his needs. He could practically hear the old fossil's voice now, sadly relating the cruel Emperor's decision to ignore the plight of the dying people of Ven.

"I have also done some looking into the mysterious Guardian of Ven," added Mugalo, somehow able to set aside the things going on there with seemingly little effort. "I have confirmed that the blacksmith, Rex Kelsar, was the last Guardian we appointed. He stopped formally reporting to us years ago, but the reports suggest that he's continued his work regardless of our approval. I'm sure that it's no coincidence that sightings of aberrations in the area are virtually nonexistent. In the rare times we did receive a report, the problem went away quickly."

"My father had mentioned him to me in the past," said Il'Vir, scratching his chin. "Half of the weapons in the Imperial Armory were made by that man, or to his exact specifications. He personally crafted the weapons and armor that the First Legion is still using. When he wasn't making arms and armor for us, he was fighting on the front lines. He's one of the most decorated Pyromancers in history. He also played a large part in convincing the Dominion to come to our aid."

Mugalo nodded slowly, adjusting his robes. "His descent into obscurity coincides rather well with the Dominion's withdrawal from our alliance, I think. Interesting."

"What I want to know is why we stopped keeping tabs on him in the first place," said the Emperor, his tone just shy of accusatory. "He's a decorated war hero, a famous blacksmith, and an influential liaison. It makes no sense that we wouldn't hold onto someone like that. I was still very young then, but you were working for the Empire. What else can you remember?"

"I... have no answer for you, my lord," said Mugalo after a long pause, and for once, he looked truly confused at the prospect. "It is as if something else worked to divert our attention long enough for us to forget about him. Perhaps he simply had a change of heart, and decided he no longer wanted to be found. Surely a man of his talents would be capable of that."

"What about family?" asked Il'Vir. "He was pretty famous, or so the stories suggest. Even if he never married, he's got to have some children in the Kingdom somewhere. Women flock to famous Adepts like moths to flame."

Mugalo paged through his files, frowning. "It doesn't say anything in the files about any family, oddly enough. That's... strange. I seem to remember... although I can't be sure... but I think he had a daughter, although there's no record of it. Perhaps my memory is truly beginning to fail."

The Emperor nearly snorted, but caught himself. Mugalo hadn't grown any older in the last ten years. Why would he suddenly start now?

"We'll have to do some digging, regardless," he said, drawing some paper and a quill out of his desk. "I'll get my researchers started on it straightaway. This... intrigues me. I find it hard to believe that the situations are coincidental. A brutal, sudden attack on Ven, far away from the Empire's eyes, and a mysterious blacksmith who disappeared years ago... Something isn't right."

"I am inclined to agree with you, my lord," murmured Mugalo. "It is unsettling. Your reign has so far avoided any great acts of terror or violence, and I can say from experience that they do not happen without reason. I will have my staff look into it as well. The Imperial Archives are vast and detailed. I'm sure that we will be able to find something."

"Vast, detailed, and cripplingly disorganized," remarked the Emperor. "I remember. Do whatever you can. We need to understand why this happened, and we need to make sure it doesn't happen elsewhere."

Mugalo struggled to his feet. "As you wish, my lord," he replied. "Until next time. I'll be sure to send the investigating unit to you once they return. They may be able to shed some more light on the situation."

The Emperor nodded, waving his adviser off. As he watched the old man hobble out of the office, dark thoughts brewed in his mind. It had been years since a Necromantic attack of this magnitude. Even longer since the Empire had been so blindsided by something like this. In the last few weeks, he had genuinely begun to believe that they were making a foothold, and that peace was tantalizingly near. But now, it seemed like peace was even further away. He wasn't sure they would ever achieve it.

The soft sound of hooves pounding on the dirt slowly pulled Wyatt out of his slumber. He hadn't slept that deeply in ages, or maybe even ever. Having to pull himself out of that pure, trancelike rest was annoying. In fact, it was making him mad. He didn't want to wake up. He wanted to keep sleeping until his head stopped hurting.

The hooves got louder, so he grudgingly opened his eyes. He could see the afternoon sun peeking through the boughs above him, although the thick pine branches blocked out most of the light. It was comfortably dark and cool under this tree, only adding to his annoyance that something so stupidly loud was trying to wake him up.

"Oh thank Adala," came Grace's voice from outside of the tree. "Tythas!"

Wyatt's heart leapt. Finally, some good news. The fatigue fled from his mind as he scrambled to get out from under the tree and meet with Tythas.

"Hold on, Wyatt," came Shem's deep voice from behind him. Wyatt paused, turning around slowly and sitting back down in the soft bedding of pine needles that littered the dirt. He sighed, not even needing to look up to know that the cat was in front of him. He could feel those golden eyes gazing at him, almost as if the emitted some kind of heat.

"You did well," said the cat softly, for once not invested in cleaning himself. "I had complete faith in your ability to defeat that creature, but I was surprised at your methods. Well done, Wyatt. Well done."

Wyatt felt a small amount of pride blossom inside of his chest, but he did his best to keep it down. "Thanks," he replied evenly, a light smile highlighting his lips. "Can you tell me what that thing was?"

"Surprisingly, yes," said the cat with a light nod. "The patron of Terramancers, who created the pass and the shrine within it, also created the beast. It guards the pass from anything that would seek to do harm to the shrine. However, it seems that its purpose has somehow been perverted. Something or someone managed to manipulate it into attacking everything that travels through the pass."

Wyatt's mouth suddenly felt dry. "What would have the power to do something like that? A Terramancer?"

"A strong one, maybe," said Shem. "But I'm more inclined to believe that it was our friend, the Necromancer. He could've bound an enslaved spirit to the creature and used that spirit to control it, or at least influence it. It would be incredibly hard work, but it would be an effective way to attack you without your awareness."

"Makes sense," mumbled Wyatt with a nod. "He's got to be a pretty powerful Necromancer, then. If he can do something like that..."

"Yes, he is," replied the cat quickly. "Be sure that you never underestimate a Necromancer, especially one as old as our foe. I'm not even certain that he's still among the living. Sometimes, those who turn their backs on Adala can end up so immersed in Death that they become something else entirely."

"It's getting easier and easier to see why there's such a stigma attached to them," said Wyatt. "Controlling the elements is one thing, but animating dead bodies, binding spirits, and immortality... those are all very, very different."

"Necromancers do not live forever, Wyatt," said the cat, his voice sharp. "Those who have turned their back on the goddess would like us to believe that they have mastered eternal life, but the truth of it is that Death will find them in the end, just as Death finds everyone. Their road has an end, and it is not a pleasant one."

Wyatt stared at the cat for a moment and then gave a brief nod. "Right. I'll remember that."

"You need to keep moving," said the cat. "Your battle, while impressive, likely attracted the attention of unwanted spectators. I'm sure Tythas already knows this, but you may want to suggest it anyway."

"Alright," replied Wyatt with another nod. "We'll get going as soon as we can. Grace still needs to rest a bit before we get on the road, but we'll do our best to keep our heads down. It should be easier with Tythas here."

"It's not going to get any easier," responded the cat flatly. "Your path is going to hurt, Wyatt. It will be full of danger and peril. It might even kill you."

"I've got to find Mom," said Wyatt quickly, his voice hard. "It doesn't matter if it hurts, or if it's hard or whatever. It just... doesn't matter. I will find her."

"Wyatt! Wake up!" came Grace's sudden call, at considerable volume. Wyatt glanced over his shoulder, suppressing a snicker.

"Yeah, I hear you," he yelled back. "Give me a minute."

He looked back, but Shem had already disappeared. He shrugged and touched the sword on the ground next to him, receiving a satisfying hum in return. He turned again, crawling out from under the tree and into the open evening air.

"Nice of you to join us," said Grace from her seat at the campfire. Wyatt looked over at her, and winced at how tired she looked. He suddenly remembered that she had been keeping watch while he slept, and hadn't had the chance to get any rest. She probably felt worse than he had when he had gone to sleep.

"Yeah, he said quietly, giving her an apologetic look. "Sorry. Go ahead and get some rest, Grace. I can take over the watch."

"Now that Tythas is here," she said, looking very upset at the prospect of not being able to sleep, "we should just keep going. We're not that far from Wayton, and I can rest in a real bed when we get there. Besides, Jag will be waiting."

"Grace, my dear, you wouldn't make the trip," said Tythas pleasantly. "And your brother is just fine, albeit quite unconscious. Go rest for a few hours. It will give Wyatt and me a wonderful chance to talk and learn about one another, especially now that he's gone and shown off his power."

Wyatt stared at the old man for a moment before remembering what Shem had said. So Tythas could sense another Adept using their power, even from miles away. That would mean that other Adepts, at least other skilled ones, could probably do the same thing.

"Yeah, I agree with him," Wyatt said suddenly, still looking at the old man. "You used your power a lot more than I did, and you were tired when we went in there, Grace. Get some rest. You won't be any good to us if you're burnt out."

She got up from the small stump she was seated on, muttering protests. But she could see that she was outnumbered, and conceded defeat. She mouthed a "thank you" to Tythas before disappearing under the boughs of the pine tree.

"She's a tough girl," said Tythas, tying off the horses before sitting down by the fire that Grace had made. "But she has a bad habit of ignoring her limits. I worry that someday she'll push herself too far. Her gift is, in some ways, the most dangerous of the six."

Wyatt walked over to the fire, sitting down near Tythas. "She had mentioned that. It sounds like a lot of responsibility for one person."

"Vitamancers are rare," continued Tythas. "The spark is careful about the individual in which it manifests, but even more careful with Vitamancers. Grace is made of a certain stuff that isn't found in many other people."

"So you sensed me using my power," said Wyatt suddenly, no longer able to keep it inside of him. "Doesn't that mean that other Adepts would be able to, also?"

Tythas shrugged. "Only another Aeromancer. And he'd have to be talented, and powerful, and paying attention, unless he was very close to you. Being that you were more or less inside of a mountain, I think that we'll be okay. But we won't tarry here for too much longer. It would be unwise to tempt fate."

"Good," said Wyatt, very relieved. "I was worried that I'd have Adepts from the Council on my trail now, in addition to a crazy Necromancer."

Tythas rubbed his stubbly chin. "Yes, about that... it's a very strong possibility that sometime soon, we'll run into resistance of some kind from the Empire. They have a pretty firm stance on people breaking the law on Necromancers in the Empire, and we've been smuggling them overseas for about two years now. We were hoping that Ven would be a good place to quietly relocate a few, but... well, here we are."

Wyatt watched the fire, thinking. "I... honestly, Tythas, I don't know what I'll do if it comes to that. I haven't made up my mind about the situation yet. The only Necromancer that I've ever met tried to kill me, after all."

"His name is Apep," muttered Tythas absently. "Apep the Snake. He's old, even by my standards. I thought he was dead, but Necromancers have an uncanny ability to survive. He was one of the ones stirring up trouble and making a bad name for Necromancers, all those years ago.

He was essentially the central cause of the last war, and the war before that as well. Although I suppose they're really all just little parts of the same war. Regardless, whatever he's up to now is very concerning."

"Would the Empire know anything about him that we don't?" asked Wyatt hopefully.

"I doubt it," said Tythas, his voice betraying just a hint of bitterness. "I was the one who reported him dead. Unfortunately, we're going to have to piece together the puzzle ourselves, and your part in this is right in the center. Why Ven? Why you?"

Wyatt's answer came simply and honestly, and after a moment, he found himself telling Tythas the whole story, even the parts that he had left out to Jag and Grace. Everything came out: finding the sword, the earthquake, his mother getting sick, learning about his family's powers, and the exploding house. He suddenly felt sick and lost, and had no idea where he was going to go to find his mother and grandfather.

When Wyatt finished, Tythas was silent for a time, processing the information. Wyatt fiddled with his own fingers awkwardly as he looked into the fire, feeling as uneasy as he ever had in his life.

"Apep has some old associates in Wayton," said Tythas, breaking the silence. "Not necessarily allies, but… associates. We'll track them down and see if we can get a lead on his location. Right now, we can put our group's mission in the background. Something is going on, and you and your family are at the center of it."

Relief flooded over Wyatt, and for the first time since all this had begun, he felt a little bit of real, glimmering hope. The pressure of his secrets had been weighing down on him, but telling Tythas his story had helped that weight to ease from his shoulders. He felt that hope take hold of him and breathe an energy into him that he had been missing.

"I want to learn more about my power," he said, looking over at Tythas. "What I was able to do back there… it's how I can save them. But even more than that… using my power in the pass to make lightning made me feel complete. It was like… a hole inside of me was filled by that power, and now I can feel it there, waiting to be put to work. Almost like a muscle I never knew I had."

Tythas grinned at him. "That's precisely how you should feel, my dear boy. Never take that power for granted. It is a part of you, much like your arms and legs and heart. It isn't just a tool; it's a vital part of your being, and it needs to be embraced. All Adepts learn this lesson to varying degrees, but a rare few try to run from it. They turn their backs on their power and try to forget it. But that's impossible. It'd be like trying to forget you have toes."

"I don't think that I would ever want to," said Wyatt, mortified at the thought. "I loved it, it was like-"

Tythas suddenly held up a hand, looking at the eastern sky. The air around them stilled, and Wyatt could just barely feel Tythas's subtle influence on the weather. Wyatt looked to where the elder Adept was staring, and he saw what Tythas was looking at. Four black dots were gliding along the horizon, circling the peninsula on the other side of the mountains. They briefly hovered through the air before descending again behind the huge stony peaks.

"Imperial Adepts," muttered Tythas. "Led by an Aeromancer, using the wind and those gliders to fly across the country quickly. That's clever. A few Aeromancers can fly unassisted, but those gliders would make it a lot easier. They're probably investigating the damage in Ven. Reports travel even faster than I remembered."

"Do you think that they can see us?" asked Wyatt quickly, trying to extend his senses toward them. But he felt like he was trying to move a boulder. In his calm state, his power seemed to not want to do what he wanted.

Tythas continued watching the eastern sky. "Not likely, but if they were in the area when you blew up half of the mountain, they might have picked up on it. We will need to keep a low profile for now."

Wyatt gave up on trying to sense the gliding Adepts and looked back into the fire, trying to relax a little bit. As long as they remained far away, he didn't need to worry about those Adepts.

"You should really get some more rest," added Tythas, turning his attention back to Wyatt. "What you went through would've killed a lesser Adept with so little training. It probably would've done great harm to most Adepts in general. I'm sure Grace wouldn't mind if you take the other side of the tree."

Wyatt did still feel pretty wiped out. It wasn't as bad, but he knew he was going to need a lot more sleep to be fully recovered.

"Alright," he said, standing up and dusting his pants off. "You'll keep watch, then? I don't know how long I'll be out, but I think Grace might sleep for a week if we let her."

Tythas chuckled. "I certainly hope not. But yes, I'll keep an eye on things while the two of you rest. Jag will be out for another day or two, with any luck. Don't worry."

Wyatt nodded and thanked Tythas again before walking to the pine tree. Their journey was just beginning, and he was somewhat surprised to find that in spite of how tired, scared, and lost he sometimes felt, he still had some excitement in his mind. This was probably the most exciting thing he'd ever do in his life. He pushed aside the boughs and ducked into the tree. It was dark, but he could hear Grace's deep, even breaths. She was already sound asleep. He laid back down on his bedroll and quickly drifted off to sleep, falling back into the deep restorative trance that he had woken from just a short time ago.

Tythas stoked the fire quietly, his expression neutral. A prickling sensation crept up his neck, and unconsciously, he looked up at the stump that Wyatt had been sitting on. A tan, short-haired housecat was perched there, staring at him with strange, luminescent eyes. The two stared at each other for a short time before the cat finally broke the silence.

"You know what I am, then?" asked the cat quietly, his voice impossibly deep for such a small body. Not at all the voice Tythas would imagine a cat to have.

Tythas cocked his head. "Know? Not at all. I have my suspicions, sure, but I would hazard a guess that not even you know what you are anymore. Not truly. Time has a way of... eroding us. Even the strongest among us."

Shem didn't move. "Perhaps. But I do know you, Vance Tythas. Even buried deep in a cave, I sometimes heard things. And I have heard of you."

Tythas smiled. "I'm flattered. What do you want with the boy?"

"I'm not entirely sure, to be honest," remarked the cat. "Perhaps you should ask him what he wants with me. He found me, after all. Those things rarely happen by chance. And I do believe that I wasn't supposed to be found. But I can see something inside of him, something different. Something entirely unique."

"I would have to agree with that," said Tythas, his eyes still locked on the cat. He felt unusually tense. "I would imagine that this Necromancer we're chasing isn't a coincidence either, considering that he's supposed to be dead. I did kill him once, after all."

"None of them will stay dead if Apep reaches his goal," muttered the cat, his glowing golden eyes finally leaving Tythas's, to look up at the darkening sky. "He hasn't given up the search that you killed him over during the war. I don't think he'll ever give it up. He's making progress."

Tythas nodded softly, not at all surprised by the cat's news. "I had suspected as much. I assumed that you were some kind of safeguard, left behind in case that path were ever walked down by any Adept."

"I am, in some ways," said Shem. "I am also much more, and much less. Unfortunately, that's about all I can say about the subject. Thanks to the magic of the sword, I am unable to speak of it."

"Perhaps that is fortunate," muttered Tythas, with a small, silent smile, directed at himself more than anything. "I will need to train Wyatt. You have no objections?"

Shem looked back down to Tythas, again meeting his gaze. "You are more qualified than I, I think. I am a cat, after all. But I think you'll find that he doesn't need very much instruction. He's a natural, more so than any Adept born in centuries. His blood is rich with Adala's life, and his destiny is too great for us to understand right now."

"I'll do my best to teach him everything I know," said Tythas with a slow nod. "Hopefully he will learn quickly, as you've said he might. He will need to be ready for the worst."

"He will be," said Shem, no trace of doubt in his voice. "I won't be able to appear to you very often. It's difficult for me to make myself visible to anyone other than Wyatt. Technically, it's breaking the rules, but I have been known to do that on occasion. If I need to, I will speak through him. Take care of him, Vance Tythas. Teach him well."

Before Tythas could respond, the little cat was gone, his form fading and blowing away with an errant gust of wind, as if it had been composed of nothing but powder. Tythas watched that spot for a time before returning his gaze to the flickering fire.

"Time erodes us," he remarked again, mostly to himself. "I should know what is going on, but my mind grows cloudy with age. Adala guide us."

CHAPTER NINE

The ride back to Wayton was quiet and mercifully uneventful. Tythas was less talkative than usual, being too preoccupied with keeping their location hidden.

"Little tricks," he had said, with a wry smile. "An artist will color a painting in a certain way, in order to direct the eye. So too can an Adept, provided he can see all the colors."

Wyatt hadn't understood that, but the old man offered no further explanations of it.

In truth, Wyatt had a small suspicion that something was troubling the older Adept, but Tythas was not exactly easy to read. He still told the occasional joke or story, but he somehow seemed less spirited than he had previously. That was concerning, but what really gave Wyatt pause was the sword. It was equally quiet, its usual vibrant humming replaced by only the occasional dull twinge. Shem's presence was absent from Wyatt's mind, for the time being. It was nice to have the privacy, but it was also strange enough to give Wyatt pause.

Luckily, the rest that Wyatt and Grace had finally been afforded had gone very far in restoring their energies. Wyatt's new task was simply to learn to control his power on a very basic level. Ever since he had touched the statue, he found that his power flared up at the slightest hint of emotion or loss of focus. Halfway through their trip, he had nearly set himself on fire when he was staring at some distant birds. He had only just noticed the electricity arcing over his hands. Much to his relief, neither his companions nor his horse had noticed.

"Once we get into town, I want you both to cover up with your cloaks and keep to yourselves," said Tythas quietly, breaking the silence. "Wayton isn't... the most pure place in the world. Keep your heads down, and above all else, do not stray from my side."

"What about my sword?" asked Wyatt, looking down at the glittering hilt on his hip, surely a glaring target for any would-be highwaymen. "Should I try to hide it?"

Tythas rubbed his chin, thinking. "It probably wouldn't hurt, to be honest. I hate to hide a weapon like that, but I don't really think that we have a choice. Just keep it close at hand. It could go a long way in preventing an uncomfortable situation."

Wyatt adjusted himself for a moment, unclasping the sword from his hip and raising it behind his head, just where the baldric went around his shoulder. With his pack over it, the hilt would barely stick up, and his cloak would do well enough to cover the rest of it. Everything situated, he drew that cloak tightly around him and pulled the hood up, just as Wayton came into view.

Growing up in a small, secluded place like Ven, Wyatt had always assumed that cities in the real world were marvelous and huge. Wayton, however, was a sobering picture of what could happen to the real world when society struggled to keep the peace. Ramshackle houses and buildings had been gathered in a seemingly random smattering, barely allowing for roads between them. No building stood over two or three stories, the architecture amateur at best. Few people were in the streets, but Wyatt could see openly-worn weapons on nearly everyone who was. Some of these men and women eyed him hungrily as he rode past, making his skin prickle.

"The inn we're staying at is a hidden gem," murmured Tythas as they rode slowly through the narrow, winding street. "The innkeeper is an old friend, and he owes me many favors. His building is one of the only truly safe places in the city. We'll be able to talk more once we get there."

"I don't like this place," said Grace quietly. "I can... it's like I can feel Death here, sapping my energy. What happened here, Tythas?"

Vance scanned the streets, his gaze steely. "I believe that our friend has been here, as well. I thought I smelled it, when I first arrived. Having you here has confirmed my fears. Apep the Snake has been in Wayton, and has done something foul."

Grace shivered absently. "How has nobody else noticed?"

"Wayton is a neutral territory," replied Vance as he urged his horse forward. "A dead zone of sorts between the claimed territory of the Dominion of Flame and the chartered Imperial land. As a result of that, there's no system of formal law here, no governing body."

Wyatt was doing his best to keep his eyes ahead, but it was hard not to stare at everything around him. Scarred faces practically begged him to challenge them. But he ignored his discomfort and focused on the little space between his horse's ears.

"What keeps outlaws from running it, then?" he asked, focusing hard to keep his energy down. "It looks like some sort of control is held over the people. At least... a bit, anyway."

"Adepts," replied Tythas, a bit of pride in his voice. "A fair few who have removed themselves from politics entirely and deemed neutrality their best option. One of them runs the inn we'll be staying at. The others are here. You can't see them, because they're exceptionally good at blending in. But they're here. Watching."

Wyatt's eyes drifted to a haggard old shopkeeper who was washing out the horse trough in front of his small shop. He glanced at Wyatt, and for a moment, their eyes met. The old man winked, and Wyatt's jaw nearly fell open as he waggled his fingers, filling the trough with fresh water from a completely unseen source.

Suddenly, Wyatt felt a lot more comfortable riding through Wayton. He understood now why all these people seemed just on the edge of a fight. They knew better.

"It's just up here," added Tythas, pointing up at a building ahead of them. A creaking sign hung above it, featuring a rather disheveled painting of a bearded man in dirty robes. The structure itself looked just as run down and dirty as the rest of the city, but Wyatt could hear music and laughter echoing from inside. They dismounted, tying off their horses.

"Really, Vance?" asked Grace dryly as she surveyed the sign. "A hidden gem? The Drunken Priest?"

"Judge not the package that thine eyes can see," replied the old man silkily as he took the lead and stepped inside. "Wait instead for the contents and reap thy rewards."

Grace rolled her eyes.

Tythas slipped through the crowd effortlessly, not even seeming to need to excuse himself as he quickly reached the other side of the building. Wyatt and Grace, however, did not fare nearly as well; they awkwardly stumbled their way across the tavern floor, bumping into many people as they did their best to cause as little chaos as possible. Wyatt got a lot of dirty looks, but he made it to the other side relatively unscathed, and nobody seemed to be paying either him or Grace much attention.

Tythas was waiting for them by the stairs, smiling pleasantly in spite of their scathing glares. The smirking old man led them up the stairs to a lone hallway, with five rooms on each side. Wyatt knew that there were likely some outbuildings that held rooms as well, but he had the feeling that not many people stayed in Wayton for very long. Tythas motioned to the two doors on either side of the hall at the very rear.

"Our room is there, Wyatt," said Tythas, pointing to the right. "Jag should still be asleep in the other."

Grace pushed past the both of them, walking into the room on the left where her brother was waiting. Wyatt and Tythas followed, doing their best to navigate into the cramped little room.

"About time you showed back up," growled Jag from the bed, staring at Tythas with disdain. "I've been awake for quite some time, old man. You've got to use more of that stuff next time if you want to keep me down."

"Well, more of it probably would've killed you," replied Tythas with a merry chuckle. "But, if you really think-"

"Tythas, shut up," snapped Grace as she quickly made her way to her brother, sitting down on the bed next to him. She leaned over him, putting her hands against his chest and closing her eyes. Golden light flashed underneath her fingers, a sure sign that she was using her power.

"That feels great, sis, but I'm mostly better anyway," managed Jag, gently nudging her away. "Vance made me some sort of vile concoction that actually ended up healing me pretty well." He looked equal parts amused and intoxicated as he prodded her. Grace was probably overdoing it a little, being that he was her brother.

She finally leaned back, withdrawing her hands and letting the light fade. She looked over him nervously, biting her lip. "You'll be okay to ride again in the morning, I think. You should go for a walk though. You need to move those recently healed muscles. I would imagine it'll be a little hard. You'll probably be stiff for several days."

"Perhaps you should take him around the town, Grace," suggested Tythas with a smile. "I have some business to attend to before the evening arrives, and Wyatt can come with me."

Wyatt blinked. "You want me to come with you? Why?"

"So that you might learn something, young Adept," replied Tythas with a not-so-subtle wink. "We're going to have to get you up to speed somehow. Might as well start today."

Wyatt opened his mouth to speak, but Jag cut him off as he slowly swung his legs over the bed. "Just go with it, kid," he said with a low chuckle. "We've both been put through Tythas's 'lessons' plenty of times. We lived, and so will you."

"Just don't pay too much attention to, well, really anything he says," added Grace, smiling devilishly at her mentor. "Otherwise, you'll notice all the holes in his logic and he'll get frustrated."

Tythas's eyes turned on her, his expression sour. "I see you both missed the lessons on respecting your elders," he replied dryly. "I'll remember that. You two both still owe me, you know, and I'm running low on acorns."

Grace and Jag visibly recoiled, gaping at him. "Not again," whined Grace, shaking her head. "You can't make us do that again. Vance, come on." She looked as if he had suggested torture.

"I don't want to know," said Wyatt, shaking his head. "Tythas, I'm going to go leave some things in our room. Come and get me when you're ready to leave. Glad to see you're back in one piece, Jag." With that, he left the room, suddenly feeling a little awkward around his companions.

He walked into the other room and removed his elaborate wrappings.

Setting everything aside, he sat down on the bed with his sword across his knees and rested his head in his hands. The sword hummed in sympathy, but Shem's voice was nowhere to be heard.

He was beginning to realize how strange it felt to be a part of this group. He could tell by the way that they interacted with each other that the three of them had been fighting together for a long time, and those shared risks and fears had forged a bond between them that Wyatt just didn't have. He felt like he was intruding on that, somehow, as if his presence could break up their familial bonds.

But mostly, it just made him miss his own family. His mother. Desmond. Even Kelsar, who had only been a friendly figure for most of his life, not a grandfather. But all of them felt so far from him, now.

The door to the room opened, and Tythas quietly stepped through. He set his pack aside and looked over at Wyatt.

"Let's get going," he said, nodding at the younger Adept. "Get your cloak back on. And bring the sword. In this town, you never know."

Wyatt swung the cloak over his shoulders, this time leaving the hood down to bunch up over the hilt. It may make him look like a bizarre hunchback, but at least it kept people from thinking he was a wealthy noble. He and Tythas made their way out of the inn quietly, back onto the dangerous streets of Wayton.

"Here we are," muttered Tythas, motioning up at a shoddy, squat building in front of them. "Our destination."

"This person we're here to see," said Wyatt as he appraised the small house, "they are an associate of this Necromancer? Apep, or whatever it is you called him?"

"Were," replied Tythas smoothly. "Were an associate. During the war, the man we're about to see defected from Apep's troops, at great personal risk I might add, and was absolutely invaluable to the Empire. His intelligence and his willingness to fight other Necromancers, to counteract their abilities, was a central part of the Empire's victory. He's a good man who wanted freedom for his people, but didn't want to achieve it with Apep's methods. In the end, he retired here, free of the Empire's ability to exile him. He lends his power to keeping Wayton safe. It's not an easy life, but it's better than the alternative."

"It doesn't look that safe," mumbled Wyatt in response, glancing around him at the rest of the street.

Tythas knocked three times on the thick wooden door. "True, but if you were to watch the city for a little longer than an afternoon, you'd find that there's actually very little crime within the city itself. Just outside the city, I'm sure terrible things can happen. But the Adepts who police the town do a good job of keeping everybody civil while they're here. They don't stay long, and as a result the economy struggles. But they stay peaceful, which is the most important part."

Wyatt eyed the house warily, waiting. There was no response, however. He glanced at Tythas, who knocked again.

"Interesting," said Tythas, trying to look into a nearby window, but the curtains were drawn. "He is almost always in his home in some way. I didn't expect this. Perhaps we should check back later."

The sword on Wyatt's back suddenly gave a hefty jolt, and Wyatt's gaze turned back to the house. Without even thinking, without even realizing it, his breathing slowed and his senses branched out, as if he were extending his hands into the shoddy building. He could smell the air coming from the house, feel it touching his skin. He could almost see it, see the blackness of it. It made his skin crawl. All of his senses told him that something in this house was very, very wrong.

"Tythas," he said quietly, looking at the old man, who was watching him with interest. "Something... isn't right. Look closer."

Tythas watched him intently for a moment before turning to the house. He stared for a moment and then sniffed, his expression souring.

"Death grips this place," whispered the elder Adept, suddenly very tense. "We need to go inside and deal with whatever is going on. I... don't believe that my old friend is here any longer."

Wyatt drew his sword on instinct and nodded once at Tythas, feeling oddly calm and nervous at the same time. Tythas tested the door, and, finding it unlocked, he pushed it open and the two of them slipped inside. Wyatt followed closely, keeping his senses extended. The sword was awake again, buzzing hungrily in his hand.

The smell of decay assailed their noses as soon as they entered the hallway. Thanks to the dim light floating in through the partially covered windows, Wyatt could just see dark stains on nearly every surface inside. His stomach threatened to turn, but he gripped the sword tighter and swallowed, focusing hard on keeping his calm.

"Stay focused," whispered Tythas, taking the lead and walking slowly down the hall. "There is still... something here. I recognize the signs."

They exited the entry hall and went into the main room of the small house, gazing around warily as they slowly walked through the doorway. The light here was even poorer, making it hard to distinguish furniture from simple shadows. Worse yet, the thick stench of death hung thick in the air, making it hard to catch a real breath.

"Shem, any suggestions?" whispered Wyatt, glancing at the sword in his hand. The sword continued to hum, but the cat's voice was suspiciously absent. Fear and annoyance bubbled up within them. Either the cat thought they could handle it, or he was refusing to help. But Tythas was with him. He had to believe that the two of them were more than capable of-

Suddenly, the wall to their left exploded in a cloud of debris and dust. A huge, shadowy form burst through with a wail that sounded like the voices of hundreds of tortured souls. Wyatt and Tythas reacted simultaneously, dancing backward to avoid the raining chunks of wood and taking defensive positions. Wyatt crouched low, his sword ready, unconsciously forming a bubble of swirling air around him. Lightning danced along the blade of his sword.

The beast that stood before them was equal parts monstrous and mysterious. It appeared to be composed mostly of shadow, and any distinguishing features it might have were somehow concealed, as if it were an inkblot that Wyatt had smeared with his thumb. But it was shaped like a large man. He could just see white, glowing eyes on what he assumed was its head. It was taller than the hall they stood in, and had to crouch low to fit. Its arms were thick and long, reaching down to its knees and ending in thick claws. It had no mouth, but, somehow, it managed to roar at them again as it sprang.

Tythas reacted first. With a flourish that splayed his robes around him, he sent a fist of flame and wind slamming into the creature, catching it in midair and tossing it back into the hole in the wall from which it had emerged. He glanced back at Wyatt.

"We need to get out of the building and into the street," he growled, motioning Wyatt back toward the door. "It'll be weaker in the sunlight, and there might be other Adepts nearby. Go."

The beast roared yet again, blasting more of the wall apart as it charged back at the two of them with abandon. Tythas swung another flaming fist at the monster, but this time it was ready: it smashed one huge, clawed hand into the floor, anchoring itself to the ground and blasting the fist apart with a grunt. Tythas sent yet more fire and wind slamming into it, but the creature held strong, using its huge claws to crawl toward them.

"Run, Wyatt!" yelled the old man, doing his best to keep the thing busy as he backed up. Wyatt made a mad dash for the front door, kicking it open and diving out into the dazzling sunlight, Tythas just behind him. The two of them skidded into the dirt and turned to face the doorway, awaiting the screaming beast that had chased them out of the house. They could hear it still, growing nearer.

Wyatt realized there were people standing in the street staring at them. "Run!" he yelled, motioning for them to clear out. They stared back at him, as if he were speaking a different language. A few even looked as if they may challenge him.

"You idiots!" he added, snarling at the nearest citizen and stepping forward aggressively, his cloak billowing out behind him in the wind. "There's a monster loose! Get away from here! GO!" As he yelled, the wind picked up, throwing the man in front back into the dirt and rolling him down the street. Thunder boomed in the sky. The townspeople, suddenly realizing that two Adepts were telling them to run, bolted in terror.

The front of the building blew apart as the beast leapt out into the street, sending yet more debris flying toward the two warriors as it landed in front of them. The nimbus of wind that Wyatt had wrapped himself in scattered any that came near him, and Tythas didn't even seem to notice as the bits of wood raining near him were incinerated by the heat of his aura.

The two Adepts reacted at the same time. Tythas flourished his hands again, summoning a gust of wind behind the beast just as he rammed a ball of fire into its front. Wyatt, untrained as he was, simply swung his sword through the air, releasing an arcing blast of lightning that snarled out from the tip of the blade and collided with the creature at the same time as Tythas's flaming hand.

This time, the beast howled in pain as motes of shadow and bits of rotten meat were blasted off of it, raining down around them. But it was still on its feet, staring intently at Tythas with pure white eyes, preparing to charge yet again.

Wyatt could feel the fatigue creeping up on him already, but he ignored it, his blood pounding in his ears thanks to the danger they were in. Tythas eyed the creature warily, waiting for the proper moment to strike. He seemed like he had dealt with something like this monster in the past. He seemed like he knew what they needed to do.

"Don't let it touch you," whispered the old man, his eyes forward. "Not even a little bit."

Wyatt nodded, but before he could voice any response, his words were cut off by an earsplitting explosion. The ground beneath the beast cracked and broke, shattering apart as black fire burst forth, surrounding them and reaching for them.

"Up!" yelled Tythas, leaping up into the sky as a massive gust of wind caught him, whisking him quickly away from the fire. Wyatt gaped up at him.

"Up!?" he shouted, looking at the old man incredulously. "How in the hell do you expect me to do that?!"

"Just jump!" shouted the older Adept, his voice frantic. Wyatt looked around. The flames were feet away from him, and the beast was charging. He yelled unintelligibly as his frustration broke and, feeling exceptionally foolish, jumped.

Some combination of Tythas's power and his own managed to catch him and lift him into the sky. The old man was breathing heavily with concentration as he held his hands out, focusing on lifting Wyatt away from danger. He wasn't going to be able to fight if all of his efforts went into keeping them aloft.

Wyatt saw the darkening clouds above his head, and he suddenly understood. He closed his eyes, focusing on the clouds, focusing on their darkness. He could feel the potential for destruction hanging in the air, calling out to him, begging him to open the door and release it. All he needed to do was influence it, will it into motion...

Thunder boomed in their ears, louder and more violent than anything he could create from his bare hands. Wyatt envisioned pulling that energy above him downward. As he focused, he felt a mighty pull at his navel as a massive bolt of searing lightning streaked down from the clouds above them, white and terrible as it struck the shadowy creature with titanic force.

The beast was ready. It raised both hands, trying to catch the bolt and deflect it. But the monster was no match for Wyatt's rage, and it buckled under the blast. The pure, unstoppable white light shredded the beast into pieces that flew in every direction like an exploding tree.

Tythas stared at Wyatt in shock for a few moments before steeling himself. He motioned with his hands for a few moments and the wind gently set the two of them back down in the street.

"Old man," wheezed Wyatt, taking a knee as fatigue crashed into him in waves, "what in the world was that thing?"

Tythas watched him for a few more moments before stepping forward to survey the area. He kept a wary eye on the writhing bits of shadow-stuff that were left in the dirt, wriggling around them like horrible little snakes. Wyatt wasn't sure at first if Tythas had even heard him. But finally, he got an answer.

"A bad sign," murmured Tythas, not looking at all winded, compared to Wyatt. "A very bad sign. Something I haven't seen since the war. That was a Shender, a kind of... golem, made by a very powerful Necromancer."

"A... golem?" asked Wyatt, plopping down in the dirt, no longer able to stay on his feet. He could feel blood trickling from his nose. "Made of what?"

"Another Necromancer," said Tythas sourly, his eyes dark. He raised a hand, and a wave of fire erupted from his palm, rolling over the remaining wriggling bits of the Shender and scouring them from the dirt. "His blood was all over the walls in there. That beast is fueled by the soul of a bound, unwilling Necromancer. Its form is constructed from the flesh of cattle. It is one of the most perverse uses of that particular Aspect, and I had thought that I would never see one again."

Wyatt's stomach gave an uneasy lurch, threatening to turn again. "So one Necromancer kills another one, and then binds his spirit to this… thing made of dead cows? That's… I can see why people are so uneasy around Necromancy. If this was common in the past…"

"It wasn't," replied Tythas sharply, walking to Wyatt and helping the younger Adept to his feet. "It never was. It's an abomination, and any Necromancer that hasn't completely lost it would tell you that. But all it takes is one well-publicized event to send people into a panic. The war… lasted a long time, Wyatt. And things like that were on the front lines of the other side. Couple that with just the right spin, just the right amount of fearmongering… never mind that they were doing this to their own people. Somehow, the common folk just glazed over that little fact." His voice was bitter, and Wyatt could tell that this was a sore subject.

Together, they walked slowly down the street, Wyatt leaning on Tythas more than he would've liked to for support. He was really getting tired of feeling exhausted, and although the strength was creeping back into him, he still wished he could've felt well rested for a little bit longer.

"It seems like the situation is very complicated," said Wyatt after a time. "Both sides seem to have their arguments. But it sounds like your friend, the one who… it sounds like he was a good man. Necromancers can't be the only ones who've gone rogue or turned evil. What about others, Aeromancers and Aquamancers and the like?"

"Bearers of every Aspect fought on both sides of the war," answered Tythas carefully. Not all of them agreed with the goals of their leaders. Adepts, for the most part, are just soldiers. Those of us who want to think for ourselves ended up leading one side of the conflict, or breaking away entirely. Eventually, I did both. But yes, you are correct. Our aspect doesn't decide our morality. There is no outside decider. The choice is ours."

"Tythas!" came a female voice from down the street. "What happened?"

Grace came sprinting into view with Jag just behind her, looking a little bit green. He may not have been as recovered as they let on.

"Golag is dead," said Tythas quietly, helping Wyatt find a place for us to sit. "We found what was left of him. A Shender, left behind in his home to lie in wait for whoever might seek him out."

Jag and Grace stared at their mentor, stunned. They looked to each other for a moment before looking back to Tythas. Grace was first to speak.

"A Shender," she said, her voice trembling slightly. "Tythas, no Necromancer has dared create a Shender since the war. If the person who did that were caught anywhere in the Empire, they'd be immediately executed."

"I'm well aware of that," replied Tythas flatly, looking up at the sky. "But we don't have time to talk about it right now, and we're not exactly in the Empire. Several buildings were destroyed in the area where we found it, and Wyatt and I put on quite the spectacular show trying to stop the thing. Wyatt here can call lightning like a master Aeromancer."

Grace looked over at Wyatt, blinking. She knelt down in front of him, taking his hands in hers. Golden light flowed around her fingers, and he felt his exhaustion fade a considerable amount.

"Thanks," he breathed, very relieved. He pulled his hands away when he felt well enough to move again. "That's enough for now. We need to get out of Wayton. If those Imperial scouts we saw are still in the area…"

"Wait," interrupted Jag with a sputter. "Imperial scouts? Okay, I realize I was unconscious for a couple of days, but I fail to see how that didn't get mentioned."

Tythas helped Wyatt to his feet again and the four of them took off at a very quick pace toward the inn. "Before we rode into the town. We saw them on the horizon on gliders, crossing over the mountains. Any Aeromancer that can control four of those simultaneously would be able to pick up the amount of power Wyatt and I were throwing around with ease. We need to get going, before they show up and start asking questions. I have a few friends here, but virtually the entire population would sell information about us to anyone for the right price. Even the Empire."

The quartet quickly pushed their way through the chattering crowd at the inn, ignoring the questions and discussions about the commotion in the streets. Wyatt even recognized the man who he had sent tumbling down the road. They locked eyes for a moment, and the man quickly looked down at his drink, white in the face. Wyatt didn't give him another look and followed the others upstairs. They gathered their things quickly, paid for their rooms, and hastily walked from the inn, anxious to get away from the prying eyes of the people.

"Are you okay?" asked Grace quietly as she and Wyatt saddled their horses in the stable. She glanced at him briefly as she asked, but didn't look at him otherwise.

Wyatt adjusted the blanket, not looking back at her, either. "Yeah, I guess. Why wouldn't I be?"

Grace fidgeted with a buckle, adjusting the girth and making sure the strap was properly tight. "I don't know. You saw... a Shender. I've never seen one before, but I know how they're made. I know all about that. I... I don't know, I always thought that side of Necromancy was pretty terrifying. But I can't help but have a curiosity about it, too. I just..."

"It was disgusting," said Wyatt, a lot more sharply than he had intended. But bringing up the Shender again was threatening to turn his stomach. He took a few deep breaths and forced his nausea down, idly rubbing his horse's neck as he focused hard on keeping his calm. "Absolutely... heinous. I can see why Necromancy is such a sore subject. Even one bad example can ruin any amount of good with something like a Shender."

"That's not even the worst of it," said Grace with a sigh, mounting her horse. "Study of higher Necromancy is forbidden in the Empire, but

Tythas has told us some things. Some really twisted stuff went on in the war. It was pretty easy to spread the anti-Necromancer agenda. Still is."

"I'm starting to get the image, yeah," Wyatt said flatly, still trying hard to keep the sights and smells from that house out of his mind. He mounted his own horse, patting it on the neck before urging it out onto the road with his other comrades. "I can't say that I can make a decision on this yet, Grace. But if I keep thinking about it, I'm going to get sick. So let's drop it, okay?"

Wyatt stared at the road while doing his best to keep his mind blank. He could feel Grace looking at him, and was pretty sure Jag and Tythas were as well.

"Yeah, sorry," she said finally, her voice quiet and far off. "I don't know what you saw back there, Wyatt, but sometimes it's easy to get desensitized to the stuff. I've been around it all my life."

"Grace," called Jag's scolding voice from the rear. "Leave the boy alone. You're going to make him sick. Let's talk about where we're going next."

Jag and Tythas rode up on either side of Grace and Wyatt, much to Wyatt's relief. He didn't want to even think about the Shender ever again. Grace, looking a little defeated, dropped the subject.

"It seems to me that we're without a plan here," remarked Tythas with gentle amusement. "Although it's not the first time, in this situation it's a little more troubling. Does anyone have any ideas?"

It was Wyatt who answered first. "You said that Wayton is in a neutral zone between the Dominion of Fire and the Empire, right?" he asked, scanning the road and the skyline as he did, trying to broaden his Adept senses and feel the wind around them.

"That's right," replied Tythas, scratching his chin. "The Empire and the Dominion have a non-aggression agreement. At least, for the moment anyway. Wayton and any other settlements that lie in the overlapping territories are considered neutral ground."

"Well, if you were a Necromancer looking to unseat and destroy the Empire, where would you head next?"

Grace and Jag had blank looks, but Tythas seemed to understand, and he spoke up. "The Dominion, obviously," he said with a sigh. "But that's not an easy road to go on. Citizens of the Dominion are famously xenophobic, and their ruling council even more so. It would be difficult to travel through their lands without attracting attention to ourselves. Which, considering the Dominion's hostile tendencies, may be the least of our worries."

"I can't ignore the fact that my house was blown up in a great ball of fire, though," replied Wyatt, rubbing his eyes. "It just seems like the next logical step, for both us and Apep. If I were in his position and looking for help, the Dominion of Fire seems like the place to go. They're always fighting with the Empire."

"And they've been allies in the past," said Jag quietly, concern etched on his face. "The Dominion and Necromancers, I mean. There were strong Necromancy sympathizers in the Dominion during the war, even if they did eventually side with the Empire. They probably still hold some amount of power, and the relationship between the Empire and the Dominion isn't exactly great these days. Since the war, since losing a common enemy, the two sides don't have much else to do besides poke each other."

"I would think that their relationship would get better with no wars going on," said Wyatt thoughtfully. "What went wrong?"

"The two have never exactly been friendly," responded Tythas, adopting an almost professorish, lecturing tone, "but recently, the Dominion doesn't approve of the Empire's blanket stance against Necromancy. While their core beliefs place Pyromancers above all other Adepts, they still believe that every Aspect is a manifestation of Adala and deserves reverence. They've offered refuge to Necromancers in the past, which has irked the Empire. It's hard to say, at this point, where they truly stand. But I think that you're right, Wyatt. We should make our way north, to the volcanic lands of the Dominion."

"I'm going to send a message to our allies in Triat," said Grace, mostly to Tythas. "Someone should know where we're at, in case something goes wrong or we need help. The Blazelands... aren't exactly the friendliest place."

Jag nodded at his sister. "That's a good idea, Sis. Triat is a long ways from the Blazelands, but at least we have some backup there if we need it. Tell them we'll update as we can, and that if there's any kind of long silence, they should send someone to check on us. Preferably a Pyromancer. I think there's one or two down there that still owe me a favor."

"I agree," added Tythas. "The border of the Blazelands is still a few days from here. That gives everyone ample opportunity to rest, and Wyatt can catch up on his reading while we ride."

Wyatt blinked. "My... reading? Um, did I miss something?"

Tythas produced a book from under his robes, tossing it to Wyatt with a pleasant smile on his face. He caught it, turning it over and reading the cover aloud.

"*Historia Arcanum*," he said dully, inspecting the worn cover of the book. "That's High Script, isn't it? We studied it a bit in school. The traditional language of the Adepts?"

"Correct," said Tythas with altogether too much cheer. "Unfortunately, the book is written in simple common script. The Council all but abandoned High Script centuries ago, and it is now nothing more than a traditional formality. Most Adepts only know a handful of words."

"Okay then," said Wyatt in response. "What is the book for, then?"

"It is the most accurate account of how the world was before Adala's ultimate sacrifice, and immediately after," explained Tythas. "The author is unknown, but his or her accounts are widely accepted as factual. Some speculate that it was written by one of the Six. That book will give you more insight into your purpose as an Adept."

"It'll also put you to sleep," commented Jag with a smirk. "It's probably the most boring book I've ever had to read. I think the boy can figure out his purpose without a book helping him, Tythas. He's already throwing lightning around like an old hand."

Tythas opened his mouth to retort, but Wyatt beat him to it. "No, Jag, I think that I want to read it. We didn't learn much about magic or Adala or whatever in Ven. Not much exposure to it, living so far out of the way. We didn't even have a Guardian Adept like bigger cities do. So it'll be good for me."

"Very smart of you, Wyatt," said Tythas with a proud smile. "It'll answer a lot of your questions, I'm sure. So get to reading. Your horse will follow us without you guiding it."

Wyatt nodded and squirmed around in his saddle, doing his best to get into a comfortable reading position atop the horse. After a few moments, he opened the book and shut the rest of the world out, which proved to be a wonderful distraction from the excitement of the day. He felt the sword at his hip give a subtle twitch, and finally, he was able to relax.

Wyatt,

I know, it's only been like a week and you haven't even written me back, but I have a lot of free time riding with the convoy. Don't hold it against me! You know I get bored easily.

Riding through the mainland has really opened my eyes. We're headed for the border between the northwestern part of the Empire and the Wilds, but we're riding through all the contested areas between the Dominion and the Empire to get there. There're a lot of little towns and hamlets that remind me of home, but everything here is so run down and harsh. The community leaders don't want to pledge to either side, afraid that they'll mark a target on their town. So they stay neutral with the Empire and the Dominion patrolling either end of the cities. It's madness.

The army is an interesting place, but I fit right in. I was always very sure that this is what I wanted, but now that I'm here I know I was right. The freedom to travel and see the world, to help people where I can and fight for our Empire… it's a good life, Wyatt. It's really good.

I hope you and Nora are doing well. Has Kelsar burned the shop down yet? I just know he's lost without me.

Des

CHAPTER TEN

Far to the north, within the sweltering heat of a volcanic mountain, a thin form hobbled deep into the rock, following the path of a narrowly winding cave. Veins of glowing magma shone on the walls all around the figure, casting an eerie red light around the skeletal woman. Her clothes, mostly rags at this point, threatened to combust as they brushed up against the hot stone walls. With every step, the bare skin of her feet was seared on the stone surface beneath her, leaving smoking black footprints behind her as she walked.

Of course, closer inspection would show the bloody wounds and blackened patches which marred the skin of the once-beautiful woman. Spots of skin on her hands had been completely worn away, allowing stark white bone to shine through. Her formerly sleek blonde hair was now tattered, matted, and falling out in many places. Her eyes, once blue and pure, now bulged out of her head, bloodshot and dry. But whatever ailment had claimed her beauty and marred her flesh didn't seem to be of much bother to her. She carried through the cave with quiet strength and determination, seemingly unaffected by the constant searing of the skin on her feet.

After several hundred yards, the cave finally opened up into a large cavern at the heart of the volcano, a cavern that was painstakingly carved into a hexagon. At the center stood six statues, arranged evenly along the points of the hexagon. Each held a different color stone reverently in its hands. All around them, the walls were carved with ancient texts. These were the words of those who had created this place, words forgotten by all but the wisest of men.

The woman hobbled into the cavern, not at all surprised in finding this place. Another followed her through the doorway, stepping much more carefully. He was tightly robed and wore a bone-white mask on his face. Like the statues, he clutched a gem in his hands; a great sapphire, slightly larger than an apple, which twinkled with an impossibly blue light. Unlike the leader, his steps were much more careful, and the sour expression on his face could be seen even through his mask.

"Master," breathed the second, squeezing the gem nervously as he glanced around the room. "I do not understand why we needed to come down here. Surely we could've waited until we had the sacrifice?"

The woman slowly walked around the statues, her hand reaching up to stroke the stones reverently. Here, the heat seemed to have abated; her flesh didn't burn at all inside the circle. She paused, reaching up to touch the hand of one of the statues. It held in its hands a stone as black as night, a stone that seemed to absorb the light around it.

"Yes, Apep," she said slowly, her voice unnatural and not at all feminine. "We could have waited. But I needed to be sure it was here before committing to this path. I needed to feel her, to be sure that she was here." The master let her hand drop and walked further around, stopping in front of the statue holding a fiery red gem. She gazed up into its hooded face.

Apep watched his master warily, raising his eyebrow. "I do not understand, master. Your essence has touched this place. Surely, you remember it?"

"Time and memory have a strange relationship, Apep," replied the woman evenly. "You are old, by human standards. Surely you do not remember every landmark that you have seen? The earth has changed greatly since I was last upon it. And being locked away from everything has… blurred some of my memories."

"This is the correct place, though?" asked Apep hopefully as he looked around the cavern. The cavern certainly looked right, but only his master could truly be sure.

"Yes, this is the place," she replied, still staring up into the hooded figure holding the red stone. "My sister gave her power in this very spot, in the center of this circle. I can feel her here, even now. I can feel her anger and her rage, aching to burn into me. Placing this here was very clever. Of course, she would've required help, and she received it from the usual source. She believed herself of great power and import, my sister. But in the end, the most important and influential was another: the one who made these seals. Her works have lasted; the rest have faded with time."

"Perhaps we should return to a safer place, now that we've verified the location of the shrine," said Apep warily, clutching his blue stone tightly. "This gem is the only thing keeping my body unharmed, and your form... master... your body is falling apart. We will need to find you a new host soon, perhaps this time we can find a stronger host that is more... compatible."

The woman finally turned to stare at her comrade, an amused smile on her cracked, bloody lips. "Are you offering yourself, Apep?" came the deep, guttural voice of that which resided within her. Her eyes glowed a malicious, bloody red. "You would be more compatible than any, I think."

Apep withered before his master's glare, averting his eyes and bowing his head. "My lord, that would be... unproductive. I believe I still have value to you."

"Your connections have value to me, Apep," replied the master scathingly. "But that which you value about yourself more than anything... your power, Apep, means nothing to me. Know your place. There are other servants."

Apep bowed deeper, but managed to keep his calm. "My apologies, my lord. I meant no offense. I simply want to see our goal realized, and that will be difficult if your body fails us in an inconvenient place."

The master turned back to the statues, stroking the red stone with a strange affection. "You have a point. We need a sacrifice, first. Blood must mingle with this stone... the blood of my sister's get."

Apep glanced nervously around the cavern once again, his hands fidgeting with the stone. "I already have a plan for that, master. But this gem will not last much longer. I must retreat soon."

The woman laughed, her voice cruel and cold. "You fear the heat, don't you? I had forgotten. Your protections don't stand up well to the pure fire of a Pyromancer. The dark, fleeing from the light."

Apep squeezed the stone nervously, but he held his ground. "My form, without these protections, is fragile. I have lived longer than even the greatest Necromancers, my lord. I have forged myself in your image and mastered Death!"

The master paused, considering Apep's statement, before walking out of the circle to approach her servant. A trickle of blood slowly drained from her eye, sliding down her face to drip on the floor with a sizzle.

"You are useful, I will admit that," she said quietly, fixing an intense stare on her servant. "But you are a fool. To master Death… if that were true, Apep, you would've given in to it when it came for you. You would've gone to my mother willingly, not fled from her embrace like so many before you."

Apep opened his mouth to speak, but the master cut him off. "You fear what comes next, Apep. I can smell that fear. It wraps around you like a shroud, powering your Necromancy and staying the hand of Death. Fear is the secret to your power. But eventually, that fear will become too great a burden to bear, and it will consume you. In time, you will make a mistake."

Apep shrank back, cowering in front of his master as her form drew closer. She towered over him, casting a great shadow; a shadow that was impossibly huge and twisted, not at all reflective of her physical form. Glowing red eyes stared at him as he knelt on the ground before her, red eyes that betrayed two millennia of anger, pain, and madness.

"There is no escaping Death, Apep."

As the days passed and the four travelers continued north, Wyatt was beginning to see why their destination was called the Blazelands.

The temperature grew and grew the further they went, made even worse by the still air and the utter lack of moisture. It was becoming harder and harder to read without sweating on his book, but Wyatt had managed to absorb a good portion of the book in the time that they had been riding. He found the material fascinating, and he had learned a great deal about the origin of Adepts and the rise of humanity.

According to the book, the world had been created by three gods. Wishing to turn an empty world into a full one, the three decided to create life. The eldest, a wise and patient god, created plants and animals. He created a system that kept everything in balance. The second saw what her elder had created and decided that it was good. But her wishes were different than his, and so she set to her own work. She also created life, but only one kind of life. She created intelligence, and choice, and individuality. She created humanity, and instilled morality and goodness within them.

Adala's children, in their infancy, lived in harmony with the world. The plants and animals served them, and they in turn served the plants and animals. The two gods were pleased with what they had created together.

But the third god was young, and quickly became jealous of the two. He wished to top the both of them, to leave a lasting imprint on the world and the works of his fellows. He created terrible, twisted creatures. He instilled in them not morality and goodness, but savagery and cruelty. They rose, and the other two wept at what their brother had created.

It was a dark time for the world. Plants burned, animals died, and humans suffered. The elder two did not know what they could do; they loved their brother, and had promised one another long ago that there would be no fighting among them. But he was hurting their world, hurting the things which they loved so deeply. They had to do something.

It was Adala who chose to act. She could allow her children to suffer no longer. She created six more humans, but these humans would be different than the others. In these humans, she invested a piece of her own power, a spark of her own light.

Six demigods. Six Aspects of Adala. She broke herself into six pieces, and gave those pieces to humanity. She instilled in her creations the gift of magic, and gave them the power necessary to survive. And as humanity was empowered, Adala was no more. She gave her life into their making.

Soon, these six demigods led humanity to greatness. They organized nations and armies. They fought for their brothers and sisters, and for the humans that had died under the cruelty of the third god's creations. And they were victorious. They destroyed the vile creatures that had oppressed their people for so long. Free of their evil, humanity flourished. The other two gods, dismayed at the sacrifice of their sister, left the world behind and went their separate ways. The Six passed their gifts on to their children, and the Adepts continued to lead humanity and fight against anything that tried to harm them.

"Of course, a lot of that is exaggerated," said Grace matter-of-factly as Wyatt finished the book. He'd been asking a lot of questions of his three companions whenever they came up. "It's largely fictional. The things discussed in that volume happened thousands of years ago. With the exception of that book, written human history doesn't date as far back as the beginning. It's all conjecture, and there's no evidence to support that book's authenticity, aside from how long it's been around."

"Grace is right, of course," commented Tythas knowingly as he surveyed the road ahead of them. "The book is a fundamental cornerstone of religion, as well as human culture. That story has existed for as long as humanity can remember. It is one of the first things we ever wrote down. Those who worship Adala cite it as being a central pillar of faith. That story has endured the passage of time, the passing of kings… it has always been the same."

"But not everyone worships Adala," remarked Wyatt.

Tythas inclined his head. "True. That is yet another line that has divided humans and Adepts alike for centuries. But even those who don't worship the goddess generally consider that text important."

"I'm not sure what to believe yet," admitted the young Adept. "It's difficult when the facts seem to change daily. I just have to wait and see before I can… choose sides."

The truth was that while Wyatt enjoyed the company of his new companions and was starting to feel a certain level of kinship toward them, he still wasn't sure about their overall goal. He wanted to fight with them, but he also knew that he had only seen their side, only walked their path, and he wasn't about to cling to one point of view before he allowed a few more perspectives into his sight.

"A wise choice," said Tythas, smiling at Wyatt as Jag and Grace gave each other uneasy looks. "I must confess that I see something special in you, Wyatt. But while I would very much like having you on our side, I do understand your hesitation. You are right; there is a great deal more for you to learn. The three of us will show you the world, but we will not try to force you to think a certain way. You are with us so that we can figure out whatever is going on and find your mother and grandfather. With luck, we can track down a rogue Necromancer on the way. But if you choose to eventually go your own way, we will not stop you."

Wyatt nodded, smiling back at him, trying not to look too relieved. "I know that, and I greatly appreciate it. The three of you have done much more for me than I could have ever expected. I'm thinking about these things daily, and honestly… I want to stay with you guys, I want to fight for your cause, once I learn more about my power. But I have to be sure that it's the best cause before I can commit to that. And I'm still not sure."

"Take your time, kid," said Jag with a nod. "I doubt we're anywhere near figuring this mess out. No pressure."

"Well, maybe a little pressure," added Grace with a wink. "I for one don't want you running off anytime soon. You're dead useful, and good for the three of us."

Wyatt smiled and opened his mouth to reply, but stopped short as Tythas held up a hand ahead of them. Together, the four slowed their horses, coming to a stop atop a tall hill and surveying the landscape ahead of them.

"The Blazelands," murmured Tythas, staring out toward the wavering horizon. The heat was playing tricks on their eyes. "We are drawing nearer to Shebal, the only true city the Dominion occupies. From here on out, we must be on our guard. There will likely be scouts in the area."

Far into the broad, flat landscape that was the Blazelands, Wyatt could just make out the perimeter of an enormous settlement. But, unlike the cities that Wyatt had seen paintings of in his youth, there were no magnificent towers or castles. In fact, the entire place appeared to be an impossibly huge collection of tents and wagons.

"City?" said Wyatt, squinting to try to get a better idea of what he was looking at. "That doesn't look like a city. That looks like a huge camp."

"The Dominion is not in any way like the Empire," said Jag, checking the sword at his hip, his expression dark. "They're largely nomadic and tribal. They have only one city, Shebal, which is ahead of us. In times of war, Shebal is deconstructed and relocated as their forces require. Even in times of peace, they move it every few decades to satisfy their need to roam around. Anyone who can prove their strength or their worth can be adopted into the Dominion's ranks. The strong rise to power, and the weak are trampled underfoot. They are barbarians."

"We'll be going to visit Flamelord Salif, who is one of the six commanders of the Dominion's military," explained Tythas. "He holds a great deal of sway with the Overlord, their leader. And while we are here, none of you are to mention my dual Aspects. I am a Pyromancer, not an Aeromancer. That is very important."

"Do you really think that lying about that is a good idea?" asked Grace carefully, looking at her mentor with a somewhat startled expression. "Tythas, if they find out… I know how the Dominion deals with criminals. It would be bad for you. It would be bad for all of us."

Tythas shrugged. "I saved Flamelord Salif from a very sticky situation shortly after the war, when relations between the Dominion and the Empire first fell through. He knows the truth, and he suggested that while I am in these lands, I only reveal 'the more favorable part' of my power. Having a Pyromancer amongst us will make our group much more welcome with the Dominion while we attempt to find a lead, so that is what I shall be. These people know me and respect me as such. It's unfortunate, but unavoidable."

Wyatt, not listening as intently as he probably should have been, was instead watching the distant camp. Movement caught his eye, and he suddenly realized that a group of horses had broken rank and was headed up the hill toward them.

"We've been spotted," said Wyatt, his voice low. His hand drifted to the sword at his hip, which gave a light hum in response to his touch. "Keep your guard up."

"Easy, Wyatt," admonished Tythas, pulling his horse a little ways ahead of the rest. "I will handle this."

The four of them waited in silence as the group of horses drew closer. Wyatt lifted his hand off the hilt of his sword, opting to grip his reins instead, trying not to be as nervous as he felt. After a short time, he could finally see the men atop those horses; clad in painted leathers, lean, and armed to the teeth, each cut a slightly different yet incredibly imposing figure. They had bronze, tanned skin and dark, hard eyes. Wyatt would not want to battle any one of them, Pyromancers or not.

"You ride on the lands of the Dominion, outsiders," called the leader as the pack came to a halt before them. "Explain your business here." Unlike the three men behind him, the leader had a tongue of flame painted on his forehead. His armor was the most brilliantly colored, and on closer inspection, Wyatt could see that it was battle-scarred, just like the man wearing it.

Tythas raised a fist, clapping it to his chest and then extending it out to point toward the leader. "The Blaze unites us. Greetings, Scoutmaster. I am Vance Tythas, friend of the Dominion, here to commune with Flamelord Salif. These are my students and friends."

The leader cocked his head, staring at Tythas intensely for a while as his horse moved restlessly before them. Finally, he returned Tythas's salute, his fist held out. "The Blaze binds us. Greetings, Vance Tythas. I am Scoutmaster Tahl, leader of this unit. I have been with the Pack for some time, and I know your face and your deeds. You and your companions are welcome in the Land of Fire."

Tythas clapped his fist once again to his chest, and the Scoutmaster did the same. "Very good," replied Tythas cheerily. "Your wisdom burns brightly, Scoutmaster. Could you perhaps point me in the good Flamelord's direction? I am afraid that when I was last in the Land of Fire, Shebal was very different."

Scoutmaster Tahl nodded, a light smile framing his scarred lips. "Flamelord Salif is currently in council with the Overlord and his five colleagues. You will find them at the center, which I'm sure you do remember. You will have to wait for their council to end, but I am certain that he will see you once he is able."

"Wonderful," said Tythas, nodding in reverence to the Scoutmaster. "Thank you for your assistance, Scoutmaster. Burn brightly."

The Scoutmaster nodded in kind. "Burn long, Vance Tythas. If you should need anything while you are in our lands, call upon me."

With that, the four scouts kicked their horses and headed off toward the camp, back to whatever patrol route they had been on. Wyatt and his companions waited silently, watching the horses ride off down the hill. After a few minutes, they all let out a collective breath.

"Barbarians though they may seem," said Tythas quietly, fixing his eyes on Jag, "they revere respect and honor above all else. Their preference for tents over castles does not make them savage, Jag. Much like the Necromancers who you fight to liberate, the people of the Dominion are not evil. They may do things differently than you, but they are just people. Remember that."

Jag nodded silently, watching the camp with a subdued look. Grace seemed uneasy, but she didn't say anything, either.

"Come now, let's go find our Flamelord and leave this place before it claims our eyebrows," said Tythas, his usual mirth back in his voice. "All of you must be on your best behavior. If anyone addresses you, respond in kind. Remember, they are a very reverent people."

The three of them nodded to Tythas, and together they all made their way down the hill, toward Shebal. Unlike the scouts before them, they did not ride quickly, but took their time making it into the camp. Wyatt was glad that Tythas was leading them slowly, as he wanted to get a look at the camp from a distance before they were inside. He wanted to have a perfectly clear idea of exactly what they would be getting into.

Shebal was unlike anything Wyatt had ever even read about in his life. The city was built in enormous concentric rings, the center of which was a tent of goliath proportions. Each ring contained many smaller circles, where families or clans collected their wagons together. Other rings contained groups of wagons where men and women sold their goods and services for gold or other valuables. Short, well-worn roads connected the rings, but they started and stopped in different places, making the path through the city oddly tedious. As they drew closer, Wyatt could see that there were more people here than he had ever seen in his life. People of all shapes, colors, and cultures had all gathered under the banner of Ignis and joined the Dominion. It was a motley collection, but there seemed to be a sort of harmony to the group.

After riding for several minutes, they finally reached the outermost ring and the closest grouping of tents. People stopped what they were doing to stare openly at the four of them as they rode into the camp. Wyatt had never seen people like these before—dressed in skins and painted with unique designs, they were a stark contrast to the simple, conservative folk that he had grown up around. Throughout the ranks, Wyatt saw the occasional flame-painted forehead, just like the Scoutmaster. Pyromancers, he assumed.

"Stay close, and don't stare," muttered Tythas, leading them straight into the heart of the camp, or as straight as he could with such a winding path. Although the terrain was uneven, Wyatt could just see a massive tent poking into the sky ahead of them. People stopped what they were doing to stare at their group as they rode down the path, making Wyatt feel uneasy. He could feel the sword twitching at his hip, which certainly wasn't helping his mood.

They rode toward the large tent for quite some time, moving at a leisurely pace. Tythas appeared to be the only member of their group who wasn't tense; he occasionally made eye contact with a warrior and traded a small gesture of respect. Other times, he simply waved and smiled at some old friend. Clearly, he had spent a good deal of time with these people. Wyatt envied his calm.

After a good deal of slow riding and watching Tythas interact with the people of this bizarre city, they finally reached the center. Before them stood a massive semi-permanent tent, large enough to fit hundreds of people if it were necessary. From the top, Wyatt could just see a large column of smoke steadily rising out from an appropriately-placed vent. The tent itself was a patchwork of hides; some were the usual size, while others looked to belong to things larger than any beast he'd ever seen. All around the tent stood a massive wooden fence, spiked at the top. There was only one entrance, where a line of guards stood to block access. He could just barely hear the scraps of a heated conversation, but not enough to make out any words.

Tythas motioned for them to dismount, leading the horses over to a nearby corral. Wyatt was starting to think there was a horse corral every ten feet; it seemed everyone who lived in Shebal owned at least one horse, even the children. Several horses were already tied up there, but Tythas didn't seem to be concerned with adding theirs to the mix.

"Tythas, we will get our horses back, right?" asked Jag quietly, eyeing the people that were tending the horses cautiously. "We paid good gold for these."

"Your fears are misplaced, Jag," responded Tythas sternly. "They are an honorable people, and would not steal from an outsider without provocation. We are guests in their city, and they will treat us as such. Also remember that I am known here. Our horses stand out, and will be left alone."

"Right," muttered Jag quickly, suddenly very interested in his saddle.

"Vance Tythas!" came a deep, jovial voice from behind them. "I knew you would return to our lands! Come to join our ranks at last? I would've preferred that you had done so before you were so wrinkly!"

The four of them wheeled around, coming face to chest with an enormous, deeply tanned beast of a man. He stood a clear foot taller than even Jag, and his chest was like a barrel. Scars covered his skin, decorating him like a tapestry dedicated to war. His jet-black hair was pulled back into a tight tail, complimented by a bushy beard jutting out from his chin. His scars and tanned skin made it nearly impossible to tell his age, but despite his obviously hard life, he had laugh lines and gentle eyes.

Tythas's face broke into a grin as he stepped forward, clasping forearms with his bearlike friend. "Hakim, you old dog! It has been far too long, my friend. The Blaze unites us."

Hakim laughed, pulling Tythas off his feet and into a bone-crushing hug. "Forget the formalities. We're both far too old for that."

Tythas laughed again, attempting to pat the gigantic Hakim on the back with moderate success. Finally, the huge Pyromancer put him down, and Vance gestured toward Wyatt, Jag, and Grace.

"Hakim, these are... students of mine. Jag, Grace, Wyatt, this is Hakim. I told you that I spent a good amount of time here when I was younger. Hakim was my strongest friend, and he saved my life on more than one occasion. He's one of the men who teaches the Pyromancers of the Dominion how to use their powers."

Hakim turned to face Tythas's young companions with a warm smile. "Students, eh? Never would've figured you for the teaching game, Vance. Always on the front lines, you were. Are all those wrinkles finally catching up to you?"

"Hardly," replied Tythas with a cool smile. "I still am on the front lines, Hakim. They're just located in different places these days."

Hakim studied the three of them closely, leaning down to look into their eyes. His were big and dark, but surprisingly warm. He paused to look at each of them, his gaze intense. When he reached Wyatt, he cocked his head and, to Wyatt's surprise, sniffed him. Wyatt blinked.

"This one... he doesn't smell like a Pyromancer, but he sure feels like one," mused Hakim, scratching his bushy beard with a huge hand. "In a weird way. Well, boy? Are you?"

Wyatt blinked again, glancing over at Tythas. The elder Adept's smirk had disappeared, replaced by a furrowed brow.

"Er, no sir," he said, holding his ground. "I'm an Aeromancer."

Hakim sniffed him again, frowning. "Huh. Must have some Pyromancer blood in you, then. I am rarely wrong about these things."

"His grandfather, I believe," said Tythas quickly, staring at Wyatt with a hard to read expression. "A rather famous blacksmith, from the war. Rex Kelsar."

"Yeah," agreed Wyatt, clamping down on his anxious thoughts about his family before they got the better of him. "Could be more, too. I don't really know much about my family."

Hakim clapped him on the shoulder with a grin. "I've heard of him. Good stock, even if you got the wrong Aspect. Too bad, too. You look like you'd make a good one. You've got that fire in your eyes."

"He's useful for some things," said Jag with a smirk. He held out his hand to Hakim. "Jag Mercer, of the Circle of Blades. I'm no Adept, but I have a few other talents."

"Circle of Blades, eh?" replied Hakim as he shook Jag's hand. "They tell stories of your unit even here. I wonder if you could match with the elite troops of the Dominion?"

Tythas patted Jag on the shoulder before he could reply. "This young man is one of the most deadly swordsman I've ever encountered. He was dangerous with a blade from the day he was old enough to pick up a dagger. His whole life was dedicated to protecting the Emperor, and he put those skills to use on more than one occasion. I don't know that I would ever want to cross him."

Wyatt could see Jag swell with pride at Tythas's compliments, but Hakim only laughed him off. "We shall see, old man. We shall see. And what of this one?" He turned to Grace, smiling warmly.

"I'm not a Pyromancer either, I'm afraid," said Grace, smiling up at Hakim. "Grace. I'm a Vitamancer."

"Not many of your kind left, my dear," said Hakim as he inclined his head reverently. "May the Blaze keep you safe. Humanity cannot afford to lose Vitamancers. Even the most zealous among the Dominion hold those like you with a certain reverence. You will always be safe in these lands."

Wyatt blinked, a little startled. He knew that Vitamancers were rare, but the way Hakim had worded it made it seem like the situation was much graver. If she was really that valuable to the world, it was important to keep her safe as long as he could.

Grace smiled brightly back at Hakim. "Thank you, sir. I am not the most experienced of Adepts, but if there are wounded and sick among you, I will do what I can for them. Unfortunately, my power can only stretch so far."

Hakim chuckled, giving her a gentle pat on his shoulder. "There are thousands of sick and wounded in this place. A pup like you wouldn't make much of a difference. I appreciate the offer, young one, but save your strength for your friends."

She nodded softly and looked away, and Wyatt could see that she was fighting to keep her expression neutral. She really just wanted to help, and not having the power to help everyone really took its toll on her.

"I'm here to see Salif," said Tythas, once again grabbing Hakim's attention. "We're... chasing a lead, you might say. Any idea when he might be available for a meeting?"

Hakim scratched his beard, looking back toward the big tent at the center of the city with a frown. "Hard to say. The council's been in there for nearly two weeks now, debating this and that. They haven't gotten done with a meeting at a decent hour in years. All they seem to do is argue and yell until they lose their voices, and then break to drink. It really is something special."

Tythas chuckled. "I see not much has changed, then. Well, while we wait, is there anything that these three can do for the Dominion?" He looked to his young charges, all of whom blinked, standing up a little straighter.

Hakim eyed the three of them once more, scratching his beard yet again. "Oh, I'm sure we can find some work for them. There's always something that needs done around here."

Tythas blinked, looking over at Wyatt as if a brilliant idea had just burst into being in his mind. "Actually, I have a special request for this one. Call it a personal favor. He recently acquired a sword, and he needs to learn how to use it. Right, Wyatt?"

Wyatt looked at Tythas, and then to Hakim's hulking size, and then back to Tythas, his mouth slightly agape. "I, er, guess?"

Wyatt staggered slightly as Hakim laughed and clapped him on the shoulder heavily. "The Blademasters of the Dominion are not only the finest swordsmen in the land, but also the finest teachers! It is rare for an outsider to learn their ways. But I see no harm in teaching this one. He looks a little bit too raggedy to do any proper damage with a sword, even if we did teach him how to use the thing. Wyatt, tenth ring, south side. Big fighting ring, you can't miss it."

The sword at Wyatt's hip gave a merry buzz at this suggestion, and Wyatt got the distinct impression that Shem was pleased at this new turn of events. Wyatt couldn't disagree, as he'd felt pretty awkward running around swinging a sword that he had no idea how to use. It would probably be good for him, and it would be a good way to release some stress.

Hakim turned toward the others, motioning to Grace first. "As for you? Your gifts would serve the healing tents well. Eighth ring, east side. Don't use your powers too liberally. Only in cases of great need. Mostly, you should try to learn from the healers that we have. Their mundane methods are greatly effective, and useful for any traveling healer. It might save you some energy down the road, and they need every available pair of hands they can get."

Grace nodded once, standing at attention. "Yes, sir."

Hakim chuckled, turning to Jag. "Mercer. Report to my son in the security tents. Third ring, northwest side. He told me that they've been having some security issues here in the city. Problems with goods being smuggled in and out. We could use someone with your skills to help us sniff out the leak."

Jag seemed to fall into a soldier's mindset, snapping to a salute that Hakim probably didn't even understand. "Sir."

Vance nodded approvingly at his three young companions. "Now then. When the council meeting is over, you'll hear loud horns playing from the center of the camp. I want you to drop whatever you're doing and meet me back here when that happens. You won't miss the horns, so don't worry about that. We'll see each other around the camp, but I want the three of you to focus on your tasks for the time being."

They all nodded in agreement. After saying their farewells, the three young companions set off in different directions, leaving the two old men to chat and reminisce. Wyatt felt equal parts excitement and nervousness bubbling up within him. He was going to train under real soldiers!

CHAPTER ELEVEN

Again!" shouted Yasmir, backing up several feet and taking a defensive position, which Wyatt found highly ironic from his awkward position on the ground. Yasmir readied his sword, and as always, looked completely unfazed. His iron stare was infuriating.

Wyatt groaned inwardly, picking himself up off the dirt yet again. That marked the eleventh time in a row that Yasmir had bested him, and at this point, he really wasn't sure what his instructor expected him to do. Every inch of him was throbbing, the product of what he imagined would be a tapestry of bruises and welts all over his body. He was starting to think he wouldn't be able to lift his sword much longer.

But he wasn't about to give up.

Wyatt readied his practice sword again, trying to calm his mind and push his frustration away. A ring of spectators had gathered to watch him train yet again, ever present and not at all quiet. Some jeered and hooted, amused by the outsider's lack of skill. Others tried to help him, telling him that emotion would be of no help to him in a fight. But that was easy for them to say. They weren't the ones being taunted, beaten, and taunted some more.

This was the second week of Wyatt's brutal training. They had expected the council meeting to be over after two or three days, but whatever they were debating, the argument was still raging with no sign of letting up. He wasn't sure how much more of this combat training he could take, and was really hoping that the meeting would be over soon.

Without another word, Yasmir leapt into action, striking like lightning toward Wyatt's right side. Wyatt parried and returned with a thrust of his own, toward Yasmir's abdomen. Yasmir spun, easily dodging the blow and clipping Wyatt on the cheek with a punch as he did. Wyatt staggered to his left, doing his best to keep his feet steady while the inside of his head rang like a bell. He created some distance between them, spitting blood from his mouth and smiling at his instructor as flippantly as possible.

Yasmir returned Wyatt's attitude with another leaping strike, which Wyatt dodged hastily. Just as he found sure footing again, however, Yasmir was already there with another strike. Wyatt parried again, wincing as his arm tingled painfully. Even with protective padding on the swords, blocking a square blow like that still hurt. Each parry made it harder to grip the hilt and lift the sword again. He was wearing thin.

He returned Yasmir's blow with one of his own, a glancing swipe to the side that his instructor easily deflected. Wyatt had been hoping for that, though, and continued with the motion, twisting and aiming a kick at Yasmir's exposed ribs. In a moment of what was surely perfect harmony, his opponent lifted his arm just right, and Wyatt's kick connected squarely in the chest. His heart leapt. That was the first real hit he'd ever given Yasmir!

His elation was short-lived, however. Yasmir clamped his arm down on Wyatt's foot and lifted, upending the rookie fighter easily and dumping him on his back. Wyatt's head slammed painfully into the ground, dazing him yet again. He sent a wild slash toward his teacher, but his grip wasn't sure. The elder swordsman parried easily, sending Wyatt's sword tumbling off to the side. Before he knew it, the tip of Yasmir's sword was tickling Wyatt's throat.

"Yield," said the older man quietly, his gaze eternally iron. Wyatt groaned again.

Yasmir set his sword aside, extending a hand toward Wyatt. "You lack foresight, you seem incapable of strategy, and you are foolishly emotional. But you have heart."

Wyatt took the offered hand, slowly rising and taking a moment to dust off his sore frame. He spat more blood out of his mouth and rubbed his head, looking at his instructor warily. "Heart doesn't seem to help me win, though."

Yasmir clapped him on the shoulder, shaking his head. "Heart does not help you win. It helps you survive, helps you endure. Strategy, foresight, and calm can be learned. Heart... heart cannot. You will get there, Rashmi. Fear not."

Wyatt nodded, wiping the sweat from his eyes. "Rashmi... this is another word in your tongue?"

Yasmir nodded, retrieving Wyatt's sword from the dirt and passing it back to him. "It means more than one thing. In this case, it perhaps means... 'wide-eyed doe.' Or 'young student,' although for now both may apply."

A normal man would have perhaps followed his joke up with a laugh or a smile, but Yasmir continued to look ahead, stoic as ever. At first, Wyatt had found his utterly dry humor amusing, but it was becoming frustrating. He never knew if he should be offended or not. In fact, he had no idea if Yasmir even liked him. It was unnerving.

Yasmir motioned to the tent at the edge of the fighting ring, and Wyatt nodded. He pushed the flap aside and ducked through. Yasmir followed, quickly behind him, taking Wyatt's sword once more and returning both weapons to their homes on a rack inside.

"Sit," said Yasmir quietly, motioning to a stool at the center of the tent. Wyatt obeyed his master, his joints protesting angrily as he slowly lowered himself onto the squat little stool. He took a moment to steady himself and surveyed the inside of the tent. It was a little more spacious than some of the others, but it was still nothing like Wyatt was used to. The people of the Dominion of Fire lived so minimally, which constantly amazed Wyatt. He'd never seen people like this before. It was both educational and humbling.

"We are done for the day, I think," said Yasmir while he rummaged through a small chest at the foot of his cot. "If I push you any harder you will hurt yourself."

Wyatt's blood rose. "I can keep going," he protested, although he didn't know why. He knew that Yasmir was right, but he didn't really want to have to admit it.

"Swallow your pride, Rashmi," admonished Yasmir quietly. "Save it for a time where it will help you. This is not one of those times. You have no audience in here."

Wyatt opened his mouth to protest again, but Yasmir cut him off, handing him a small jar. Wyatt took it from his teacher, peering at the opaque paste inside.

"This is a salve that will help your sore skin heal," explained his teacher, sitting down on a stool near Wyatt. "It will also help you sleep through the pain. Use it tonight when you sleep, and you will be able to stand up tomorrow."

Wyatt stowed the jar away, nodding lightly at his instructor. "Thanks," he said, a little bit sourly. He wasn't terribly excited for yet another day of training. The council meeting really needed to end soon.

"You will be seeking to join the Dominion, then?" asked Yasmir evenly as he reached for a waterskin. "Even an Aeromancer can find status and direction in our family."

Wyatt shook his head. "No, I don't think so. I mean, I haven't really given it a lot of thought, but I have... a lot of things to work out right now. And I'd imagine if I'm ever going to master my powers, I'll have to go to the Adept Council and train with them."

Yasmir shrugged. "They are not the only Adepts in the world, Wyatt. Anyone that would lead you to believe otherwise is either ignorant or a liar."

Wyatt was well aware of that. He was traveling with two rogue Adepts, who were at best on uneasy terms with the Council, and at worst had already been declared apostates. Wyatt didn't really know.

"I know that," he said quietly. "But I'm not really concerned with all this political drama that seems to motivate everyone else. I just want to learn how to control my powers. Once I do that... Well, then I guess I can figure out where I stand."

Yasmir offered a slight nod. "You are not without wisdom, Rashmi. There are many men in this camp who would want you to join our cause for selfish reasons. Be wary of them. Stay true to your path, and you'll-"

Suddenly, the sound of a large horn being blown echoed through the air, cutting off their conversation abruptly and sending strange vibrations through Wyatt's chest. He blinked in confusion and looked up at Yasmir, who was staring toward the exit of the tent.

"The council meeting has ended," said the older man quietly. "You should gather your things and find your friends. Your time here may be coming to a close."

Wyatt didn't need any further motivation for that. He quickly gathered his pack and sword from the chest that Yasmir had offered to him, lifting the baldric over his head and strapping it in comfortably. He was starting to feel odd if it wasn't at his hip.

"Your sword... it is a unique blade," commented Yasmir with interest. "You wear it well. It fits you, which is strange to say, being as you are still so untrained."

"Maybe in just sword combat," said Wyatt with a smirk. "But I'm not defenseless, Yasmir."

Yasmir gave a short laugh, a very rare thing. "So confident. Youth is amusing. Go find your friends, Rashmi. If you decide to stay, come back here and we will continue your education."

Wyatt thanked his instructor for everything and then ducked out of the tent, anxious to get back to Tythas and the others. If this Salif could tell them anything about Apep's whereabouts, they might get that much closer to finding his mother and grandfather. He had been feeling restless for two weeks, and now he finally could have some direction again.

Wyatt had intended to run to the spot where he had agreed to meet the others, but he quickly discovered that his body wasn't up for it, so he instead settled for an awkward jog that he would probably regret later. But he didn't care; he wasn't about to miss this. He'd been waiting far too long already.

After what felt like hours of laboring through the camp, Wyatt saw Jag, Grace, and Tythas standing by the horse corral where they had all separated two weeks before. Grace was peering through the throngs of people that were gathering by the center tent, probably trying to find him. He slipped between the crowds and made it to his friends, resting his hands on his knees and panting heavily as he came to a stop.

"Well, you look like you've been having fun," said Jag with

amusement. "Don't fall over just yet, Wyatt." Wyatt eyed him sourly, but said nothing.

Grace leaned down, putting her hand on his back. "You do look a little wore out, Wyatt. Are you okay?"

He stood up straight, nodding quickly and shrugging her hand off of his back. "Yeah, I'm fine," he said, giving her a confident smile. "Tired and sore, but I'm okay."

She touched his arm, frowning at him. "Really? Okay? Because it feels like you're barely on your feet. Let me patch you up."

Wyatt shook his head. "Save your strength. If I'm going to get used to this life, I have to learn how to heal on my own. Bruises and scrapes are nothing compared to the real wounds I could get from a real fight. We need you strong. Besides, my teacher gave me a healing salve for tonight. I'll live, Grace."

She looked like she wanted to argue with him, but Tythas spoke first. "He's quite right, Grace. Besides, you aren't giving the boy nearly enough credit. He's still standing, is he not?"

Grace sighed and nodded, taking her hand away and rubbing her eyes. Wyatt knew that she didn't like it, but there wasn't much that she was going to be able to do about it. He really didn't want to start relying on her magic touch every time he got hurt. That would just lead to even more problems for him in the future. He loved magic, but he also was beginning to realize how complicated it really was.

Tythas was eyeing the large council tent patiently. "The horns blew a little while ago. The council should be emerging any moment here. Hopefully, Salif will have a moment to speak with us, and we can get on with our journey. Wyatt, I know you need some rest, but I want you to be ready to ride soon. Can you do that?"

Wyatt nodded grimly, thinking of his mother. "Yeah. I'll be fine, Tythas."

Moments later, the huge flap that hung over the door was drawn inward and up, and a group of heavily painted men emerged. Each of them was adorned with the finest furs and leathers, and each of them bore an elaborate painted flame on his forehead. Except one.

To the rear of the group, deeply in conversation with one of the council elders, walked a withered old man. He carried a confidence and strength of a man a quarter his age. He, too, wore furs and leathers, but they were a much different style, from a much different land. A bone-white mask covered the top of his face, but there was no mistaking his identity.

"Apep," whispered Wyatt in shock, his hand immediately reaching for his sword as he stepped forward. Jag's reaction was nearly identical.

Wyatt felt a strong hand grip his shoulder, holding him in place. He saw a hand on Jag's shoulder, as well. The two young warriors looked at each other briefly before glancing back, to see Tythas' grim face between them.

"Stay your weapons," he whispered, staring ahead at Apep with obvious contempt and distaste. "If you draw steel in aggression here, we will all die. This is a peaceful city. You know that. Use your heads."

Wyatt swallowed and tried to relax, fighting back the anger that was rising in him like bile. His hand grudgingly left the hilt of his sword, but he could still feel it twitching and buzzing at his hip, almost as if it were trying to leap out of its sheath and strike at the Necromancer. Clearly, Shem was as pleased to see him as the rest of them.

Apep paused briefly to finish his conversation with the large elder. The other elders paused as well, and for a time, stood at the entrance to the tent, still beyond the fence. To a normal person, Apep probably looked like a sprightly old man. He was smiling, shaking hands, and not at all threatening. But Wyatt knew better, and he could almost smell the blood and decay in the air, hanging on his shoulders like a shroud. Wyatt knew what he was capable of. Just looking at the old man made his skin crawl.

"What in the hell is he doing here?" hissed Jag angrily, staring at Apep as if he were trying to ignite the older man with his eyes. "And why isn't anyone attacking him?"

Tythas shook his head. "I don't know. I don't like it either, Jag, but you need to calm yourself. A hand on a weapon in this place could be taken as a challenge. You're no good to us dead."

Jag eyed his mentor warily, but eventually he relented and released the hilt of his sword.

The four of them stood in the crowd for some time, watching Apep socialize with the elders of the Dominion. Eventually, the group of elders again started walking, through the gate and into the crowd that awaited their return. There, the group broke up and went their separate ways. Apep followed two of them off into another part of the camp, and soon he was lost from sight, swallowed by the immensity that was Shebal.

Tythas eventually stepped forward, raising a hand as he did so. Wyatt felt a very subtle change in the air, almost as if Tythas had directed just enough wind toward him to turn heads and tousle hair. Nobody else seemed to notice, but Wyatt felt the small trick, and he smiled a little as he saw several people, including a tall elder, turn their heads. The man saw Tythas and quickly broke off from his fellows, smiling as he approached their group.

So close to the rest of his wild-looking colleagues, this man seemed very different. His black hair was cut short and slicked back with some kind of oil. Gray kissed his temples, the only clue as to what his age might be; otherwise, he appeared youthful and healthy. He was fit and lean, wearing leather pants and a simple shirt. Even the emblem of fire painted on his forehead was smaller and less grand than the others Wyatt had seen. He appeared to be calm, quiet, and composed, having no need for extravagance or swagger.

Tythas held out his hand and smiled at the elder, but they did not shake. Before they could, the elder motioned for them to be silent and follow. Without a word, he walked directly past them at a brisk pace through the city. Tythas nodded at the rest of them, and the group followed, puzzled.

And they walked. Wyatt hadn't spent much time exploring the city during his time there, but this walk made him truly appreciate the vastness of the Dominion's population. They walked past so many tents and huts and dugouts that Wyatt lost count. There weren't just families in this place; there were entire clans, generations of blood relatives all living together in the same circles. It was astounding to see so many people together in such a way.

After nearly forty minutes of walking, they still hadn't even cleared half of the city yet. Worse yet, Wyatt was starting to worry that his legs were going to fall off. He knew that he wouldn't be able to keep this up much longer. He needed a rest.

"Here," said the elder suddenly, his voice breaking their silence for the first time. He pointed to a large tent that was a little separated from the rest, secluded by its distance. It even had a sort of makeshift space around it, giving it added privacy. The tent itself looked large and inviting, and Wyatt was sorely hoping that there would be something soft to sit on inside.

The five of them entered, and the elder closed the tent flap behind him. He secured the flap with wooden fasteners, and then paused to stroke the edge of the doorway with one finger. Wyatt felt power swell around them, startling him.

Runes flared up all around, glowing all over the material of the tent. They swam and swirled through the leather itself, tracing every inch of it. Suddenly, they flashed brightly, momentarily dazzling Wyatt. When he blinked several times and looked again, they were gone. A brief silence followed.

The elder's tent was larger inside than it had appeared; perhaps forty feet long and twenty wide, it was actually quite spacious. The interior was adorned with a large table at the center, which had maps and papers haphazardly scattered across it. Several chairs sat around the table. Off in the corner, there was a large bed, partially obscured by thick curtains.

"Interesting," said Tythas quietly, peering at the door as he scratched his chin thoughtfully. "I wouldn't think something like that would be necessary here, Salif. Things must have changed since I was last here."

Salif motioned for them to sit at the table, nodding softly. "Yes, they certainly have, old friend. I'm sorry I couldn't meet with you sooner. I was alerted to your presence in the camp when you arrived, but unfortunately that meeting took much longer than we had expected. I hope you have been treated well."

"Yes, yes, of course," said Tythas with a wave of his hand.

"What was that?" asked Grace suddenly, still eyeing the doorway where the glowing runes had first appeared. Wyatt was still wondering the same thing, but he could see no trace of the runes on the doorway, or any other part of the tent.

"A very uncommon kind of magic," said Tythas quietly, looking over at her. "Something that very few Adepts know how to do. Fewer yet know how to do it well. Runic inscription like this... where ever did you get it, Salif?"

"An inscriber lived among us for some time," replied Salif evenly, shrugging. "He joined our ranks, but died shortly thereafter, having been sick when he got here. I think he just wanted a peaceful place to die. He was an Aeromancer, but his talent for inscription was unheard of in this age, so he was easily brought in. When I realized that my privacy was becoming a concern, I asked him to make this tent."

Tythas walked over to the nearest wall, studying it intently. After a few moments of silence, he poked it with an outstretched finger. Runes glittered around the spot he had touched momentarily and then faded again. He peered at his finger for a moment, frowning. He then looked back to the wall, leaning in to sniff it.

"Ahh," he said, suddenly seeming to understand. "The airflow... this manipulates the air around the tent, making our voices not carry. I imagine that even if I were standing just on the other side of this wall, I would hear nothing but the roaring wind. But I can hear out of the tent perfectly. Clever, Salif. Very clever."

Salif nodded approvingly. "And you are just as clever as ever, I see. It's good to see you, Vance. Who are your companions?"

"Wyatt Arden, Jag Mercer, and his sister Grace," said Tythas with a wave of his hand to each of them. "Jag and Grace were... charges of mine, when I was still with the Council. When I left, they came with me. Wyatt is more of a recent acquaintance, but he's proven himself to be a valuable ally and a dutiful student."

Salif shook each of their hands, nodding with approval. "You're all in very capable hands with Vance. He's just a few goats shy of a herd, but also wise beyond his years. He makes it work."

Jag held the elder councilman's gaze with a sour look on his face, seemingly unaffected by the Pyromancer's joke. "Can we skip the formalities? I want to know what Apep the Snake is doing here, negotiating with the Dominion."

Salif sighed, nodding. He walked around the table, sifting through the piles of papers for a moment. Eventually, he laid three maps out on the surface for them to look over. They appeared to be battlefield maps, covered with notes and markers for strategy.

Salif motioned to the first map. "Apep came to us a few months ago, shortly after a skirmish with an Imperial regimen left a lot of members of the Dominion dead. He's campaigning for our help in his efforts against them. Essentially, he wants us to declare war on the Empire, and he's offering to assist us if we do."

Tythas took his offered seat near the table, studying the maps closely. "These are Imperial. He brought them to you, I assume."

Salif nodded slowly. "Yes. According to his account, he came upon a detachment of Imperial troops preparing to attack an important outpost on our borders. It was a small group, by Imperial standards. Two thousand Imperial soldiers, preparing to crush a few hundred soldiers guarding an obscure encampment, close to the Wilds. From what he said, he snuck up on their camp in the dead of night, and used the final Darkshard to eliminate them."

Tythas's face went pale, falling into his hands. "I didn't think he had the last one. I thought it lost. Dear Adala, preserve us. Two thousand."

"Darkshard?" asked Wyatt, confused. Looking at Jag and Grace, he realized he wasn't the only one, as the both of them looked equally puzzled.

"An artifact from the Old Age, when the Six still walked among us," said Salif quietly. "Darkshards were created by Necron, the patron of Necromancy. He… crystallized his blood, fastening to the crystals massive pieces of his power. He gave them to his children, so that they might have a secret weapon with which to fight back."

Tythas nodded, rubbing his eyes. He looked decades older, now. "Breaking a Darkshard causes every nearby human soul to become dislodged from its body, leaving a lot of corpses and loose energy behind. It's painless and instantaneous. A talented Necromancer can use those conditions to make a great number of Drones. The process of making them was supposedly very taxing, so Necron made only three. The first was used nearly a thousand years ago, by accident. The second was used by Apep as the first blow that ignited the war. We had thought the third was lost, thrown to the bottom of the sea some time ago. If his account is true, we were wrong."

"He is telling the truth," said Salif quietly, while Jag and Grace sat down, both looking pale and horrified. "I've seen the Drones myself. Two thousand mindless monsters, held at the will of an incredibly powerful, incredibly unstable Necromancer. Plus whatever menagerie of undead things he's been stocking up over the years. It's a grim sight."

"So he's offering his support to the Dominion, then, in a joint campaign," said Wyatt, leaning over the table to look at the maps. It clicked into place in his mind, and his expression darkened. "He wants the Dominion to openly attack the Empire, and during a large-scale battle, he'll position his own army for a surprise attack. The Imperials will be flanked and obliterated, and then he'll use his talents to expand his army even further."

Salif looked up at Wyatt, surprised. He nodded. "Exactly. That was the problem we encountered during the Great War. Any time Apep and the rest of his Necromancers won a battle, they won themselves thousands of new Drones. Each battle got harder."

"He's at a disadvantage right now," mused Jag, tapping his chin with one finger. "He has a small force, but any kind of organized army would defeat it and send him into retreat. But if he uses the Dominion as an anvil, his own army can act as the hammer. It doesn't need to be bigger, just thorough and effective, which Drones certainly are. And just like that, he'll multiply his forces."

"He's stirring the pot," said Tythas evenly. "Trying to push two bigger forces into war so that he can build his own forces. Salif, I'm sure he will help you crush the Empire. But the moment he has enough Drones, the moment that he's positioned himself just right, he'll stab you in the back. He'll destroy both sides of this silly war and plunge the world into darkness, like he tried to do decades ago."

"I share that belief," said Salif sadly, regret plain on his face. "But unfortunately, the recent actions of the Empire and Apep's smear campaign against them have caused tempers to run hot and memories to fall short. Apep committed a lot of atrocities during the war, but most of the Council has seemingly forgotten them already. At the very least, they're willing to ignore them if it means finally defeating the Empire and taking control of their lands. They're so focused on finally defeating the Empire that they can't see the real dangers of what they're doing. I failed to dissuade them, Tythas. I'm sorry."

There was a silence among them, hanging in place like a heavy weight. It took some time to digest what was happening, for them to really process it.

"They're going along with it, then?" asked Grace quietly, bravely defeating the silence. She looked nervous.

"Yes," said Salif with a deep, resounding sigh. "Yes, I was outvoted. The campaign will start soon. Within a few months, we will openly declare war on the Empire. Perhaps sooner. Many people will die to serve the pride of a few childish men."

Wyatt was pacing now, his aches somehow forgotten. "There's got to be something going on here that we're not seeing. Apep came to you months ago, but he tried to kill us in Ven only a few weeks ago. He left a Shender for us to find in Wayton. And I can't help but think that he was somehow involved in the explosion at my house. He's got to know something about where my family is."

Tythas sighed, standing and walking toward the wall of the tent to stare intently at the fabric. He looked to be struggling with something.

"What do you know, Vance?" asked Salif quietly, staring at his old friend.

Tythas was quiet for a few more moments before finally responding. "He's searching for the seals," he replied quietly, looking older and more tired than Wyatt had ever imagined he could. "He has the same goal as he had during the Great War: to throw the world into chaos so that he may serve it up to Necron."

Salif's head went into his hands as Grace, Jag, and Wyatt stared at their mentor. Jag was sputtering in disbelief.

"Necron?" he asked, absolutely incredulous. "What do you mean, Necron? The patron of Necromancy? The... the demigod?"

Tythas nodded, looking a little sick. "Yes, that Necron."

"I don't understand," said Grace, shaking her head. "The demigods are... they're gone. They left, all six of them, thousands of years ago.

Moved on to be with Adala, leaving mankind to their devices. That's what the books say. That's what all of the books say, Tythas. All of them."

He shrugged, turning to face her. "The books are wrong. History has been reshaped and twisted in order to pacify the masses more than once. It's true that the demigods left this realm and joined their mother thousands of years ago, at least as far as any mortal knows. All but one, anyway."

Salif nodded at his friend. "Shortly before that happened, Necron went insane. Not completely, mind you. But he lost his love for humanity, lost sight of what Adala had charged him and his siblings to do. He wanted to rule, wanted to control his siblings and humankind. This short period of time is when Necron created the Darkshards and taught his children the darker, twisted side of their powers. He taught them to create the Shender, the Strigoi, and other horrible monsters."

Tythas walked back over to his chair and sat down, continuing for Salif. "The other patrons tried at first to pacify him, but when he started killing mortals by the hundred, they quickly intervened. As he was an immortal like them, they couldn't kill him. I suspect they didn't want to kill their brother, even if there was a way. So they united their collective powers and bound Necron deep within the earth. They locked him away behind five great seals, each attuned to a different Aspect and hidden in a different part of the world. The knowledge of these seals was passed down to a select few, and has been ever since. As a former member of the Adept Council, I know. I imagine that the elders of the Dominion all know, and perhaps a few others."

"And Apep found out," said Jag sourly, wringing his hands together. "He's after the seals."

"Their locations are not fully known," said Salif. "Last I knew, we were only aware of two. One is in the heart of the Empire, deep beneath the castle in Farillyon. The capital city was actually built there with the purpose of guarding that seal, although very few actually know it is there. The other seal was found by Apep during the Great War. It's at the bottom of Lake Eryth. When he found it, he kidnapped an Aquamancer and used her blood to break it, sacrificing her to Necron. To our knowledge, the other three remain hidden."

It hit Wyatt like a fist in the stomach. He sat down quickly, trying to compose himself. "Ven. There's a system of caves near the town. My friend Desmond and I used to play there when we were younger. It's huge and complex, full of all these glowing crystals. The night before my house blew up, there was an earthquake. A bad one, bad enough to damage the buildings in Ven. Afterwards, the crystals weren't glowing anymore. That's why Apep was there. He found another seal, and he razed the city to add some Drones to his collection while he was in the area."

Tythas and Salif shared a look. "When Apep broke the Seal of Aquilon, the waters of Lake Eryth boiled for days. Eventually, the water completely evaporated, leaving it completely empty and devoid of life. It took the combined efforts of many Aquamancers and Terramancers to restore the lakebed and return the lake to its former condition."

Jag looked at Salif, the tension on his face obvious. "Salif, I realize that the Dominion has always been incredibly secretive to outsiders, but you're an Elder. If anyone, anyone at all in the Dominion knows the whereabouts of Ignis's seal, you need to come clean about it right now. If Apep finds out where that seal is, he'll be heading there next. All this talk of war… he's just lulling all of you into a sense of security, giving you a big bone to chew on so that he can explore your lands freely and find the seal. Or, better yet, so he can find out where it is from one of you."

Salif sat back, looking at Jag with surprised. "I am not used to being addressed to frankly by one so young. You are a brave man, Jag Mercer. But I understand your position, so I will ignore your lack of tact. I do not know where the seal is, but it has long been rumored that its location is made known to each Warlord when he or she first steps into power. If we are to believe that, then it is safe to assume that the keeper of that secret is the Warlord's steward. The same family has served as stewards to the Warlords of the Dominion since the beginning."

Everyone stood, except Salif. "We need to find that steward," said Tythas, giving his friend an imploring look. "There's no chance that the Warlord will tell us, but Salif, we have to try. Apep could break the whole world if he finds that seal."

Salif sighed and nodded, getting to his feet. "You're right, of course. I don't know what we can do to get him to tell us, but… this is the Dominion of Fire, and I outrank him by leagues. If anyone can get that information from him, it'll be me. Meanwhile, you all need to lie low and stay out of sight. There's no telling what kind of eyes Apep has in the camp. With the friends that he's made in the last few months, he could probably have all of you killed, and I'd be powerless to stop it."

Everyone in the room opened their mouths to protest, but Salif quickly brought his fist down on the table. A wave of heat rolled out from his body, causing Wyatt's eyes to water.

"I respect your determination," he said slowly, staring at Tythas with hard, dark eyes. "And I understand. But believe me when I say that if you defy me in this, you will all die, and Apep will be that much closer to his goal. He did not see you earlier today, which is fortunate. We must not tempt fate. I cannot stop him from winning more allies in this camp and driving the Dominion to war. That is already done."

He slowly leaned over the table, his gaze sweeping over them all. "Our only hope is to catch him off guard, at the seal. If we do that, we may just be able to defeat him. But I won't be able to do it alone. So stay here, keep your heads down, and wait. I will send for you when the time comes."

Tythas sighed, sitting back into his chair once more. "He's right. Apep has more friends here than we do. If we get spotted by him… at the very least, it will greatly hamper our plans. Most likely, we'll all be killed. We need to stay put."

Jag gave an exasperated sigh, flopping back down into his chair with clear frustration. Grace was fidgeting with her nails, but said nothing. Wyatt got up and resumed his pacing, trying his best to ignore the sword's humming presence at his hip. He could almost feel Shem's energy rolling off of it, coursing through him like hot blood. The cat was clearly ready for a fight.

"Stay calm, and be patient," added Salif, heading for the tent flap. "This should not take me long. I'll send for you all in a very short while, I'm sure."

Wyatt absently patted the sword's crossguard, as if he were mentally trying to tell the cat to be good. Shem didn't respond. He watched his fidgety companions for a time, realizing that waiting was not going to be easy for any of them. This was going to be a very long "short while."

The four of them watched Salif leave, everyone silent as they attempted to find something to do with themselves. Wyatt's exhaustion came crashing back into him like a tidal wave, and he quickly steadied himself at the table, sparing his throbbing legs any more effort.

Grace suddenly turned to him, her gaze intense. "I realize that you want to recover without any help," she said carefully, sitting down near him. "But if we have to go chasing off after Necron, you're not going to get the opportunity to get the rest you need. If you don't get that rest, Wyatt, you're going to be a burden on all of us, and you might even get yourself killed if we do get into a fight. So I'm going to patch you up, and you're going to shut up and like it."

Wyatt blinked and opened his mouth, but finding no words to fill it with, he closed it again. She gave him a poisonous glare and pushed him down into his chair, crouching down and resting her hands on his knees. He could hear Jag's snickering in the background. All at once, a tingling warmth flooded his body, replacing the pain in his muscles. Unlike the times before, Grace wasn't just giving him energy. She was healing him. It took his breath away, and he had to catch the moan in his throat before it escaped. He felt like he was melting.

A few seconds later, or perhaps several weeks, she pulled her hands away and the tingling sensation faded. Like coming awake after a long nap in the sun, Wyatt opened his eyes, taking a deep breath in. He looked at Grace sluggishly, feeling a little dumbfounded.

"Don't get so beat up again," she said flatly, wiping a bead of sweat from her forehead.

Wyatt nodded mutely, savoring the lovely lack of pain that he was experiencing. In fact, he felt the exact opposite of how he had felt before. He felt energized, like he could run for miles.

"Grace, you should meditate and try to get some of your strength back," said Tythas from the corner of the tent, scratching his chin as he studied a map that was hung on the wall. "Wyatt, you should-"

Suddenly, everything just... stopped. Tythas's mouth was open, and he was in the middle of a gentle gesture at Wyatt, but no sound came from his mouth. Jag had stopped in mid-stride halfway across the tent, and Grace was frozen in her chair, picking at something on the table. The hairs on the back of Wyatt's neck began to prickle, but before he could become well and truly alarmed, he saw a pair of luminescent yellow eyes on the table across from him, and he realized what was going on.

"And now the pieces fall into place," came Shem's deep, booming voice, echoing in Wyatt's mind as well as the tent around him. "Apep seeks to break the seals laid by the Patrons and bring Death itself into this world. He's been locked away behind magic and stone for nearly two thousand years. He was insane when he was bound, but he was still rational. Now... I have to wonder if anyone stands a chance."

Wyatt leaned back in his chair, taking a deep breath as he studied the cat's eyes. "I haven't really read a lot about them yet. How powerful is Necron? Can the Adept Council stop him?"

"Perhaps if they had Necromancers on their side, in order to block his powers," replied Shem. "But, as you already know, there are no Necromancers left on the Council. Or anywhere in the Empire, for that matter. I doubt any that are still alive would stand with the Council, after the persecution brought down upon them by virtually the entire Empire after the war. Apep played this masterfully. Pitting the Empire so strongly against Necromancy, he outwitted them into alienating their only allies in the real conflict. He's been planning this for decades."

Wyatt looked over at Grace, frowning. "What about the Vitamancers? Surely their powers can counteract his acts?"

Shem followed Wyatt's gaze, falling on Grace's frozen figure. "True. But Vitamancy... well, that's another problem, isn't it? Your friend here is one of a very select breed. There are very few left, Wyatt, and fewer yet are born each generation."

"Lovely," said Wyatt as he rubbed his eyes. "So our only hope is to stop him before he can break the other seals. I know you can't tell me what you are, but you seem to... know a lot, which means you're probably pretty old. Do you know where the other seals are?"

Shem shifted uneasily. "I did," he replied after a moment. "But nearly two thousand years have passed since I last visited those places. I've spent most of that time locked in a sword, buried in a cave. As I told you when we first met, I heard some things over the years, and occasionally I was able to stretch my awareness out to the world at large, but... I doubt I could still find Necron's seals."

Wyatt sighed, running a hand through his hair and leaning back in his seat. "Yeah, because that would be too easy," he remarked, although he hadn't really expected the cat to be of much help.

"I don't know that I would be able to tell you anyway," added Shem, padding around in a circle at his spot on the table. "As you know, my binding tends to keep important information in my head. So it's a lost cause, either way. I will be of no use to you in your hunt for the seals."

"I thought you were supposed to be some kind of... weapon, against this kind of thing," said Wyatt, looking up at the cat. "That's why you were bound in the sword in the first place, isn't it?"

"Precisely why, I'd guess," said the cat smoothly. "Although Necron may not have been the foe my binders had in mind. But I am a weapon against anything that would threaten humanity. You just have to figure out how to use me."

For the first time in his life, Wyatt wanted to hit a housecat.

"Do not act as if I have been useless to you, Wyatt Arden," chastised the cat quickly, cutting off Wyatt's bitter thoughts. He sauntered to the edge of the table, leaning close to Wyatt's face. "It was my mental influence that attuned you to your power and brought about control faster than you ever could have alone. And it was I who saved your life in Ven, as well as the lives of your friends. Without me, Apep surely would have destroyed all of you."

Wyatt sighed, nodding his head. "I'm sorry, Shem. I know you've been useful, and I know that you saved us. The situation is just very... bleak."

"You have all the tools you need," said the cat, batting Wyatt's forehead quickly with an oddly long outstretched paw, "right here. And in your heart. Have faith in your companions, Wyatt, and have faith in yourself. The rest will come in time. It always does."

"I need you to try your best to remember anything and everything you know about these seals," said Wyatt, his voice hardening. "If you think of anything and you can actually tell me, please do. You could save everyone, Shem."

"The seals were deliberately placed by their respective makers," said the cat. "Aquilon built his seal at the bottom of a lake, where he thought only his kind could reach it. Victus built his in the heart of human society and culture, close to life. Every demigod had an affinity for his or her own element, and would've placed their seals accordingly."

Wyatt nodded. "That's something. So Ignis's seal is probably somewhere nearby."

"I'd count on it," said the cat with a nod. "Perhaps at... the source? Aah, I should remember..."

Wyatt blinked, leaning toward the cat. "The source? You mean there's something here that actually causes all this heat?"

Shem was pacing the table now. "Aside from geography? In a sense. I think the seal may even play a part in it. Ignis was particularly irate with her brother's situation, and she put a lot of energy into her seal. She and Necron were very close before Necron's fall. So the stories say, anyway. Fire and undeath don't get along very well, either. She put the seal... here, beneath the ground. In the stone. But high, high up... no, that doesn't make sense..."

Wyatt had never seen the cat appear so flustered before. It was refreshing and strange at the same time.

"Wait," said Wyatt suddenly, staring at the cat. "Beneath the ground, but high up. Shem, is the seal in Mount Trajhnheim?"

The cat halted in place, returning Wyatt's stare. "Yes. The cauldron... it's a fake, built atop the real cauldron to hide the seal. There's a small fissure in the rock, a tiny passageway near the very top. At the end of the passageway is a chamber, built atop the cauldron. No mortal, aside from a skilled Pyromancer, could get near that place without being incinerated."

"I have to tell the others, then," said Wyatt, springing to his feet. "The volcano is only a few hours from here. We can scout it out, and wait for Apep there. We can stop him!"

Shem sat back, his eyes boring into Wyatt. "Tythas said that when

Aquilon's seal was broken, Lake Eryth's waters boiled for days. Wyatt, if Necron breaks that seal, Mount Trajnheim will erupt. Even being several miles away… an explosion like that could decimate the Dominion's population. Everyone here could die."

Horror and revulsion crept into Wyatt. Necron could start his army right here if the volcano erupted.

CHAPTER TWELVE

yatt's heart jumped in his chest as the world suddenly started moving again.

"-perhaps consult with your, uh, guide," Tythas continued, looking over at Wyatt from his spot in the corner and completing his soft gesture. He was seemingly oblivious to the conversation that had just occurred. "He may be able to advise us further, if he is willing."

Jag and Grace looked over at their mentor, both looking very confused. "Guide?" asked Grace, cocking her head. "Vance, what are you talking about?"

Wyatt was staring at the spot on the table where the cat had been just moments before, still trying to get his bearings. But the cat had already vanished. As he registered what Tythas had said to him, a part of him wanted to curse the old man. But a much bigger part of him realized that it was probably time for his secrets to come out. For now, they had more pressing matters than his strange companion's identity.

"I already have," said the young Aeromancer bitterly, nearly kicking his chair aside as he walked out from behind the table. "He thinks that the seal is in Mount Trajhnheim. He's fuzzy on the details, but considering that we're in the Blazelands, it makes sense that it would be somewhere in the area, what with all this heat."

"He was there, then?" asked Tythas quietly, his eyes never leaving Wyatt.

"It looks that way," replied Wyatt evenly. "In some form, anyway. He's been locked away for a long time, though. A lot of his knowledge has been locked away with him. There's no telling how reliable it is, but… it's the only lead we've got. But Tythas…"

"What in the world are the two of you talking about?" interrupted Jag, looking at his mentor for a long moment before redirecting his gaze to Wyatt. He looked equal parts confused and alarmed. "Wyatt? Who do you mean?"

Wyatt held up a hand, which he knew would only frustrate his friend further, but kept his eyes on Tythas. "He also thinks that if the seal is broken, the release of energy could cause Mount Trajhnheim to erupt. Shebal's current location is too close to the volcano. Not only is this their sacred city, but there are also thousands of people living here. Thousands of innocent people who could die. Think about what Apep could do with that, Tythas."

Tythas rubbed his eyes, his weariness and age again plain on his face. "There's no way of knowing that for sure, but given what happened with Aquilon's seal… it's certainly possible. That much violent death in one place could fuel a lot of dark, dark stuff. We have to tell Salif."

"It's not safe for us to leave just yet, though," said Wyatt quickly, lifting his chair up with an extended toe and sitting back down with a troubled sigh. "We're stuck here until we know that Apep isn't out-"

Suddenly, Grace stood. "I'm getting very tired of being left in the dark here. How do you guys know all of this?"

Wyatt and Tythas looked at each other for a few moments. Tythas's eyebrow raised, and Wyatt sighed, nodding. He drew the sword, setting it on the table before his friends. It hummed lightly in response to his touch.

"Touch it," he said quietly, motioning to Grace. She walked over to his side of the table, and after a brief pause, she reached out to touch the hilt, biting her lip.

"It's… it's vibrating," she said faintly, looking at the blade in startled confusion. "And… I can feel something. It's… it's alive?"

Jag stood and walked to join his sister, coming up behind her. He reached out and lightly touched the sword for a few moments before withdrawing and looking at his fingertips. "What is it, Wyatt?"

Wyatt sat down and leaned back in his chair, rubbing his hands together. "I have no idea," he admitted, more than a little frustrated. He took a moment to collect his thoughts before relating the story of how he found the sword, Shem's role in their battle with Apep in Ven, and the conversations that had taken place between Wyatt and the strange cat.

"I don't like it," said Jag, once Wyatt had finished his tale. "We were always told that all of the old things from before the Six were gone. Dead, sealed away, or wherever immortals go when they get tired of this world. Nothing is supposed to be left of those days, save for some stones and stories. Nobody in this lifetime or the last has even heard a whisper of something like that."

Wyatt took the sword up and sheathed it once again, feeling Shem's energy ripple through him. "From what I understand, he's supposed to be some kind of weapon or tool, to be used against... something. I don't know. He's not able to reveal much."

"I've been thinking about it a lot, since Shem first revealed himself to me outside of the pass," said Tythas. "He's certainly powerful, and that sword is unlike any magic I've ever seen. But he could be a lot of things. A dragon, maybe."

Wyatt, Grace, and Jag all stared at the older man, dumbfounded.

"A dragon," repeated Grace flatly, her disbelief evident on her face. "Come on, Vance."

"The dragons were hunted and killed by the Six," said Jag. "That's what the legends say. They were the biggest threat to humanity, and the reason Adala broke herself in the first place. They were vicious, bloodthirsty monsters."

Wyatt was still reeling. "Wait... dragons are real?"

Tythas shrugged, not seeming to understand how big of a revelation this was to Wyatt. "They were. There are some bones in the Imperial Castle. But they all died out before Necron was even sealed away. Unless the Six kept one around and didn't tell anybody. Dragons were supposed to be smarter than any living creature, which is why they were so dangerous. Maybe the Six wanted to keep certain pieces of knowledge alive."

"I guess it's possible," said Grace, shifting uncomfortably. "I can sense the life inside of that thing. It's... big, way bigger than anything

I've ever felt before. No human feels like that. No Adept, not even the strongest, has this kind of... magnitude. I don't know how that little sword can contain it."

"We need to focus on the problems at hand," said Tythas evenly, pacing around the tent. "We can't leave. Apep could still be in the camp, and we have no idea where Salif went. But we also can't just sit here and let Apep run off to break the seal. With every seal that breaks, Necron grows stronger. It's like trying to stop a snowball from rolling down a hill. We know that one seal has already been broken. Likely, he broke one in Ven. He's on his way to the third. We are running out of time. The time may come where we have to split up."

Jag looked like he wanted to kick something. "You know that's a bad idea, Tythas. Without you around, Apep could decimate the three of us easily. I can fight as many Drones as you want me to, but I'm not match for an Adept like Apep. Wyatt has certainly done well, but he's not even half trained with a sword or with his powers. And we can't risk Grace."

Grace gave her brother a scathing look. "You sound like him some days, you know. I know what I'm doing. I know the risks, and I wouldn't be here if I weren't willing to take those risks. Stop treating me like I'm a child."

Jag seemed to deflate a bit under his sister's glare. "Listen, I'm not trying to say that you're weak or... a liability, or whatever. I just think that it's stupid to put you in unnecessary danger. Vitamancers are getting rarer and rarer these days, and you're a particularly strong one at that. And, well... come on, Grace. You're my sister. It's my job to protect you."

"What about YOU?" she said incredulously, taking a step toward her brother and jabbing him in the chest with her finger to emphasize her words. "You've been running off and diving into danger since the day I met you, Jag Mercer! Nothing seems to make you want to slow down, to stop being so brave and heroic and STUPID! It's your job to protect ME? Whose job is it to protect YOU?"

An uneasy silence settled over the group as the two siblings stared at each other. Jag looked just a little terrified as he stared at his sister with an alarmed expression. Her red hair and fiery expression made her look truly scary, and Jag was already withering under the pressure. Wyatt glanced at Tythas, whose expression suggested that this had been brewing for a while. Perhaps it was good for them.

"It is my job to protect the both of you," said Tythas quietly, stepping between them and resting a hand on their shoulders. "Wyatt, too. And if any of the three of you go gallivanting off after Apep, he could bring the entire Dominion down on your heads. If he's declared you enemies, even if I'm with you, it would be bad. He's their ally now, remember? That makes it even worse. But he doesn't know that I'm involved with any of you, and he would be wary about attacking me here if I'm alone. He might ignore me entirely. And he also doesn't know that I have the birdshape amulet, which means I can scout out the seal freely. It makes the most sense for me to go on ahead."

"That doesn't mean we like it, Vance," said Grace, sitting back down in her chair with a huff, not looking at Jag. "What if he finds us here?"

"I won't be gone long," he replied. "I just want to find out where he's at, and if we can even make it to the seal before him. It's the best that we can do right now."

"Get going then," snapped Jag, walking to the edge of the tent to stare at a spot on the wall, as if he could set it on fire with his eyes. "And get back here quickly. I'm getting restless."

Tythas looked over at Wyatt. "If Apep does come while I am gone… Wyatt, you are the best hope the three of you have of surviving it. Anyone who attacks you is an enemy, and you have to do whatever you must to protect yourself, Jag, and Grace. Jag learned these lessons at a young age, but you… There isn't any blood on your hands, Wyatt. It'll be hard, if you have to take a life. Be ready, and stand firm."

Wyatt nodded and swallowed, not really sure how to respond. He couldn't seem to find the words. He hadn't even considered that he'd have to fight people other than Apep, much less take a life. It was one thing to battle the Necromancer, but entirely another to have to do harm to people who weren't even his enemies. He felt a knot developing in his stomach as he thought about it.

"Be safe, Vance," said Grace quietly. "Come back here to us quickly. I'm not ready to bury you just yet."

"Always, little one," replied Tythas with a grin and a shine in his eye. With that, he turned toward the exit, stepping forward with unmatched confidence.

Salif stepped through the tent flap, halting Tythas before he could make it out of the tent. The Pyromancer held up a shaky, blood-soaked hand. His face was pale and his expression dark.

"The steward is dead, and the Warlord is missing," he said quietly, staring at Tythas's shocked face. "Apep slipped away from his friends and is currently unaccounted for. The city is in an uproar. Fingers are being pointed everywhere. I tried to tell the other elders about the seal, but none of them would listen. They're blaming the Empire."

"We need to move," said Tythas, gripping Salif's shoulders tight. "We think that the seal is on Mount Trajnheim, but we can't be sure unless we get there. Get us your fastest horses, Salif. If he breaks the seal, the volcano could erupt. I don't need to tell you what that would do to your people."

Salif vanished through the tent flap without another word. Tythas turned back to the others. "I'm still going on ahead," he said, giving them all a resolute look. "I can get there faster than any of us, and someone needs to stall him. We're going to have a fight on our hands today. Prepare yourselves."

Tythas slipped out through the tent before the three of them could protest. They ran out behind him, watching a dark shape leap up into the sky as they got outside. They watched the shadow fly off toward the great mountain that loomed in the distance, leaving them behind to wait for horses and curse under their breaths.

Wyatt had never ridden a horse so hard in his life. He, Grace, Jag, and Salif were galloping madly to the north, toward the towering Mount Trajhnheim. They were still miles away, and Wyatt could feel the tension rising with every second. Salif especially was on edge; Wyatt had explained their theory to him, and he seemed to feel exceptionally foolish for not coming to that conclusion himself. The volcano was in danger, and if it erupted, it could decimate the population of the Dominion. He was even more worried that in the resulting chaos, those who were left would blame the Empire yet again, and Apep's underlying goal would be even easier.

They rode hard without speaking. The whipping wind and sound of hooves on the road made it virtually impossible to carry any sort of conversation, but truthfully, Wyatt was glad for the break. They had done enough talking, and now he knew that nothing else needed to be said. They finally had caught up to the crazed Necromancer and might have a shot at stopping him. With any luck, they'd have answers to some of their questions, and Wyatt might even learn of the fates of his mother and grandfather.

Suddenly, light flashed on the horizon, at the base of the mountain. They were several miles out, but Wyatt could see gouts of fire erupting from somewhere and shooting up into the sky. He leaned in closer, trying to see what was going on, unconsciously drawing the wind closer around him. He could feel an echo, like someone was manipulating that wind ahead of him. He could hear whispers riding on the air.

"Shem!" he shouted, feeling a little manic as an idea came into his head. "I'm going to need your help with this one!" He drew his sword in a quick, fluid motion. The other three looked over at him, looking confused, but he had already made up his mind.

"I'm going on ahead!" he yelled to Grace, although he doubted she'd be able to make out his words. "Tythas is in trouble!"

At another time, Wyatt probably would've found it harder to call the wind to him. But the pressure of what was happening and his burning desire to see Apep fall had hardened his resolve and sharpened his will, and without any resistance, he focused his power, wrapping a nimbus of air around him. It was an incredible feeling to have it react so easily. It felt like he was flexing a muscle that ached to be used. And use it he did.

A great gust slammed into Wyatt's back, lifting him off of his horse and carrying him above and ahead of the group. He could just make out

Grace's surprised yelp as he shot ahead of them like an arrow, cutting through the air with ease. He could feel the sword humming in his hand. Shem was pouring strength into him through that connection, reassuring his control and erasing doubt from his mind. At this moment, Wyatt was unstoppable.

Moving faster than he ever had in his life, Wyatt closed the gap between himself and the fire within minutes. He couldn't help but feel a little bit giddy; the rush was incredible. It wasn't long before he could make out Tythas alone amidst a sea of Drones, feverishly blasting them back with flame and wind. But they were gaining ground; it looked to Wyatt like Apep had sent his entire horde after the old man. But the skeletal Necromancer was nowhere in sight.

Another idea popped into his head. Without even thinking, he raised the sword above his head in both hands, as if to prepare a downward slash. He laughed, the absurdity of what he was about to do clear in his mind as he drew near the sea of dead things. Flexing his power again, he felt some strength drain out of him as it pulled from his navel. But the adrenaline was flowing in full effect, and nothing would deter him. He didn't need to look up to know that the lightning was coming. He felt it rumbling in his chest as he descended toward the mob.

The air sizzled as a blue light slammed into Wyatt's sword, wrapping him in an aura of power and destruction. His whole body was vibrating in response to the power he had summoned, exhilarating and terrifying him at the same time. With a final nudge of his will, Wyatt slowed his descent just enough to keep the fall from killing him as he rained destruction down from the sky.

Wyatt impacted the ground like a cannonball, landing atop the shoulders of a Drone in the center of the largest group. Lightning exploded out around him, cutting through the monsters in every direction. The Drone he landed on was completely obliterated. As his feet found solid ground, power roared around him, uncontrolled and awesome.

Panting hard, Wyatt fell to a knee as the lightning ceased. His ears were ringing as he tried to get his bearings, but he wasn't afforded a break. More drones shambled in toward him, completely undeterred by his display of power.

Lightning crackled along the blade in his hand. Without another thought, Wyatt leapt forward, swinging the blade in a great arc in front of him. Electricity surged outward, scything through even more Drones with ease. Wyatt swung with wild abandon, spinning and dancing away from the horde wherever he had an opening. At that moment, he wasn't thinking about his mother, his friends, cats, seals, or demigods. He was lost in the moment, engrossed in a fight like never before.

He could just make out Tythas through the shambling masses, equally amazing in his display of power. The distraction that Wyatt had caused had allowed the elder to create some space between him and his foes, and now a great dancing ring of fire swirled around him, incinerating anything that got close. He swung his hands outward like a conductor, and great plumes of fire swept over the Drones in response.

In time, Wyatt and Tythas moved closer to one another. The ring of fire broke, and Wyatt suddenly found himself back to back with the old man, surrounded by a seemingly unlimited number of drones. The two of them leaned into one another, blasting and searing the shambling mob with furious certainty. It was the freest Wyatt had ever felt, and the most fun that he had ever had.

After one final swing of his sword, all of the Drones were gone. A sudden, almost vacuous silence settled over the duo as the two of them tried to find their wits. Wyatt clutched his sword tightly in his hand, still ready for more fighting. He half expected more Drones to rise up out of the ground.

"Of all of the things that I was expecting to happen," said Tythas, panting and still at Wyatt's back, "that was certainly not high on the list. I don't even want to begin to know where you got the idea to do that, but it certainly worked. Well done, Wyatt. Well done."

"Where's Apep?" asked Wyatt as he sucked in deep breaths. The adrenaline was fading now, and he could feel cold fatigue creeping into him like ice. "He's got to be close."

Tythas pointed up at the mountain, finally separating himself from Wyatt. "He's already inside. I caught up to him here, but he apparently anticipated being caught. He must've known I was in Shebal all along. He hid his drones under fresh soil, and as I tried to engage him, they rose up around me and caught me by surprise. Before I knew it, he was gone and I couldn't catch him. I... I fear it may be too late, Wyatt."

Wyatt called the wind around him yet again, preparing to fly up the mountain and catch up to Apep. But before he could, Tythas caught him by the shoulder. Wyatt's hold on the wind broke, suddenly disrupted by Tythas's power.

"You will die if you try to follow him in there, Wyatt," said Tythas quietly, gripping Wyatt's shoulder tighter than he probably needed to. "The temperature inside that volcano is not something anyone but a Pyromancer can survive, not without help. I can, but I lack the ability to protect the both of us from the heat and defend myself at the same time. And there is no telling what sort of things Apep has left at the entrance waiting for us. We can't do anything else here. We need to do our best to evacuate the Dominion, to move on before we suffer even more damages."

Wyatt bucked Tythas's hand off of his shoulder, giving the old man a glare that could cut steel. This was the only lead he had on his mother, and he wasn't about to give it up.

"I can't just let him get away, Tythas. He knows what happened to my family. I can't give that up!"

"I know," replied Tythas quietly, watching Wyatt with a truly pained expression. "I know, Wyatt. But that doesn't change the fact that you will die here if you go after him. If we both go, we will both die. We cannot fight him there. And once he breaks that seal, we may be the only ones who can help thousands of innocent people survive this. Is your family more important than the lives of thousands?"

Wyatt let out a frustrated scream as he kicked the fallen form of the nearest Drone, sending bits of it flying everywhere. Thunder crashed in the distance as lightning lit the sky, echoing his rage. He slammed his sword into its sheath, blood pounding in his ears. He was letting go of his only lead, and he knew he had to do it. He wanted to level the entire mountain.

Stay calm, Wyatt, came Shem's firm voice in his mind, easing his nerves a bit. He felt the sword's soft hum at his hip, felt Shem's determination coming from it. *Don't lose hope.*

"Where are the others?" asked Tythas, looking out on the horizon. "I would've assumed that they would be close behind you."

"They're coming," said Wyatt, pointing toward where he knew the rest of the group would be. "But I took off ahead of them, and I was moving a lot faster. I'm not sure how long they will be, or if their horses will even make the rest of the trip. They were riding pretty hard."

"I think that you should fly ahead to meet them," said Vance, raising a hand to shield his eyes from the sun as he looked off toward where Wyatt pointed. "Intercept them and tell Salif what's going on. I'll fly ahead to the camp and start making preparations, once I've scouted out the area. We'll meet up there."

Wyatt nodded at Tythas, signaling his agreement. "Yeah, that's fine," he said flatly, trying to keep his displeasure in check. Shem had helped to calm him down, but he still felt a little bit volatile.

Tythas clapped him on the shoulder once more. "I am sorry, Wyatt. I don't like it either, but we have no choice. I promise you that we will find your family. This isn't the last we've seen of Apep. We tracked him down once, and we can do it again."

Wyatt nodded dully. "I know, Vance. Let's get going. We don't have a lot of time."

Tythas clutched his amulet, his form melting into the shape of a great shadowy bird. He took flight, his huge wings thundering in the wind as he did. Wyatt was envious of his amulet; that kind of flight would certainly be less taxing. But lacking one for himself, Wyatt called the wind once more, wrapping it around him like a warm cloak. He leapt up, letting it carrying him into the sky, this time at a much slower, more even pace.

It wasn't long before the rest of his companions came into view, their horses leaving a cloud of dust behind them as they rode. Wyatt waved his arms and landed a safe distance ahead of them, giving them time to slow down. He stood in front of them, waiting for what he imagined would be a hail of anger.

"What happened?" asked Grace as the horses came to a stop, looking down at him. "You took off, faster than I've ever seen an Aeromancer fly. Where did you go?"

"Tythas was in trouble," he replied, motioning behind him. "He found Apep, but he got ambushed by Apep's drones. They were hiding in the dirt beneath him. Apep got away, and he's inside the volcano already. There isn't anything we can do. We need to get back to the city and start helping to evacuate the people. There's no telling what kind of damage that volcano is going to do when it erupts."

"What do you mean, there's nothing we can do?" asked Jag incredulously. "He's in there! We need to charge in after him and put a stop to it before he breaks the seal!"

Wyatt shook his head. "No. We're too late. None of us can follow him in there. Salif might be able to shield us from the heat, but he wouldn't be able to defend himself if he did. Tythas said the same thing. And there's no telling what other lovely little traps he's left for us on the way up the mountain. He left about a thousand Drones down there for Tythas. We don't have time to find out. We need to get the city evacuated. If those people die, Apep is going to have even more power at his fingertips."

Jag looked like he was going to protest some more, so Wyatt cut him off. "I have already argued your case to Tythas, Jag, but it's not the right move. He's protected from the heat, but we aren't. Tythas already went on ahead, and Salif can't keep all of us safe and defend himself at the same time. We can't go in there. We need to get the city evacuated."

Salif nodded. "He's right, Jag. Keeping everyone safe from the heat is beyond me. Apep is hoping to collect power by killing thousands of my people. Preventing that is going to be the most harm we can do to his plans at this point. There are innocent lives at stake here. You're a soldier, Jag. You know it to be true."

"They're right, Jag," said Grace, reaching out to grab Jag's shoulder and get his attention. "We don't have time for this. You know they're right."

Jag looked positively murderous, but he finally relented. "We grabbed your horse when you took off," he said to Wyatt, obviously trying hard to keep from kicking something. "Get up there so we can get moving."

Wyatt looked up, just in time to see Tythas's huge, shadowy form flying over them, headed in the direction of Shebal. "Tythas went on ahead," he explained as he climbed up into the saddle. "He'll be getting the process started, but we will need to catch up. At least we don't have to worry about Apep waiting for us."

The four of them turned, riding back toward the city with Jag and Salif in the lead. Grace looked over at Wyatt's subdued expression with a frown.

"I'm sorry, Wyatt," she said, just loud enough that Wyatt could hear it. "I know you were hoping to learn something about your family, but… I really think you made the right decision here. I wish I was wrong, but…"

Wyatt nodded, but didn't say anything in return. He was beginning to hate being right.

As Shebal finally came back within view, a strange feeling began to crawl over Wyatt. It felt as if a rock were growing inside his abdomen, slowly expanding and becoming more painful. It made him feel cold and lethargic, making it difficult to do anything at all, much less ride a horse. He was sweating and tired, and he hated it. He felt like the situation was trying to pull him in two directions: his mind, telling him to rest and recuperate, and his heart, telling him to never quit.

But the feeling in his gut was just making that even worse. He focused on it, trying to figure out what was going on. It wasn't sickness, he realized; it had something to do with whatever was going on in Mount Trajnheim, something to do with the horrible thing that was about to happen. He was dimly aware that he could feel the mountain, like a fresh wound that beat along with his heart. He could feel it coming, as if he were standing on a precipice, and knew that he could not catch himself before he fell. But he knew that he wasn't the one on the precipice. It was the entire world.

He grimaced, tightly gripping the hilt of the sword as if he could draw more strength from it. Shem's presence touched his mind, and calm reassurance flowed into him. The blade hummed softly, subdued, like a soft whisper in his ear. It wrapped around him and washed over him, whisking away some of the pain and anxiety in his stomach. Shem, although sometimes difficult, was there to help him. There was no question of that now.

They were drawing nearer to the city, and Wyatt steeled himself for what was going to be a hard road ahead. A part of him had known it before, but now there was no doubt in his mind. People were going to die, a feeling that he would never be able to be okay with. It was like a pressure on his heart that would not go away.

Suddenly, Tythas's birdlike shape dropped in front of them, landing about fifty feet ahead. All four riders slowed their horses, coming to a halt just in front of the gigantic raven. There was a flash of light and feathers, and Tythas's form returned to normal. He held up a hand, motioning for them to stop. They slowed their horses and came to a halt close to him.

"Salif, you need to keep going on ahead," he said to the Pyromancer, his expression grave. "The camp is a complete chaotic mess, and your supporters are losing ground. Lines are already being drawn. Farooq, Apep's biggest supporter, has taken temporary control of the council in lieu of a Warlord. He'll probably be vying for the position. You're the only one who can oppose that, Salif."

Salif's horse whinnied unsteadily, and he did his best to calm it. "Farooq has wanted me dead for at least five years now. I imagine he's already spitting his propaganda against me, trying to get me removed from my seat."

Tythas nodded gravely. "Yes. He's revoked my position as an honorary member of the Dominion," he added with a deep sigh. "He's trying to pin the whole thing on the four of us. Saying that you plotted to murder the Warlord and take his position for yourself, and that you hired the three of us as your assassins. And, my favorite part, that you worked with me because of my ties to the Empire, and you're planning on surrendering the Dominion's lands and people to the Emperor so that you could have more gold and a noble rank in the kingdom you truly serve."

Salif looked like he wanted to be sick. "If I don't get there soon, the damage isn't going to be able to be undone. I'm sorry, old friend, but I don't know how long it will take to undo this. If I even can. You may never be welcome back with those people, Vance."

Tythas shook his head sadly. "Do not worry about that right now. You need to go to them, to save your people. Do whatever you can. Just make sure that Apep can't kill thousands. We don't have a lot of time."

Almost as if on cue, the ground beneath their feet rumbled. The knot in Wyatt's stomach gave a painful jolt, and his skin prickled as the feeling of dread suddenly spiked into his throat, making him nauseous and shaky. He leaned over in his saddle, clutching his stomach and crying out, unable to keep his pain inside.

The others looked over at him with a frown as the horses started. Tythas watched him briefly before looking off toward the looming shape of Mount Trajnheim. Smoke had begun to seep from the peak, a sure sign of bad things to come.

"The seal's been broken," managed Wyatt, trying to shove the pain back down. "It's... I can feel it. Everything is unstable. We need to go, and we need to go now."

Grace's horse trotted over to him, and she put her hand on his arm, her brow furrowed in concern. She stayed like that for a few seconds before pulling her hand back, looking puzzled.

Wyatt shook his head, unable to speak. They weren't listening to him, which just made him even angrier and made him feel even worse. The ground rumbled again, stronger this time, spooking the horses yet again.

"He's right," said Tythas, trying to settle his horse's nerves with gentle pats. "I can feel the energy releasing as we speak. Salif, you can probably feel it, too. We need to go, now. We can't do anything more here. We must move forward, on to the next seal, and hope that we can stop Apep there."

Salif's horse took off at a full gallop toward the camp. He gave Tythas one last apologetic look before setting his eyes forward, his gaze firm and steady, the look of a man willing to do anything to save his people from certain death.

Tythas pointed toward the south. "We have to get out of the Blazelands. I have no idea what kind of damage the eruption is going to cause, but the entire area could be thrown into discord. There's no telling what else might wake up with that kind of power being let out of the seal."

Grace slid off of her horse, offering it to Tythas so that he could direct them. She walked over to Wyatt's, climbing up behind him. He could feel her healing energy lightly roll over him. It wasn't trying to undo any damage, but instead was just warming him, reassuring him. Jag gave her an odd look, but didn't say anything.

Tythas climbed up on to the offered horse, settling into the saddle. "These horses have had a hard ride, and I don't know how much more we're going to be able to push them. Grace, I know you want to help Wyatt, but you may need to save your energy for them. We have a long way to go, and there aren't a lot of safe places to camp between now and there. We are all going to have to be strong."

Grace nodded, and the warm sensation that had washed over Wyatt diminished somewhat. But it didn't go away entirely. Grace was too stubborn for her own good, he thought. But he appreciated it.

Tythas looked them all over once more, as if he were trying to silently assess their mental states. But all three of his young companions had iron in their eyes. None of them was even close to being ready to give up. He smiled proudly at them for a moment, a small smile that perhaps only he was aware of. And then he turned to the south, that same determination hard in his own eyes.

Jag, Grace, and Wyatt followed, eyes set on the far horizon.

CHAPTER THIRTEEN

yvarion Il'Vir strode into his office, trying hard to ignore the pounding headache that had crept into his skull in the last twelve hours. Part of it had to do with the lack of sleep, he knew, as he hadn't gotten a good rest in weeks. But mostly, it was out of worry.

The Emperor wasn't one to worry, normally. He was Tyvarion Ironhide, Ruler of the Empire, Commander of the First Legion, master Terramancer. He was as steady as stone.

Usually.

Lately, though... it didn't seem to matter what he did or whom he did it for. Everything was falling apart. His power and his reach were shrinking, and he wondered for how much longer he'd be able to protect even the people in his own capital, much less those in the furthest parts of the Empire.

Ven had been destroyed. Their scout unit had returned with the news that they had found bodies littering the countryside. Most of the city had burned in some kind of fire. They also reported evidence that an Atumen had, at some point, rampaged through the city. That itself was a nightmare to even consider.

First, it was Ven. And just last night he had woken from the middle of his uneasy sleep, as he felt the earth itself beneath him shift and groan and cry out in pain. It made him shake and shiver, and he knew that something terrible had happened. It took a lot of energy for the earth to call out like that, and only a Terramancer like himself could feel it happen.

Now he was unsure of everything. Something was going on, just out of sight, weakening the strength of his Empire and blinding the sight of the Council. He knew that there was a very powerful Necromancer behind all of these events, judging by the events that had happened in Ven. The bodies had shown the unmistakable signs of Necromancy. But he could tie the crime to nobody, and the Council was likewise at a loss. A haze hung over all of them.

Things were not going well.

"My lord," said the woman who was in his study waiting for him, getting to her feet. "I know that you have a lot on your plate at the moment, but we really need to talk. It is urgent."

"What is it, Rose?" asked the Emperor as he walked past her and sat down at his desk. Rose Veratha, Magistrix of the Arcane Academy of Farillyon, usually stayed out of his business. Although she sat on the Adept Council, she was largely concerned with education and left running the Empire to others.

"It's about the enrollment this year," she replied as she took a seat across the desk, idly brushing some of her graying-red hair out of her eyes. She adjusted her expertly-tailored dress, giving him a very uneasy look. "The number of new students, as you know, has been dwindling for years now. But this year... we don't have a single new Vitamancer enrolling at the Academy."

Emperor Il'Vir blinked, looking at her in bewilderment.

"It's not as if we didn't look for them," she said hastily, fidgeting in her chair. "We searched and searched, all over the kingdom and a few other places, too. But we haven't found one that was the proper age to begin learning. We actually... only found three, total, all of whom are but children. One was still sucking on her mother when we arrived. It'll be at least five years before the next is old enough to enroll."

Tyvarion began searching through his papers, trying to find the ledger he kept of enrollment numbers over the years. After some chaotic searching, he found the paperwork and scanned the numbers quickly.

"That's a very sharp decline," he said quietly, looking over their numbers. In the past, over a hundred Adepts joined the Academy every year, on average, and the numbers were always split pretty evenly among the six Aspects. But that had been long ago; in the last two decades, the numbers had slowly shrunk, but they had never had a certain Aspect not enroll. Last year, they still had one Vitamancer enroll. This year... none?

"I know," she replied gravely, folding her hands in her lap. "I don't know what to make of it. We've been finding Adepts in the most obscure, distant places for centuries. If they are out there, we should be able find them. Which means that either something is blocking our ability to detect them, or... they just aren't out there anymore."

The Emperor stood, walking over to the window and staring out over the rooftops of the capital, his home for all of his life. He loved this city, but the effects of the Great War and the Empire's slow slide into chaos were becoming more evident every day. It hurt his heart to look out at the city and see poor people in the streets, shops closing up, and women carrying daggers for protection.

"I'll get someone to look into it immediately," he said softly, his headache flaring again. It was like there were some sort of creature inside his skull, frantically pounding as it tried to escape. "Although I can't promise you any good news. The road ahead looks to be long and dark for all of the Empire, Rose."

The Magistrix stood, walking over to him. She paused a few feet away, looking out the window as well. "I've never seen you look this tired before, Ty," she said quietly, lingering behind him.

If anyone else had been so informal with him, they would've faced a punishment. But he and Rose had been friends since childhood, and he knew it was hard for her to think of him as her Emperor. There would always be a part of them that remembered those better days, when they were just young, dumb friends, without any of the responsibilities they now carried.

"I haven't been sleeping well," he replied after a time, glancing back at her. "I can't seem to rest for more than an hour or two at a time. Either I have nightmares or someone rushes in to wake me up, needing a signature here or a decree there. This castle is incapable of running itself, I swear."

"You should have said something to me sooner," she said softly, moving a little closer. "I can help with that, Ty. You know I can."

Help. He had never been good at accepting help, although he probably needed it a lot more than he knew. Rose had always been there to offer it, throughout his whole life. She was a true friend, even though he had never treated her the way she really deserved. He was too busy, too much in the middle of everything anymore to see it.

"I've definitely felt worse in my life, Rose," he said with a halfhearted chuckle, shaking his head. "I think I'll be alright."

She stepped even closer, resting a hand on his shoulder. The characteristic warm, tingling feeling that came whenever a Vitamancer used their power washed over him, nearly making him sigh with relief as the pain in his head and his joints subsided. He wanted to fall into that feeling, to not feel hurt and tired for just a small span of time.

But he was Tyvarion Ironhide, and he was most certainly not a normal man. He had learned at a young age that if he relied on anything other than his own resolve, he would eventually falter, stumble, and fail. He wanted so badly to accept her help, and he appreciated what she was doing. But it wouldn't help him in the long run. He didn't need a crutch; he needed to stay strong, to keep his eyes ahead.

He shrugged her hand away, shaking his head again as the tingling sensation faded and his headache filled the void it had left behind. "I appreciate it, Rose. But I'll be fine. You have a lot on your plate too, and you need to save your strength for that. If I feel like I'm getting worse, I will send for you. But it's not necessary right now."

She sighed, shaking her head and leaning away. A cold, awkward silence settled between them, making him feel, in a strange way, worse than his headache had.

"I'll get my researchers looking into the problem right away," he offered, breaking the harsh silence. "There's a lot of history in the Imperial Archives, and there may be some kind of precedent. It could be nothing, Rose. Things just… ebb and flow, sometimes. I don't need to be an Aquamancer to know that."

The Magistrix sighed again and walked over to the door brusquely. "Thank you for your time, Emperor," she said stiffly. "I eagerly await the results of your research."

Tyvarion nodded as he heard that familiar sadness echoing in her voice. He'd heard it so many times before, disappointed her so many times before. But she never gave up on him. For some reason, she never left his side, even when he broke her heart.

"Thank you for bringing your concerns to me, Magistrix," he said flatly, staring out at the descending sun as he felt the weight of so many things resting upon his shoulders. It was a weight he knew well, having shouldered it for his whole life.

She disappeared through the doorway without another word, leaving Emperor Tyvarion Il'Vir very much alone in his study.

"Master?" came Apep's tentative voice, calling out through what remained of the volcanic cavern. He squinted into the hazy darkness, trying to see through the thick dust and ash that hung in the air. He coughed, clutching a rag over his mouth to try to keep those things out.

His master had warned him that the mountain would explode, but he hadn't really been prepared for the amount of violence that was released by the earth. It was a magnificent show; he had never seen a power like that, such magnificent destruction wrought in one place, seemingly from nothing. But the tension that had already existed within the mountain coupled with the glorious breaking of the seal was a combination too great to contain. It had been more than enough to create an awesome, terrible eruption.

"Master?" he called again, listening to his own voice echo weirdly around him as he tried to navigate his way through the dust. Somehow there was still a surface beneath his feet, but the ceiling and walls of the cavern had not survived the eruption. He could tell that if he were to walk too far, he would find that the floor was gone too, leaving nothing but a lake of magma beneath them. The cracked and broken seal was now suspended over that great cauldron, held in place by narrow stone bridges.

"Here, Apep," came Necron's deep, icy voice, blasting the dust away as it fell upon him. A figure rose up from the center of the broken seal, casting an impossibly large shadow behind it, a shadow wreathed in flame that resonated with a dark, chilling power.

The figure took a slow step forward, and the shadow seemed to shrug those flames off, casting them aside. The last remnants of fire quickly faded away, swallowed by the growing, strengthening darkness.

"My sister's rage persists, even after her power has been broken so definitively," mused the figure, stepping forward again. Apep could now see that Necron had left behind the frail, decaying form of the Terramancer and had stepped into the body of the Pyromancer they had sacrificed. He had been the Warlord of the Dominion of Fire while he was alive, and now Necron held his spirit in Death. He would use that spirit, use the heat and rage from within it to break the remaining seals.

Necron flexed and stretched, as if he were testing the boundaries of his new prison. His form seemed to twist and shift further than a human body would allow, but when Apep blinked, his master looked normal again. Necron's new body was fresh and unmarred, and he looked almost entirely normal, aside from his shadow. Huge and monstrous, it was a sign of just how close the Lord of Death was to being whole again.

"We are so close, Apep," came that icy voice again as Necron looked up in to the open air above them, as if he could see the sky through the smoke and ash. "Soon, I will shed this weak shell and walk this world in my true form. Then we shall know the true mettle of my siblings."

Apep nodded excitedly, one hand still clutching a blue crystal that protected him from the heat. "We will destroy them all, Master. I care not for anything in this life. We will cast it all into Death and make a new world, a kingdom built in your image."

Necron's eyes seemed to glow with a crimson light for a moment as he fixed them on Apep. "Do not underestimate our foes, Apep," chided the master. "Children though some of them may be, they are not without talent or power. And something else... something else has risen to battle me, to assist them and keep me bound as I am. Or perhaps, to help them do what my siblings would not, and finally cast me out. My memories stir, but... too much has changed, too much has been diluted by time and stone for me to know what it is. But I can taste it on the air now, Apep. I can feel it in these borrowed bones. Be careful."

Apep cocked his head, frowning as he looked at his master curiously. "Something... else?" One of the others? Ignis, maybe, woken by this eruption... or maybe even Victus, come to stop his foil?"

Necron shook his head. "Something else, Apep. Something forgotten by everything and everyone. Something, which until very recently, may have ceased to exist some time ago. Exactly what it is or what it has become... time will tell. Time will tell all, Apep. It always does. Time and Death are twins, after all, conjoined at the hip. They walk together."

Apep had no idea what Necron was trying to say, so he merely nodded. His master knew so much more than he, had seen so much more and simply was so much more. He had long ago cast aside fear, admiration, and most other human traits. Even so, he found that in the presence of Necron, he felt very, very human.

It had only been an hour since they parted ways with Salif, but that time felt like an eternity to Wyatt. Time crept agonizingly forward as he and his companions rode south with wild abandon. But eventually, it caught them.

Wyatt finally felt the air change as the tension inside of him, the tension inside of earth's very mantle, finally snapped. A breathtaking release of energy preceded a great groan from the earth beneath them, and the skyline was lit with a brilliant orange as Mount Trajnheim erupted.

They were far enough away to avoid the magma, but ash and debris were still a concern. It was Tythas who saved them from that. His experienced eyes had been ready for it, and as the wave of destruction came, he raised his arms and called a great wind that wrapped them in a protective barrier. He then closed his eyes and went into a trance, his arms outstretched and his face tilted up toward the sky. Wyatt knew that the wind might save them from the debris and the ash, but the heat could still be enough to harm them. But when the great cloud finally descended upon them, it hadn't felt like anything other than a hot gust of wind.

From that point forward, the ride was quiet and somber. Grace held onto Wyatt with a desperation that he hadn't expected, and he realized at some point that she had started crying. She could probably feel the lives behind them being snuffed out, those unfortunate souls who had not been able to survive the eruption. Apep had struck them a great blow, worse than he probably knew.

Tythas, meanwhile, had sorely needed rest after using so much of his power to protect all of them. Jag, in a moment of soldier's ingenuity, had produced some leather straps and quite literally tied the old man to his back. From that point forward, Tythas had fallen into a deep meditation, one that didn't seem to be interrupted by the bobbing and flopping he was doing on the back of a horse. His own horse followed without a rider that day; Grace had declined it, wanting to be near to someone. After the first day of rest, the old man seemed to regain his energy, and took up his horse once again.

On the third day of hard riding, Jag's horse misstepped and broke its leg. It was a soldier's reflexes that saved Jag's life, but nothing could save the horse. The unfortunate beast lost its footing entirely and went face-first into the dirt, leaving Jag just enough time to spring from the saddle and land a few feet away in the dust. The beast let out a few horrible, pained noises before going still.

"That was lucky," breathed Jag, panting a bit as a result of the sudden surge of adrenaline that came with nearly being thrown from a moving horse. He looked up at Grace. "Thanks, sis. You saved my life."

Grace quickly hopped off of Wyatt's horse, rushing over to the fallen steed and dropping to her knees in front of it. She pressed her hand against its neck, a pained look on her face as she tried to save the unfortunate animal.

"It's gone, Grace," said Wyatt carefully, sliding out of his saddle and walking over to her. He had seen animals die in the fields before, and as a result he knew the signs. White foam was collected around its mouth and its eyes were rolled back. It had given Jag and the rest of them everything it could give, and died because of it.

Grace ignored him, pressing both of her hands into the horse as a honey-colored light flowed from her hands and into the beast. She had already been using a lot of her energy to help keep them going and Wyatt knew that if she wasted any more of her power, she'd be risking her health and their mission.

Wyatt knelt down next to her, resting a hand on her shoulder, doing his best to project confidence and reassurance into her, even if he didn't feel very much of it himself. She needed that right now, needed him to be strong for her, like she had been for them so many times.

"Grace," he said softly, squeezing her shoulder lightly. "We need to keep moving. There's nothing you can do. I know you want to help, and I know it hurts. But there's nothing that you can do." He saw tears streaming down her face as she frantically worked to save the unfortunate creature.

"I may be able to do something," said Tythas quietly, sliding off his own horse and walking over to them. "Please, Grace, stop. You're wasting your energy, and we're too far from our goal for that. You've done more than enough, more than what would ever be expected of you. But you have to let it go, and let me take over from here."

Grace stood and walked away quickly, turning her back on all of them and walking ten or fifteen paces off. She stopped there, silently staring out at the countryside as tears continued to fall from her eyes. Wyatt watched her, wishing he knew what he could do for her, feeling just as powerless as he had when they had let Apep escape. He noticed that Tythas was preparing to do something, so he backed away from the fallen horse.

Tythas closed his eyes, holding his arms out with his palms up as he looked up to the sky. A soft wind tousled Wyatt's hair, a wind he hadn't felt before. Suddenly, a bright flash fell over the horse as a pillar of golden fire descended above it, washing over it with pure, shining light. Within moments, the fire had consumed the horse, and Wyatt could see that it was quickly turning the animal to ash.

"May this flame light the path to your Father," said Vance softly, opening his eyes and staring into the flames. "Rest well, and know that the fire will keep you safe as you walk from Life into Death."

With that, the elder Adept took a step back, coming to stand with Jag and Wyatt. The three of them watched the flames slowly burn the horse away. After a few minutes, the heat subsided as the last of the fire went out, leaving nothing behind but a pile of ash that slowly blew away in the wind. Grace still stood away from them with her back turned, not wanting to watch what Tythas had done.

"You said 'father'," said Wyatt quietly, looking at Tythas as sudden curiosity came over him. "Who are you talking about?"

Tythas continued to stare at the ashes, lost in thought. "Adala created humanity," he replied, his voice soft and distant. "But animals, and the rest of the life that populates the world, were created by another."

Grace finally walked over to the rest of them, looking down at the ashes. Her eyes were red, but she had stopped crying. "I'm sorry," she said with a sniff. "I just..."

"We know, Grace," said Jag, first to reach her. He rubbed her back softly and looked into her eyes, showing a sincerity that Wyatt had never seen from the soldier before. "Don't worry about it. It's hard on all of us. You don't have to explain anything."

"We're getting close to a small farming settlement," said Tythas, motioning off to the southwest. "One not unlike Ven. There isn't much there, but should at least be a barn we can sleep in and somewhere to buy some supplies. After that, we need to find a larger town, somewhere to do some research about the remaining seals."

Jag was next to speak, looking over at his mentor. "I was thinking about that, actually. We know the seals of Fire and Water have already been broken. We can pretty safely assume that another was broken in Ven, around the time that Wyatt's house blew up and his family vanished. So that's three. There are only five total, and we know that the seal of Life is beneath the castle in Farillyon. I don't have any idea how Apep plans to get at that one, but we can't do much there either. I would think that just based on its location alone, it is pretty safe."

"I would also say it's a pretty safe bet that the seal Apep broke in Ven was the seal of Earth," added Wyatt, walking around restlessly as he spoke. "The fact that there are so many caves out there filled with glowing crystals, and the earthquake that happened just after..."

"I agree," said Tythas with a nod at Wyatt. "Which leaves the seal of Air. The questions then become, where is it, and where can we learn of its location?"

"I think I know where we can find out," offered Grace with a sigh, as if she were unimpressed with her own idea. "None of you are going to like the idea, but it's probably our best shot at this point."

Jag blinked at her, but his confusion only lasted a moment. A horrified expression fell over him as he seemed to realize what she was referring to.

"You want us to go there?" he asked incredulously, gaping at her. "There. Are you insane?"

"I fear that she may be right, Jag," said Tythas with a pained look on his face. "She's also right that I really don't like the idea. Going back there could, at the very least, get two of us killed."

"I know that, Vance," she replied hastily, pinching the bridge of her nose. "But that's the only place that has texts old enough for us to find what we're looking for. If that information is written anywhere, that's where we're going to find a record of it. Maybe even the original."

Wyatt ran a hand through his lengthening hair, exasperated. "What in the world are the three of you talking about?"

His three companions started, collectively remembering that he was still there. They all shared a look for a moment before Tythas gave a slow reply.

"The Imperial Archives," he said carefully. "In Farillyon. While we're there, we could possibly check on the seal as well, to make sure it's protected. If necessary, I may be able to leave a surprise for Apep, should he manage to infiltrate the castle."

"Why is going to the capital such a bad idea?" asked Wyatt with a frown. "I realize you guys aren't exactly loved by the Empire, being vigilantes and all, but would they really try to kill you?"

"Just Tythas and I," replied Jag, looking over at his sister. "We... oh, dammit guys, I'm just going to tell him. He's with us; he needs to know." Tythas and Grace didn't offer any objections, so he looked back to Wyatt and continued.

"We told you that we fled the Empire after Necromancers were removed from the Adept Council and started working to protect them," he said, holding Wyatt's confused gaze. "What we did not tell you is that... Grace, my sister, is Grace Il'Vir, the only legitimate, surviving heir of Tyvarion Il'Vir, the Emperor."

Wyatt stared at him, dumbfounded. He looked to Tythas and Grace, both of whom were silent, not offering any dispute up to Jag's claims.

"Wait," said Wyatt, his confusion only growing. "You're her brother. But your surname is Mercer. That's an unclaimed name. I don't understand."

Grace walked over to Jag, resting a hand on her brother's shoulder. "He is my brother," she said with a smile. "Before he met my mother, our father sired Jag with a servant girl. When he found out that she was pregnant, he decided that an illicit child would only be another blemish on his already imperfect reign. So only days after he was born in secret, Jag was given away to the Blades, leaving them to raise him as a nameless warrior."

Jag's eyes were hard and proud as he looked at Wyatt. "One day, my father came to me in secret and told me the truth. He apologized, saying it was the only way. He said that this way, I had a real chance. He had me raised by the Blades so that he could keep me close. I was the best, you know. Tyvarion Ironhide was my father. I may not be an Adept, but I'm the finest swordsman in the kingdom. I've watched over him for my whole life."

"Meanwhile, Tythas was my favorite teacher at the Academy," said Grace, looking over at their mentor. "And he was one of the few Adepts who shared my feelings about how the Empire was treating Necromancers after the war."

"One day, an assassin tried to kill Grace," said Jag. "We never figured out who sent him. I killed the man and saved her life, but it sent the Emperor into a fury. He pulled her from her classes at the Academy and more or less locked her inside the castle. She was always to be with an armed guard, never to leave the grounds. His paranoia got the best of him."

Tythas walked around, stretching his legs. "Jag came to me at that point, to discuss the issue and see what we could do. He knew that I was close to his sister. We hadn't met each other previously, so I only knew him as the famous Blade, not the Emperor's illicit son. When he confessed to me his origins, I was skeptical at first, but research in the Archives confirmed his claim. When he told me what had happened to Grace, we planned to secretly spirit her out of the castle. We both felt that she needed to continue her education and her training."

"Jag approached me with the idea, and I couldn't wait to get out," said Grace. "I was living inside of a cave, and it was impossible to have even a little bit of privacy. When I needed to dress or bathe, there was a female guard in the room with me. When I wanted to walk the halls, there was always a guard behind me, his armor and weapons clanking and rattling. I hated it, and I honestly felt like I was going crazy."

"So in the dead of night, about three years ago, we kidnapped the princess," said Jag, unable to keep the amusement from showing on his face. "It really was a great plan, and before the Emperor even knew what happened, the three of us were gone. We revealed my origins to Grace, and for the first time in our lives, she and I both felt like we had a real family."

Wyatt looked between the three of them, now pacing as he tried to process all of this. He suddenly felt very awkward. He had slept in the dirt with Grace. The two of them had fought monsters and nearly died together, saving each other's lives in the process. And she was the princess...

"The Emperor found out, however," said Tythas with a disappointed shake of his head. "I should've suspected it would happen, but I was too focused on the outcome. One of my allies, a man named Mugalo, told the Emperor what he knew. I had needed his help in getting access to the inner part of the castle, and he had provided it readily. When he told the Emperor, he said that I had threatened his family and taken what I needed forcibly. It was assumed that since he disappeared at the same time, and had been seen in my company in the weeks leading up to the kidnapping, that Jag had been my willing accomplice. The two of us are wanted for high treason in the entire Empire. Most places are perfectly safe, but... the capital is another matter."

"I wasn't exaggerating when I said that I am the finest swordsman in the kingdom," said Jag, adjusting his sword unconsciously. "At one time, nearly everyone in the castle knew my name. I fought off seven assassins at once and saved my father's life when I was only sixteen. In the middle of the castle's Grand Courtyard. Hundreds saw it happen."

"Meanwhile, my exploits during the Great War are still spoken of amongst soldiers and in taverns across the kingdom," said Tythas. "Perhaps somewhat due to my own rumormongering ways. I served as High Chair on the Council during the war, and after my retirement from politics I taught at the Academy. Even after being gone from there for so long, Jag and I are still very well known in Farillyon."

"Which means if we go there and we get caught, Vance and I will die, she'll be locked up again, and you'll be imprisoned and subjected to questioning, at the very least," said Jag to Wyatt, very seriously. "From there, you'll most likely be found as an apostate and… well, that's just not a good thing for anybody."

"Well, what if we just don't get caught?" offered Wyatt with a pause.

The other three stared at him, dumbfounded. Wyatt felt a little bit stupid for suggesting it, but he certainly felt it was a valid point.

"Look," he continued, before they could offer their sputtered responses. "Farillyon is a big place, and even if people might recognize you, they're certainly not going to be looking for you. Grace, you haven't been seen by anyone but the castle staff and guards for years. All we have to do is disguise you three to the best of our abilities and get in and out as quickly as we can."

Tythas scratched his chin thoughtfully. "The boy does have a point. The Archives are just outside of the market square, in the middle of the city. As long as we avoid Hightown and the Education District we should have a decent chance of success. We've worked on worse odds before."

"Maybe it would be a better idea if the two of you didn't come with us at all," said Grace quietly, biting her lip. "I know my way around the Archives just as well as anyone, and Wyatt is a complete unknown. He and I can just be a couple of students, doing some research in the Archives for our latest term essay. I'm not going to get recognized there. At least… I don't think I will."

Jag shifted his feet uncomfortably, giving Grace another one of his strange looks. "I don't know if that's very smart, sis. What if the two of you get caught? Wyatt's good, sure, but if Tythas and I are there we'll have a much greater chance of escaping."

"And a much greater chance of getting caught in the first place," said Tythas decisively. "I concur with Grace. She and Wyatt will infiltrate the city and get what we need from the Archives, while Jag and I enjoy the beautiful scenery of the hills surrounding Farillyon. It's going to be dangerous, Wyatt. Are you sure you are ready to do this?"

Wyatt nodded, his mind already made up. "We need to find Apep so that I can find my family and we can prevent Necron from killing all of us. I don't know why I'm involved in all of this, but I'm going to do what I can to help. So let's get going."

Tythas nodded. "Good man. Jag, you can ride with me. We're only a few hours from Graysdale. Once we get there, we'll get some supplies and fresh horses and set out for Farillyon. I wish I could say we had time for a proper rest, but we don't. We can't risk Apep beating us to the next seal."

The four of them mounted their two remaining horses and set off toward Graysdale, their energy returning ever so slightly. They had a plan now, and that made all the difference.

Wyatt,

It's crazy to think that I've already been gone for so long. Over a month! Where does all the time go?

The time here with the Army has been absolutely crazy. You know, I'd heard a lot of things about wildlings and the Wilds in general, but it never prepared me for the way this place is. You've never seen so many trees so close together, Wyatt. It's almost suffocating, sometimes. They can navigate it somehow, but I swear the paths that we find move around when we're not looking at them. It's a very strange place.

We haven't run into any real conflict, though. Occasionally we run into a wildling scouting party, but they have only engaged us once, and I think only because they had food on them and thought we were going to take it. They fled after we killed a few of their men. Honestly, that's the most action I've seen, aside from sparring with the boys on a daily basis. Have to keep sharp, after all. I wish they would relocate us to the contested zone with the Dominion. At least the guys stationed there get their fighting in more frequently. But supposedly they want the more experienced soldiers there, since relations are so tense right now. Don't want any silly rookies starting an incident.

I've been wondering about you, though. How are things? I heard about some kind of commotion in Ven, but it's hard to get any real news this far removed from society. Fill me in, brother. Tell me all the news from home. Did you and Annie get hitched yet? If not, get going! She's cute AND makes apple pie that rivals your mother's. That's the dream, Wyatt.

We don't find a lot of anything up here, so I don't have a souvenir to send along with the mail just yet. But I'm looking for just the right thing, I promise!

Tell your mom I said hi and kick Kelsar for me next time you see him. Are you getting my letters? I still haven't heard back from you. Write me something and let me know you're alive!

Des

CHAPTER FOURTEEN

They had told Wyatt that Farillyon was magnificent. They had warned him that he had never seen as many different people over the course of his entire life as he would see in one moment in the Starlit City. But nothing could have prepared him for it. Now he knew that the various descriptions they had given were akin to someone trying to describe a master painting with a crude pencil sketch.

Farillyon was impossibly vast, an incomprehensible sea of people and stonework. Tythas said that it was so large that a walk from Lowtown all the way to the castle took an entire day. Wyatt hadn't believed him at first, but he now saw that it would probably take longer. He and Grace were slowly making their way through the street, fighting the crowds and the masses. There were so many people, just going about their business as they moved from place to place.

All around them, Wyatt could see buildings of every size, shape, and purpose. He could see the smoke coming from chimneys blocks away. He could hear the blacksmiths in the Market District hard at work crafting their goods, reminding him of distant days in Kelsar's shop. He could smell the horses and donkeys in the street. He watched as an Aquamancer patrolled the street, cleaning the waste from the roads. Above his head, Wyatt could see tall stone aqueducts that brought water to the entire city. He had no clue where the source of that water might be, but in a great center of magic and science like Farillyon, he had little trouble believing that everyone had running water.

What they had not warned him about, however, was the hostility he would feel in the streets. They had not told him that so many of the people would watch him with dark, shifting eyes, as if they were sizing him up or expecting him to attack them. How they would clutch tight to their purses, daggers, or cloaks, and keep almost solely to themselves.

As he and Grace walked, they noticed other things as well, peeking through the cracks. They saw homeless and sick people on the streets, begging for help or food or money. In most situations, people ignored them. But every so often, they would see a homeless man being beaten by a city guard for begging, or a sick child being spat on by a well-dressed woman for daring to clutch at her skirts and ask for a warm home. Wyatt was disgusted by it, but he knew that he could do nothing to help. They didn't want to draw attention to themselves, and he knew that these were just symptoms of a much greater problem.

"It was never like this before," whispered Grace as the two of them moved through the crowds. "I grew up here. This city is supposed to be beautiful. It's the Starlit City, not the city of sadness and filth!"

"It's not entirely bad," responded Wyatt halfheartedly. Truthfully, the reality of the city's obvious problems had quickly shattered the illusion of magnificence and grandeur that he had built up in his mind. Looking at these people now, at the corruption that seemed to have taken hold of everyone, he realized that he missed the simple life in Ven. Fresh air, cool wind, and nice people who didn't want to stab him and take all of his money.

"I don't understand," said Grace sadly as they fought the crowds. "I've only been gone for a few years… how could this have happened in such a short time?"

Wyatt merely shook his head, his attention more focused on the people around them than it was on their conversation. He noticed several men eyeing Grace with smiles on their faces. It made him nervous at first, but then he realized that they didn't suspect her of being a princess; they were looking at her and smiling like that for entirely different reasons. A hot rage began to grip his chest, and his hand went to his sword.

What happened to keeping a low profile? echoed Shem's voice in his mind, brushing his rage aside disinterestedly. He blinked the red away and looked down at the hilt of his sword subconsciously. Even Shem had disguised himself; the sword was no longer brilliantly crafted silver, but instead simple steel. Anyone who looked at it would see a simple military weapon, not the blade of a rich Knight or Lord.

She knows they're looking at her, echoed Shem again. *You acting chivalrous is only going to get you in trouble. If you want to protect her, protect her from harm, not the leering eyes of foolish men.*

Wyatt nodded, his rage washing away as regret for his own foolishness came over him. Trying to do anything would definitely get them noticed, and there were bound to be more men just like these all over the city. He didn't want to fight unless he had to, either. He took his eyes off of them and kept to looking for dangerous men, not deviants.

"Wyatt? Are you listening?" Grace's voice sounded from beside him, and he blinked, looking over at her. Her eyebrow was raised at him, and he suddenly realized that his inner-dialogue had caused him to miss whatever she had said and to forget whatever they had been talking about.

"Sorry," he said sheepishly, rubbing his head. "These people make me nervous. I guess I was a little lost in my own paranoia. What did you say?"

Grace pointed ahead of them, toward a towering white building several blocks away that stuck out above the smaller houses and shops around it.

"That's the Archives," she said with a nod at the building. "The upper levels are mostly tables and study areas for students. The actual storage section, where we're going to have to search for our information, is underground. Some sections are open to the public, others aren't. We, uh, may have to break into one of those restricted sections."

Wyatt responded with a simple nod, already having figured as much. The Empire wasn't going to keep its greatest secrets open to the public, after all. No doubt he and Grace would have some sneaking around to do. With any luck, the archives would be a big enough place that sneaking around the guards wouldn't be that hard to do.

As they finally reached the Archives, Wyatt noted two things that he hadn't expected. The first was two guards stationed outside the doors, momentarily accosting everyone who tried to enter the door behind them. The second was that every window on the upper levels was dressed in heavy iron bars, blocking anything from getting in or out.

"Well, that's new," muttered Grace as they stood a short distance away, appraising the guards and the rest of the building. "The city really has changed. I don't like it. Just what in the world has my father been doing?"

"Dunno," replied Wyatt, his voice low as he eyed the guards. "But I guess we should get it over with. Do you recognize either of them?"

Grace shook her head. "Nope. They both look pretty young. Judging by the insignias on their collars, I'd say fresh recruits, doing the job nobody else wants to do."

Wyatt shrugged. "I guess we don't have a choice. Let's go in."

The guards scrutinized the both of them with heavy gazes as they approached the doors of the Archives. As they drew near, the guard on the left raised an arm, blocking their passage.

"Citizens!" came the gruff, dispassionate voice of a city guard from beneath his polished helmet. "In compliance with the Imperial Protection Decree, you will be required to surrender your weapons upon entry to the Imperial Archives. Failure to do so will result in arrest for non-compliance."

Wyatt and Grace stared at him, but he let his arm drop and resumed scanning the other people in the square. In fact, as the two of them continued to stare at him, he continued to ignore them entirely, as if to imply that they no longer existed. After a few awkward seconds, Grace and Wyatt slipped between the two disgruntled guards, going slowly in case the guards changed their minds. Wyatt's mind was already racing. If he gave them his sword, would they be able to figure out that it was something more than a normal weapon?

Don't worry, Wyatt, reassured Shem's deep voice, echoing in his mind. *I can keep a low profile. They won't have any idea what I am, but you'll be without my help until you leave. So be careful, and don't do anything stupid.*

That was enough to ease most of Wyatt's tension, but he still didn't like the thought of being that far away from Shem. He had come to greatly appreciate the comforting strength that emanated from the sword, and he wasn't sure anymore that he would feel right without it.

The interior hall of the building had a window cut out on the left, revealing what appeared to be a large locker filled with people's belongings. A wide counter was pushed up to the window, where another bored-looking guard sat in attendance. At the far end of the hall stood yet another guard, keeping watch in front of a set of magnificent, finely-carved wooden doors.

"Weapon check," said the bored-looking guard flatly, not looking up from the book he was reading as he slid a ledger to the edge of the counter. Wyatt and Grace stepped up to the window, both unstrapping their belongings. Wyatt was first, and he reluctantly passed his sword through the window to the guard.

"Name?" asked the guard lazily, finally looking up as he took the sword from Wyatt and hung it on one of the hooks behind him.

"Wyatt," replied Wyatt quickly. "Wyatt, er, Garden."

"Just the sword, then?" asked the guard disinterestedly as he wrote Wyatt's name down in the ledger. "No knives, daggers, clubs, whips, crossbows, polearms, riding crops, axes, lances, throwing stars, boomerangs, staves, or siege engines?"

Wyatt stared at the guard, flabbergasted. "Um. No, just the sword. Where on earth would I keep any of that?" he asked after an awkward pause, looking down at himself.

"You'd be surprised," said the guard dryly, shifting his gaze over to Grace. "What about you?"

"Susie Crane," she said cheerfully, stepping up to the window and handing the guard a pair of daggers that Wyatt had never seen before. He found himself wondering where exactly she had been keeping them hidden, and then quickly shut down that line of thought as his face got very hot. The guard wrote her name down without interest, taking the daggers and hanging them alongside Wyatt's sword behind him.

"You two will get your things back when you're done here," said the guard, handing receipts to the both of them. "We close at sundown, and I don't care if the sun is still up, either. If we tell you we're closing, we're closing."

They both took their receipts and walked toward the guard at the far end of the hall, who asked to see their receipts. He eyed them both momentarily before turning to unlock the doors and allow them entrance. Wyatt let out a low sigh as they walked into the main part of the Archives. So far, things were going well.

The main floor of the enormous library appeared to serve largely as a directory. Large signs pointing in virtually every direction let the patrons know where they could find what they sought. The signs for this level pointed to areas for administrative offices, security rooms, and conference rooms. Wyatt could see stairs leading up to the study rooms that Grace had mentioned earlier. Judging by the size of the building, there were at least five floors above him.

But the texts themselves were below, and that was their destination. Judging by the signs at the stairwell, the complex beneath them was even larger than the building above. Wyatt's nervousness was quickly displaced by his excitement. He had never seen as many books in his whole life as the Archives promised to hold in one place. The things he could learn here, the things he could discover...

"This way," said Grace quietly as she moved ahead of him to take the lead. The two of them slipped down the stairs, trying to attract as little attention as possible. They passed two armored guards on the way down, but the two seemed preoccupied with official business and paid them little mind. Wyatt was grateful for that. Now that they were in the building, they stood little chance of getting away if they were caught. There were bound to be other Adepts inside too, ready to fight for the Empire if ordered to do so. Wyatt did not like the odds.

They followed the stairs down for several floors before finally reaching the bottom, where Grace took an immediate left, leading Wyatt down one of four main halls. Above them, a large sign reading "HISTORY" hung over the entryway, giving Wyatt an idea about where they might be headed. Looking down the hall, he could see that this major artery had several branches on either side, with signs hanging above them to notate their contents. The walls and ceiling were covered in a strange bumpy material, and the floor was carpeted and soft. The halls were all lit by heatless orbs that hung in the air every ten feet or so, bobbing merrily in place.

Grace led him further and further down the hall, and Wyatt could see the dates on the signs getting older. They were looking for something written about a time before the Empire, before the history of mankind had even truly begun. Wyatt couldn't wait. He wanted to stay down in the Archives for days and read everything he could find.

Finally, they reached the back of the hall. Here the wall was simple stone, faintly etched with a design that Wyatt didn't recognize. A lazy-looking guard stood watch, keeping an eye on the few people that drifted this far down the hall. He eyed the two of them with equal parts disinterest and suspicion as Grace and Wyatt came to an awkward halt before him. Wyatt felt a little strange, and he had no idea why Grace had brought him to the back wall of all places.

"Sir," said Grace with a sudden commanding presence that Wyatt had never seen from her before. "Captain Vilhauer sent me, from up in the Main. He said to tell you that "the eagles are in flight" and that if you didn't get your sorry ass up there as soon as possible, he'd be eating his meals using your pension."

The guard experienced a litany of emotions all at once, his face changing from annoyance to anger to abject shock. As Grace finished speaking, his jaw quite literally hung open as he gaped at her.

"I- you- we- DAMMIT!" he shouted suddenly, abandoning his post in a heartbeat and sprinting down the hall at an awkward, clanking gait. The carpet and strange walls had the odd effect of muffling the sound, and as he ran out of sight, Wyatt found very quickly that he could no longer hear the clanking.

"What was that about?" asked Wyatt after the guard was out of earshot.

Grace stepped up to the wall, ignoring his question. She studied it for a moment before nodding in approval and pressing her right hand onto one of the small, faintly-etched symbols.

The etching on the wall came to life, glowing with a warm blue light that made Wyatt blink in surprise. The markings twisted and shifted as the stone surface rippled, as if it were a pool of water into which Wyatt had just tossed a stone. After a few moments, the rippling surface parted in the middle, opening a doorway in the wall just large enough for one person to enter at a time. Even opened as it was, the rest of the wall still rippled and glowed with life.

"Hurry," whispered Grace, and she slipped through the small opening without another word. Beyond, Wyatt could only see darkness, which made him a little uneasy. Grace had obviously done this before, which made him feel a little better. He sighed, steeled himself, and stepped through the opening into the darkness beyond.

Wyatt could hear the rippling stone seal itself behind him, the sound something between a squelch and a splash. He blinked, trying to see something, anything in the dark space which he had stepped into, but he couldn't make anything out.

"Give your eyes just a few moments, Wyatt," came Grace's faint voice from beside him, nearly making him jump. "They'll adjust in a bit."

"What did you say to the guard back there that got him so spooked?" asked Wyatt in a low voice as he blinked and blinked, trying in vain to force his eyes to adjust. "Something about eagles?"

"Old guard code," she whispered back. Wyatt couldn't see her face, but he could almost sense the proud smirk on her face. "I wasn't sure if they had changed the codes, but it certainly worked."

"And what did it mean?" he asked as he looked around. Faint shapes were beginning to come into Wyatt's field of view as he adjusted to the dark. He now realized that it wasn't pitch black in here as he had originally thought. Rather, it was lit by a very dim red light which emanated from an unseen source. There were no shadows, but even after his eyes had adjusted, he found that he had to focus on what he was looking at to make it out.

"Last I knew, it was code for the castle being attacked," replied Grace. "That's the signal for every guard in the city to mobilize into one armed unit, rather than just the small separate guard units they normally divide into. I don't think they've had to use it in a very long time, but I was glad to see that they didn't change the code. That could've been awkward."

Wyatt chuckled, shaking his head as he surveyed the room. Now able to see it properly, he found that it was very unlike the rest of the Archives. The room around them was vast and cavernous, holding a number of enormous shelves. The walls around them were lined to the ceiling with cubbyholes containing scrolls and other unbound writings. At the center sat a handful of tables for study and conference. He could smell the books and scrolls without even getting close to them. The whole room smelled of aging wood and parchment, which Wyatt loved. Luckily, the room was empty of any scholars or Imperial officials.

"This is the Restricted Archive," whispered Grace, scanning the shelves. "I've only ever been in here once, and it was with my father. We were looking for a text about the history of the Dominion, when the most recent tension started building between them and the Empire."

"I think what we're looking for is going to be much older," replied Wyatt, eyeing the scrolls with a heavy sense of dread. They might be down in this cave for days and not find a single thing of use.

Grace inclined her head, walking ahead quietly and looking at one of the walls of scrolls. "Yeah, and I think we can discount the books for that reason. Binding like that didn't really become common until a few hundred years after the Empire was established. Which means we're going to be sifting through the scrolls. They are… somewhat arranged. I think."

Wyatt sighed and approached one of the other walls, looking over the rolled parchment and vellum scrolls carefully. Now that he was closer, he could see that each cubby was labeled with a small metal plate, containing a generic description about the topic of the scrolls, and the number of scrolls that the cubby would contain.

But as if things couldn't be hard enough, only some of the cubbies had the proper number of scrolls. Some had extras, and others had too few. Even worse, some of the scrolls looked so ancient that they might fall apart if Wyatt breathed on them, much less unbound and unrolled them. He hoped that whatever they might be looking for would be in better shape than some of the others.

"The scrolls are still somewhat of an unknown," said Grace quietly carefully reading every metal plate on her wall as she slowly walked the length of it. "The stories say that when nobody is in the room watching them, they rearrange themselves. Or something else does it. Either way, some of these really old things were written directly by the Six. Some even say that Adala herself wrote some of the things that are stowed away down here."

Wyatt could suddenly feel Shem's distant power buzzing in his mind, trying to offer assistance to them from afar. But the distance between them was too great, and Wyatt couldn't get any words from him, only a general sense of reassurance. Wyatt could still hear Grace talking, but he closed her out again, concentrating on whatever message Shem was trying to get to him.

Without even realizing what he was doing, Wyatt began to walk. He was focusing entirely on Shem's distant, thrumming presence. He didn't even hear Grace questioning him, trying to get his attention. He continued to walk around the Archive, his hand sliding gently along the wood cubbies. He could feel each metal plate beneath his fingertips, cold and smooth. He walked and walked, finally reaching the very back of the room. His pace slowed slightly as he furrowed his brow, tuning everything else out as he focused on Shem.

Suddenly, his fingertips stopped on a metal plate, and his feet were rooted in place. He awoke from a daze, taking a deep breath and feeling like he had just come up for air after a deep dive. He stared at the cubby, his fingers still locked onto the small metal plate, suddenly realizing what he had done. He drew his hand away, hoping to read the plate beneath them, but whatever it had once said had long ago rusted away.

"Wyatt!" hissed Grace, tugging harshly on the back of his shirt. "What in the name of the Six are you doing?"

Wyatt shook his head. "Sorry," he whispered, trying to clear his head. "Shem was trying to reach out to me, and... I don't even know, Grace. I just started walking, I guess, and I ended up here. Whatever he wanted, he's gone now. But I think he led me to this cubby."

The cubby itself was stuffed with scrolls of all shapes and sizes. Wyatt sighed and began scooping all of them out, wrapping his arms around them carefully as he pulled. To his surprise, many of them were several feet long, and he realized that the cubbies were much larger than he had thought. He stepped back with his arms full of parchment and walked to the closest table, carefully setting all of them down. All in all, there looked to be nearly thirty scrolls of varying shape and age.

For the next hour, the two of them read through every one. Six of them were written in a language that neither Grace nor Wyatt even recognized, so they set those aside for later. Ten of the scrolls featured ancient versions of popular children's tales; Vardish, a clever trickster who Wyatt had sung about as a child, was written of as Vaerdishe, a commoner who learned that he had dragon blood and fought with the Six against the monster Uresh, the most horrible of the dragons. And that was only one; each of those scrolls wrote about fabled heroes as if they were real people. After reading so many, Wyatt was starting to question everything he thought he knew about history.

"Hey," said Grace quietly, snapping Wyatt out of his reverie and spreading a scroll out in front of him. "This... this might be something, Wyatt. I don't know for sure, but..."

Wyatt moved around the table next to her so that he could read it properly. Over her shoulder, he could see a simple song written in flowing, loopy handwriting. It was short, and reading over it, Wyatt realized that it was a song he already knew.

> Bright *Fire sleeps in sulfurous heights*
> *Protected by her dangerous art*
> *Fair Earth rests within deep and dark*
> *Stone and ore make up her heart*
>
> *Far beneath the crushing waves*
> *Quiet Water slumbers in depths unseen*
> *At the highest point is Air entombed*
> *Through storm and cloud, gaze still keen*
>
> *Good Life himself, great king of all*
> *Lies beneath most regal feet*
> *All to keep poor Death at bay,*
> *Locked in Black, his wrath so sweet*

The two of them stared at the song for a while, reading and rereading it many times. This version, Wyatt realized, was a lot different than the song he had learned as a child. The version he had sung when he was young didn't speak of sleeping or resting, but instead was about the Adepts and their different powers. This... this was certainly something different.

"At the highest point is Air entombed," read Grace carefully, staring at the scroll as if she were trying to see something she couldn't. "So it's on top of a mountain?"

Wyatt nodded, running a hand through his hair. "Maybe, yeah. There're a lot of mountains around the Empire, but don't really know my geography this far west. What do you think?"

Grace continued to study the scroll. "The highest point... well, the highest charted mountain is the Mount of Light, to the northwest of here. That... would actually make a lot of sense."

Wyatt scanned the scroll for something else that might tell them more about it. There was no author named, symbol of penmanship, no date, and no other markings to speak of. Even stranger, the parchment initially looked to be fairly new. But when Wyatt leaned in closer, he noticed that the ink was moving slightly, quivering as if it were tense and itching to spring.

Suddenly, the words on the page uncoiled like snakes, wriggling in every direction for the edge of the paper. Grace and Wyatt both instinctively recoiled, and that brief moment where they removed their hands from it was enough. Cracks formed along the surface of the paper, and within seconds, it began to break apart. The paper separated into hundreds of little pieces which blew away on an unfelt breeze, separating in every direction and scattering into different cubbies.

The two of them stared mutely at the space on the table where the scroll had been for several moments. Wyatt blinked once, and then again, before looking to Grace. He'd never seen anything like that, and in spite of the fact that they'd just lost the scroll, he let out a low chuckle.

"Magic," he breathed, trying not to laugh, "is incredible. Have you ever seen anything like that?"

Grace shook her head. "No, no I haven't. I guess the stories were true. But I think we have our lead. The Mount of Light. That's going to be... complicated."

Wyatt waved a hand. "We should get out of here. We can worry about the next step when we're back with the others. Right now, we need to get out of the Archives and out of this city without attracting any more attention to ourselves."

The two of them made their way back to the strange wall, and suddenly a thought occurred to Wyatt. He held up a hand, halting Grace.

"Um, Grace..." he said, unease creeping up his back like thousands of tiny spiders. "We came in this way, and we got past that guard, but... won't he be waiting on the other side for us?"

Grace stared at him for a moment. Evidently, neither of them had bothered to consider that possibility. He suddenly felt like an idiot, cursing himself for allowing this to happen. They might have to get in a fight to get out. They might have to hurt an innocent guard who was just doing his job.

But before Grace could muster a response, the wall ahead of them rippled like water as the runes upon it flared to life, illuminating them in blue. Wyatt and Grace leapt to either side of the portal, pressing themselves against the cubbies and staring at each other in mute alarm.

The wall opened. Through the portal, a stooped, elderly man stepped into the room. He was clad in fine silken robes and many rings adorned his fingers. His face was equal parts wrinkled and sharp, and his thin graying hair was combed straight back. Despite his advanced age, he carried himself with an air of importance and confidence. Wyatt could feel his presence as well as see it; this little old man was obviously a very, very powerful Adept. Grace raised a finger to her lips and stared at Wyatt intensely. He gave a single, slow nod in response. He wasn't going to say a word.

The portal closed behind the old man, leaving them once again in the faint red light. The ancient Adept dusted himself off, blinking a few times before turning to look directly at Wyatt.

"I have been wondering where the two of you had gotten yourselves," he said quietly, his voice surprisingly strong considering his age. "You have the guards in an uproar, you know. Intruders in the building, although they couldn't actually find you. Of course, only an Adept could enter a restricted room. Only a member of the royal family or Adept Council could enter this particular restricted room."

Grace noiselessly crept up behind the man, looking like she were ready to pounce on him like a cat. Before she could reach him, however, the old man spoke again.

"I do not recommend it, Princess," he said quietly, still looking at Wyatt. "I do not need to see you to know that you are there. I can feel you from here."

She sighed, and the tension left her body. "Mugalo," she said, a hint of venom in her voice. "Am I to assume that there's a legion of guards waiting for us on the other side of the door?"

The older man chuckled, his face wrinkling into a smile. "Not at all. They're still scouring the building for you, but I do not think they know who you are. For now, you two are free to do as you will. My happening upon this room was pure coincidence. Why, though, would long-lost Princess Il'Vir and a heretofore unknown Pyromancer be lurking about the Imperial Archives, with danger so close at hand?"

"I'm an Aeromancer," replied Wyatt evenly, still unsure of Mugalo. He remembered Tythas mentioning something about him, but couldn't quite recall what. He could tell already that the elder Adept wrapped himself in secrets and deception. It was unsettling to be able to see that about the man, while knowing nothing else beside it.

"Are you now?" said the old man, cocking his head and leaning in a little closer, looking puzzled. "You do so smell like a Pyromancer. Perhaps my old nose is just going bad after all of these years. But my question stands. Just what exactly are the two of you doing down here, of all places?"

Grace stepped past Mugalo to stand next to Wyatt. "Research, Mugalo. An independent study. And we've found what we needed, so we're going to be leaving now."

Mugalo gave another chuckle, a sound that made Wyatt feel even more uneasy. "Again, Princess, I wouldn't recommend it," he said with mirth, looking back to the door for a moment. "While there isn't a legion of guards standing outside, they are still looking for you. And they have very good memories, my dear. If you go as you are now, you will certainly be captured."

Grace opened her mouth to retort, but Mugalo held up a hand, cutting her off. "If, however, you were to use one of the secret, long-forgotten tunnels that lead out of the belly of the Archives and into other parts of the city, you might just escape without notice. That, my dear, is entirely up to you."

"What are you talking about?" asked Grace sharply, looking around the room. "There aren't any ways out of here other than the door."

"That you know of," responded Mugalo with a sly, almost reptilian smile. "I, however, possess a knowledge of this city's secrets which is unparalleled. I could tell you how to escape."

Wyatt and Grace both eyed him with distrust, but he waved a hand at them dismissively. "Come now, if I wanted the two of you taken, I would have merely subdued you both myself. The exit is at the back of the chamber, hidden behind the cubbies. Find the slot labeled "Unlikely Histories" and press on the iron plate. The doorway will open, and you'll come out somewhere in Lowtown, amidst what I imagine to be a large amount of dung. I haven't used that exit in quite some time."

"We need our equipment," said Wyatt suddenly, thinking of the sword that he left with the guards as alarm flared within him.

"Ah," said Mugalo, inclining his head as he fished around on his belt. He unfastened a small pouch, and wordlessly he drew an impossibly long roll of canvas from within it. Wyatt blinked several times, but his eyes were not deceiving him. The old man winked at him as he set the bundle on the floor and fastening the pouch once more at his waist.

"I took the liberty of confiscating everything you signed in," said the old man happily. "Which, by the way, was very curious and certainly made this entire endeavor worthwhile. My boy, you really shouldn't leave a magnificent item like that just lying around. In the wrong hands, it could kill all of us."

Wyatt unrolled the canvas and handed Grace her daggers before hooking the sword once more to the baldric at his hip. "I'll keep that in mind," he said flatly as worry crept up into him. If Mugalo had already realized what the sword was...

"Now, I'm going to go about my reading," said the ancient old man with a nod at them. "I suggest that the two of you vanish before any other prying eyes enter the room. There's no telling what the others would do if they caught you down here. Apostacy is a high crime in the Empire, young man. Be sure you work on that."

Grace grabbed Wyatt by the wrist and led him to the back of the chamber without another word to the elderly Adept. They found the section that he had suggested, and Wyatt pressed his thumb against the iron plate. He felt it give slightly and they heard a "click" as the wall shifted. Grace pushed on against it, and the perfectly balanced door swung inward on a silent hinge, revealing a dark passage and tall stairs beyond.

The two of them looked at one another for just a moment before Wyatt took the lead, ducking into the passageway, his hand on his sword. Grace followed without another look back.

Mugalo smiled as he watched the secret door swing back into place. His old eyes had seen many things, but today, he saw his salvation. The pieces were all falling into place, just as he had always known they would. If she had been with anyone else, he would've sold the sneaky little Princess back to her father without another thought. But the arrival of that boy and his sword were the signal he'd been waiting for. The boy could not yet be held back, being far too important to Mugalo. He would have to be tested.

No, Mugalo had to let them go. And now, he had work to do.

CHAPTER FIFTEEN

The space on the other side of the door was so dark it was almost suffocating. It was a kind of tangible darkness, so thick that it pressed down upon anyone unfortunate enough to be inside of it with unrelenting force. It was making Wyatt nervous.

They shuffled about in the dark for a few moments before a shimmering light flickered into view, revealing Grace's outstretched arm. Her hand was open and raised up toward the luminescent ball that had appeared above them. Wyatt was grateful that control over light rested within the domain of a Vitamancer, as the last time he'd been caught deep underground in the dark, it was only the wind that had saved him. And there was no wind in this place.

The soft light of the orb illuminated a small room with no doors of any kind. There were no books or scrolls here, either. The floors, walls, and ceiling were all unmarked, rough stone, giving the room a very basic look. As best as Wyatt could tell, it was a dusty stone closet, not at all a secret exit.

Fear bubbled up within Wyatt. Had Mugalo locked the two of them inside this small room so that he could call for help and turn them over to the Empire? Was he about to be dragged off to the castle with a bag over his head, a collar around his neck, and chains binding his wrists?

"Look," whispered Grace, pointing to the far wall. "It's a ladder, Wyatt."

Wyatt blinked and looked at the spot where she was pointing. It was barely visible in the dim light, but Wyatt could see what she was pointing to. A narrow gap had been carved into the rear wall where a number of metal rungs were slotted. The ladder led straight up into a small hole in the ceiling, just enough space for someone to crawl up into what was hopefully a secluded and seldom-traveled alleyway. Relief flooded through him as he nodded his agreement, walking forward to inspect the ladder.

"It certainly hasn't been used in a while," he observed, running a fingertip over one of the steel bars and removing a thick layer of dust. "I wonder how many people even know about this."

"Not many, I would bet," said Grace as she stepped up next to him. She peered up the hole above them, trying to see further into the darkness. The orb she'd created bobbed toward them and floated lazily up the chute, shining light into the very narrow space. Considering they were several stories underground, the ladder was expectedly tall. Wyatt could just make out what looked like a trap door at the very top, but it was hard to tell from so far below.

"You first," said Grace, motioning to the ladder. "I have no clue what might be on top of that door, but if it's hard to move you're going to have a better chance of getting it open than I am. You're a lot stronger than me."

Wyatt nodded and grabbed a rung, quickly starting up the tall ladder. He could hear Grace following close behind him, so he kept his pace steady and even. Coated in a thick layer of dust, the rungs were all perilously hard to get a good grip on, so Wyatt had to take a moment with each step to brush them off. The last thing he needed was to fall all the way back down this chute.

It took some time, but after a great deal of pausing and dusting, Wyatt reached the top of the ladder. He inspected the trapdoor as best he could, as his own shadow was blocking out most of the light from the orb below him.

"Send that thing up here, would you?" he called to Grace, finding a reasonably comfortable way to perch on the ladder. "This door is… funny."

Wyatt heard her mumble a reply and the ball of light bobbed up next to him, momentarily dazzling him. He did his best not to look directly at it and squinted at the door, trying to make sense of what he was seeing.

Deep runes were etched into the oaken trapdoor and the dark iron bindings that held it together. For as old as this door probably was, it appeared to be perfectly preserved and still as strong as the day it had been made. He knocked on it lightly, receiving deep, muffled thumps in return. The door was just as strong and thick as it looked. He'd never be able to force it open normally, much less from an awkward position.

He studied the door further. It had no lock, no handle, nor mechanism of any kind that would allow it to be opened. From his place atop the narrow stone chute, it looked less like a trapdoor and more like the stopper on a tall bottle, meant to keep whatever was inside from spilling out.

"What do you make of this?" asked Wyatt, calling down to Grace below him. He pressed himself close to the ladder, trying to give her as much space as possible to see. She climbed up a bit closer and stuck her head out to see past him.

"It looks like runework," she replied after a few moments, doing her best to study the door from her position. "Which means it was made by an inscriber, which also unfortunately means that I know nothing about it. Inscription is a lost art. There are still a handful of people who know the basic craft, but something like this is well beyond that. I don't know, Wyatt. Maybe we should turn back."

Wyatt reached out a hand and touched the door. As his fingertips brushed against the cold iron banding, the runes on the entire door flared to life with a steady blue light. He tried to make sense of them, but they may as well have been a picture drawn by a child. They had no discernible pattern or meaning that he could detect.

Wyatt closed his eyes, pressing his hand more firmly into the door. If he couldn't read the runes, he would do his best to feel them. His breathing slowed as he narrowed his focus, concentrating on the connection between the door and his hand. He could feel his pulse thumping in his fingertips, thrumming against the door like a rhythmic drum beat. Whispering voices danced in his ears, speaking unintelligible words as he drew further into the door.

Blood.

His eyes snapped open as the voices spoke one clear word that crashed through him like thunder. He started, nearly losing his grip. Clutching the ladder like he was caught in a thunderstorm, he took several moments to try to slow his beating heart. He glanced down, and upon seeing Grace's puzzled face, relaxed a bit and felt exceptionally foolish.

"Don't ask," he said hastily, shaking his head. "Just pass me one of your daggers, would you? I have an idea."

She gave him an odd look for a moment, but reserved any questions she might've had, wordlessly pulling a dagger from its sheath and passing it to him handle-first. He adjusted his footing, looping his left arm around one of the rungs to steady his balance while he held the knife in his right hand. He sighed, shaking his head, and made a small cut in his left palm, drawing blood from the meat of his hand as he winced in pain.

"Magic and blood," he muttered, more to himself than anything. "This is the second time. What is with these people? Couldn't I just give the door a secret handshake?" He could feel Shem's amusement rolling out of the sword, but the cat didn't say anything. Lacking any better option, Wyatt wiped the blade off on his shirt and passed it back down to Grace, who was eyeing him with deep bewilderment. He shrugged in response.

After she took the blade, Wyatt took grip of the ladder with his right arm and secured himself firmly in place. He took a deep breath, trying to keep his mind from imagining all the horrible things it was imagining as he steeled himself. After a moment, he plunged his hand upward, smearing the blood against the wood and iron.

He felt a slight tug at his navel, the feeling he normally got when using his power. He watched in stunned disbelief as his blood swam over the door, flowing into the runes as if it were alive and congealing in the carved spaces in the door. The light within the runes warped from blue to crimson, and suddenly, the whole door flashed with a bright red light.

Wyatt let out a startled noise and looked away just a split-second too late. He was caught off completely off guard and looked right into the door as it flared to life, dazzling him completely. He blinked and blinked, trying to clear the frustrating spots from his sight. He could suddenly hear noises from above them as the dismal smell of Farillyon's streets rolled over him.

"The door..." said Grace from below him, sounding more than a bit stunned. "It's just... gone..."

The infuriating glowing spots cleared from Wyatt's eyes enough for him to see again, and he could see that she was telling the truth. The door had vanished entirely, revealing an open hole in to the world above. Wyatt could just make out the walls of tall buildings as he peered up through the opening.

The two of them scrambled through the hole, climbing to their feet, ready for an entire armada to be waiting for them on the other side.

But there was no armada. They were in an alley, in a narrow space behind several stacks of wooden crates. Completely hidden from the street, this was as good a place as any to step out of a hidden hole in the ground from a forbidden, secret underground room.

"Wyatt," said Grace suddenly, sounding a little breathless. Wyatt turned around to find her pointing at the spot the two of them had crawled out from, but instead of the hole in the ground they had exited, there was only a seamless section of cobbled alley street.

The two of them stared at it for a few moments before Wyatt let out a low whistle, shaking his head.

"A magical, secret door that requires blood to open," he said with a grin that he couldn't help. "That's very fairytale-ish, but I think at this point I'm starting to expect it."

Grace smirked at him. "Magic, mayhem, and adventure. How do you feel, farmer? Ready to quit?"

He laughed, shaking his head again and turning to the crates that were blocking them from the rest of the alley. "Well, it worked out in our favor, I guess. Mugalo didn't try to stop us."

"That still worries me," said Grace, shaking her head. "He's the man who betrayed Jag and Tythas to my father. Even when I was younger, he always gave me the creeps. He's my father's chief adviser, and was chief adviser to my father's father, too. He always reminded me of a snake. His eyes are too beady and clever. Getting older has only made him shiftier. He likes to play the part of the doddering old man, but he's the furthest thing from it."

"Yeah, I got that impression too," Wyatt said as he tested a foothold on one of the crates, nodding with satisfaction. We can climb up here, I think. I don't know how well these are balanced, so I'll go first. If they all fall, I'll have a better chance. I'll hopefully be able to call the wind and stop them from crushing me."

"Gallant and optimistic," said Grace, sarcasm dripping from her voice. "Alright, Mr. Hero. Get climbing, then."

Wyatt shook his head with a smirk and scaled the crates with ease, hopping from the top of them down onto the street below. Mugalo's unlikely assistance had improved his mood greatly. Now that they were out under the sky and he was reunited with the sword, he didn't feel nearly as uneasy about getting away.

Grace landed next to him, barely making a sound as she came to a crouch with the landing. The two of them surveyed the alley together, still ready for an ambush.

"Any ideas where we might be?" Wyatt asked, glancing toward Grace on his left.

"Not a clue," she replied, looking up at the side wall of the Archives. "The Archives is shaped like a big cross, so it's hard to say which side we came out on. I won't have a good idea until we get out into a proper street. But it seems like we're in the clear, Wyatt."

He nodded and motioned for her to take the lead. "Let's get moving, then. You can go first, since you know where you're going. It looks good, but I'm still nervous. Let's just get out of here."

She nodded and started off ahead of him. Wyatt went to follow, but stopped as the hair on the back of his neck prickled. The street was roughly forty feet in front of them, and from where he stood, it appeared to be empty. He glanced back, around the pile of crates. That street was empty, too. The sword at his hip gave a sudden, rough jerk, and alarm found its way into Wyatt's body, making him tense up. He reached out wordlessly and grabbed Grace's arm. She looked back, opening her mouth, but he cut her off with a quick motion of his hand. At that, he pointed out to the street ahead of them, and then behind them.

She looked ahead for a moment, and then to the other street. She seemed to realize what he was pointing out and ducked backward to crouch next to him by the crates once more.

"What do we do?" she hissed, one hand going to her daggers automatically. "They're obviously waiting for us."

Wyatt pointed up. "We fly," he said, although he wasn't entirely sure he'd be able to carry the both of them. If he could, it was definitely going to be slow progress. But he didn't really have any other options.

Grace nodded, looking very nervous. She slipped behind Wyatt and wrapped one arm over his shoulder, the other under his arm, making a tight knot around his chest and clasping her hands together tightly. The flowery smell of her hair washed over him, and just for a moment, he forgot what he was doing. But he caught his wandering mind and focused, knowing that he had much more important things to think about.

Wyatt called his power, aware of Shem's steadfast presence in his mind aiding him as he did. The wind picked up around them with ease, and a familiar calm flooded through him. Touching the wind as he was, he felt like he was reuniting with his oldest, strongest friend.

Wind wrapped tightly around the two of them, sending Grace's red hair into a fiery dance. Her head looked a bit like a campfire. Wyatt tensed, ready to leap, and asked if she was ready. She bit her lip and nodded.

With that, the two of them jumped into the air together, just as a strong gust blew through the alleyway, carrying them up and forward at a respectable speed.

They flew out over the rooftops, coming out over the street that they had avoided running into. Wyatt could see dozens of city guards below them, armed and scouring the streets, obviously looking for them. One of the guards looked up, pointing at Grace and Wyatt and shouting something to his comrades.

Suddenly, Wyatt's grip on the wind faltered as another gust blew in direct opposition to him and Grace. It stalled their rise and suddenly,

Wyatt found himself fighting to stay aloft. On a nearby rooftop in front of them, Wyatt could see an older man dressed in decorative robes, his arms outstretched.

Wyatt could see the wind wrapped around the robed man, too, and his expression soured. Another Aeromancer, who no doubt had way more experience than Wyatt. They had been prepared. Mugalo must have warned them after all.

"Grace, you're going to have to let go of me!" he shouted suddenly, struggling against his foe's power. The two of them were virtually stationary in the sky as the opposing winds battled one another. "I can't beat him with you on my back!"

Grace squeezed tighter. "What do you mean, let go of you?! In case you forgot, I'm not an Aeromancer, and we're eighty feet above the ground!"

Wyatt's face scrunched up with concentration. "Just trust me! I'll take care of you, I promise!"

Grace screamed something that sounded suspiciously like a curse word, and a moment later, flung her arms open and kicked off of him like a squirrel leaping off of a tree.

From deep within him, Wyatt called more power than he had ever tapped into before. He could feel it roar out of him like a tidal wave, and he knew that whatever he was about to do might kill him.

As if Aeris herself had swept Grace into her arms, an unstoppable gale blew over the city, catching the young Vitamancer and spiriting her away faster than Wyatt had believed possible. He watched in bewilderment as what appeared to be a small tornado appeared beneath her and carried Grace away toward the edge of the city. He could see the wind wrapped protectively around her, almost like it was trying to protect her.

The other Aeromancer tried to reach out and grab her, but his power was no match for whatever Wyatt had wrought. Relief flooded through him as the wind carried her over the city wall and out of sight.

He gripped the hilt of the sword in his hand as he focused his power, breaking the other Aeromancer's grip and making to follow her. But once again, the wind around him destabilized. He looked back to the roof, and dread hit him as he saw two more men beside his original foe, their arms outstretched as well. Their combined power buffeted him from all directions as he fell, preventing him from being able to grip the air.

As quickly as he could, Wyatt twisted and drew the sword. He felt Shem's power as surely as his own, and the two of them together managed to call one more gale at the last moment that slowed his descent. He landed roughly on the stone amidst a sea of armed guards, his weapon drawn. Theirs were drawn, as well, and he knew that there were at least twenty swords pointed at him.

"Apostate!" called one of the guards, stepping forward with his sword drawn. He had officer's wings pinned to his collar, distinguishing him as the commander of this particular unit. "Drop your weapon and submit to Imperial Law!"

Wyatt grinned at the officer as that defiant little monster in his chest woke up. He knew what he was going to have to do.

"Shem!" he yelled, still smirking at the officer with an almost manic look in his eyes. "I hope you're ready!"

The soldiers all blinked at him, trying to decipher some hidden message within whatever he had just said. The officer shifted his feet and opened his mouth to say something else, but paused as he caught the sound of something that was slowly coming into the foreground.

It was the sound of roaring. It sounded distant and distorted at first, but as the tense seconds passed, the guards seemed to realize it was coming closer. They all started nervously looking around the alleyway, forgetting for a moment that Wyatt was there. After a few seconds, the sound was loud enough to vibrate the pebbles lying in the street. Wyatt thought his ears were going to burst, but suddenly, the noise stopped.

A great ring of fire blossomed into view above them, and through that ring leapt a great lion. But it was no ordinary lion. His eyes glowed with a blazing yellow light, and as he roared with bestial fury, his mane flared to life, a mane of fire and lightning.

At that, chaos broke out. Some soldiers charged, intent on killing Wyatt and whatever demon he had summoned to slay them. Others, perhaps realizing they were not paid nearly enough to face certain death, fled in abject terror.

Wyatt met the officer's sword with his own steel as electricity from Wyatt's own fingers crackled along his weapon. As their blades connected, the power surged, slamming into the officer and blasting him backward into his own men to lie there in a smoking heap. Wyatt spun, deflecting other swords and blasting soldiers aside with ease. He was lost in the battle, not even aware of the toll that using this kind of power was taking on his body. Dimly, he was aware of Shem's hulking form, tearing into the straggling soldiers with merciless, hungry intent. It wasn't long before those who were still left standing turned and fled, realizing that Wyatt was no ordinary Adept.

Then, without warning, Wyatt found himself in a sudden, painful silence. Shem paced behind him, his claws and muzzle stained with blood. Wyatt surveyed the damage, that familiar fear of killing innocents waking within him. But as he looked around, he realized that Shem had only wounded his prey, and Wyatt hadn't killed anyone either.

The three Aeromancers floated warily down around them, falling slowly down like drifting leaves. They landed several feet away from both Wyatt and Shem, keeping distance on both sides. All of them looked nervous.

"Apostate," said the one in fancy robes quietly, raising a hand as a stalling gesture. "We want no more blood. Please, come quietly with us and you will not be hurt."

"You'll just be collared like a dog," growled Shem, his booming voice echoing throughout the street with unearthly strength. "Wyatt, do not be afraid to fight. I am with you."

Wyatt leveled his sword at the eldest Aeromancer, ignoring the cat. "You came into this expecting an easy fight," he said hotly as lightning crackled along his sword. "What you didn't expect was fifty of the Emperor's men to be beaten so soundly by a teenager and a cat. So my suggestion? You three scurry back to your castle and tell your Emperor that I've got better things to do than kill my own kind. We're on the same team, even if you're all too stupid to realize it."

The elder Aeromancer held his gaze, although he still had an air of nervousness about him. "We are not the only Adepts here, boy," he spat, scowling at Wyatt. "Besting normal soldiers is one thing, but several experienced Adepts at once? Not likely. Come with us if you would like to survive the day."

Wyatt sent Shem a mental signal, and he felt the cat's agreement. He pulled at his power again, hoping that they were too oblivious to notice what he was about to do.

"That," he said with solemn confidence, "is not going to happen."

Shem leapt just as Wyatt's power called the lightning above them. A full bolt of lightning snarled through the air, slamming into the Aeromancer behind Wyatt. Wyatt felt his resistance rise at the last second, but Wyatt's bolt shattered that barrier with ease and slammed the man into the ground with unbound fury.

The elder Aeromancer raised his hands and shouted, pointing them toward the airborne Shem. Lightning snaked out from them, crashing into the cat. But strangely, it continued to flow into Shem, seemingly with no ill effect. He narrowed his eyes in concentration as Shem continued to bound forward toward him. His focus changed to alarm as he realized that the cat was absorbing his lightning. But before he could act, the cat was upon him.

It only took one crushing bite for the Adept to crumple. Shem spat out a mouthful of bloody robes and turned to face the last remaining Adept menacingly. He roared again, releasing the energy that had been channeled into him. The electricity blasted outward, and the Adept staggered backward, caught off guard.

As Shem stalked toward him, the Adept realized his mistake and turned to flee. Shem made to follow him, growling and preparing to leap. But Wyatt was ready for it, reacting in time.

"Enough," he said quietly, his mind clamping down on Shem like a firm hand holding a leash. Shem growled again, but instead of following after the fleeing Aeromancer, he padded back over to Wyatt.

"We've done enough damage already, I think," said Wyatt quietly as he sheathed his sword. He walked over to the remaining man, the Aeromancer whom he had called lightning down on. Crouching down, Wyatt found the man's neck and pressed down with two fingers. Wyatt felt an unsteady, faint pulse... and then felt it cease as the man died beneath his fingers. He watched the body for a long time, silent, shocked. He got to his feet with a sigh, shaking his head at how unnecessary it had all been. These guards were just doing their job. They weren't his enemy. He swallowed, pushing the pain and the sickness he felt away. He didn't need it right now.

But Wyatt had a job to do, too. More than ever, looking at the decaying capital around him, Wyatt knew how important that was.

"You fought well," observed Shem, padding over to Wyatt and inclining his great, furry head. "I am proud. Not the farmer you were when I found you." The swirling fire around his mane had greatly diminished, looking just like normal fur. In fact, the cat looked almost entirely like a normal lion would now, save the eerie luminescent eyes that Wyatt had come to know so well.

Wyatt gave him a wry smile, reaching up to scratch the cat behind the ear. "Maybe you just didn't look close enough."

The cat gave a low, rumbling growl. "Maybe."

"I think we should get out of here before they send more soldiers or Adepts," Wyatt said sadly, motioning at the unconscious, groaning pile of bodies around them. "I don't feel like fighting any more. So back in the sword, Shem."

The cat nodded again, touching Wyatt's forehead with his nose. The great beast's whole form blazed with light, and for a moment, Wyatt's vision swirled with fire as a warm sensation rolled over his entire body. His senses went away entirely and just for a moment, he knew only the light of the cat.

He blinked, his breath coming in a deep, desperate gasp. He was still standing in the street, the limp forms of several Imperial soldiers lying all around him. Shem was nowhere to be seen.

"Impressive," came a voice from behind him. Wyatt groaned and turned, his hand drawing his blade again. Striding down the street toward him was a tall, thin man in robes of dark blue. His hair was dark and long, tied back in a messy tail. Gray kissed his temples. His skin was ghostly pale, a stark contrast to the dark colors of his clothes. Most concerning of all, Wyatt could see bands of flowing water wrapped around his forearms, swirling between his fingers like living gauntlets. He bore no marks of rank or insignias of nobility, but Wyatt could tell even from across the street that he was no ordinary Adept.

"I hope you aren't here to stop me," said Wyatt wearily, adopting a battle stance. He could feel Shem in the sword, distantly wanting to be let out again. But the energy had already been spent, and the cat wouldn't be able to help him anymore. Sweat dripped into Wyatt's eyes, making him blink.

"I'm afraid so," said the pale Aquamancer quietly, coming to a halt a ways down the deserted street. "You see, they only let me out of the castle in very specific situations. Most of the time, I'm locked away underground, kept in a special room completely devoid of moisture." Some of the fallen soldiers were coming to, crawling or staggering away into the safety of alleys or open buildings. A cold wind blew down the street as the two Adepts sized each other up.

Wyatt blinked, staring at the Adept in puzzlement. "Why?"

"Because I'm of mixed blood," he said simply, now pacing slightly as he watched Wyatt with hard eyes. "Aquamancer and Necromancer. Neither side really wanted me. I was not enough like one and too much like the other for either side of my family to claim me. They chained me up and stoked my hatred like a flame. When troublesome scamps like you make their lives harder, they let me out and let me do what I do best."

Wyatt couldn't help but feel pity for the elder Adept, but maintained his distance. There was a madness in the Aquamancer's eyes, a madness that contorted his face into a mask of fury. Wyatt could feel it in the air, and he knew that he'd never faced a foe quite like this one.

The Aquamancer reached up, lifting up the front side of a stone collar that had been hidden by his robes. "This is a different kind of collar than the usual ones. I'm told that it was made by the Emperor himself. If I get too far from the castle, it tightens. If I try to run, it'll squeeze until my head comes off."

Wyatt swallowed, trying to find something to say to keep the crazed man at bay. But he had no words for something like this. He had nothing to say that could make the man's circumstances better.

"So I do what they say," he continued with a dry laugh, still pacing as the water around his wrists began to coil around his upper arms, resembling icy snakes. "If I do, I get a little sunshine and they let me release some of my aggression."

Wyatt raised his sword.

"I'm sorry," he said simply, holding the man's gaze firm. "I know that it means nothing to you, but I really am. If I survive this, I'm going to do my best to find a way to help you."

The Aquamancer laughed, the sound cold and harsh and devoid of any emotion. "I would certainly like to see that, little Aeromancer. But you have no idea what they are capable of."

Wyatt heard it before he saw it. From the aqueducts above them, water rose in great tendrils, snaking down from the sky toward him with lethal intent. It was the sound of rushing water that saved him as he looked up just in time.

Instinctively, he pulled at his power yet again, calling up a great and mighty gust of wind that he threw toward the Adept like an enormous fist. The stabbing tentacles of living water were caught by the blast, broken into thousands of droplets that scattered in every direction, coating the entire street in spray.

The Aquamancer was already running, his face a jagged snarl as he leapt at Wyatt with both hands. He held no weapon, but his fingers were open like the claws of a cat as he leapt.

Wyatt remembered his lessons with Yasmir, his memories of the daily beatings he'd received still fresh in his mind. He remembered what Yasmir had done, his body already moving before he realized what he was doing.

He met the leaping Adept with a boot that connected squarely to the man's sternum, taking the air from his lungs in a great rush. Wyatt misjudged his momentum, though, and the both of them went tumbling apart as Wyatt felt something in his knee flare with pain.

The Aquamancer tumbled backward, coming to his feet with a dark scowl as he coughed and wheezed. Wyatt also got to his feet, trying to test the damage to his knee without alerting his enemy. He could put some weight on it still, but he wasn't going to be able to run while it was in this condition. He wrapped a tight glove of air around his entire body, making him feel lighter and offering protection from the rushing waters.

"You're not as wide-eyed and young as they made it seem," remarked the man between deep, choking breaths. "I'll have to… adjust my approach, it seems."

Wyatt sighed, raising his sword. He said nothing, his eyes set with grim determination.

The water that Wyatt had blown apart around the street came rushing back, settling around them and filling the street. To Wyatt's astonishment, the water held itself in place, gathering to a depth of several inches. A narrow area around Wyatt remained dry, the water pushed back by the wind that swirled around him. Everywhere else, he was surrounded.

Swords, hands, claws, spears, and knives of water all surged to life around him, grabbing, stabbing, and slashing at him with quick, deadly efficiency. He threw a hand out, sending gusts of wind out around in all directions. Anything that managed to come through the wind was cut apart with his sword. He danced backward, lopping off hands and cutting tendrils in half. As he separated them from the rest of the water, they briefly lost shape, falling back into the water below them.

He wasn't going to be able to keep this up, he realized. He frantically spun and leapt around the street, trying to get away from the water, but it was all around him. He had no escape.

Suddenly, the Aquamancer was there, catching him completely off guard. Wyatt saw horribly pale hands reaching out for him. His free hand batted them away and sent wind blasting into the Aeromancer's torso like an angry fist.

Their hands, just for a moment, came into contact. That moment was apparently enough; Wyatt's entire free arm went numb as he felt his very essence pulled from his body through the small spot where their skin had touched. As the Aquamancer tumbled back once more, Wyatt gasped and blinked as his vision went hazy.

The water calmed momentarily as the Aquamancer flashed Wyatt an eerily white grin. "You should never let a Necromancer touch you. Didn't anyone tell you that?"

Wyatt's panic was now rising in full effect. His free arm, the one that had touched the pale man's skin, wasn't working right. He was trying to shake it and clench his fist in an effort to get the feeling back, but he was rewarded only with awkward, jerky flopping as his muscles failed to coordinate with one another.

Wyatt, came Shem's voice in his mind, although from a great distance. *You need to go. You've done enough. Run.*

That only made him angry. He was going to win this fight.

Wyatt reached deep within himself once more, deeper than he had ever had to reach before. Distantly, some small part of him was aware of how tired he was becoming, but he didn't care. He grasped the inferno in his heart that he had come to know as his power. He drew on it again, knowing that he would only be able to do this one more time. It would have to be enough.

Thunder boomed in the sky above them, rattling the windows as lightning flashed. Steady rain began to fall as the clouds darkened and swirled. Wyatt stared at his foe, his eyes steady and hard. He raised his sword once more, letting his other arm hang limp at his side.

The Aquamancer laughed again, his eyes manic. "You fight an Aquamancer and give him more water? Boy, are you really that stupid?"

Wyatt held his ground as thunder boomed again, reverberating in his chest. More rain fell, and after a few moments Wyatt could barely see his foe through the thick sheet of water. It fell all around him, but he held his grip on the tight bubble of air around him, keeping him completely dry. Rain was all he could see, all he could hear. He shut his eyes as he felt his foe take hold of the water, taking it from Wyatt's grasp.

Wyatt gave one last great pull at his power, and lightning crashed down just as the Aquamancer touched the water. Terrible and awesome, the snarling blue light slammed into the street and buildings around them. Everything was lit up with the fury of Wyatt's power.

Electricity surged through the water around them, and Wyatt could feel it snaking toward the Aquamancer with hungry intent. The pale man tried in vain to push the water away from him, but the damage had already been done. From all directions the current flowed into him as he frantically tried to disconnect himself. But he was too late, and the surging power connected, tearing through his body with abandon.

Wyatt let out a breath, and as he did, the sky above him seemed to match. The rain stopped falling almost instantly, and the clouds calmed and settled. The water, no longer held by the Aquamancer's power, flowed down the street, trailing off into gutters and drainage ditches. Wyatt looked around, trying to find whatever was left of his foe.

The Aquamancer lay against one of the nearby buildings, having been thrown into it by the force of the electricity when it hit him. His robes were smoking and burnt. He was still conscious, staring at Wyatt with a crazed, hungry expression, but his body didn't seem to be working properly. His limbs jerked and twitched awkwardly, but he couldn't seem to control anything.

Wyatt walked over to him slowly, sheathing his sword. He could feel his fatigue down to his very bones. He hoped he'd have enough left to get out of the city.

"I told you," he said simply, leaning down a little closer to the Aquamancer. "I'm not playing. Tell your Emperor that. Tell him that there are bigger things going on here, and for right now he's better off leaving me to my devices. His daughter, too. We're doing something much bigger than the Empire can understand. Someday, I think he and I will probably have a long chat. But until then, there are bigger things going on. If he sends more men after me, I want you to tell him how much he'll regret it. He's not my enemy unless he wants to be."

The Aquamancer didn't seem capable of responding, but he gnashed his teeth and let out a noise halfway between a snarl and a gurgle. Wyatt shrugged, and with the last shred of his power, he called the wind again. He felt it reluctantly take hold of him, lifting him up into a slow and unsteady flight. He let out a breath of relief as he glided over Farillyon, ignoring the people in the streets who pointed and stared and shouted as he passed overhead. His exit from the city was unfettered.

As he rode that soft wind out over the city, he nearly fell asleep. In the sky with the wind at his back, Wyatt had never felt more alive.

CHAPTER SIXTEEN

hey've been gone a long time," said Jag, staring out toward the enormous capital city as he fought to keep his nerves at bay. "Too long. And that storm… I think we should go get them, Tythas."

The two of them were seated atop a hill a few miles from Farillyon, looking out over one side of the capital. Vance sat comfortably beneath a large oak tree, while Jag had been alternating between restless pacing and a fidgety sort of meditation. From their vantage point, they could see enough of the city to know that something was going on.

Tythas watched the storm with increasing worry. He had already felt Wyatt throwing power around with abandon, but this storm was something else entirely. Part of him agreed with his young colleague, but he shook his head.

"No," he said quietly, his eyes heavy. "We have to trust that Wyatt and Grace can take care of themselves. Grace is not the doe-eyed young girl she used to be, and Wyatt is an exceptionally talented and frustratingly mysterious individual. I still have no idea what he is truly capable of, and I must admit that this is a marvelous opportunity to see what the boy can do."

Jag raised an eyebrow, turning to face his mentor. "What do you mean? He's just an Aeromancer. A powerful one, with a dragon or some other ancient awful thing helping him out. But he's still just an Aeromancer… right?"

Tythas's face was blank. "I don't know, Jag. Some days I think he's just a farm boy who is in way over his head. And then other days, I think he's more than all of us."

Jag sighed, obviously frustrated. "I don't think I get you, Vance. He seems like a young kid who got thrown to the wolves and somehow managed to survive. I give him credit for being a quick learner and as brave as any soldier, but I don't see anything else."

Tythas chuckled. "That's because you are still young as well, Jag. You are many things, but you still have many years ahead of you. You can't be taught to see the difference between the players and the played. It's a skill you have to learn all on your own. But I wonder… do your feelings toward Wyatt have anything to do with the fondness growing between him and Grace?"

Jag scowled. "Low blow, old man. Low blow."

Tythas laughed. "My point stands. Look closer, Jag, and you might see something in him that I once saw in you. That I still do see in you."

Jag looked like he was going to retort, but stopped as thunder boomed over the city. The two of them looked out at the darkening sky, both of them frowning.

Jag squinted, peering toward the clouds. "What is that?" He pointed to something that was flying through the air, streaking toward them like a javelin. "Is that… is that Grace?"

He leapt to his feet, taking several steps forward as he tried to get a better view. Tythas followed, coming to a halt next to Jag and studying the skyline with puzzlement.

Then they heard her. She was shrieking like a banshee as an unseen force carried her with remarkable speed toward the hill they stood atop. Vance splayed his hands out, immediately trying to still the wind and pluck her out of the sky.

The wind that carried her shrugged his power seemingly without effort. He frowned, rolling up his sleeves and pressing harder. But yet again, the wind seemed to slip between his fingers. He couldn't even begin to grasp it. He threw his considerable power at it like a charging bull, but nothing could touch it. His eyes widened with shock when he finally realized what was going on.

"Adala save us," breathed Tythas in disbelief, staring at Grace with wide eyes. "That's a sylph. A living gale."

Jag looked over at him, alarm clearly etched on his face. "I assume that's a bad thing?"

Tythas shook his head, unable to find the words to accurately describe his surprise. Whatever had happened in the city, it had scared Wyatt enough that he had done something that very few veteran Aeromancers could accomplish. He had done something that Tythas himself had only dared attempt once in his life.

"Well, get her out of it!" yelled Jag, looking like he wanted to leap into the sky and catch her. "Do something!"

As Grace's writhing, screaming form drew closer, Tythas merely shook his head, all too aware of how powerless he was. "You don't understand. There is nothing I can do. A sylph is the height of an Aeromancer's power; some say they're blessings from Aeris herself. Once they're created, they can't be controlled. To an extent, they take orders from their creator. But if that Adept is too tired or weak-willed, a sylph can break free and do whatever it likes."

Jag blinked at him. "Well, how do you get rid of them?"

"They eventually dissolve and dissipate back into the sky," replied Tythas. "But until that point, they've been known to do pretty bad things if left unchecked. Blow down cities, carry entire herds of cattle across entire provinces, that kind of thing. It's a very dangerous thing, to call a sylph."

Jag and Tythas watched, stunned, as Grace was sent gently down in front of them by the living wind. She stopped screaming and fighting as she settled gently onto the ground, looking absolutely livid.

After setting Grace down, the sylph's form shifted into a small, swirling vortex that floated about twenty feet away from them, drawing up stray leaves and grass as it did. It swirled in place, as if waiting for something.

"I am going to kill him," snarled Grace with wild eyes as she tried awkwardly to get to her feet, her fiery hair in utter disarray. Having just flown over a city on the back of a living wind, however, her legs were still a bit shaky, so she flopped angrily back down into the dirt. "We were flying out, and we got ambushed. He told me I had to let go of him. I thought he was just going to set me down, but no, he summons that… whatever the hell that thing is, and away I go. I'm going to kill him."

Jag crouched next to her, putting a hand on her shoulder. "Are you alright, sis? Are you hurt?"

Grace made a face at him. "I'm absolutely fine, but that heroic idiot is back there fighting three Aeromancers and about fifty city guards on his own."

The next few seconds were filled with silent tension as the other two absorbed what she had said. Jag looked like he wanted to draw his sword and storm the city, while Tythas was already unconsciously calling the wind. Both of them knew how dangerous it was now that Wyatt had been detected in the city.

Tythas took the amulet off of his neck and threw it out into the sky. It flashed with light and took the form of a shadowy raven, which cawed with agreement and flew out toward the city.

"Before we go running back to help him, I want to scout ahead," said Tythas quietly, his eyes closed. "I can feel the other Aeromancers, but their presences are like candles compared to the wildfire that Wyatt has become. It feels like they underestimated him, so he may not need our help."

Jag and Grace nodded uneasily. "It looked pretty bad, Vance. There were a lot of soldiers. But we found what we were looking for. The seal is atop the Mount of Light. We also... met Mugalo."

Jag's expression darkened. "So he's the reason you got caught. He sold you back to the Emperor."

Grace looked down into the dirt, thinking. "I don't know. I can't make sense of it. He met us down in the Archives, but he was alone. I've seen the things that he can do. He probably could've subdued the both of us if he really wanted to. But he told us about a secret exit in the Archive, gave us our equipment, and let us go."

"Mugalo has always operated under his own motivations," said Tythas distantly, his eyes still closed. "It is possible that he has his own agenda, or may even be aware of Necron and his plans. I can't even begin to fathom how far that old snake's reach extends. He has his fingers in everything."

"Wyatt has called whatever lives within his sword for help, by the look of it," he said. "It's taken the shape of a lion with a flaming mane.

They made quick work of the soldiers, and the Aeromancers, too. Wyatt looks unharmed, although a little annoyed. I think he had to kill one of them."

Jag and Grace both looked relieved. "Good, that means he can fly over here and I can soundly beat him," said Grace venomously.

"Wait," said Tythas suddenly, his expression looking pained. "Is that... dammit all. Mugalo has to be involved. He's let Alvernon out."

Grace and Jag both grew pale. "Adala be with him," said Grace quietly. "Alvernon is as dangerous as they come, and he's completely merciless."

"They're fighting, said Tythas tensely. "Wyatt got a good kick in, but now Alvernon is using a Pool of Grasping Hands. I've never even talked to Wyatt about how to fight with another Adept. And Alvernon isn't like any other Adept, either."

"We should get moving, then," said Grace, climbing to her feet. "He can hold Alvernon off long enough for you to fly ahead and get there, and we can catch up. Let's go."

"Hold on," said Tythas, holding up a hand as the sky above the city gave an ominous rumble, the thunder rattling their teeth. "Wyatt has a plan, I think. But... it's raining. I can't see anything, now. The rain is too thick."

"Rain?" asked Grace, incredulous. "He's calling rain with an Aquamancer like Alvernon trying to kill him?"

Tythas tried to say something, but lightning flashed in the sky, a huge spike of it roaring down into the entire street where Wyatt was fighting, bathing nearly every inch of it with power and fury. The crash was deafening, and the three of them had to cover their ears.

And then, it all just seemed to stop. There was a tense silence shared by the three of them as they tried to grasp what Wyatt had done. None of them, not even Tythas, had ever seen lightning like that before.

"He won," said Tythas simply, his voice breathless and amazed. "He called the rain, and Alvernon took hold of it, not realizing what Wyatt was doing. With that much water in his grasp, the lightning went right for him. Wyatt had an air bubble wrapped around him, so none of the water touched him. I'll be surprised if Alvernon survives. He looks completely wrecked."

"Is Wyatt okay?" asked Grace, the venom gone from her voice. "I never... How does he know how to do all of this, Tythas?"

"I have no idea," said Tythas, opening his eyes. "But he's on his way back here, floating over the city. He's moving slowly, but he should be here soon."

They waited in restless silence, watching Wyatt's tornadic friend spin happily off in the distance. After several minutes, Wyatt's distant form finally bobbed over the walls of the city toward them. He settled down gently, smiling at them with fatigue in his eyes. He looked like he was about to fall over.

"You smarmy little ass," said Grace, stepping forward and punching him in the arm as hard as she could. "Don't you ever throw yourself into danger for me like that again. You should've let me stay. I could've fought with you."

Wyatt's expression soured, but he didn't flinch at the impact. His arm was hanging limp. "I didn't exactly have a choice, Grace. They were there for you. If they'd caught you, we would've been much worse off. It's one thing for me to fight them in the street, out under the open sky. It's completely different for me to do it in the belly of the castle, where I have a lot less power. I saw a chance to get at least one of us out, so I had to take it."

Tythas nodded, stepping forward to clasp his other shoulder. "Well done, Wyatt. Well done."

"Thanks," Wyatt replied, rubbing the arm Grace had punched. But he wasn't rubbing the spot she had hit; rather, he was rubbing almost the entire length of it, as if he were trying to warm it up. But it still hung limp. He gave up, motioning in the distance to the little tornado.

"Er, what is that thing?" asked Wyatt quietly, eyeing it with a mixture of awe and suspicion.

Tythas barked out a sudden laugh. "You are positively amazing, Wyatt. That's a sylph. It carried Grace here all the way from the heart of the city at your command. You created it."

Wyatt stared at it, blinking. "I did that? Wow. That's, er... neat."

There was a brief moment of silence before all of them started laughing. Wyatt walked over to the sylph with a sheepish grin on his face, shaking his head.

"Thank you for helping me and my friends, sylph," he said, reaching out to run his fingers through the swirling wind. "You're free to go now. Please be good, okay?"

The vortex gave a swirling howl, but it wasn't a howl of dismay. It was almost joyful, if wind could be such a thing. The small tornado dispersed, the wind blasting outward in every direction.

"What's wrong with your arm?" said Grace suddenly from behind him, finally noticing that it was still hanging limply at his side. "I didn't think... I didn't hit you that hard, did I?"

Wyatt turned back to the group, shaking his head. "No, it wasn't you. It was the Aquamancer I fought. Said he had mixed blood, part Necromancer. He fought with his bare hands. I didn't know why until he managed to touch my wrist. My whole arm has been numb ever since."

Grace rushed up to his side.

"Sit," she commanded. Being far too weary to offer any kind of objection, he flopped down in the dirt. She slowly lifted his arm, taking his hand and stretching the whole limb out.

"Alvernon isn't much of a Necromancer," she said quietly, studying the arm closely. "But his touch is like poison for your whole body. He draws the life right out of you, from any part of your skin he can touch. It's a very uncommon ability."

A dull tingling washed over Wyatt's arm, and he was very relieved to note that he could flex his muscles and feel it again. "I got that, funnily enough. You know him?"

"Every Adept has encountered him in some way, I suppose," she replied, furrowing her brow as she worked. "He's Mugalo's attack dog. Whenever the Empire or the Council needs dirty work done, Alvernon is the one to do it. His touch will pull the life out of anyone, even another Necromancer. He's killed many Adepts in the name of peace. That's why they keep him around."

"I promised him that I would find a way to help him," said Wyatt quietly, looking intently at a fixed spot on the ground. "I... can't even begin to imagine what his life must be like. He doesn't deserve that, even if he is a killer. There's... got to be a better way."

Jag nearly fell over. "You want to let that animal free?"

"He's an animal because of the Empire and the Council," said Grace hotly, glancing back at her brother. "Don't forget that our father had a hand in what he's become. I agree with Wyatt. There's always a better way."

Tythas shifted uneasily. "You must also realize that setting him free may mean killing him. Are you prepared for that, Wyatt?"

Wyatt remembered the Adept who had just fallen to his blade. He was certain that the memory of that man's death would be burned into his mind for the rest of his life. He knew what it meant to take a life, and what it had already cost him.

"If he pushes me to that point," said Wyatt quietly, looking up and holding Tythas's eyes with his own, "then I will kill him myself. We can give him the chance to have a real life, but he has to work at it, too. If he's too far gone, if whatever they've done to him can't be fixed… yes, I'm prepared."

Tythas nodded and clapped him on the shoulder. "You've come a long way. We need to get moving, however. Your exit from the city was hardly stealthy. I imagine they're going to mount another attack of some sort if we don't leave the area. They were overconfident, and that's what got you past them. Last time, they sent four Adepts to bring you in. This time, they'll send forty."

"The only road to the Mount of Light takes us directly through the heart of the Empire," said Jag sourly. "There are at least three Imperial towns along the way, and we'd pass not too far from a military base. Tythas, I don't know what you plan on doing, but if we go there we may have to fight our way through."

"I agree," said the older man knowingly, scratching his beard. "However, there is another route. Our travel there would be largely unhindered, I think."

Grace let Wyatt's arm drop, turning to face her mentor. Wyatt clenched his fist and flexed, noting with deep relief that it appeared to be back to normal.

"You want us to go by sea, don't you?" she asked. Wyatt could detect the slightest hint of apprehension in her voice.

"Yes," said Tythas with cheer, nodding at her. "I have an old friend who lives in Triat, to the south. He runs a shipping company that brings rare goods from the Scattered Coast and Cape Pride. I'm sure he wouldn't mind taking us up the other way toward the Mount of Light. The back end of it is right on the coast, and there's even a small trail on that side that very few people know about."

"Triat is the Empire's port, right?" asked Wyatt, trying to remember the last time he'd actually looked at a map of the Empire. "I remember reading about it."

"The City of a Thousand Sails," said Tythas with a smile. "The city of my birth, incidentally. You're right that it's the Empire's port, but it isn't technically Imperial land. It's run by a sovereign governor who keeps a good relationship with the Empire without becoming a part of it. It's a wonderful city. I always preferred it to Farillyon, as it's much friendlier."

"Well, the horses are tied up down by the river," said Jag, pointing over the far side of the hill. "I figured they needed a drink and a chance to cool off. Triat isn't a far ride from here, and with any luck we'll have a chance to rest while we ride on the boat. If we do meet up with Apep at the Mount of Light, at least we won't be ragged and tired like we are now."

Grace looked seasick already. "I can't believe you are going to make me get on a boat. I'll remember this."

Jag snickered. "You'll be fine, sis. It's necessary. We can't exactly go gallivanting around in the open in Imperial land, especially when three of us are wanted outlaws."

Wyatt blinked. He hadn't even realized it, but Jag was right. Wyatt had assaulted a number of Imperial officials and fled capture. He was just as wanted as the other two. There would be no collaring or forcing into the Academy now. If they caught him, they'd probably just kill him and move on with their lives.

Tythas noticed Wyatt's faraway look and smiled at him. "In the company of thieves, Wyatt. When Apep's intentions become known to the Empire and what we've been working toward becomes apparent, they will retract whatever price they have on your head. Don't worry too much. It'll be over soon."

Jag walked over to Wyatt, wrapping an arm around his shoulder as the group began to walk for the horses. "Besides, being an outlaw isn't all bad. The women love it. I bet if I took you into a tavern in Triat, you could walk out with three of them on your arm and- OW!"

Grace had kicked him. Hard.

"Well anyway," he continued, rubbing his leg and glaring at his sister, "you're with friends, and Tythas is right. When all this comes out in the open, when we put Necron back in his box and Apep in a deep, deep grave, we'll straighten all of this out. They might even call us heroes."

Wyatt sobered a bit at that thought, smiling lightly. "I just want to find my family and go home, Jag. Let's worry about that. If we end up as heroes, well, I guess there are worse fates."

Mugalo slid through the cold stone halls deep beneath the castle, his thoughts deep and far-reaching. Alvernon had failed to apprehend the boy, just as Mugalo had expected. It had been a fantastic opportunity to test Wyatt Arden's abilities, and the boy had performed magnificently. If anyone had a chance at stopping the rogue demigod, it would be that young boy and his interesting sword.

He had also needed to test Alvernon. The Aquamancer had always been equal parts resourceful and reckless. Perhaps as the years went on he simply lost any desire to keep himself alive. Or perhaps he was truly as mad as Mugalo had claimed when he ordered the man collared in the first place. It was hard to say what the unique Adept was truly capable of.

Mugalo stopped at the end of the hall, facing a solid door. He ran a finger over the cold iron, wincing inwardly as the chill metal bit his skin. The runes on the door stirred to life, swimming and flashing with light. He heard the mechanism click and the door swung open to reveal a large open chamber bathed in the deep shadows cast by one lonely, flickering torch.

A form at the far end of the chamber stirred as Mugalo came to a halt, closing the door behind him. He paced around the windowless room, peering through the dim light at the faint runes that shone on the walls. Runes of sealing, designed to keep moisture out and destroy any that came in.

Mugalo could hear the rattling of chains as the figure at the far end of the room moved closer to him, still concealed by shadow. Even without looking into his eyes, Mugalo could feel the heat of his hatred. Alvernon had always been much too easy to read.

"You didn't tell me you were sending me to kill Aeris reborn," growled Alvernon as Mugalo turned to face him. "That boy has more power than any one Adept should have a right to."

"So they tell me," said Mugalo dryly, although he still wasn't sure how much of the story he believed. The reports about the battle in the heart of Farillyon were varied and inconsistent. The guards would have him believe that the young man had called a demon to aid him, had defeated thirty guards with a wave of his hand, and had smote one of the Aeromancers with the hand of Adala herself. Then, after dispatching Alvernon, he had ridden away on unseen wings.

All of these things had happened, he supposed. But not in the manner that they suggested. They were uneducated fools. They were also very lucky that Wyatt Arden knew the fine art of self-restraint, as the young Adept could've slain all of them if he had chosen to do so. He even spared Alvernon, something that had greatly surprised Mugalo. The lad was unpredictable.

But he was special, and perhaps only Mugalo knew truly how special. He was the sign that things were finally coming to a close. He was the sign that Mugalo would finally be able to act after so many years of waiting.

"I'm going to kill him, you know," said Alvernon maliciously, the look in his eyes animalistic. "Slowly. He's made a fool of me, and I can't allow that."

"You have said the same thing about me every day for many years now," observed Mugalo with a smirk. "The truth, Alvernon, is that you will do whatever I tell you. Or have you forgotten our agreement?"

Alvernon stepped forward and raised his hands, pulling the chains around his wrists tight and reaching out as far as he could, his arms locked in a reared-back, ready to strike position. He glared at Mugalo with hate and venom in his eyes, looking very much like a rabid, chained-up dog. His expression was practically feral.

"I haven't forgotten," hissed Alvernon, his neck straining as he pulled at his chains, trying to touch Mugalo, who stood only inches away from him. But the chains would not budge. The stone collar around his neck was peeking out of his clothes. "But I hope you haven't forgotten that I swore on my blood and my Spark that I would be the one to kill you. And one day, I will."

Having heard this threat hundreds of times, Mugalo chuckled. "So you say, Alvernon. So you say. But you don't need to worry about them right now. Truthfully, I never expected you to succeed against Wyatt. They must be allowed to carry out their goals now. The good of the Empire demands it."

Alvernon narrowed his eyes. "You sent me to kill him and you didn't think I would succeed? Why in the world did you send me out there in the first place, then?"

Mugalo shrugged. "I needed to test his abilities, and you were the most adequate measuring stick available. You performed admirably, and I'm sure given another opportunity you may even be able to kill him, now that you know what he is capable of. But he needs to survive, for right now. I have plans for him."

Alvernon sneered at him. "You have plans for everything, don't you? Why is he so important?"

Mugalo chuckled again. "That is not something you need to concern yourself with, Alvernon. You are a tool, nothing more. I don't keep you here for your charming personality. But surely you could feel the strength that rolled off of him? Surely you could feel the boy just as well as you could the sword at his hip?"

Alvernon finally relaxed, letting the chains fall slack. "Yes, I could feel it. So what is it? A dragon or some other old beastie from the Old Age? Or maybe one of the Six? There have always been rumors that they still existed in some form..."

Mugalo snorted. "Hardly. Something much more interesting. And something key to my plans. So for now, be a good boy, stay down here in the dark, and don't hurt yourself. I will have more work for you soon."

Mugalo stepped out of the room without another word, leaving Alvernon to stare at his back and wonder just what the old snake had planned.

"It was a lion, master, just like last time," said Apep quietly, slipping through the doorway of the house they had occupied for a brief rest. "A mane of fire and lightning, with glowing golden eyes. And it took orders from the boy with the sword."

The tiny house had contained more people than Apep would've expected. A family of seven living together in such a small building reminded Apep of why he had shed his connection to humanity. People were so foolishly content with simplicity, with mediocrity. Apep knew better. His destiny was great and his life was unending. Unlike the family, all of whom now lay dead at his feet, Apep would never fall. He'd already stripped the souls from their bodies. He'd bind them later, of course, and make them do his bidding.

Necron's dark, colorless eyes somehow managed not to reflect the light of the flickering fireplace he was staring into. Apep noted with distaste that the skin on his master's cheeks was already beginning to blemish and wear thin, a sign that this vessel was already starting to break down. Soon, he would be unable to walk out among the humans again. It had lasted longer than the last, but not much.

"I should know what this is, Apep," mused Necron, his voice quiet and terrible. "I should remember. It's right there in my mind, just beyond sight. I can very nearly hear it taunting me, laughing at me. But I can't seem to remember it, no matter how hard I try."

"So this lion, this… creature, whatever it may be, is from before?" asked Apep, casually stepping over a body as he approached his master's side. "From when you walked the earth unbound?"

"Perhaps even older," said Necron cryptically, still watching the fire. "From before my siblings and I fell apart. From before humanity grew strong. The memories that stir now… are distant, but they remind me of the time before all of this. A time when I was just a young warrior, fighting against foes greater than you could ever imagine."

Apep crouched down over the body of a young, attractive woman, pressing his hand against her chest and extending his power. "So it's one of those things, then? A dragon, or one of the other monsters that you and the others destroyed all those centuries ago?"

Necron sighed, a sound that Apep had never actually heard his master make before. He was frustrated with himself, frustrated that he could not remember. Time truly had diluted his memories.

"I have no clue," said his master simply, a grudging acknowledgment of failure that Necron was not normally prone to making. "Whatever it is, the fact that it has awoken now, while I am so close to returning, does not bode well for us. We must be especially careful around it, and around the boy that wields that sword."

"They will no doubt be eagerly researching the location of the last remaining seals," noted Apep as he stood back up to view his handiwork. "They may even be waiting for us at the next one."

"Yes, I'm counting on that," said Necron, a smile creeping onto his sickly face. "The fact that they were sighted in Farillyon tells us that they already did the research they needed. They most likely got into the Archive and found some ancient text that contained the location of the seals. They fled the capital, and no doubt are already on the way to the Mount of Light."

Apep frowned. "A useful diversion, but it will not stall them long. What would you have me do?"

"Contact your friends in the Dominion," replied Necron. "We did a wonderful job convincing them that the events at Trajnheim were the boy's doing. I am certain that one of them would be more than happy to meet him there and challenge him. The Dominion are a proud, foolish lot. They will do as you ask. And while they are stalled, the rest of the Dominion will mount their attack on Farillyon. You will rouse your army to the south, and we will crush the capital between two unstoppable forces."

Apep nodded excitedly. "We will take the seal of Life with ease, with the blood of our prisoner. You will rise again, master! This world will be yours!"

"We must move quickly, Apep," said Necron decisively, clapping his hands together. The bodies in the room stirred suddenly, climbing unsteadily to their feet. Apep felt his master's cold, incredible power roll into them as each was bound, Necron using power that Apep thought was still locked away. "Get a message to your friends to begin their attack. Tonight, we leave to collect our forces."

Apep nodded, smiling at his master in awe. It was all coming true.

CHAPTER SEVENTEEN

Wyatt leaned against the railing at the prow of the boat, staring out at the magnificent shape of Triat as the sprawling city faded into the distance. Even this far out to sea, they were still surrounded by innumerable other vessels. Tythas had told him that roughly one in three were pirate ships, but they looked harmless enough. He understood now why Triat was called "The City of a Thousand Sails." Tythas, once again, had been right about it.

It was just as magnificent as Farillyon, but in a different sort of way. Where Farillyon had astounded Wyatt with its splendor, Triat astounded him with its unbridled freedom. The capital had been so controlled; Adepts patrolling the streets, armed guards at every gate, and soldiers in guard posts every few miles. It had been clear to Wyatt when he walked through the city that it was suffering, and more guards and soldiers didn't seem to be helping the issue. Farillyon's dark side was starting to show through, peeking around the edges despite the Empire's best attempts to hide it. Triat, however, was much different.

Triat had no uniformed guards. This was, at first, very concerning, but Tythas had murmured reassurance; there were city guards, but they wore plain street clothes. They could be found not only patrolling the streets, but also eating in the restaurants, helping sailors moor their boats, and giving directions to travelers. They were an incredibly friendly lot, and the effect on the people was palpable. There was a certain kind of controlled chaos to Triat, almost as if it embraced the things that Farillyon tried so hard to hide. Wyatt found it deeply refreshing to not feel the eyes of a hundred soldiers on him.

Triat served as a sort of bridge between the Empire and the Scattered Coast. It was technically a part of the Empire, but it wasn't directly ruled by the Emperor. Instead the city elected a Governor-General every ten years for that duty. The current Governor-General, a man named Judah Grayfallow, had held the position for nearly thirty years. He was wildly popular with the people, and even as he got older, was both clever and capable. Tythas had suggested that the two of them were friends, but he hadn't said much else.

Now, as he watched it go, Wyatt felt for the first time like he'd found a place he might like to call home someday. It would be easy to return to Triat after all this was over. He'd never really cared for farming, but sailing and helping to battle pirate activity in the Coast was something that certainly appealed to him, especially considering his abilities. And it would keep him away from all the bureaucracy and political drama that went on in the Empire. He could just live how he wanted.

He savored the feeling of the wind and the salt as it sprayed against him, feeling calm and refreshed for the first time in days. Out on the water, left to the will of the wind and the sea, Wyatt had never felt more at peace. His lingering worries were able to wash away, for a time. He took a deep breath, letting the scent of the sea fill his mind.

"You've been awfully quiet since we left Farillyon," came an uneasy voice from behind him. He turned to see Grace making her way toward the prow, one hand clutching the railing tightly as she did. She was not a fan of boats, as it turned out. She looked a little green, but she was braving it for the good of the group. He had to give her that.

"Just thinking, I guess," said Wyatt in response, moving over a bit to make room for her. She stepped into the gap and leaned heavily against both the railing and Wyatt, trying her best not to clutch them both for dear life. For a time, she was quiet, just watching him as he watched the sea. He started to feel a little uncomfortable, but she finally spoke, breaking the silence that hung between them.

"Years ago, when Jag and Tythas rescued me from the castle, we nearly had to fight our way out," she said softly, choosing her words carefully. "One of my personal guards figured out what was going on, and was going to tell my father. Do you know why he didn't?"

Wyatt shook his head, not saying anything.

She reached out and touched his neck, two fingers pressing into the very important vein he knew was under the skin. "Because I put a knife right there. He was prepared to be attacked by Jag and Tythas, but not by me. He died, looking at me like I was a traitor. Bled to death right in front of me. I was fourteen."

A heavy feeling settled in Wyatt's chest as he watched her, realizing that she knew exactly why he'd been so quiet since they left Farillyon. He didn't quite know how to respond.

"He was just a soldier," she said with a sigh, looking back out over the sea. "Just a soldier doing the job that my father made him do. He was nice to me, too. Gave me a little more freedom than the others. Brought me books and other things from the outside when he could, just to make my life a little better, a little more pleasant."

Wyatt nodded slowly. "And you still killed him."

"I had to," she said, a hint of frenzy in her voice. "I had to. If he had gotten to the others, had alerted the guards or father, they'd have set a trap inside the castle. Tythas and Jag would both be dead, and none of the good things that I've done would ever have been possible. I would still be locked in that castle, barely better than Alvernon. And you? You'd be a dead body, still stuck in that creek we pulled you out of when we first met."

Wyatt sighed, reaching out to wrap an arm around her shoulders. He squeezed her arm gently. "I know, Grace. You don't have to justify anything to me."

"I'm trying to tell you something, Wyatt," she said, her voice carrying more edge than she probably intended. "To SHOW you something. We warned you that you would have to take a life sooner or later. We all have. The truth is that it never gets easier, and it always hurts. I'll never forget Jaxon's face as the life left his eyes. I'll never forget how it felt to see him die, to feel him die, and to be the cause of that. It goes against my very nature."

Wyatt nodded, squeezing the rail a little tighter as their ship went over a wave. "Thanks, Grace," he said quietly. "I know that this is hard on all of us, but... it's just a lot. All of this is a lot. More than I ever thought I'd have to deal with. And honestly? Grace... I miss my mom. I miss my best friend, Desmond. I even miss Kelsar, the old ass. I miss all of them, and the simple days when I could just spend time with them. It's funny how you don't realize how important things are until you lose them."

Grace looked over at him, her expression softening. "I guess... Wyatt, I'm sorry. It's easy to lose sight of those things, and I... I keep forgetting that you're trying to find your family."

Wyatt nodded, doing his best to fight off the fear that had been inside of him for weeks now. "It's just... you guys don't have much, but you have each other, you know? The three of you have been fighting this fight for so long, helping each other out. I'm still... trying to figure out my place in all of it, I guess. I don't know if I'll ever see my family again. They could be dead."

Grace gave him a sideways look. "Wyatt, after all the times we've saved each other's lives, after all the fights and the chaos... do you really think you're not my family, too?"

Wyatt blinked, suddenly unable to find the words to respond.

"You're a part of this group just as much as any of us," she said with a soft smile. "In a weird way, you've made the three of us put aside our petty little squabbles. We used to fight a lot, used to argue. But you unite us. And you help us and protect us, even put your life on the line for us without a second glance. And we'd all do the same for you."

Wyatt smiled at her. "I guess you're right," he admitted, feeling a little bit foolish.

"Of course I am," she said with a wry smile, elbowing him. "But regardless of that, we're going to find your mom and your grandfather. And we're going to tell them about how their little farm boy from the middle of nowhere became a hero and saved the world."

Wyatt laughed. "I don't know how Mom will handle that," he said, shaking his head. "I don't think she ever wanted me to leave the farm, much less save the world. I tried to get her to let me join the Army, when Desmond enlisted. I think I nearly killed her."

Grace laughed. "She sounds like a good mom."

Wyatt smiled and nodded. "She is. And she'll love all three of you, you know. I think she loves everyone she meets. She's just... genuinely nice. I've never met anyone that she didn't get along with. I've seen her turn a bar full of angry drunks about to fight into a weeping, singing mess. She's incredible."

Grace squeezed his arm. "I can't wait to meet her. But in the meantime, you need to cheer up and clear your head. This gloomy mood of yours is going to make this trip even harder on me. Look up."

Wyatt glanced up, noticing the dark clouds above them that seemed to be following their boat into the sea. He laughed again, letting some of the tension out of his chest. Within a few moments, the clouds dispersed and the wind died down a little.

"Sorry," he said sheepishly, absently running a hand through his hair as he grinned at her. "I forget that I can do that sometimes."

"Not many Aeromancers have that kind of subconscious control over the weather, you know," she said softly, only briefly looking at him before looking away again. "You are definitely something else, Wyatt. Do you know anything about your family, other than your mother and grandfather?"

Wyatt shook his head and shifted his feet. "No, I guess it just... never really came up. I mean, I tried asking my mom about my father, but she was always really good at changing the subject. I know he was a soldier, and that's about it. Any other parts of my family are a mystery. Mom and I always seemed to have too much to do on the farm. No time to talk about things like that, I suppose. Or maybe we didn't want to."

Grace nodded. "My mom died giving birth to me. She was a Pyromancer, Dad said, and he says she had a temper like no woman he has ever met."

Wyatt gave her a glance and a sideways grin. "I can believe that."

She punched him, laughing. "Thanks. Anyway, after that he didn't seem like he ever wanted to marry again. Between the fiasco with Jag's mother and my mother's death, I think he was just tired of the whole ordeal. Had better things to do than try again, I guess."

Wyatt smiled a light smile and nodded. "Mom was like that, too. We used to go into town for supplies every week or so, and all the local farmers tried and tried to win her heart. But it all bounced off of her, as if she just didn't have the patience for any of it anymore. She was far too busy with the farm to date. She might've even liked it that way."

The boat went over a particularly large wave, forcing them both to grab hold of the railing. They clutched it for a moment before looking at each other. After a few seconds, they both burst out laughing.

"So what do we do after all this is over?" asked Wyatt, looking back out to the sea and smiling. "I mean, I don't think I'll be able to go back to being a farmer after this. That life seems so far away now, and it's only been a handful of weeks."

"Well, Apep and Necron aren't the only bad guys out there," she said with a shrug. "And we still have the issue of helping Necromancers out, as well. Making sure they get to the island safely, or bringing them back and showing them how to find lives on the mainland if they want that instead. There will always be work to do, I think."

Wyatt scratched his chin. "That does seem pretty important. But maybe after all this is over, there will be a better way to go about it."

Grace cocked her head. "What do you suggest?"

Wyatt shrugged. "Well, you guys said that after this we might actually have some favor with the Empire. Maybe we can use that as leverage in order to change the right minds. Get the Necromancers back on the Council and back into the mainland. And stop skulking around, doing all of this as outlaws."

Grace shook her head. "Apep and his men were the problem last time. He had a whole horde of followers then, but the fact remains that as long as a Necromancer presents himself as being a threat, people will attribute that to all of them. The wounds from the war are still too fresh. There's just something about Necromancy that unsettles people. The Empire has warred with the Dominion countless times over the centuries, but there's no prejudice against Pyromancers. Just Necromancers. I fear it may never go away."

Wyatt sighed. "It just seems stupid. Like we're tearing ourselves apart over prejudices and finger-pointing. Adala's children should be united, not fighting with each other. She would've wanted that, I think. She didn't give her powers to us so we could squabble over them."

Grace nodded. "You're right, but unfortunately it takes a lot more than a few rogue Adepts to change the hearts of so many people. So we do what we can to make a difference regardless."

Wyatt looked over at her. "We'll fix it, Grace. We'll undo all of this damage and make the world a better place."

Grace blinked and stared at him for a moment before letting out a laugh and shaking her head. "If it were anyone else, I would probably just brush a statement like that off. But with you... I really believe you. And I've seen you do enough incredible things for it to be easy to believe. I'll help however I can."

The waves of the ocean crested and broke around them, and the two of them continued talking for a long time. They talked of things big and small, grateful for the chance to stop, to think, and to breathe the ocean air. For that short time, they forgot their battles and just talked.

Sometime later, while studying maps and trying to decide on a course of action, Jag lost his ability to remain quiet.

Inside the cabin of the ship, Jag stalked over to the door to the outside and latched it shut. He walked quietly back to the table where Tythas sat studying a map of the Mount of Light, sitting down across from his mentor. Tythas looked up, his eyebrow raised.

"I want you to tell me just exactly how a farm boy with about a week of combat experience and no formal training managed to do that," he said evenly, trying to keep his voice from sounding overly concerned. "There is something very strange going on with that kid, Vance, and you know it. So be honest with me."

Tythas watched him quietly for several seconds, the silence hanging between them like a tense wire. The silence grew, and so did the tension. Soon, Jag was sure it was going to snap.

"I have no idea," said Tythas honestly, with a deep sigh that can only be produced by someone with deeply profound troubles in his heart. "None at all, Jag. And that is the honest truth."

Jag eyed him suspiciously, leaning back in his chair. "You have to be asking the same questions I am, Tythas. You know way more about how Adepts operate than I do. You probably know more about Adepts than about anyone else alive, and yet you just accept everything that kid does with a smile and a nod. Like you know something we don't."

Tythas leaned forward, his expression growing heavy. "Jag, 'that kid' has a name," he said sharply, his voice harsh and scolding. "And he has saved your sister's life twice now. He saved my life, too. Is that it? Are you jealous that he hasn't thrown himself into the face of death to save you? Because in case you forgot, back in Ven, 'that kid' and his sword are the only things that kept you alive when Apep bested you."

Jag visibly shrunk, leaning back in his chair. "Sorry," he said quietly, looking at the floor. "It's just... I get nervous around most regular Adepts, and here's one that is stronger than almost all of them only a month after discovering his powers. It's unsettling."

"I do agree with that," admitted Tythas, shifting and settling back into his chair, scratching his goatee. "My best guess is that it has something to do with that sword of his, and whatever old and dangerous thing is in his ear, guiding him. It may be opening doors for him that other Adepts have to open on their own. It might even be enhancing his power. It's hard to say without talking to the thing inside of it directly, which I've only been able to do once. I don't think it has any intention of talking to me again, either."

"So what do we do?" asked Jag honestly, his voice on the precipice of nervousness.

Tythas leaned back, fixing his eyes on the younger man. "Jag, you're acting like he's some horrible monster, waiting to eat you while you sleep. Again, Wyatt has proven his friendship and his loyalty to us more than once. In the span of a few weeks, he has done more for a group of complete strangers than most men would do for their own kin. He has even put aside the search for his family in order to help us defeat Apep, something that pains him more than you could possibly know. He hates himself for that decision, Jag. I saw it in his eyes, back at the volcano. He hates having to do the right thing."

Jag felt even more foolish, nodding. Tythas was right, of course. Wyatt had saved all of them with the powers that Jag was so afraid of. Maybe he wasn't giving the boy enough credit.

"But he does it anyway," continued Tythas firmly. "He puts his mother's life aside for the good of the whole world, something that is both incredibly hard and incredibly noble. I trust him completely, and when the time comes that he fully comes into the doubtlessly unfathomable power he possesses, I will follow him into battle without second thought."

Jag blinked, looking at his mentor with curiosity. "You really think that he's that important?"

Tythas gave a single, slow nod. "There are very few things that I am sure of where Wyatt Arden is concerned. But one of them is that he is special. He has a purpose, and he is here for a reason. Players of such magnitude are rarely revealed until they are needed. That is how the world works: in subtle, unseen ways. If you remember the stories, Vardish was just as much an anomaly as Wyatt. And Vardish came to be one of the most important heroes of the old age."

Jag sighed. "I feel like an idiot. He's a great kid and I'm proud to know him. I just… I don't know. It's different, not being an Adept and living in a world where small men can call lightning from the sky with a flex of their arm. As a soldier, things are much more cut and dried. But then Wyatt comes along, this unassuming little farm kid, and beats three normal Adepts, plus Alvernon, with barely a scratch…"

"You are remarkable, Jag," said Tythas with a simple smile. "You are very right, in this world a normal man is at a disadvantage. Yet you fight as ferociously as any. When you look in the mirror, you see someone with all the power in the world, not a simple soldier. And I've seen you defeat those men who can call lightning from the sky with a flex of their arm with nothing but a sword in your hand, unmatched courage, and exceptional wit. Do not forget that you are just as important to this group as any of us."

Jag smiled, finally letting some of the stress off of his shoulders.

"Thanks, Vance. I'll do my best to keep an open mind where Wyatt is concerned. He's saved us all more than once, so he certainly deserves that. But can we at least agree that he deserves a careful eye?"

Tythas nodded seriously. "We can. Don't think I'm not aware of the problems you've brought up. I've been watching him since the first day, and I will continue to do so. I'm as curious as you are to see what he is and what he will become."

Suddenly, the door wiggled, prevented from opening by the latch that held it. It wiggled again, and then a loud "thump" sounded against it.

"Hey!" came Grace's muffled voice from the other side. "Let us in! It's getting rainy out here!"

Jag got up and quickly walked to the door, unlatching it and allowing Grace and Wyatt to slip inside. He closed the door behind them, but did not latch it this time.

"Sorry about that," he said merrily, walking back over to his chair. "One of the big waves must've knocked the latch down. It's a little loose, I think."

Grace sat down at the table next to him, rolling her eyes. "Uh huh. Have the two of you come up with a plan?"

Jag motioned to one of the many hammocks hanging at the far wall. "My plan is to actually get some sleep for once."

Tythas thumped his hands on the table. "Hear, hear. That's the best idea I've heard in weeks."

Wyatt sat down at the table, chuckling. "I think Grace is suggesting that we should have a plan of attack at the mountain, just in case Apep is there waiting for us. But sleep is a good idea, too."

Tythas motioned to the map. "Well, in terms of plotted courses, there are really only two ways up the mountain," he said as if the crazy lines he had drawn on the map should make some kind of sense to them. "We chose the sea route so that we could use the secluded trail up the back of the mountain and avoid any other people. But, we do have two Aeromancers in the group, so in theory…"

Grace shook her head and interrupted him. "No, flying us up there is a bad idea, Vance. We need the two of you at full strength. You could use your bird amulet, I guess, but Wyatt doesn't have one of those.

Flying with me on his back all the way up the mountain would probably end poorly for everyone involved."

Jag gave her a strange look. "What makes you think he'd be the one carrying you?"

Grace ignored him, looking over at Wyatt and continuing. "Unless you think you could summon another sylph?"

Wyatt shook his head. "No way. I have no idea how I did that the first time, and I doubt I could figure out how to do it again unless I was under pressure. It seems like unless I really need them, my powers stay asleep."

Tythas nodded. "That's pretty normal. A lot of Adepts can do incredible, nigh-impossible things under pressure. But ask them to do it in a controlled, calm situation and they'll probably hurt themselves."

Grace looked back to Tythas. "Then flying is a bad idea. I think we'll be doing this the old fashioned way. Save our strength and take the trail. We're all in good shape, a hike won't hurt us."

Jag scratched his stubbly chin. "Well, there is something to be said for only two of us being tired, versus all four of us from climbing the mountain. The trail is what, a four hour hike?"

"Six," said Tythas thoughtfully. "If memory serves. I haven't actually seen the Mount since I was a boy. If you told me before it was a location of one of the seals, I'd have just laughed at you. But now it seems to make a great deal of sense."

Grace shrugged. "We've fought on less before. Many times. I think it's the better option. And I don't really care that much for flying, anyway."

"I don't really like the idea of getting attacked in midair again, either," said Wyatt sourly. "Knowing my luck, Apep will send some great, dead, bat-monster to try to eat us. It'll be harder to keep Grace safe if she's riding on my back."

"Who said she'd be the one riding on your back?" asked Jag, peering between Wyatt and Grace, his expression murderous.

"I agree," said Tythas to Grace and Wyatt, the three of them ignoring Jag entirely. "Hiking it is. We had best get a few hours' rest before we arrive. I suggest we take to the hammocks. Prepare yourselves for a fight, because Apep may very well be waiting for us when we get there."

Jag grumbled something unintelligible, walking over to the nearest hammock and climbing in with a sullen sort of flop. The other three watched him for a moment before all of them burst out laughing.

Wyatt,

I don't even know if you've been getting my letters. I know you won't get this one. I don't have a lot of time left… I'm losing blood pretty quickly. It's getting hard to hold a quill, so if my handwriting is bad, well, sorry. It never was very good though, was it?

I made a mistake, Wyatt. I never should've left Ven. I'm paying the price now for that mistake. The rest of them… they're all dead. I don't even know what happened. We were camped on the edge of the Wilds, just to the south. Everything was fine. We were supposed to be looking for wildling scouting parties. And sure enough, we found some. We killed all the wildlings, no problem. And then the night after, we're all sitting around the fire, drinking and laughing and singing… it was almost like home again, you know? Just friends and songs and good times. And then Ralph, he just… dies.

They all died. Everyone. The water, something happened to it, something none of us could do anything about. Knives and spears and swords, made of water but razor sharp. The horse troughs, latrine puddles, even our drinks tried to kill us.

Why am I even writing this? You're not going to get it. It's going to burn like the rest of the camp and the bodies around me. I heard that Ven got hit by something. I hope you made it. I hope you and your mom and Rex all got out of there and you're sitting on the docks in Triat or on an island somewhere away from all this death.

Where do I go? I can't walk anymore. I'm going to die here, in a heap of bodies and blood. You chose the right path, Arden. Not me. Not Desmond. I wish I coul

A gloved hand snatched Desmond's wrist, hauling him up from the ground with staggering strength. He managed not to cry out in pain as the wounds to his torso rubbed against the pile of rubble he'd been partially hidden under. He clutched the parchment he'd been writing on with an iron grip. He looked up into his killer's eyes, finding a pale, handsome face looking at him with an amused, almost sadistic smile.

"What do we have here?" said the man, his voice like ice as he looked at Desmond's hand. "Writing a letter to Mom?"

Desmond tried to say something, but the only sound that came out of his mouth was a low, animalistic growl as he struggled against the man's grip. The man laughed, prying the balled up parchment out of Desmond's hand and tossing him aside like a toy. Desmond groaned as he landed in a heap, but he kept his eyes on his enemy, his gaze like fire. He reached for his dagger, the only weapon he had left.

"Dear Wyatt," said the man aloud, his voice mocking. He continued reading the letter, and strangely, his smirk turned into a frown. He read for a few more seconds before turning his icy gaze back on Desmond. Desmond glared back.

"Wyatt Arden?" said the man quietly as he walked toward Desmond, crouching down in front of him. "You know Wyatt Arden, do you? By the sound of this, you know him very well. My, my. That's interesting. Wait here, would you?"

The man turned his back on Desmond, smirking again, and trotted off a ways. There was a horse there waiting for him. Desmond hadn't noticed the horse before. Why hadn't he noticed the horse before?

He slowly slid the blade out of its sheath, silently cursing his fingers as they began to go numb from the blood loss. He didn't have much time left, so he'd have to make this count. This guy, whoever he was, knew Wyatt. Desmond couldn't let his best friend get hurt.

Desmond watched him rummaging around in the saddle bags, looking for something. He reached in, drawing out a small leather-bound book. He opened it, and to Desmond's disgust, bit the end of his finger until he drew blood. He then smeared the blood into the page, rubbing his finger into the parchment with a scowl. Desmond clutched the dagger tight, keeping it barely concealed beneath his chest.

The pale man watched his little book for a moment before nodding with approval. Desmond thought he might've said something, but couldn't hear him from this far off. The man turned, walking slowly back toward Desmond, the sick smile again on his face. Desmond's heart thumped a little harder, and he could feel the life bleeding out of him. One chance.

"Good news," said the man. "You get to live. And you get to come with me."

Desmond waited until the man was barely a few feet from him, and then with all the energy he had left, he wildly flung his body into a roll. He made it just far enough to free his arm, using the momentum from the roll to boost his throw as he hurled his razor-sharp dagger straight into the man's chest.

The man didn't seem to react, and Desmond was sure he'd hit the mark. But at the last second, a tendril of water erupted out of the man's sleeve, snatching Desmond's blade out of the air with ease. The man didn't even look at it, still watching Desmond with that same smile as it fell to the dirt. He walked closer, crouching down again. Desmond felt the rest of his energy rushing out of him, and he knew he'd lose consciousness soon.

"You've got fight in you," breathed the man, leaning close. His breath was a toxic, sickly sort of sweet. "I like that. You're going to need it where you're going. Hold onto that, kid, and you might just survive what he's going to do to you."

CHAPTER EIGHTEEN

ythas's sailor friend dropped the four of them as close to the shore as he could, but they still had to swim the rest of the way. The mountain didn't have a beach on the rear side; instead, they'd have to climb a short rock face to reach the actual trail. Tythas had insisted on their arrival that he'd done it "many times" in the past before executing a graceful dive from the stern of the boat and swimming merrily for shore, much to Jag's chagrin.

The others followed him into the water. Luckily, the weather wasn't nearly as bad, thanks to Wyatt's improved mood. The water was cool and refreshing, and the swim was brief. They reached the rock face, following Tythas up a path of hand and foot holds that none of them had spotted without the old man's assistance. He scaled the wall easily, chuckling to himself as the other three took a slower, more sure time in climbing up the wall.

Once everyone was atop the flat rock, Tythas took a moment to dry everyone off with a subtle nudge of heat from his hands. The four of them checked themselves over for a moment before finally looking up at the mountain ahead of them. It was impossibly tall, ending not in a sharp peak like Wyatt had expected, but a flat cap. Tythas smiled up at it, nostalgia shining in his eyes for a moment. But the moment was brief, as his smile quickly turned into a frown.

Grace noticed him falter. "Vance? What's wrong?"

"Something is different," he said, sounding a little unsure of himself. "I think. It has been a long time since I was here, but... I don't know.

Maybe my old brain is just getting addled. But I remember there being a peak, not a flat part like that."

There are Adepts atop the mountain, said Shem inside of Wyatt's mind. *I can feel them from here. Something is amiss.*

"We're too late," hissed Wyatt, clutching the hilt of his sword. "They're here already. We can't wait six hours. We have to fly up there now."

"How can you tell?" asked Jag, a hand on Wyatt's shoulder.

Wyatt lifted the sword just a bit, nodding to Jag. "A little bird told me."

Tythas reached into his robes, drawing his amulet out. "I'll take Jag, as he's heavier. It'll be easier for me and less strain on Wyatt. Wyatt, conserve your strength as best you can."

There was a flash of light, and when Wyatt looked back, Tythas's shape was gone. A great shadow flew over them, and Jag jumped up and spread his arms just in time for Tythas's great, shadowy bird form to catch him by the arms and carry him through the air, toward the mountain.

Wyatt crouched down, looking over to Grace. "Come on, then," he said, smiling at her confidently. She walked over and climbed up on his back. Making sure she was holding tight, he stood and let his mind fall into his power, wrapping the two of them in the warm, steady embrace of the wind.

"If you tell me to jump off, I swear..." growled Grace. Distantly, Wyatt heard her and smiled.

He leapt, the wind catching them and carrying them upward with quickness and ease. Flying was certainly harder with Grace riding on his back, but Wyatt noted that it was easier this time than it had been in Farillyon. He'd eaten good food and gotten some sleep, and that made an extreme difference.

He could feel Shem in his mind, too, eagerly awaiting a fight and silently offering a small amount of strength to Wyatt. Wyatt took it without question, knowing he'd need all the energy he could get when he got to the top of the mountain. Wyatt found Shem's hunger for fighting a little bit unsettling, but he wasn't sure if it came from a true desire to fight or a simple need to release energy that had been built up over however many thousand years.

He and Grace soared through the sky, catching up to Tythas's gigantic flapping form. Jag gave them a thumbs-up as they climbed and climbed, the forested landscape of the Mount of Light moving quickly beneath their feet as they did. In a matter of minutes, Wyatt could clearly see the vegetation line on the mountain, where the gray peak jutted out above the trees.

And Tythas had been right. Something was definitely wrong. It looked like as if the top of the mountain had been cleaved neatly off, leaving a strange, almost perfectly flat place atop the mountain, perhaps three hundred feet in diameter. It was unlike anything Wyatt had ever seen, and for some reason that he didn't understand, it chilled him to his bones.

Wyatt and Tythas reached the edge of the flat peak, landing and unloading their cargo quickly. Tythas's form flashed with light again, and when the light faded, he was back to normal. He stowed his amulet back in his robes, the mirth gone from his expression. He looked across the flat surface of the mountaintop with heavy eyes.

The mountain was flat, save for a single, jagged crack that ran the entire length of the flat peak. In the very center, Wyatt could see the runic etchings that surely made up one of the seals. The long crack bisected the seal entirely, and if it had once glowed with power and light, it was now lifeless and broken.

There were people waiting for them, but not the people that Wyatt had expected. Three members of the Dominion stood atop the seal, the one in the center standing ahead of his smaller comrades. The forehead of each was adorned with a painted flame. The one in the middle, obviously in charge, wore a sleeveless leather chestpiece that allowed his muscular arms to show. Intricate tattoos of elaborate flames ran over every inch of exposed skin, making him look even more fearsome.

Tythas stepped forward, taking the lead. "Mubaraji, what are you doing here?"

The man sneered at Tythas. "Not even enough respect in you to observe our customs and greet me properly. You were welcomed into our glorious Dominion, Vance Tythas. Show me the proper respect as your superior."

Tythas spread his arms, his expression sarcastic and annoyed. "We're not exactly in your Dominion anymore, Mubaraji. I know you assume that everything belongs to the Dominion, but in this case, you are wrong. The Mount of Light is most certainly the Empire's land. So I ask once again, Mubaraji. What are you doing here?"

The huge Pyromancer chuckled. "I am not here for you, Tythas. As much as I would like to drag your traitorous hide back to the Warlord, I am here on a much more important mission. I have come for the demon you consort with." He raised a finger toward Wyatt, who blinked in confusion.

Tythas gaped at the man. "A demon? Mubaraji, have you lost your mind? It can be said that the two of us have never gotten along, but you have more sense than that. Demons do not exist. Wyatt is not a demon. He is just an Adept, like you and me."

"Do not think to compare yourself, or anyone else, to a great member of the Dominion such as myself," snarled Mubaraji. "Now still your tongue, old man. I want to speak with the boy."

Tythas opened his mouth to say something in response, but Wyatt put a hand on his shoulder, stepping forward. "Don't," he said quietly. "If he wants to talk to me, let him."

Wyatt stepped ahead of Tythas, holding his arms out. "Here I am."

Mubaraji nodded gravely. "You have become a problem for the people that I serve, demon. I am going to send you back into the Pit, where the other beasts like you were cast when Ignis walked the earth."

Wyatt snorted. "The three of you are going to fight the four of us? Those are long odds."

Mubaraji shook his head. "No. You caused Mount Trajnheim to explode. You brought hell upon my people. You are the problem, and you alone are my target. I may not like Vance Tythas, but boy... I hate you."

So Tythas had been right. Apep had managed to delude his allies into believing that Wyatt and the others had caused the eruption, that they had killed the Warlord and tried to destroy the Dominion. He hoped Salif was okay. Yasmir, too. But there would be no use arguing with a man like Mubaraji. That much was obvious.

Wyatt shifted his feet, unconsciously adopting a more defensive position. "What do you mean?"

Mubaraji drew a dagger, drawing the edge across his palm and squeezing until blood dripped down the hilt. "By my blood, by my power, and by my life... I challenge you, Wyatt Arden, to a blood duel." he said, his voice commanding and firm, showing no sign of pain as the steel bit into his flesh.

Wyatt looked over his shoulder at Tythas, frowning. "I think I already know the answer to this, but what is a blood duel?"

Tythas had gone pale. "It's a ritualistic battle between two warriors that sometimes occurs in the Dominion," he said, staring at Mubaraji. "But... it's more than a fight. He's laying out both his rank and his life for the taking. Wyatt, if you defeat him in a fight, you'll be a member of the Dominion. You'll assume Mubaraji's role as a member of the War Council, as well as gaining all of his property."

Wyatt blinked. "I'm not a Pyromancer," he said, confused. "How does that work?"

Tythas shook his head. "I am not aware of anyone outside of the Dominion who has ever been challenged, but as far as I know the laws remain the same. Beat him and you gain his rank, title, lands... everything his becomes yours."

Wyatt looked back to Mubaraji, incredulous. "Why? Why would you do this?"

Mubaraji gave him a flat, serious look. "Because you have committed a great crime against my people. You would not risk your life against me normally. You are shrewd and cowardly, like your companions. Unlike you, I am an honorable man, and I do not attack from behind. Now you see how serious your crimes are, and now you know how deeply upsetting they are to the people of the Dominion. We will not allow you to go unpunished. But the time for talk is over. Do you accept the challenge?"

Thoughts raced through Wyatt's head. If he were a powerful member of the Dominion, he would be able to help Salif stop the campaign against the Empire. He could actually help bring some unity back to the world. And he could use their resources to search out his mother. He might even be able to sever their ties to Apep and deal a blow to the Necromancer's plans. Mubaraji had offered him something that would be very difficult to refuse.

A great weight settled on Wyatt's shoulders as he let out a low breath. A strange calm washed over him as he looked up into Mubaraji's eyes.

"I accept," he said simply.

Mubaraji tossed the dagger across the space that separated them. "Then spill your blood on the stone beneath you, as is customary. And then we will begin."

Wyatt looked back to the others, who were watching the interaction wordlessly. Grace looked like she was going to be sick.

Wyatt settled his mind and reached out to Shem, who buzzed reassuringly. Then, without another thought, he drew the sharp blade of the dagger across his left palm.

A line of hot, fiery pain erupted along his hand, but he swallowed the pain and put it out of his mind. He held out his hand and squeezed, letting the blood drop from his clenched fist onto the stone beneath him. With his other hand, he tossed the dagger aside, not watching as it fell over the edge of the mountain.

Mubaraji removed the knives hanging around his belt, as well as the curved sword on his back. Once he had removed all of his weapons, he handed them to his two companions, who took them and retreated to the far edge of the flat top of the mountain. They were both expressionless, but Wyatt got the impression from them that this endeavor was entirely Mubaraji's, not the Dominion's as he had said.

Wyatt drew the leather baldric over his head and walked back to his friends. He handed the sword to Tythas. "Keep that safe, please. And don't let him get to you. Shem, if I die or get separated from everyone else somehow, you are to help them however you can."

Be careful, Wyatt, echoed Shem in his mind, and Wyatt thought that just maybe, the strange little cat might've meant it.

"You're an idiot, you know," blurted Grace angrily, her cheeks red. "But we don't have time to talk you out of this anymore. Don't die."

Wyatt sighed. "Grace, I..."

She shook her head, cutting him off. "I know. I would've done the same thing. So shut up and go win. Make us proud."

Jag clapped him on the shoulder. "You can beat him. Just be smart, keep your head, and stay out of the fire."

Wyatt gave him a sour look. "Easier said."

Tythas pointed to Mubaraji. "He is strong and an excellent fighter, Wyatt. But he is overconfident. He is absolutely certain in his mind and heart that he can beat you, which will be his greatest weakness. Use that."

Wyatt nodded wordlessly. He took one more moment to look at the faces of his friends before turning and walking back to Mubaraji. They met at the center of the mountaintop, standing over the cracked seal that had been Aeris's mark. Wyatt stood perhaps ten feet from Mubaraji, his heart pounding. Not having Shem hung at his hip or clenched in his hand felt exceptionally strange. He knew that without the sword, he would be weaker than normal. But he had to win. He just had to.

Mubaraji clapped his hands, and a huge ring of fire roared up around them, leaving maybe a fifty foot circle in which they had room to fight. The fire was tall, and even as far as he was from it, he could feel the heat rolling off of it.

And then Mubaraji was moving. The huge man roared like a caged lion, surging toward Wyatt with an almost impossible amount of speed for a man his size. Wyatt just barely managed to dodge a massive punch to his body that probably would have put him out.

But dodge it he did. He spun, answering the punch with a wild kick to the Pyromancer's gut as he called a blast of wind to hit him in the same spot. Wyatt's boot connected with Mubaraji's midsection as the wind roared in, taking him by the shoulders. The combined forces sent the huge Pyromancer flying backward through the air, tumbling end over end.

Mubaraji righted himself in midair, flipping over and landing on his feet. He didn't even seem fazed by Wyatt's kick, and within seconds, he was charging once again.

Wyatt skipped back, retreating to the edge of the small battlefield to try to give himself more time to think. He could feel the roaring wall of fire at his back, threatening to set his hair and clothes on fire if he got any closer.

Mubaraji paused with a smirk a ways away from him. He raised his arms as if to say, "come at me."

Thunder boomed overhead as a cold rain began to fall around them. Wyatt could hear it sizzling as it hit the wall of fire. He hadn't even noticed the darkening sky, but he was grateful that he had called the storm, even unconsciously. He stilled his thoughts and sank deeper into the wind, leaving his nerves behind. As high up as he was, as close to the sky and the elements as he was, he found a strange sort of calm.

Mubaraji looked up at the sky, his smile wavering. A flash of lightning lit the clouds, followed immediately by a deafening crash of thunder that reverberated deep within Wyatt's chest. He could almost feel that power flowing through his body, aching to release.

Mubaraji looked back to Wyatt and charged, his expression determined. Wyatt crouched down, holding his hands up and pulling at his power like he never had before.

Time seemed to slow. Wyatt could see the muscles in Mubaraji's neck sticking out and straining as he hurled himself forward. He could see the tendons in his arms tighten and loosen. Every tensely wound inch of Mubaraji's body was surging at him, ready to go for a killing blow. Wyatt felt his strength tested as his power reacted, welling up and out of him like a roaring geyser.

When Mubaraji was about ten feet from Wyatt, the sky answered his call. Lightning, great and terrible, flashed down from the sky. As close as he was, Wyatt had to avert his eyes or risk losing his sight. But he could feel it, surging through his entire body. His skin tingled. The air crackled and roared around him. A normal man would've surely been knocked aside by the energy flowing through the air, but to Wyatt it felt like a wonderful rush. He let the tingling, crackling power wash over him.

Then, silence. Wyatt opened his eyes, looking to the spot where the lightning had struck. His heart skipped a beat.

Where Mubaraji had stood before, there was now a great sphere of rock that seemed to have grown directly out of the mountain. Wyatt stared at it in bewilderment as the rain fell around them.

Then, the stone shifted. As if turned to liquid, the surface rippled, a wave moving through it that started at the top and rolled all the way to the bottom. The top opened as the liquid stone sank down, revealing Mubaraji's crouched, unharmed form glaring at Wyatt. The stone sank down into the mountain and settled, and after a moment there was no sign that it had ever been disturbed.

Wyatt gaped at him. Mubaraji got to his feet, cutting a striking figure against the rain and the flaming backdrop as the thunder rumbled. He seemed to magnify in Wyatt's eyes, suddenly a much more deadly foe than he had realized at the start.

"Wyatt!" came Tythas's distant voice over the fire and rain. "He's a Terramancer! Be careful!"

"I got that, yeah!" yelled Wyatt in response, trying to shake off the cold fatigue that was creeping over his body. Calling that much lightning had already taken a lot out of him, and Mubaraji was virtually unharmed.

"I must congratulate you," called Mubaraji over the rain, cracking his knuckles and pacing from side to side. "You have forced me to reveal the other side of my power. Only one man has ever done that, boy. Do you know who that was?"

Wyatt shook his head, slowly stepping to the side as he tried to get his back away from the fire. He needed more space.

"The Warlord whom you killed," growled Mubaraji. "A great man, and the best warrior I have ever known. He defeated me in a fight much like this one. But he spared my life, being impressed by my powers. He allowed me to keep my title and my position. And then he promoted me, appointing me to his War Council."

Wyatt shook his head. "I know what you think, but I didn't kill him, Mubaraji. Apep did. You know, deep down, that Apep isn't your ally. We're trying to stop him. But I didn't do anything to harm your people, Mubaraji, except get there too late. And for that, I'm sorry."

Mubaraji snorted. "You are beneath me, demon, and therefore not worthy of offering an apology. But do not speak to me as if I am a child. We know what the man you call Apep is, and he will only be an ally of the Dominion until we can defeat the Empire. Then, the flames will consume him as well."

Wyatt sighed, shaking his head. They had no idea. They thought Apep was just a rogue Necromancer; they had no concept of the power that was commanding him, power that he was about to unleash on the world. And he only had one seal left.

Wyatt opened his mouth to speak again, but Mubaraji raised a hand. "No more talk, demon. Now you die."

Before Wyatt could prepare himself, Mubaraji was suddenly in front of him, his fist smashing across Wyatt's face like a hammer. Pain exploded through his skull as he lost his balance, falling down onto the stone with a cry of pain.

He felt like his brain was underwater. He couldn't seem to make his body work correctly; everything was sluggish and weak. His hands were shaking as he tried to crawl away from Mubaraji. He blinked as blood fell into his eyes and dripped down on the stone.

Mubaraji kicked him in the gut, and Wyatt felt his ribs break as he rolled, crying out in pain again. He managed to create some distance between himself and the hulking Pyromancer, doing his best to shut out the pain. He kept rolling, as far as he could.

Finally, he came to his feet, finding a shaky balance. Mubaraji lounged several feet away, looking amused. Wyatt wiped the blood from his mouth and spat the rest aside. He knew that another hit like that would be the end of him. He shook his hands, trying to get the shaking and tingling to go away, and called more wind to wrap around him.

It answered the call, but not nearly as easily as before. His body calmed and his mind steadied just enough to bolster his confidence, albeit not much.

Mubaraji roared again, and the flaming ring around them intensified. Wyatt felt a wave of heat roll over them, the blast of hot air loosening his grip on the wind and making it harder to breathe.

"Fire can make its own wind, boy!" yelled Mubaraji as he circled. The ring of fire seemed to tighten around them, forcing Wyatt to move closer toward his enemy. "You are obviously powerful, but you have no idea how to fight other Adepts!"

The heat was making it difficult for Wyatt to reach the wind. The hot air was hard to work with and unpredictable. It would be impossible for him to call any kind of powerful wind while this kind of heat was flowing around them.

Wyatt pulled again at his power, focusing it into his hands. Crackling energy snarled to life on his fingertips. He sent three quick blasts out toward Mubaraji as he ran to the side, the small blue bolts bright and deadly.

Mubaraji dodged the first and threw his hands out, the stone beneath him rippling. Thin fingers of rock rose up, blocking Wyatt's bolts as they shattered to bits.

The rain intensified, making it hard to see the other side of the battlefield. Wyatt could hear the flames behind him turning it to steam, hitting and popping. He was soaked to the bone.

"Enough!" shouted Mubaraji. He held his hands out toward Wyatt, and the hair on his neck prickled.

Wyatt ran for his life, trying to dodge whatever was about to come his way. He moved to the side as a screaming gout of flame shot out from Mubaraji's hands, covering nearly half of the circle they were fighting in.

Wyatt felt his foot hit the stone, but instead of sturdy rock, he felt like it sank into deep mud. He realized his mistake too late as the stone solidified, catching his left foot and locking it in place.

He did his best to remain steady and looked up just in time to see the roaring fire overtake him. He threw up his arms, covering his neck and head instinctively as he braced himself for a painful death. Distantly, he thought he could hear Grace screaming his name.

From far away, he felt Shem in his mind. He couldn't make out any words, but he thought the cat was speaking to him. He felt the rumbling of the cat's deep voice like a pressure on his heart. The voice moved through his entire being, and Wyatt felt that voice unlock something that was hidden deep within his heart.

Instead of the searing pain he had been expecting, Wyatt felt a gentle, almost tickling warmth. He felt the fire wrap around him, but instead of burning him, it seemed to surge into him, as if he could feed off of it.

The cold fatigue that had come over him before vanished as he held onto the heat of the flame. He pulled at it as if he were pulling at his own power, drawing it in and welcoming it as it coursed through him. It energized him, strengthened him. He felt the wound on his head close and his ribs beginning to mend.

And now he could see Mubaraji. The Pyromancer's face was contorted in to a mask of rage and concentration. He was confused, but instead of breaking off his power and halting the flame as he should have, he poured more power into it. The roaring, hellish inferno intensified, making Wyatt's eyes sting from the brightness of it. Mubaraji roared with effort, taking a braced stance and giving the fire everything he had.

Wyatt opened himself to the fire with renewed vigor. He felt his ribs heal, felt every nagging ache and pain that he'd been carrying vanish. Soon, he started to worry that he wouldn't be able to take any more. He felt like the energy was going to burst out of him. It was hot and strong, and he knew that he was going to need to let it out soon.

An idea sprung into his mind, an idea he knew would finish the fight. He slipped out of his left boot, having not sunk far enough into the stone for it to grip his ankle. He braced himself, calling the wind with a wild, fiery pull of his power.

He leapt forward into the flame as a great gust of wind caught him by the back and propelled him forward like a javelin. The empowered gust cut through Mubaraji's wall of fire as if it weren't even there, meeting Wyatt's call instantly. He felt the lightning within him and called it to bear, the crackling energy wrapping around his entire body. He could see Mubaraji's stunned expression as Wyatt flew through the fire he was creating, splitting it aside without any visible sign of damage.

And he connected. The Pyromancer, baffled by Wyatt's frontal attack, reacted far too late. He tried to move aside at the last second, but Wyatt was already there. His knee slammed into Mubaraji's face, the lightning that was wrapped around him blasting into the Pyromancer from that connection. Wyatt felt bone breaking under his knee before the huge, tattooed man was hurled backward by the blast of electricity and wind. Wyatt saw the ring of fire around them weaken and falter before going out completely as he landed, rolling into a crouch as he watched his foe.

The Pyromancer also rolled, but not by choice. He flopped awkwardly as he skidded across the flat mountaintop, his limbs flailing and slamming into the stone repeatedly. But his flailing may have also saved his life, as he came to a halt just at the edge of the cliff, limp and unmoving.

Suddenly, the rain and his own pounding heart were the only sounds in Wyatt's ears. Mubaraji stirred, trying to rise with a moan. But his body was broken and his power was spent. Wyatt knew he wouldn't get up again.

He turned just to see his friends running toward him, all of them soaking wet. Wyatt grinned at them, feeling immensely relieved and quite pleased that he had managed to come out of the fight without an injury. He spat the remainder of the blood out of his mouth and started walking toward them to meet him.

"Stop moving!" yelled Grace as she reached him. She made it there first, gripping his shoulder as Wyatt felt her power flare to life. She looked concerned at first, but she quickly realized that he was not injured, and her concern switched to confusion.

"How in the world are you not hurt?" she asked as Jag and Tythas caught up to them. Wyatt looked down at himself and shrugged.

"No clue," he said honestly, looking up to Tythas. The old man had stepped aside to speak with the other two members of the Dominion, all three of them locked in a quiet conversation. Tythas was scratching his chin and nodding as the other two pointed to Mubaraji.

"I think you just earned your stripes, kid," said Jag, clapping Wyatt on the shoulder. "That was quite a punch to the face you took. The fact that it didn't take your head completely off your shoulders is enough, but then you got up!"

"I'm glad I could be so entertaining," replied Wyatt dryly, rubbing his jaw. Jag laughed.

Tythas walked back up to them, his expression pensive and subdued. "These two are called Witnesses," he said with a motion toward the other two Pyromancers. "Their position within the Dominion is to oversee trials and ceremonies like this. They are unbiased enforcers of tribal law. In this case, they were here to officially recognize the winner of this fight as a member of the War Council."

The older of the two Witnesses walked up to Wyatt, saluting with a fist to his heart. "The Blaze is strong in you, Councilman. Welcome to the Dominion of Fire."

Wyatt nodded, returning the salute, feeling a bit awkward. "What will happen to Mubaraji?"

The Witness looked over to the unconscious form at the edge of the mountaintop, his expression thoughtful. "He is alive. Should he survive the trip back to our lands, he will be healed and put in captivity. He will work as a slave until you arrive and decide his fate. Or, if you prefer, we can kill him now and be done with it."

Wyatt shook his head. "No, that's not necessary. Keep him alive as best you can. When he's healed, find him a job that can put his skills to work. He can still be of use to the people of the Dominion. I'm sure you can find a place for a skilled warrior like him."

The Witness nodded. "I can. When will you return to the Dominion? There is typically a ceremony for new citizens, winners of a blood duel, and new councilmen. You must be sworn in under the Law of Ignis, and… Well, there is much to do."

Wyatt sighed and nodded. "We've got a lot to do out here first. I wish I could come sooner, but it will have to wait. But I want you to take a message to the council. Tell them that Apep is not their ally. Tell them that he's using them to break the seals that keep Necron at bay. The final seal is within Farillyon, and if the Dominion assists Apep in sacking the capital, he'll have full access to the seal. He'll break it, and Necron will rise up and cast the whole world into Death."

The Witness stared at him. "Necron, the Father of Dread? That is Apep's goal?"

Wyatt nodded. "And he's getting close to completing it. I swear to you on my power and my title. So go, get that message to the council, and tell them that if they continue their path of war, they will find only death. Salif will stand by me."

The Witness gave Wyatt a respectful, solemn nod, and after a brief discussion with his colleague, the two of them collected Mubaraji and disappeared down the main path of the mountain.

Wyatt sat down on the stone, putting his head in his hands. Despite what absorbing all of Mubaraji's power had done for him, his whole body was beginning to ache all over. Probably from using so much power, he imagined. He just wasn't used to that kind of energy flowing through him.

"You did well, Wyatt," said Tythas quietly, sitting down near him. The other two followed suit, forming a little circle on the stone. "That was a vicious fight. Mubaraji is not a weak man, not by anyone's assessment. You did very well."

Wyatt looked up into the elder Adept's eyes as uncertainty boiled within him. "Why didn't he kill me, Vance? He should've killed me. I should be a pile of cooked meat right now, but instead, it was like… it was like I sucked his power into me and used it against him. He healed me with fire. How does that make any sense?"

The other three exchanged glances. Jag and Grace looked as confused as Wyatt felt. Tythas cleared his throat, looking thoughtful.

"There are a few possibilities, I suppose," he said, scratching his goatee. "You could have some Pyromantic abilities, passed down from your grandfather. While mingling of Aspects is uncommon, it is not impossible. I am proof of that, as well as Mubaraji. It is also equally likely that whatever sleeps within your sword had something to do with it. Why don't you ask?"

He handed the sword back to Wyatt, who took it gingerly in his hands. Wyatt's mind was a sea of confusion and anger, some of which was directed at Shem when his hands closed around the hilt.

He didn't need to ask the question, though. He felt Shem stir within the sword, felt that presence grow in his mind as the sword buzzed in response.

Tythas is right, of course, echoed Shem in Wyatt's mind. *You do have some part of Ignis's gift living within you.*

Wyatt was tempted to yell at the sword, but thought better of it. *Why didn't you tell me before?* he asked, trying to remain calm.

Because your mind couldn't understand your power yet, replied the cat slowly, his voice deep and calm. It was as docile as Wyatt had ever heard him. *I know you are angry, and I know you do not understand. But that is the point. That kind of power, especially that particular Aspect, is dangerous. You weren't ready to know what you are until you walked into that fight with no help, your head held high. You stared down death and proved to yourself that you were worthy of wielding Ignis's fire. All I did was open the door.*

So he had to try to cook me alive for you to help me? replied Wyatt scathingly, savoring the image of pummeling the cat in his mind.

He had yet to put you in any real danger, said the cat simply. While Wyatt appreciated Shem's help in unlocking his powers and saving his life, he was suddenly very aware of how much the cat probably knew and wasn't telling him. The cat claimed that his knowledge was restricted by his binding, but he wasn't sure if he believed it.

"He agrees with that," said Wyatt out loud, shaking himself out of his internal dialogue and putting his attention back to the foreground. "Smugly, I might add. I guess I'll fit into the Dominion better than I thought."

Tythas gave a long sigh. "That complicates things. Pyromancy is dangerous. It can kill you if you're careless."

Wyatt eyed him flatly. "I think any of this insanity can kill me if I'm not careful," he said dryly. "I'll keep it in mind, but we've got bigger problems at the moment."

Tythas chuckled a bit, nodding. "Just be careful. I'll be able to tell you more about it later, but we don't really have time to go down that road right now."

Grace shifted her position, looking at Tythas. "This seal has already been broken," she said, idly tracing a fingertip over the broken rune. "By the look of it, for a long time. This whole thing was just a diversion."

Tythas inclined his head. "It looks that way, yes. I think a part of the mountain broke off and collapsed. Judging by the base of the mountain, this cleft probably runs through the whole thing. But this is such a rarely-traveled part of the Empire that there may not have even been any witnesses. Some of the nearby towns might've felt a bit of a rumble, but beyond that... there's no telling when it might have happened."

"Which leaves the seal of Life," noted Jag, his expression somber. "Apep and Necron knew that the whole time. They're probably already marching on Farillyon."

Tythas nodded as the rest of them stared at the broken seal, as if it might tell them a secret for victory. But the seal did not speak; it was as lifeless as the stone it had been carved into.

Wyatt got to his feet, growling in response to his sore body and his depressing allies. "So let's stop sitting around here worrying about it," he said harshly, "and go find them. Let's go stop them and finish this."

"It's a long walk," said Jag, looking up at him. "We sailed for nearly a full day on a straight course with strong wind at our backs. It'll take a lot longer to cover that distance on foot. And we're not exactly friends of Farillyon, either."

"Then we had best start walking," said Grace, flashing a light smile at Wyatt. "We're the only ones who can warn the Empire about what's coming. If we can get there before Apep does... we might have a chance."

The other two got to their feet. "Aren't you worried about what they might do, though?" asked Jag, glancing up at Tythas. "I mean, the whole kingdom is still looking for us, right? What if we get caught?"

Wyatt clapped him on the shoulder. "I don't think we really have a choice, do we? The heroes in the stories never do, either. But they always do what they have to do. You said it yourself, Jag. So if we're going to be heroes, let's do the thing right."

Jag groaned. "I should never have told him that."

CHAPTER NINETEEN

Tyvarion Il'Vir was in a sour mood. His children and their frustratingly talented friends had somehow managed to vanish from Imperial lands without leaving even a hint at where they might be headed. Alvernon had been sent to track them, but had so far turned up no results. The Emperor was keeping a close eye on the unpredictable Aquamancer, but it was becoming more and more difficult the further he strayed from the capital. Despite Mugalo's assurances that Alvernon was tamed, the Emperor did not trust him. Worse yet, the eruption at Mount Trajnheim had sent the Dominion into such a flurry of patriotism and xenophobia that any kind of peace talks had all but ceased. They had retreated into the Blazelands, further than Imperial scouts could safely follow.

He quickly scanned over a dozen or so scouting reports, noting that not one of them held a shred of useful information. For someone who had once prided himself on the extent of his knowledge and reach throughout the country, the Emperor was now feeling incredibly blind. He needed to get the advantage back, but he had yet to figure out how to do that.

A knock echoed from his door. That was strange. Normally, it was understood that while he was in his office with the door closed, he was not to be disturbed. Except, of course, in cases of extreme emergency. Either he had a particularly thick-headed aide who needed his signature (and a cuff on the head as well), or something very bad had just happened.

"Enter," he spoke, his voice low and commanding. Sometimes he marveled at how much his voice had changed. In his youth, he'd been a military commander. Then, his voice had been loud and harsh. Now that he was in command of everyone, his voice wasn't loud unless it was absolutely necessary. But even a whisper stopped his subjects in their tracks.

The door creaked open as four hooded figures slipped inside. Alarm and caution flared inside of the Emperor, and he quickly reached for the inscribed bell near his desk that, when rung, would ring the others linked to it and signal an alarm to the castle. He already began to call at his power, a reflexive action that caused the stone walls around them to creak and shift in sympathy.

The first figure moved with remarkable, almost inhuman speed, his cloak billowing open as he hurled a heavy wood-handled knife. Just behind him, the second figure made a motion with his hands, and the papers on the Emperor's desk flew in every direction as a great wind blew through the room. Just before his hand reached the rope to pull the bell, the knife slammed into the base of it with an unnatural speed, pegging it to the wall with a brief "clank" before the bell silenced itself.

Three rings meant that there was an emergency. Two meant that the Emperor could use some help, but it was no emergency. A muffled clank generally meant that he accidentally bumped into the bell and nobody should pay it any mind. They wouldn't think twice about it.

The stone bracelets around the Emperor's wrists, holdovers from a different time, began to shift and writhe, to come alive at his gentle call. He fell back into a defensive crouch as his arms were sheathed in razor-sharp spikes of black stone.

"Emperor, I beg you, still your power," said an unmistakably familiar voice from underneath the second hood. The cloaked figure who had spoken stepped forward, drawing back his hood and revealing the aging, dignified face of Vance Tythas. "We are not here for a fight, unless you force one upon us."

Il'Vir kept his expression neutral, but if Tythas was here, the other three were doubtless his wayward children and their exceptional new friend. He'd have to bring the whole castle down to win this fight, something he was certainly not willing to do. So he relaxed, the stone on his arms reshaping and becoming simple bracelets once more.

"Hello, Father," said a cool voice as the first figure drew back his hood. The proud, hard, strong eyes of his lost son, his greatest regret, stared back as the Emperor did his best to control himself. He ached to tell his son how proud he was, but he knew that anything he said to the young man at this point in his life would be met only with spite. That bridge had been burnt to cinders years ago.

Grace drew back her hood as well, but said nothing. She was watching her brother with an apprehensive expression on her face. The final figure also drew back his hood, revealing the youthful face of the Adept who had vexed the entire Empire so. He had defeated more men single-handedly than many would boast about defeating in their lives. And he'd managed to not kill a single one of them, a true testament to the boy's character. He looked now like he felt exceptionally out of place. The Emperor didn't blame him; this little family reunion that had fallen in his lap was not likely to be a happy occasion, especially considering the bounty that he'd put out on his own son's head.

"Why are you here, then?" asked the Emperor, relaxing his posture and returning to his seat at his desk, not bothering with the scattered papers. He felt extremely tired as he looked up at them. "And more importantly, how in the Pit's black shadow did you get in?"

Tythas sat down at one of the chairs on the other side of the desk, his manner diplomatic and pleasant. The door opened behind them again, and Mugalo slid into the room. The Emperor had always wondered how the man could stand to be so disgustingly snakelike. He really did seem to slide places at times, a surefire sign that he was up to no good.

"I let them in, your Grace," said Mugalo, sitting in the chair next to Tythas, who shifted uncomfortably. Evidently he shared the Emperor's distaste of the wily old Pyromancer. Not really that big of a surprise. Tythas had always been a reasonable man, which was perhaps his downfall.

Il'Vir gave Mugalo a flat look. "Enlighten me then, Mugalo, as to why you would let a number of wanted criminals into my office. Or my castle. Or my city."

Mugalo offered a wheezy chuckle. "Because the situation deems it necessary. I serve you, Emperor, but I also serve the Empire, which is far more important than your poorly handled familial drama. Fear not, as they are not here to discuss any philosophical differences. They are here because for the last month, they have been fighting the battle that you, that we, have been blind to. They are here now because they have nowhere else to turn, and neither do you." The Emperor watched Mugalo for a moment before his eyes drifted to the Aeromancer at the back of the room, who was still silent. The boy was looking out the window, his demeanor equal parts pensive and commanding.

"I don't quite follow, which I'm sure was your intention," admitted the Emperor, looking back to Mugalo. "But you have my attention."

Tythas nodded, taking over. "Several months ago, while I was traveling with your children and trying to undo some of the damage wrought by your anti-Necromancy decree, I happened upon some information from one of the Necromancers that we smuggled out of the Empire. He said that he had been approached by a very, very old Necromancer who promised him unending wealth and power if he were to offer his help in completing a few tasks. Supposedly, the old Necromancer reeked of corrupted power. You know the smell, I believe."

The Emperor nodded, not at all liking where this story was headed. "I remember."

"In short," continued Tythas, "he made the man we helped sick. Our friend was a true Necromancer, not one of the twisted ones. He served Death as a faithful servant, and had not been corrupted by the power. He refused the old man's offer."

Il'Vir listened without comment, watching the weathered lines on Tythas's face as the story went on.

"We halted our normal work and put some effort into tracking this old Adept down, as the description that was given to me did not sit well with my memories of the war. A little over a month ago, we tracked him to Ven. I'm sure you know how that turned out. We saw your scouts flying overhead shortly after we left. What they wouldn't have been able to tell you, I imagine, is that the Necromancer we had been tracking was Apep the Snake. He somehow survived the war, survived my fight with him, and has been continuing his work in secret."

Shock flooded through the Emperor, but he did his best to remain outwardly calm. His mind was racing. "He found a seal in Ven," he said, the portrait of that event suddenly becoming a lot clearer. The earthquake. The ruined buildings. The Atumen that had inexplicably woken up.

Tythas offered a nod. "Yes, and he broke it. From there, we chased him into the heart of the Firelands, where he had been toiling for months in an attempt to curry favor with the Dominion. He quite cleverly turned them against us, and it wasn't long before we realized that he had spun a remarkable tale and twisted their views so badly that they would actually blame the eruption of Mount Trajnheim on the Empire. The eruption, by the way, was caused by Apep sacrificing the Warlord and breaking the seal with his blood."

The Emperor felt a pang of regret. The Warlord was a good man, a great fighter, and a reasonable diplomat. During the war, the two of them had fought side-by-side against Apep's hordes of dead. That would be a difficult blow, and would explain why the peace talks between the two groups had been all but abandoned.

"We arrived here, to search the Archives for the location of the remaining seal. We knew that he had already broken the seal of Water, during the war. That left Aeris's seal, as we knew that the seal of Life was buried beneath this castle. Grace and Wyatt infiltrated the Archive, but you somehow learned of their presence, and an unfortunate circumstance was forced upon us."

Wyatt, the Aeromancer at the window, shifted his feet uneasily as he looked out over the city. He didn't look at all like the unstoppable force that the guards had described. He looked almost... reluctant.

"We chased him to the seal of Air, but we arrived instead to find the seal long broken, and three Pyromancers of the Dominion waiting for us. Mubaraji, having been goaded into the chase by Apep, believed that Wyatt had been the cause of the volcanic eruption. He challenged Wyatt to a blood duel."

The Emperor stiffened. If that was true, and Wyatt was alive and standing before him, then...

"Which he won," said Jag with pride, looking over at Wyatt, who ignored all of them.

"Yes, which he won," said Tythas with a little nod and a smile. "Wyatt is now not only a citizen of the Dominion, but a member of the Dominion's War Council, having gained Mubaraji's status and title. The Dominion which is marching on Farillyon, burning your lands in their wake."

The Emperor froze, staring at Tythas. "What do you mean?" he asked, very puzzled. There had been no reports to suggest any great activity from the Dominion, especially not mobilization of an army.

"It's quite true," commented Mugalo, handing a new batch of reports to the Emperor. "They are coming for us like an arrow to a target. A big, flaming arrow that tears through anything in its path without pause."

The Emperor scanned over the reports quickly. Small villages along the path to Farillyon had been razed. Hundreds were dead. His army was still spread out, fending off pirates in the southeast and wildlings in the northwest. Somehow the Dominion's forces had slipped past them completely. He still had the city guard and the Blades, but that would be far from enough.

"To make matters worse," continued Tythas, "Apep has pledged his own support to them. He has spent the better part of the last thirty years collecting, preparing, and preserving the dead. There is no telling how large his army is, but he likely has thousands of Drones at his command, and no doubt a few other surprises beside them."

Memories of the war flashed through Il'Vir, memories of his own men rising from the ground to bite and claw at him with savage, mindless intent. He suppressed a shudder.

"They close in on the capital, Emperor," said Mugalo with a grave sort of weight. "We've already received reports of the dead army moving toward us. No doubt their plan is to flank us and attack from both sides. We will be overrun."

"Apep is doing all of this so that he can get to the seal, of course," said Tythas. "He has no intention of actually following through with his alliance to the Dominion. Once he has raised Necron from the ground, they will cast the entire world into decay."

The Emperor didn't want to believe them. He wanted to say that Tythas killed Apep all those years ago, or that they were wrong about

Necron, or that the Dominion wouldn't align themselves with a Necromancer. But he had been to the secret place where the seal rested. He had put his hand upon the stone, upon that inscription that Victus had infused with his power. He had felt, with his heart and his hand and his power, what lingered beneath it. He knew in his chest that they were all telling him the truth. They wouldn't be here otherwise.

"What do we need to do?" he asked with resolve, looking at Tythas. Despite their differences, they had a common enemy, and he knew when necessity dictated an alliance. A temporary one, maybe. But it was necessary.

"We need to know where the seal is," said Jag, his voice flat and emotionless. "So we can put some defenses in place. At that point, we need you to draft up an emergency peace treaty. Wyatt can serve as the liaison between the two sides. Even if he's not popular in the Dominion, after defeating Mubaraji so soundly I doubt anyone will challenge his position, at least for now."

Tythas nodded at Jag. "If we can sway the Dominion to our side, even temporarily, we can use their armies to help battle off Apep's Drones and hopefully keep them out of the city and away from the seal. And if he does manage to breach the defenses, we can at least make an attempt at stopping him at the seal. That's our only hope, at this point."

"I could perhaps try to collect our forces," began Il'Vir, but Mugalo cut him off.

"They'll arrive on our doorstep within two days, Emperor," said the old man with a somewhat condescending smile. "The bulk of your army is at least a week out. They'll never make it in time. Farillyon will be burnt and dead by the time they arrive."

The Emperor gave a resigned sigh and nodded. "Very well. Let's go to the seal, and I shall draft up this treaty. It does seem to be the only way." He got to his feet and walked past them, motioning for them to follow.

The castle was vast, a labyrinth unlike Wyatt had ever seen. It reminded him to a degree of the caves that he and Desmond had spent so much time exploring as children. But where those caves had been natural, smooth, and wild, the castle was cold, perfectly shaped, and a little harsh. It was full of corners and edges. The natural, strange shapes of the caves had possessed a kind of life; the castle was shaped without emotion. It was harsh, and Wyatt hated it. He ached for the sky and the sea.

They walked down a seemingly endless number of stairs. Several times, they would walk down stairs only to walk to the other side of the castle and walk up stairs. Passage after passage they walked without speaking. The whole ordeal seemed like a giant waste of time to Wyatt. Why would anyone want to live in such a massive castle? It seemed to be in direct opposition to accomplishing anything.

Finally, after what seemed like an hour of walking, they arrived in the belly of the castle and the Emperor stopped them short in the middle of one of the dimly lit halls underground. He stepped up to the wall ahead of them. Reaching under his shirt, he drew an ancient silver amulet from around his neck and pressed it up to a blank spot on the wall.

To Wyatt's amazement, the amulet actually sank into the wall. Soon it had been completely swallowed, as if it had been dropped into a pool of mud. Glowing white runes flared to life along the whole wall as the bricks twisted and pulled inward, revealing an arch-shaped doorway.

"Magic," he muttered, shaking his head.

The Emperor quickly led them through the doorway, which contained a short dimly-lit hallway and an enormous circular stairway. They descended the stairs quickly and noiselessly, the silence among the group becoming the loudest sound among them. It grated on Wyatt's mind; never before had he felt so out of place, almost as if he were intruding on something very important and very secret. Tythas was at odds with Mugalo, and Jag and Grace were at odds with their father. Wyatt was very much the outsider here.

The Emperor allowed Mugalo to take the lead down the stairway, murmuring a few instructions to him before hanging back to fall in next to Wyatt. Wyatt felt the middle-aged king's stony gaze fall upon him, and he knew that there would be silence no longer.

For a few more moments, they just walked. Finally, the Emperor's demeanor softened a bit and he let out a long sigh.

"You fight well," he said softly, almost an admission of respect for Wyatt. "Were the situation different, I would ask that you join my employ and fight for the Empire. But as I understand it, that isn't really an option."

Wyatt gave him a light smile, the tension between them great and heavy. "No, I don't think so," he replied. "Although I appreciate the sentiment."

The Emperor nodded, his right hand idly tracing the stonework on the wall as they descended the long stairwell. "When this is all over, I hope that you will afford me the opportunity to explain my side of the story. I promise you that nothing I do is done without reason and consideration."

"That's not a bad idea," said Wyatt with a nod. "Although I hope you'll offer me the same. I have no desire to be shackled in irons and thrown into a cell... well, wherever it is you hold apostates."

The Emperor shook his head. "There must be a misunderstanding. Our laws on apostasy exist to protect Adepts from themselves. It's important for us to know if an Adept hasn't been trained by the Council or the Dominion, because if they haven't then they could be a danger to themselves and the people around them. An untrained Adept with powers that have woken up is very, very volatile."

"And the collars?" replied Wyatt sharply, the very real fear finally breaking through to the foreground of his mind.

The Emperor was silent for a time, considering his words. Jag and Grace were shooting each other furtive glances, but the rest of the group was silent, either purposely ignoring the conversation or simply remaining mercifully silent.

"The collars were..." began the Emperor carefully, "built for other reasons. They were actually made centuries ago, by inscribers. They were created so that we would have a way of controlling those Adepts who were driven insane by their power."

"Necromancers, then," said Wyatt pointedly.

"Not necessarily," replied the Emperor. "Although it's true that those mental issues are more prevalent with that particular Aspect, it can happen with any of us. Aquamancers, for instance. Aquamancy is perhaps the least understood of Adala's gifts; control over water is the standard, but very occasionally, an Aquamancer will be born with some ability to peer into the future."

Tythas looked back to the Emperor, as if a thought occurred to him, but he seemed to decide to not say anything at the last minute and turned his eyes back ahead.

Wyatt blinked. "To see the future? How does that work?"

The Emperor shrugged. "I have no idea, and the best explanation I was ever able to get from one of them had something to do with viewing reflections in fresh rain puddles. Aquamancers are often… well, wishy-washy, if you'll forgive my pun. But I do know that if those individuals aren't properly observed and trained, sometimes their minds can get lost in their visions of the future. They slip completely out of reality and their minds are lost, like a ship out to sea with no sail."

"It can happen to any of us, though," noted the Emperor as he continued. "Sometimes a Pyromancer who isn't careful can burn himself with his power. But the burns are internal. Sometimes, the damage is done to the brain, and they cease to function like normal people. An Aeromancer can lose himself in the wild, untamed nature of the wind and never really come back. I've seen that happen myself, actually. The wind unhinges some part of the mind that is needed for rationality, leaving the Adept an animal with devastating power."

"So if the collars were designed to control those people, why are they being used on apostates?" asked Wyatt.

"Most of what you heard has probably been hyperbole," replied the king thoughtfully. "I suspect a lot of my reign has been treated as such. Collars are used to bring in rogue Adepts until we can figure out what to do with them. Twice in my career have I ordered Adepts permanently collared. Once was Alvernon, whom you have met. I shouldn't need to explain that one."

"And the other?" asked Wyatt.

"The Aeromancer I mentioned earlier. He grew up far from our control, raised by one of the pirate groups of the Scattered Coast. Southlanders are notoriously difficult when it comes to magic, and they refused to bring the boy here to be trained. He did his best to control himself, but children are emotional things. By the time he was a teenager, he lost control. Killed hundreds. We were forced to intervene, but by the time we got the collar on him, he was already lost. I ordered the collar to protect everyone around him."

Wyatt got the impression from the tense shoulders of his friends that there was a lot more to the stories being told, but he didn't feel like pressing it here. He changed the subject.

"What about Necromancy, then?" he asked, his question eliciting a deep breath from Grace. "Why these policies outlawing something that people can't control or change?"

The Emperor scratched his ear. "A combination of political pressure from a great number of influential people and bad timing. I had my misgivings about that particular law, but sometimes when the people want something badly enough, not even a king can stop it from changing. If my career has a great failure, you have found it. Perhaps I should have worked harder to change the minds of my colleagues. Perhaps... well, there were many things that could have been done differently, but the law is what it is. I haven't pursued this little group of vigilantes as closely as I could have for a reason, you know."

Jag and Grace looked back at their father, their faces incredulous. If the Emperor noticed them, he didn't say anything.

Abruptly, they reached the bottom of the stairwell, which opened into a flat foyer before a great stone door. Heatless orbs of light bobbed merrily in the air, flooding the room with a honey-colored light.

The six of them stopped before the huge door, and the Emperor turned to face Wyatt again. He was tall, and now Wyatt could see how truly huge the man was. He and Jag had a similar frame, but where Jag was leaner and quicker, the Emperor was all muscle, all power. He was probably a fierce warrior in his own right.

"When all this is over, we all have things to talk about, I think," said Il'Vir, his voice grave. "But I promise you this: if what you all have told me is true, your crimes against the Empire will be forgiven. All of you. If you are able to prevent that which I have so foolishly missed, I will be greatly indebted to all of you."

Wyatt glanced at his companions for a moment, sharing a look with each of them. Grace looked like she wanted to say something to her father, to yell and scream and cry and hug and get it done with. Jag was solemn and pensive, a soldier's mask, but Wyatt could tell that he wasn't as sure about his father as he'd been when they arrived. Tythas, meanwhile, was as unreadable as ever.

Finally, Wyatt nodded. The Emperor returned his nod and moved to the door, standing before it with a heavy kind of authority hanging from his shoulders.

Drawing a knife out of his sleeve, the Emperor studied his palm for just a moment before making a neat cut, cupping his hand and letting the blood pool. He dipped two fingers of his other hand into the blood, reaching up and painting a simple rune on the stone. Much like the one they had encountered in the Archive, the door glowed as the runes etched into it came alive and absorbed the blood. The light twisted and intensified, but instead of disappearing, Wyatt heard a number of clicking noises, and the door swung inward as the light faded.

"This is the seal," said the Emperor, ushering them through the door. Inside was a large, open room. The walls were roughly cut stone, making it feel almost cavelike. The floor, also roughly cut, was perfectly flat and held a great glowing rune in the middle, a hexagon. The mark of Adala.

Grace paused wordlessly before her father, taking his large hand in her small ones and channeling her power into him. He studied her for a few moments, offering no objection. After a time, she released his hand and looked up into his eyes. For a moment, the two of them looked at each other. But eventually, she walked away from him and joined her brother at the far end of the seal.

The Emperor gestured toward the great glowing rune on the floor. "It's hidden, of course, behind those two doors. Without royal blood and the right rune, entering this room is very difficult. You should be able to set up whatever safeguards you want here, but I'd be-"

A sharp intake of breath interrupted his words as three inches of sharp, bloody steel erupted from the upper-left side of his chest. He choked and blinked, trying to make sense of what was happening as he looked down at the short blade jutting from between his ribs. Crimson blood dripped from the tip of the blade onto the floor beneath them.

Mugalo stood behind him, barely resembling the doddering old man that he had always appeared to be. Although he hadn't actually changed any, his demeanor and bearing were so different that Wyatt barely recognized him. He seemed so much... larger, so much more inhuman.

Wyatt and the others recoiled in shock as Mugalo quickly drew his short blade out of the Emperor and pushed the dying man forward, causing him to stumble and fall onto the seal. He struggled and tried to find his feet, but blood was quickly pouring out of his chest, splashing onto the stone beneath him.

There was a sharp ringing noise as Wyatt drew his sword and advanced on the elder Pyromancer, anger searing in his blood. But before he could take another step, a great wall of black fire erupted between them, nearly reaching the ceiling. Mugalo's sharp laughter could just be heard from the other side, and through the dark flames Wyatt could just make out the old man's silhouette.

"So young, so foolish," mused the old Pyromancer, his voice strangely clear over the sound of the fire. "All of you. Even you, Vance. How you ever dared to trust me is beyond my comprehension. But it doesn't matter now, I suppose, does it?"

Grace had reached her father, and was crouched over him with her eyes closed, pouring energy into him as fast as she could. Jag looked sick as he watched, powerless.

"Why, Mugalo?" shouted Tythas, his expression stricken. The Emperor was the key to this. They needed him.

"Why not?" replied Mugalo with amusement. "I have my reasons, old friend. Unfortunately those reasons are much greater than you or your little companions. This is just another piece of the puzzle, I'm afraid. Another move on the board. Strategy. Something that even after all of these years, you remain woefully ignorant of."

Wyatt made to step forward, confident that his newfound affinity for Pyromancy would protect him from the hungry flames. But before he could reach it, he felt Tythas's hand grip his elbow like a vice, stopping him just short with strength he didn't know the man possessed. His hand, mere inches away from the flame, suddenly flared with pain and heat. He withdrew it quickly and stepped back with Tythas, clutching his fingers in pain.

"I trust none of you will go anywhere?" asked Mugalo with mocking amusement. Grace was crying, her healing energy pouring into her father, who was still somehow hanging on. Her tears dripped down onto his shirt, glowing with the same golden light that wrapped around both of their bodies. Meanwhile, Mugalo's silhouette had disappeared behind the veil of fire. He'd probably already retreated back up the stairwell on the other side.

Wyatt rushed to Grace's side, resting his hand on her shoulder. He barely noticed his sore hand now, too concerned about the Emperor and the anguish his friends were feeling.

"Don't you dare die on me, Dad," growled Grace as she poured energy into her father, more than Wyatt had ever seen her use. "You have too much to tell us. Too much to answer for."

The light around them faded. Jag rested a hand on his father's shoulder, and Wyatt watched in awe as years of repressed anger and pain evaporated. Maybe it was only temporary, but in that moment the only thing that Jag knew was that his father was dying. No anger would help him here.

"Too much damage has been done," whispered Grace, struggling to maintain her composure. "I... I can't save him."

"I'm sorry," managed the dying king, his voice rough and broken. "I... I'm so sorry. Both of you... both of you are so much more than I ever was. I'm so proud of you. I love you both. I... I'm sorry..." His voice faded. He reached up to touch the faces of his children, and for just a moment, he held the connection. But his hands fell, his body stilled, and an eternal silence settled into him. Wyatt felt it, felt the energy leave him. He could almost see Tyvarion Il'Vir leave this world behind.

They were quiet for what felt like a long time, although Wyatt really had no idea how much time had actually passed. He felt frozen, as if the weight of the moment had solidified the air around them.

Finally someone moved, breaking the silence that was almost physical, holding the four of them in place. Tythas crouched down, leaning over his two charges and resting his hands on their shoulders. Grace and Jag looked up at him, very much young children once again.

"I know," he said quietly, his voice low and raw. "I know. But we can't do this here. We can't. We need to get back up to the surface and try to stop Necron and Mugalo and anyone else that threatens the well-being of our people."

He squeezed their shoulders tightly, confidence and steel coming back into his voice. "We must save our grief. We must use it. Remember this feeling, for a time will come where you will need it. And when you call upon it, it will fill you like a raging storm. Remember your father. Fight for him."

Jag and Grace looked at each other for a moment. They seemed to find something in each other, some kind of foothold where together, they could hold fast. They both nodded. Grace closed her father's eyes, and the two of them stood, tall and proud and angry.

"Should I burn the body?" asked Tythas gently, looking at Grace.

She shook her head. "Il'Vir kings are entombed with their ancestors in the Royal Crypt. He will rest with his father and their fathers. He... he deserves that. No matter what, he did do some good."

"There has got to be a way out of here," declared Wyatt, walking around the cavern to inspect the walls. "Deep caverns like this were always built with escape chutes, in case the main route caved in. That's what we need to find."

Tythas moved to the other wall, inspecting it in kind. "I think you may be on to something, Wyatt. Look for runes, like the kind that were on the doors that led down here."

"Why don't we just stay and wait?" asked Jag, his voice full of menace. "We can fight them here. The four of us should be more than enough..."

Grace shook her head, wiping tears from her eyes. "They're right, Jag. If we wait here we'll have, at the very least, Apep and an army of

Drones to worry about. Now add in whatever Necron is and maybe Mugalo, too... I don't think we'd stand a chance. We need to think about the people of Farillyon, too. They don't know what's coming. We need to get people out."

Wyatt pressed his hand against the wall, and a glowing web of runes appeared, snaking outward from his touch and lighting up a small portion of the wall. The others moved to him, peering at the runes.

"The same as the other door, then," said Tythas quietly, looking over at Grace.

She nodded, reaching for her dagger, but Jag beat her to it. He sliced into his hand without a second thought and carefully drew a rune on the stone with his blood, the same rune that his father had drawn onto the door behind them.

For a moment, nothing happened. Jag looked almost uneasy, as if this would disprove their belief that he was an Il'Vir. Maybe he feared that the door would not open, that only the magical Il'Virs were the truly important ones. Or maybe he just feared that it wouldn't open at all, and they'd be stuck down here until Apep and Necron came for them.

But the runes twisted and the solid stone wall melted away, drawing in on itself and revealing a narrow space and the iron rungs of a ladder, much like the basement of the Archives. A very tall ladder, which Wyatt suddenly realized they were going to have to climb in order to escape.

"Always ladders and blood and secret doors with these people," he muttered, taking the initiative and putting a hand on one of the iron rungs.

His companions followed, but he was glad to be in the lead. He wanted the opportunity to talk to Shem, and being at the top would let him climb without thinking too much.

Necron is going to break out, isn't he? asked Wyatt in his head, nudging Shem's presence with his mind.

There was no response for a moment, forcing Wyatt to listen to the sounds of four people climbing an iron ladder in a narrow stone shaft. He couldn't even see the top of it.

Yes, replied Shem softly, his normally booming voice smaller and more distant. He felt the sword stir to life as Shem's presence came into his mind.

Once he broke the second seal and was able to possess a body... we never really had a chance at stopping him, did we? We can't make new seals, we don't have that kind of power.

We may have been able to stop him even with two seals broken, explained Shem carefully. *Or at least weakened him to the point where the three remaining seals would have held him down longer than your lifetimes. But there will always be another Apep, another mind that he can twist and warp for his purposes. Truthfully... after the first seal was broken, he would have eventually escaped.*

That's why you're here then, isn't it? thought Wyatt, finally voicing a suspicion that he'd held for a good while now. *You're here because whoever put you in that sword knew Necron would escape and wanted you to wake up and try to stop him.*

Again, Shem's response was delayed. Wyatt climbed and climbed. His whole body was getting tired already, and his hand ached where Mugalo's fire had burned him. But he hadn't spoken up because Grace needed her strength, especially now. He didn't think that a sore hand would hinder him too badly. He could still move it, it just hurt.

I am not the hero here, Wyatt, replied Shem finally. *I do not think I was put here to stop Necron. Were that the case, I would have stopped him the last time he went on a rampage. No, I was put here to help. To help you.*

Again, Wyatt was given the impression that Shem knew a whole lot that he wasn't telling Wyatt. There was no doubt in Wyatt's mind that these secrets had something to do with his sudden abilities as a Pyromancer, with his inexplicable strength and constantly growing powers.

So help me, Shem, he replied, a hint of command in his inner-voice. *Help me to see what I am missing, what we need to do to stop Necron.*

I am helping you, said the cat, his echoing tone reproachful. *You already know what you need to do, Wyatt. You need to climb out of this hole and fight.*

I broke part of your binding already, thought Wyatt suddenly, reminded of the first fight against Apep when he gave his blood and partially released Shem from his prison. *That's why you can appear as a giant lion, right? What happens if I release you the rest of the way?*

I would cease to exist within this sword and assume my true form, replied Shem slowly. *Or whatever my true form has become after all these centuries. I am not entirely sure what form I would hold anymore.*

And what would happen to me? asked Wyatt, reminded of the amount of energy and blood he'd had to offer up in order to release the first binding. He'd nearly passed out.

You would die, replied Shem flatly. Wyatt had expected that answer. *Which is why it would be horribly foolish of you. Wyatt, you operate under the assumption that I am some great and powerful being that would be able to destroy Necron and save the world. But I do not know what I would be able to do, Wyatt. So don't cling to the delusion that freeing me and sacrificing yourself would be a good idea.*

Wyatt hadn't exactly termed it as a good idea, but it had crossed his mind. Even now, he knew at least that if there were no other options, Shem's unbound form might be able to help them in some way, might be able to save them from certain doom.

Shem, began Wyatt after a pause. *Whatever happens up there... thanks. For all you've done. You've saved my skin more times than anyone should have a right to. You've probably done more for us than anyone will ever know, more than I'll ever be able to explain.*

There was no response, and Wyatt could feel Shem withdraw into the sword, his presence fading. He was still there, but Wyatt got the distinct impression that their conversation was over. He mulled over Shem's words in silence for a time, wondering just what the cat was.

He sighed and continued climbing.

CHAPTER TWENTY

 herever Wyatt had expected to end up, this certainly wasn't it. In fact, this was about the furthest thing from what he'd imagined.

He reached the top of the ladder, pulling once more on his aching arms and climbing out of the shaft. He crawled out onto what he assumed would be a stone road or walkway, but instead of another part of the castle or one of the nearby streets, he found soft, cool dirt beneath his fingertips. Instead of ending up in another part of the castle or a nearby alleyway, he had somehow ended up in an earthy-smelling forest clearing.

He blinked, looking around. All manner of plant and animal life surrounded him, sewing together a tapestry of sound and color. Squirrels chattered from nearby trees, birds flew through the expansive sky overhead, and flowers of all shapes and sizes bloomed in every direction. Wyatt had never seen a place quite like it. It was like looking at paradise.

Wyatt glanced behind him, expecting to see Grace and his other companions climbing out of the hole in the earth. But there was no sign of the ladder or the narrow shaft he'd climbed out of. Wherever he had gone, his friends had not followed. He reached out mentally to Shem as his hand reached for the sword at his hip. But the blade wasn't there, and Shem's distinct presence was nowhere to be felt. He was alone.

"Welcome, Wyatt Arden," called a voice, deep and strong and unlike any Wyatt had ever heard. He didn't just feel the voice calling his name; he felt it in his bones, his blood, and his soul.

Wyatt turned back to see a towering form lumber out of the woods. Nearly ten feet tall and covered with brown, shaggy fur, it almost reminded Wyatt of a huge bear, the kind he knew to roam the hills north of Ven.

But where bears walked on all fours and occasionally stood up, this creature seemed comfortably bipedal. Silver fur crisscrossed the brown, bearing a striking resemblance to the silver runes that Wyatt was beginning to associate with powerful magic. He wore a necklace of leaves and berries. As he walked, the whole forest seemed to lean in nearer to him. Flowers bloomed wide in his presence. He was obviously the maker of this place.

Wyatt eyed the thing warily, trying to summon up some wind to use if he needed to protect himself. But he couldn't seem to get a grip on it in this place. It slipped from his grasp as if he were trying to hold water in his hands.

"None of that, now," said the bear, walking toward him. "Your power will not work here, child, however great it may be. This is not Adala's domain."

Wyatt sighed, realizing the futility of his paranoia. Whatever was going on, it was obviously far above him. He took a breath and relaxed.

"Who are you?" he asked, glancing around the glade, still somewhat awed by its beauty. The forest stretched out in all directions around them, impossibly vast and deep. He knew that he'd get lost almost immediately if he tried to wander off, especially with no grip on his power.

"My name is incredibly long and humans are usually incapable of speaking it," said the bear-thing, sitting down in the grass and fixing his strange black eyes on Wyatt. "For the sake of conversation, however, I am typically referred to as Roshafel."

Wyatt nodded, his mind racing. He had heard that name somewhere before, or at least he thought he had. But he couldn't remember where. He sat down in the grass across from the bear. He wasn't really sure why, but it seemed like the right thing to do. "I'm Wyatt Arden, but I guess you already know that."

The bear gave a great nod with his shaggy head. "Indeed. I know a great many things, Wyatt Arden. But we should get your questions out of the way first, I think."

"What are you, then?" asked Wyatt, peering around the glade once more. He had never seen nature grow so openly and purely in the world, never even heard of a place like this.

"Roshafel the Sower, Roshafel Deep-root, Roshafel the Gardener," replied the bear slowly, gesturing with a paw as he did. "A good question. I am called these things because so very long ago, I created all of the plant and animal life in this lovely, troubled world of ours."

Wyatt blinked. He had heard the name before, although not exactly like that. The books all called him Roshashela, if they referred to him at all. The books had discussed the existence of other gods, like Adala, who had walked in the world during her life. The history of the world was long-debated and murky, but most scholars agreed that Roshashela had once existed in some form or another.

"The books called you Roshashela," said Wyatt quietly, peering at the bear.

Roshafel rolled his eyes, a strangely human thing to do considering that he was a large bear. "They have called me a lot of things. Humans do love their themes. I imagine they referred to me as that because it sounded more like my sister's name."

"Adala," Wyatt breathed, suddenly aware of what exactly he had just stumbled into. "You really are him, then. You created the plants and animals. You're Adala's brother. You're... you're a god."

"Quite," said the bear with another great nod. "Human scholars have argued and argued for centuries over what went on before my brother and sister got into their little spat. But yes, you are correct. I created the playground upon which the creations of my siblings trod."

"Siblings?" asked Wyatt.

"Roshafel, Adala, and Wyrdax," explained the bear. "The three children of the Sun and the Moon. We three, the architects of life, are the reason that you exist today in all your dramatic, human glory."

Wyatt suddenly realized why this place felt so different than the rest of the world he'd seen. He probably wasn't even on the same continent anymore; this had to be Roshafel's sanctuary, wherever he had retreated to watch the ages pass by.

"Why did you bring me here?" he asked, looking back to Roshafel with a bit of apprehension. Was he going to be able to leave?

"To make you an offer," replied the bear, reaching out to collect a squirrel that had scampered over to him. He held it up in one large paw for Wyatt to see. The squirrel chattered at him for a moment before retreating up Roshafel's arm, finding a safe perch atop the bear's huge head. Roshafel chuckled, not at all bothered by it.

"And what offer would that be?" asked Wyatt warily, still watching the squirrel. In another time and place, he might've laughed at the sight, but there was something very wrong about the entire situation that Wyatt couldn't seem to shake. He looked into the bear's eyes. "The scholars might argue over your name, but the one thing that I do remember them agreeing on is that you want nothing to do with humans, Adept or not."

The bear nodded, the squirrel hanging on for dear life. "Somewhat true. I didn't mind humans nearly as much before my younger brother started trying to kill them. They were smart, but they respected the earth. They used nature to their advantage, but they preserved it out of necessity. They created tools of wood and stone, but they cultivated the land and consumed only what they needed. They worked with nature, and in doing so, created a special kind of harmony. This was the design, the system, which we had hoped for."

The bear gave a long sigh. "And then Wyrdax, my shortsighted little brother, got jealous. He was always the one who was most easily swayed by his emotions. He wanted to be like me, to create animals. So I let him, curious to see if he could create something that I had not devised. And he did. He created dragons. Massive, ruthless, and incredibly intelligent, the dragons were almost the perfect beast. They were just as smart as humans, but lacked the compassion that my sister had instilled in her humans. Some could breathe fire, or hurl thunder. The strongest among them could change their shape, hiding among humans. Wyrdax wanted the humans to die, so his dragons hunted them."

Wyatt nodded, silently listening to Roshafel's story and trying to take all of the information in.

"In order to save the creations which she so loved, my sister invested godly power in mortals," continued the bear. "She broke herself into pieces and invested nearly all of what she was within them, leaving nearly nothing behind. We had long ago promised our father and mother that we would never directly oppose one another, you see. She couldn't fight Wyrdax in the conventional way because if she did, she feared that the Sun and Moon would fall out of harmony and the world would die. And even though they killed her children, she couldn't bring herself to fight the dragons, either. She had too much love in her heart."

The bear sighed again. "My younger brother was foolishly power-hungry and jealous of his older siblings. My younger sister possessed a blind, all-encompassing love of her creations and did not see the flaw in her plan to empower them. Truthfully, in those days, it was hard to see what they would become. But their true nature was there, buried deep. The jealousy, the greed, the constant need to compete and grow stronger. My sister was an emotional thing, and she created humans in her image."

"Emotion isn't bad, though," said Wyatt, his head cocked. "Emotion has been the power behind some of humanity's greatest victories. Not to mention things like art and poetry and music."

"Those wild emotions are the cause for the same problems they solve," said the bear, his voice almost bitter. "Regardless, after my sister broke herself, she was mostly gone from the world, instilled in her creations. My younger brother saw this as an opportunity to finally finish the deed and subject humanity to his rule, but he constantly underestimated Adala's strength. Even divested amongst her children, her power was more than enough to stop him, especially coupled with human ingenuity. Her children defeated my brother's monsters one by one, isolating them and hunting them down, just as the dragons had done to them for so long. And when they had defeated all of them, they turned their sights on Wyrdax. Unable to kill a god, they used their mother's power to create a place now known as the Pit, an eternal prison. And into the Pit they hurled Wyrdax, never to return."

Wyatt had heard of the Pit, of course. It was still referred to in the stories about the Six and their adventures and conquests. Legend went that departed souls whom Adala rejected were sent to the Pit instead.

"And now humans run rampant," continued Roshafel, gesturing with both paws. "Without a foe to oppose them, they now target one another. They have lost the harmony that Adala wished upon them, and your world now lies in chaos. Necron, my foolish young nephew, has gone insane and threatens to destroy all life, not just human life."

"So what do you want me to do, then?" asked Wyatt. "I appreciate the story, but I'm already trying to stop that from happening. I think my friends and I are the only chance the world has."

The bear nodded. "I know. Your efforts have been valiant and brave, Wyatt. But I am not asking you to stop it. I am asking you to let it happen."

Shock flooded through Wyatt and he recoiled, leaning back on his palms. "What do you mean, let it happen? You want Necron to destroy all life?"

The bear shook his head. "No. Not all life. However great his power may be, Necron cannot reach this place. I want him to destroy everything back where you came from. When the rest of the world lies burnt and broken, I will leave this place for the first time since my sister's death. I will take my foolish nephew by the scruff of his neck and hurl him into the Pit. And then I will create life, just as I did in the beginning. The world will start over."

Wyatt was sickened by the thought of it. One of the self-named architects of life wanted him to let it all die just so he could reset the world.

"I don't mean to suggest that you should let all of human life die," added Roshafel, his casual tone making Wyatt feel disgusted. "In fact, quite the contrary. I have seen how humans can work in harmony with nature. That was the original intent, after all. You are a good man, Wyatt. I will let you stay here while Necron destroys the world. I will bring your friend Grace here, and other humans that I have selected. And this small group will restart everything, will birth humanity anew."

Wyatt stared at the bear, utterly baffled.

"You do care for her, do you not?" asked Roshafel, leaning toward Wyatt to study his face. "If there is another human whom you desire more, I can bring her instead. Or perhaps both. You can lead them, Wyatt. You can be the father of the new race, the wise and humble race that serves nature instead of walking upon it with disinterest."

"I do care about Grace," said Wyatt slowly, still staring at Roshafel in bewilderment. "And I care about the rest of my race, too. Even the ones who oppose me. Everyone has a right to fight for life. We don't need to start over."

"Don't you see how much easier it would be?" asked Roshafel, his voice plaintive. "You wouldn't have to worry about Necron or Alvernon or any of the other evils in the world that wish you ill. Thanks to the children of my siblings, the earth has become a den of madness. My creations, my children, suffer for it. Your people suffer from the evils of one another. But if we do this, Wyatt, we can put an end to all of that. You can give up your powers and live like you were originally meant to, without any godly influence at all."

Wyatt climbed to his feet, his chin held high, defiant even in the eyes of a god. "Roshafel, your offer is tempting. But as nice as the outcome may seem, giving up even one life to get there is not worth it. I could never live with myself if I willingly let anyone die. I reject your offer. I will fight and stop Necron and repair the damage that my people have done. But I will not sacrifice any lives for an easy way out."

The bear sighed, shaking his head. "So blind, so emotional," he said sadly. "Just like your Mother. No foresight, no desire to work for the greater good. Headstrong and foolish."

"You're a gardener," said Wyatt, pointing to the plants around them. "Which means that when a weed grows, you pull it out and toss it aside. It's easy for you. And that's why you'll never understand. This isn't about easy. It's about right."

The bear shrugged. "I tried. Your fight is a long and hard one, Wyatt Arden. I hope that if Necron does destroy everything, in your last moments you remember that you had a chance to survive. I will still restart life after he does his work. But there will be no humans in the new world."

Wyatt turned his back on Roshafel, walking toward the edge of the glade. He didn't know where he might be going, but he didn't care as long as it was away from Roshafel the Gardener.

Wyatt walked through the treeline, coming around the corner of a building that he hadn't seen before. The smell of the forest and the flowers of Roshafel's glade vanished instantly, replaced by the unmistakable scent of the city. A few butterflies fluttered around his head, but they were the only sign of the strange forest from which he had ventured. He'd arrived back in Farillyon, in an alley of some sort. He tried to get his bearings by looking up at the sky, but the buildings around him were too tall. There was no way of telling where in the city he had ended up.

He felt the sword at his hip, and Shem's presence blossomed in his mind. He could feel the cat's curiosity nudging at him.

"I'll explain later," he muttered.

A nearby sewer grate suddenly clanked loudly and flew open, slamming into the stone beside it. A hand appeared first, and then a head of vivid red hair appeared as Grace quickly climbed out of the sewer, looking angry, dismayed, and a bit dirty. She quickly turned to help Jag and Tythas climb out behind her.

"Still no sign of him," she said to Jag as she helped him up, her voice low. "He just vanished, right in front of me. I don't understand. Apep doesn't have magic like that. Nobody does." Evidently she had not seen Wyatt when she climbed out. Jag hadn't noticed him either, but Tythas quickly met his eyes as he rose from the sewer, his demeanor as dignified as possible considering the situation. He nodded at Wyatt.

"I wouldn't worry any longer, Grace," said Tythas, nudging her toward Wyatt.

She turned toward where Tythas was pointing, finally spotting Wyatt. He grinned sheepishly and waved.

She ran toward him, closing the short distance in the span of a heartbeat. The look in her eye went from sad, to surprised, to happy, to angry in the span of a blink. She stopped in front of him, and Wyatt was expecting a hug. He raised his arms. She punched one of them.

"You dolt," she growled. "Don't grin at me like that. We were worried about you! What happened?"

Wyatt rubbed his arm, giving her a sour look. "Hey, it's not my fault. I got abducted. It's not like I just ran off and left you behind."

Tythas and Jag came forward. Jag gripped his sister's shoulder, and she looked back at him briefly before she looked at Wyatt again, her expression softening into something resembling embarrassment.

"I... Wyatt, I'm sorry, I shouldn't have done that. I just... you were gone, and... sorry."

Wyatt nodded. "I know. It's fine."

"You were abducted, you said," said Tythas, eyeing the butterflies that were still fluttering around the alley. He sniffed the air with interest. "Am I correct in assuming that you were visited by the Sower?"

Wyatt nodded glumly. "Yeah. I guess he took me to wherever he's taken refuge."

Tythas motioned for them to walk and headed down the far end of the alley. Wyatt followed beside him, with Grace and Jag in tow.

"So what did he have to say?" asked Tythas softly, looking up at the sky as they walked down the alley. "He's appeared to Adepts before, but none that I know of while I have been alive."

"He wanted to make a deal," said Wyatt simply, shrugging. He was still angry, but he didn't want to let it show. "One that I wasn't willing to make. That's all that really needs to be said about it."

Tythas nodded thoughtfully. "Fair enough. I hope you didn't completely ruin that relationship, though. If he's taken note of you, he could be a valuable ally."

"No," said Wyatt firmly, shaking his head. "He's a lot of things. He's more powerful than all of us combined, and he could probably stop Necron without too much effort. But he's too... different. Alien, almost. He has no emotion. He's not enough like humans to understand why we fight and why he should help us."

Tythas eyed him for a moment before chuckling softly and shaking his head. Wyatt cocked an eyebrow.

"We've only been together for a short time, Wyatt," explained Tythas, still smiling. "But you've grown so much."

Before he could respond, Grace tugged at his arm. He glanced back at her, and from the look on her face he got the impression that she wanted to talk. Tythas nodded knowingly at him, and Wyatt slowed his pace a little so he could walk next to Grace. Jag sped up, filling Wyatt's former position, and he and Tythas began talking loudly and pointedly about the weather.

"They're idiots," she muttered, glaring at her brother. Wyatt snickered.

Grace looked at him, her expression soft. Her eyes were still red. "Wyatt, I... I shouldn't have hit you. I'm sorry. That was stupid of me, really stupid. You didn't deserve that."

Wyatt squeezed her arm. "It's okay, Grace. You just lost your father. You're allowed to be a little bit crazy right now. In fact, you're probably allowed to be a lot crazier than that."

She nodded, lowering her gaze. It was obviously still bothering her.

Wyatt gave her a sideways smile. "Next time you want to go crazy, just hit Jag instead. We both know that's okay, and he's used to it."

She laughed, looking back at him and smiling. They shared a look for what felt like forever.

"I heard that," said Jag with a smirk, glancing back at him. "Powers or not, I can still take you, kid."

Grace and Wyatt laughed again. For a moment, it was hard to remember that they were facing down the fight of their lives. For just that brief, fleeting little bit of time, they were just friends having a laugh.

They exited the alley and stopped to get their bearings. They were somewhere in the Lower City, the worst part of Farillyon. The day was clear and bright, but Wyatt knew that they were mere hours away from it getting a lot gloomier. They were already short on time.

"We don't have a lot of time left," said Wyatt, looking at the city around them. People were going on with their lives, ignorant of the doom that was looming. Wyatt could still remember what it was like to not know.

"I think the time has come for us to split up," said Tythas with a sigh. "We really have no other option at this point. Wyatt, you need to fly north, to head off the Dominion's army and try to put a stop to whatever it is they are planning. You're a member of the War Council now, and you've proven yourself on their most sacred proving ground. If anyone can convince them not to attack Farillyon, it will be you."

Wyatt nodded. He was already planning to do that. "But what about the three of you?"

Tythas looked at Jag, and then Grace. "The three of us... well, one of us needs to rouse the city guard. Jag, I think that's your job."

Jag looked back at his mentor. "I'm a wanted man in Farillyon, Vance, you know that. I might get killed, or arrested."

Tythas smiled. "I also know that your men are more loyal to you than they are to Mugalo, even if you have been gone for a few years. The Emperor is no longer here to give orders. Convince your men the truth of what has happened and take back your role as guardian of Farillyon. You are Jag Mercer, the greatest soldier I have ever known. A man capable of things even Adepts hesitate to consider. They will follow you. Once you have them on our side, you can evacuate the city."

Jag nodded, his expression distant.

Wyatt clapped a hand onto Jag's shoulder, just as Jag had done to him so many times. "Heroes, remember? You'll do fine." He looked back to Tythas. "What about you and Grace?"

Grace and Tythas shared a look for a moment, and Grace nodded, as if she were accepting whatever Tythas had in mind without even knowing what it was. Tythas smiled at her.

"Grace and I..." began Tythas, looking at Jag and Wyatt with that same soft smile. "Grace and I will fly south. We will lie in wait for Apep's army of Drones and spring a trap on them. We will stall them as best we can."

There was a moment of silence, followed quickly by a litany of objections that came from Jag and Wyatt. They both began talking so quickly and loudly that it was difficult to hear either one of them.

Grace held her hands up, silencing both of them before they could finish. "Please, both of you," she said pleadingly. "You both have important roles to play in this, defending the city and swaying the Dominion to our side. So do I. Fire works great against Drones and other undead, but do you know what works even better? A Vitamancer.

My presence is enough to disrupt them, and I'll be able to give Tythas the edge he needs to overcome them. We'll be fine. I can heal him, he can protect me, and we can both destroy Drones by the hundred."

"I hate it," said Jag staring at his sister. "This isn't... this isn't the way it was supposed to be. You're not supposed to get in the fights. That's my job. You..." his words trailed off as he closed his eyes. He took a deep breath, and when he opened them again, some of the Jag Mercer steel had returned to them. "Don't you dare get killed."

Grace nodded, smiling her bravest smile. "I'm your sister, remember? You've taught me more about not getting killed than anyone. You and me against the world, Jag. I'm not going anywhere."

Jag, ever the soldier, saluted her with a fist. She grinned at him and looked over at Wyatt, who was struggling to keep his composure.

Grace took a few steps, walking right up to him. She reached up and tugged at his baldric, tightening the strap a bit and adjusting his ruffled shirt fondly. Resting her hand on his chest, she smiled up at him, a small smile that said a lot more than either of them currently could.

He smiled back, and they both nodded. For a short time, his fear seemed to dissolve, replaced by a warm, buzzing feeling in his chest that had nothing to do with the sword.

"Keep yourself safe," she said quietly, her hand lingering. "Or I'll punch you again."

He laughed a small laugh. "You, too. And keep the old man safe, would you? We don't want his heart giving out."

Tythas gave him a sour look. "I will remember that when you need to learn the secrets of your powers, young Adept."

All four of them laughed. Grace finally dropped her hand and walked back over to Tythas, adopting a regal, resolute expression. Jag, too, looked so different than the day that Wyatt had met him. Even dressed in simple clothes, wearing a simple soldier's sword, he somehow managed to look like a leader. Today, with his chin high and his eyes ahead, he looked like a king.

Jag gave a wink and a sideways grin before dashing down the nearby side alley, disappearing from sight. The sound of his footsteps faded as the three of them were left behind.

Tythas drew his amulet from within his robes, calling on its power and taking the shape of a great, shadowy crow. He rose into the air, his wingspan barely short enough to allow him flight in the street. He took off above the buildings, and Wyatt could see him turning, preparing to take Grace by the shoulders and fly her to their destination.

Grace and Wyatt looked at one another once more, and suddenly she was there again, kissing him. And everything just... went away. Necron, Apep, Mugalo... everything was gone, slipped between his fingertips like fresh drops of rain. That kiss was everything he knew, everything he was. It roared through his blood and his heart like a wildfire, like a power he'd never felt before. He held her tight against him as she bit his bottom lip.

She stepped back, and the world slammed painfully back into place. But it was a different world, a brighter world. His heart pounded in his ears as they locked gazes, and whatever fear Wyatt might've had in him seemed to have vanished. He had to fight. They had to win, otherwise he'd never get to have a kiss like that again.

Grace's cheeks were slightly flushed now. She looked like she wanted to say something, but Wyatt beat her to it. "We'll talk about that when we both come out of this alive."

She gave him a beautiful grin and nodded. He took the last few seconds that he had with her to drink her in; the shape of her smile, the quality of her eyes, the way her red hair flared out when she was stressed and made her look just a little bit manic...

And then Tythas swooped in closer. She raised her arms and jumped just at the right time, his huge talons gripping her by the shoulders. They vanished in a flash, the great, dark form of the bird flapping into the distance. Wyatt watched them go, unmoving.

"They'll be fine," he whispered, thinking of the kiss. "They'll be fine."

A soldier rushed into Mugalo's office, his metal armor clanking and jangling as he did. Mugalo had always thought they looked so silly, bouncing about with such urgency.

"Sir!" shouted the captain, snapping into a salute. Mugalo hated that. Why was he shouting? They were the only ones in the room, and it was quite quiet. He sighed, looking up from the items he was packing away and appraising the guard.

"They've escaped the lower levels, sir," he said, mercifully without shouting this time. "It looks like they broke off into different directions. The anomaly flew north after the rest of his companions left. Since he disabled the only Aeromancers we have that can fly, we weren't able to follow him."

Mugalo nodded. That had, of course, been the plan all along. He'd known about the exit path in the seal room, having assisted in its construction. "Good. And the others?"

"Mercer is still in the city," said the captain. "It looks like he's trying to rouse support from some of his old friends. We're probably going to have a mutiny on our hands very soon."

Well, that could work. Mugalo nodded again. "And the other two?"

"South, with the aid of Tythas's birdshape amulet."

"To meet Apep's army of Drones, I'd guess," said Mugalo, scratching his chin. "Just as well. Go back to your barracks and wait for Mercer, captain. When he arrives, give him this."

Mugalo reached into his desk and drew out a tightly bound scroll. "This is a patent of nobility that belongs to him. It should have been given to him when he was a child, but Il'Vir was too easily swayed by suggestions that a bastard, non-magical child would have ruined his early career. But it is as valid now as it was the day it was written. When the rest of the Blades see this, they will know that Jag Mercer is our new Emperor. They will follow him without question, and you will let them."

"Sir?" asked the captain, obviously confused.

Mugalo nodded at him. "Yes, I know. Just go along with it. You served alongside him, so he should be able to trust you. He will assemble the entire Guard, and the Blades. Suggest to Mercer that after evacuating, they should march north, to establish a perimeter and wait for the Dominion's arrival. He will go along with it. Despite the time he spent there and Tythas's avid love for those people, Mercer still harbors a deep distrust of them. Even I question whether or not they will honor Arden's newfound position."

"We're taking the guard out of the city?" asked the captain, looking surprised. "Shouldn't we be here? Even if we evacuate, it is still our city."

Mugalo shook his head. "Captain, this castle is the last place you want to be. It's just a building, surrounded by more buildings, with a wall built around them. Keep your people alive. That's the key here. Use the tunnels under Lowtown. They lead to the hills to the south. With any luck, the Drones will have moved past already, and you'll come out behind them. Send a small detachment with them, only what you can spare. Order them to head for Triat until all this settles. Now go, and you will get everything I ever promised you and more."

The captain saluted again. "Sir!" He disappeared from the office, clanking down the hall as he went. Mugalo watched the door close, and after a brief pause, walked over to the cabinet in the corner that sat securely locked at all times.

It looked like a normal cabinet. Normal lock, too, but Mugalo knew that no key could unlock it. He pressed his finger into the small opening, a circular opening just large enough to accommodate. He flexed his forbidden power, channeling just a bit of heat into the metal. He felt the mechanism shift as the lock began to glow red. Finally, it clicked.

The cabinet opened, revealing a single shelf that held an inscribed stone basin filled with a thick, reddish-brown substance that had dried and caked onto the sides of the bowl. Blood.

Mugalo picked up the stone knife that sat next to it and cut a narrow wound in his palm. He hated how easily this flesh was marred. He set the knife aside and reached out, making a fist. A few drops dripped into the basin, and the blood already inside of it reacted instantly. It swirled and moved as if once again alive and fresh, and within a few moments, a face appeared in the blood, taking a vaguely humanoid shape.

Mugalo drew the wounded fist across his chest, offering a salute. "My lord. We proceed as planned. Necron will be released, and they will surely destroy him."

The face twisted a bit. Being made of blood, it was slightly difficult to determine the expression on the face, but Mugalo took it to mean that his master was pleased.

"Good," bubbled the blood-face, its voice sickly and distant. "My son, you have served me so well. I am proud of you."

Mugalo bowed his head, resisting the urge to smile. "It has been my pleasure, my lord. All of the pieces are falling into place. Soon, my dear father, your work will be complete."

The face in the basin grinned wickedly at him. "I understand that Alvernon has found something interesting. What would that be?"

This time, Mugalo did smile. "Arden's best friend from his childhood. A purely non-magical friend. Young and strong, he was a soldier. He survived Alvernon's attack through sheer resilience and courage."

The blood stirred again. "Then we have already begun the next phase of the plan. Once again, my son, you defy every expectation. Keep him safe, Mugalo. He is too important to lose."

Mugalo spread his hands, still smiling. "I will do everything in my power to teach and protect him, my lord. He will be yours."

"Go, then," hissed the face. "Before Necron arrives here and devours you." The blood in the bowl settled, drying out and once again caking to the sides. It looked as if Mugalo had never even disturbed it.

Mugalo collected the rest of his things, placing them within a special bag that had been made for him so long ago, a bag capable of holding much more than appearance would suggest. Finally, he placed the basin and the knife safely within it and buttoned it closed. He drew the bag over his shoulder and slipped out of the room, locking the door behind him.

After a few minutes of walking, Mugalo reached the roof. He made sure the bag was secure on his shoulder as he walked out to the center of the roof, far from any of the towers or battlements. Confident that he had enough space, he lowered himself to his knees, unlocking a part of him that had been hidden for so long.

He screamed in pain as his body began to change. His skin darkened as his arms and legs elongated. His face stretched and lengthened, his teeth sharpening. Strange protrusions erupted from his back, breaking through his simple robes. His skin continued to darken, becoming the deep color of crimson and hardening to an almost sparkling sheen. Close inspection would reveal scales where regular skin had been, scales that were now the size of saucers and as hard as diamonds.

The protrusions on his back grew, snapping and cracking as they branched outward. Membranes of flesh appeared between those branches, stretching out and connecting them. Soon, the wings were complete. A great tail stretched out behind him, tipped with a spike of bone.

He was nearly the size of the entire roof now. Very few of his kind had ever reached this size. He was the last of them, the oldest, the strongest, and the wisest. He had survived when all of the others had died. For centuries, he had worn the shell of a man, stuffed into a weak and fleshy body that he detested. But no longer. Now he would fly freely again.

Mugalo roared with fury, his great wings stretching out and flapping once. The sound was like a clap of thunder, and anyone on the roof would've been thrown into the distance by the strength of the gust he created.

He set his weight before surging forward at a run. His huge body lumbered across the roof, cracking the stone and sending booming noises throughout the castle. He leapt from the edge as his wings caught the wind, flapping them again with all the strength in his great body. The wind lifted and carried him up as he flew to the west, over the mountains and out to sea.

The humans would see him go. They would point and shriek as his huge crimson form flew overhead. He rained fire down at them, something he hadn't been able to do in far too long. It brought back distant memories of his youth, from before he was Mugalo.

No. He was Mugalo no longer. He was once again what he had always been: Crydax, the greatest of the dragons.

CHAPTER TWENTY-ONE

Jag's hands gripped the wooden rungs as he climbed. He was maybe ten feet off the ground now, climbing the southern wall of a flower shop at the very edge of Hightown. The roof of that flower shop was precisely the necessary height for someone with exceptional physical ability to make a flying leap over the wall that blocked off the castle. That person could then execute a well-timed forward roll to soften their landing, arriving on the other side of the wall amidst the large, soft, and conveniently placed flower beds of the Royal Gardens.

This was something that Jag had done more than once in his life. He had deliberately left this particular hole in the castle's defenses off of any of his security reports, just in case he ever needed to get back into it someday. As his captain had always said, it never hurt to have a backup plan, but it often killed not to.

Jag reached the roof of the flower shop, peering out over the gap between the wall and the roof. The gap was several feet wide and it required a running start in order to clear the distance. He'd never really been worried about missing, but looking at it now, he realized that it had either gotten larger, or he'd gotten saner. Either way, he was going to have to do it again.

But to his surprise and distaste, someone had installed large iron spikes atop the wall around the entire perimeter. Nearly ten inches in length, they were firm and looked wickedly sharp. Probably to keep out thieves or to deter birds from gathering along the wall.

Either way, it was going to make this harder.

But Jag Mercer was not some common thief. He was the most famous soldier in Farillyon, and a few iron spikes were not going to be enough to keep him from getting where he needed to go. He excelled at working on his own, and this certainly wasn't going to stop him.

He scanned the roof, looking for something that might assist him in his venture. If he had been given the time to prepare, he might've brought a rope or some other kind of climbing equipment. But sadly, he was a well-known fugitive in this city. Even if he found a shopkeep who was willing to sell him something at this hour, he ran the risk of the wrong person catching him. All would be ruined if he didn't get to the right people first.

He was going to reveal himself to the public, but only after he had the Blades on his side. They might take a little bit of convincing, but he had risked his life for all of them more than once. They would listen to him, and if the Blades followed, so would the City Guard. He just had to make it that far, to convince his old friends of the danger that was about to befall them.

In the corner of the flat roof sat a large barrel. Next to it was the trapdoor that led back down into the shop. The barrel, he realized, probably made for an effective lock of the door. He distantly recalled that the florist had two children, and they'd be about in their teenage years now. He suppressed a laugh. Not exactly subtle, but effective nonetheless.

But the barrel had what he needed. He fumbled with it for a moment and drew the thick wooden lid from the top with a satisfied nod. It was just large enough for what he planned. The idea he had was more than a little crazy, but Jag didn't really see any other options. He wasn't just going to waltz in the front gate where there were guards on alert. Besides, he excelled at crazy.

He walked to the far side of the roof, taking a few seconds to mentally plot his path. He had perhaps twenty feet to run. He knew he'd made the jump before, but the spikes definitely added a new twist. It really did look further than he remembered, but he was pretty sure his plan would work. Mostly sure.

Clutching the barrel lid tightly in his right hand, Jag ran as hard as he possibly could. In just a breath he had cleared the roof, and his foot came down on the very edge of the building. He leapt with all his strength, lifting the barrel lid over his head to give his legs room to move. Distantly, he wondered if it might catch the wind and help carry him further.

In midair, he tucked his leg, making just enough room for him to slip the barrel lid underneath his feet. His aim was perfect; as he neared the wall, his legs stretched out, the barrel lid now firmly underfoot. Angled just right, he was still moving forward without the lid sliding away. He reached the wall and pushed down with all his might, driving the lid onto the spikes with a "thud" just as he reached the wall.

Before the spikes could fully penetrate the wooden lid, he kicked off of it, diving ahead and sparing his feet the painful impalement that the wall had promised. He cleared it with ease, leaving the lid behind him. Firmly secured to the wall, it would probably offer a good perch for any birds that had been put out by the spikes.

Now for the hard part. The wall was perhaps twenty feet high, and he now had that far to fall before making his landing. The ground beneath him would be the soft soil of a flowerbed, but he could still break something if he didn't land just right. Much too late, he prayed that he wouldn't land on a bed of roses.

Tucking forward, he executed a perfect roll as he landed, smashing into the flowerbed and scattering multicolored lilies in every direction. He got to his feet, quickly dashing out of the open view of the garden and into the shadow of a nearby rosebush. He took a moment to catch his breath and slow his beating heart before taking a breath and peering out into the garden.

The patrolling guards hadn't spotted him. One of them had his back to Jag, lazily strolling down one of the paths. The other within sight was leaning against a tree sleepily. His head was bobbing up and down and he let out a snort every so often, which seemed to only briefly wake him back up.

Who in the world was training these inept twits?

Jag darted out from behind the bush, using the opening he had to slip into the service entry for the castle. The groundskeepers and servants used this entrance in order to keep them out of the view of the public. Jag had also used it many times in his life, as it was a less-conspicuous way to get in and out of the castle.

His entry was largely unobstructed. Slipping through the doorways, he adjusted his demeanor and walked openly down the halls as if he belonged there. The servants, the only people ever walking the halls at this time of night, were unlikely to even look him in the face if he carried himself like this. They were trained to not draw the eye and not interact with the nobility. Jag, having protected the nobility his entire life, knew exactly how to act. He put on his best scowl and walked with a boisterous swagger.

The walk through the castle itself was uneventful. Servants ignored him, as he had expected. There were a scant number of guards. The ones Jag did come across were not difficult to avoid. He knew every hallway and corridor in the massive structure. Within ten minutes he reached the inner entryway to the Imperial Barracks.

It was the inner entryway because it also had an outer entryway, the main entrance that most guards used. Only the Blades knew about the inner door, which served as a quick route to the Emperor in case of an emergency. He suspected that a few of the servants probably knew about it too, and many other secret doors besides it. He had once unlocked the door to the private training room of the Blades to find Sim, one of the oldest and most decrepit servants in the castle, slowly carrying weapons back to their racks and tidying up the room. Sim had bowed over and over, spewing apologies, but before Jag could digest that Sim had been locked in a room with one door, the old man disappeared out of the Barracks.

Jag pulled on the torch bracket that opened the secret door, stepping quickly into the training room and noting with pleasure that it was empty. He was hoping to reveal himself to his closest allies first. He didn't fancy the idea of getting tossed into a holding cell full of rats and bones.

He stopped to check his weapons. The sword and his many knives were all secure. He didn't like the idea of getting into a fight, but he knew there was a possibility that he would have to blacken a few eyes for them to listen to him. The other Blades were formidable fighters, but none as good as him.

With a final calming breath, he pushed open the door and stepped out of the training room, strolling into the main common area of the Barracks. He recognized several faces instantly, and was pleased to note that the soldiers that were nearest to him had been his close friends in the Blades. Mason, the closer of the two, stood six and a half feet tall and outmuscled nearly every man in the city. He was an imposing sight and a fearless warrior. Jag had once seen him carry three wounded soldiers on his back for nearly a mile. Brok, the other, offered a stark contrast to Mason. Smaller than even Jag, Brok was as unassuming as any farmer. But he was a deadly marksman and as silent as the night when he wanted to be. He defeated an entire guard unit in training without ever being spotted. The two of them looked up from their meals, staring at him in shock.

A great many things happened all at once. Jag raised his hand as if to say "hold on now, don't kill me just yet" just as Mason and Brok sprang from their seats. Several other guards followed suit. Jag rested his other hand on the hilt of his own weapon, but chose not to draw it. This was the crucial moment that would decide if he won them over or got stabbed to death.

"Hang on!" he yelled, his hand still up. Mason and Brok glanced at one another, nodded, and stepped forward to block the other guards from reaching Jag. They were the only other Blades in the room, but their actions would give every one of those guards at least a moment of pause. Jag had a chance here.

"I'm not here for a fight," he said slowly, staring at Mason. "There're many more important things going on right now than my arrest. Hear me out, soldiers. Mason, Brok, you two know that I'm not evil. You've seen it. You've worked with me, bled with me. Nearly died with me."

Mason and Brok glanced at one another again. Finally, Mason nodded at him. His voice was low and slow, his words careful.

"Alright, Mercer. What are you doing here?"

Jag lowered his hand, his other still on the hilt of his weapon. "The

Dominion is marching on the city. We have a day, maybe two, before they arrive from the north. To the south, Apep the Snake has raised an army of thousands of Drones, and they march north. The two forces will arrive at the same time, obliterating the city if we don't do something. The army is scattered and the Guard is not going to be prepared unless I can get this warning out. With the time we have, we can evacuate the people, mobilize every soldier we have, and make a stand."

Mason and Brok looked like they wanted to laugh. "Mercer, you've always been colorful when you get to storytelling. But let's be realistic. You're a wanted fugitive. Why should any of us believe you? Even if we are friends, Jag, you still betrayed the Empire."

"Because he's right," called a voice from the back, before Jag could offer a response. Every head in the room turned to see Captain Reynolds, his armor polished and as noisy as ever, walking through the crowd. The captain was a large, burly man in the height of middle age. His face was scarred and craggy after decades of combat, but his eyes were always bright. He reached Jag and immediately held out a tightly-wrapped scroll. Jag stared at it, puzzled.

"The Emperor is dead," he said loudly, so that the whole room could hear.

There was a collective intake of breath as Jag winced. He had been hoping to break that news to them himself, but he had to recognize the small part of him that was relieved to not have to do it. Reynolds had virtually raised Jag, and was one of the biggest reasons why Jag became the soldier he was. Jag took the scroll, puzzled.

"What is this?" he asked, peering at the wrapped up roll of parchment.

"Your patent of nobility," said the captain with a wry smile. "I should've given it to you long ago. I wanted to, but the Emperor forbade me from doing so in order to protect his career, and as he said, protect you. But he is dead now. We found his body in the seal room beneath the castle."

Jag blinked, looking down at the scroll. "A patent... of nobility?" he asked as his confidence, his Jag Mercer self-assurance, vanished. He knew what he was holding, and he also knew what the captain was suggesting. As if there were a great unseen object attached to the scroll, he could almost feel the weight of it settle on his shoulders.

The captain turned to face the rest of the men, giving Jag a moment to collect his thoughts. "I give you my word, men. The Emperor is dead, slain by Mugalo. I saw the scouting reports myself, reports of the Dominion closing in from the north. We are about to be overrun, and the Emperor is no longer here to lead us into battle."

The soldiers sheathed their weapons, looking stone-faced and serious. Jag was still staring at the patent in his hand, trying to keep his heart rate from rising. He was barely even hearing the captain's words.

"The man standing before you now," continued Reynolds, gesturing to Jag, "is Jag Mercer. As you know, he is the most decorated soldier amongst you. Some of you were his friends, some of you envied him, and some of you disliked him. But every one of you has respect for him. What you do not know is that Jag Mercer is the bastard son of Tyvarion Il'Vir. The Emperor was pressured at Jag's birth to keep it a secret in order to avoid a scandal. So Jag's care was entrusted to me, to the Blades. He's been here longer than any of you, been a part of this place since before he could walk."

Jag numbly unrolled the scroll, looking over its contents. Reynolds had told the truth; the scroll was a notarized patent of nobility for Jag Mercer, the one and only son of Tyvarion Il'Vir. It bore the seal of the Royal Historian and the faint glow of magic. And now, in the hands of the only son of the Emperor, it meant something much, much more.

The soldiers were all staring at Jag. Mason was smiling. Jag looked up at them, unable to even open his mouth to speak. His job had been to win them over, but this... he hadn't expected this.

Reynolds turned back to him, saluting with a fist to his heart. "That also means that he is the rightful heir to the throne. Never before has a non-Adept king sat upon the throne. But here he stands before you... your new Emperor."

With that, Reynolds dropped to a knee, bowing his head and holding his salute. Every other soldier in the room followed suit, and Jag suddenly found himself in a room full of kneeling soldiers. He rolled up the patents, stowing them away in his pack. He stood there awkwardly for a few more seconds before gesturing a bit wildly with his hands.

"Get up," he said hoarsely, gripping Reynolds by the shoulders and actually hauling the man to his feet. "All of you. We don't have time for this! You can all salute me later. Right now, we have a lot of work that needs to be done and not a lot of time to do it."

The captain laughed and got to his feet, and Jag felt the tension in the room lift as he did. The rest of the men got to their feet, and most were smiling. The soldiers were going along with the captain. He had done the work and won them over for Jag.

"What is your plan, Emperor?" asked Reynolds, motioning to the table. Brok, his timing perfect, appeared with maps of the area and spread them all out for those in the inner ring to see.

Jag felt incredibly awkward being addressed as Emperor, but he also knew that he'd have to get used to it. He wasn't exactly happy with this turn of events, but what choice did he have? There was nobody else for the job. Grace was a strong Adept and much smarter than him, but she was still very young, and he knew his sister well enough to know that she had no desire to be in charge of anyone. She was a healer first, and that's all she ever wanted or needed to be.

He looked up at Brok. "I need you to recall all the castle guards, all of the Blades, and all of the city guards. Get everybody here as quickly as possible. Sound the disaster alarms, as we're going to need the people to start packing. We need to find a way to get them out of here. And get the word out that the leadership has changed. We don't have time for squabbles over who follows who. If the captains don't want to comply, motivate them. Demote them if you have to. Just get it done."

Brok nodded, and after a brief salute, vanished through the doorway. If anyone could round up the entire city guard so quickly, it would be Brok.

Reynolds eyed the map. "Even if we draft the city guards, we're not going to have enough forces to meet both armies. Maybe if the rest of the army was here... but they aren't, so it doesn't matter. What do you suggest?"

Jag pointed to the south. "My sister and Vance Tythas flew a little ways south to meet the Drones. They will, at the very least, stall them. Wyatt Arden, the Adept who made that big scene outside of the Archives and trounced Alvernon, flew north to meet the Dominion."

Mason's eyes went wide. "He's going to try to fight the Dominion's army on his own?"

Jag shook his head. "I hope not. He defeated one of their councilmen in a blood duel, which is… well, it's a ritual sort of fight where the loser forfeits their lands and title to the winner and becomes their servant. It's very rare, but it's a way for up-and-comers to gain power in the Dominion if they don't want to go through the traditional route. One of their higher-ups challenged Wyatt, and Wyatt won, so he's on their War Council now. He's going to try to convince them that marching against the Empire is a mistake, and that they need to unite against Apep now and work out the problems later."

Reynolds pointed to the map. "That's where the last scouting reports put the Drones at. No doubt they'll be closer, but Drones move slowly."

Jag inclined his head, pointing to another spot. "This is where I would estimate the Dominion's army to be, based on the reports I saw. Armies move slowly, too. Once Wyatt reaches them, he may buy us some time. All in all… I expect we have a day, at most, before the two forces reach us."

"So where should we go?" asked a nearby soldier from the back.

Jag scratched his chin. "First priority is securing the people of Farillyon and evacuating them. Not everyone is going to want to go, and we don't have time to force everyone. Brok is going to sound the alarm and notify the Guard. Once that's done, we'll need a small group of soldiers to lead them out."

Reynolds pulled another scroll out of his pack. "I've already been working on that, Emperor. I took the liberty of digging up the old maps of the tunnels beneath Farillyon. I don't think anyone has actually been in them in a few centuries, but provided they're still there, we can get our people out discreetly."

Jag nodded. "That's good. That should put them behind the Drone army. From there, they can go to Triat and wait it out. Even Apep would think twice about marching on a city full of mercenaries and pirates. As for the rest of us… we will stand firm and defend the city against whatever may break through."

Reynolds shifted his feet. "Emperor… if I may… I have never

trusted any member of the Dominion further than I could throw them. You've shared similar sentiments with me in the past, Emperor."

Jag had to agree with that. "Yeah, I know. But Wyatt's an amazing kid. The things that he's already managed to do... If you could've seen him in that blood duel, captain, he'd have made a believer out of you, too."

The captain shrugged. "I'm not saying he hasn't already. I saw what he did to the city guard, three Aeromancers, and Alvernon. But I'm not worried about him. The Dominion is full of snakes and traitors who would all gladly stab each other in the back to gain a higher seat on the War Council. One of them could have it out for him, and that would be enough. He could be killed in his sleep. I think we should go back him up."

Jag didn't like it. He hated the thought of leaving Tythas and Grace alone, and he knew that the seal needed protecting.

"No," he said swiftly, making a decision all at once. "I trust Wyatt to get the job done. We evacuate as best we can and send our Adepts south to back up Tythas and my sister. Two Adepts, however strong they may be, cannot hope to survive against that many Drones without help. That army cannot be dissuaded, unlike the Dominion. Wyatt will come through. The rest of us will hold firm and keep the city safe."

Captain Reynolds gripped him by the shoulder. Jag felt a sharp spike of pain as if he'd been cut, but before he could respond, everything went white for a moment.

"Sir, with all due respect, this Empire has a long history of being betrayed by the Dominion," said the Captain, his voice low in Jag's ear. "We need to send our forces north to meet them, because they are not going to honor their agreement."

Jag's mind felt sluggish and dull as the Captain's words resonated within it. Finally, he seemed to wake up again, the pain and the strange sensation fading out of his memory. He considered the Captain's words for a long moment before nodding.

"You're right about that," he said. "Besides, we know how they fight. I think the Guard and the Blades will be enough to handle them. We've recalled the army, so if nothing else, it'll be enough to stall them."

The captain nodded approvingly. "I will make preparations to mobilize our remaining forces."

Jag looked to Mason. "I know most of our Adepts are in the field, but there are some who are still here. Recall whoever you can, and if any of the older students at the Academy are confident enough in their abilities, call upon them as well. We need all available hands. Don't waste your time trying to persuade. Yes or no, that's all we have time for."

Mason saluted and ducked out the door that Brok had used. Jag looked up, scanning the room, the faces that looked at him expectantly.

"It's been a while since I was last here," said Jag softly. "But I took an oath a long time ago to always serve this great Empire. Every man and woman in this room has bled for the cause, for their people. Every one of us has given of ourselves so that the Empire could stand strong. We're on the advent of a turning point in history. It is in our hands to make sure that this Empire survives, that it rights its wrongs and makes progress in the right direction. I pledge to you, my soldiers, that I will lead you down that path. I pledge myself to you, men."

Jag saluted them with a fist, and the room erupted in a rallying cry that strengthened the steel in Jag's heart. Jag didn't know it, but he looked more like his father now than ever before.

Grace and Tythas surveyed the landscape, peering out over the low valley that stretched out before them. They were lying atop a merry green hill, several miles south of Farillyon. In the distance, at the very end of the valley, they could see the great shadowy mass slowly making its way toward them. This far away, it almost looked like a great cloud of darkness, like a low black fog rolling out over the land.

But they knew better. They knew that that cloud was full of writhing limbs, of shrieking and growling corpses. What was moving into the valley was much worse than a dark fog. It was a machine of death.

"Remind me again how you were able to talk me into this?" asked Grace in a low voice, her displeasure evident.

"You, my dear, are a lot like me," replied Tythas with far more cheer than should be allowed. "That is to say, prone to acts of great bravery and laughable stupidity. The two details are closely related. As your brother always likes to say... we specialize in crazy."

Grace let out a very unwomanly grunt. "Alright then, what's the plan?" she said, doing her best to keep her cool. She'd been in battles for her life before, but this was bigger than anything she'd ever imagined. She never expected to be staring down thousands of Drones with one crazy old man as her only backup.

"This valley is the only path north through the flats," said Tythas, pointing out over the valley. "We have a rare, perhaps even singular, opportunity to trap them here. At the very least, we can use the valley as a choke point and try to hold them for as long as we can."

"How many do you think there are?" asked Grace. It seemed like a stupid question, but she couldn't resist asking it anyway.

Tythas squinted off at the hoard. "Thousands, I'd imagine. Remember, he had a Darkshard. He killed thousands of people just to bolster his army. Not make, mind you. Bolster."

Grace sighed. "Alright. This is the ambush point, then. No doubt Apep is planning the attack to happen at night, but it's still sunny out right now. That'll give us a bit of an edge. Drones don't like the sunlight, after all."

Tythas inclined his head. "I think we should set some traps down in the valley. There's not a lot of offensive power in your repertoire, so I'd like you to just save your energy for now and try to find your center while I go down into the valley and leave a few surprises for our new friends."

Grace raised an eyebrow. "What sort of traps are you thinking of setting, exactly?"

Tythas got to his feet, chuckling. "My dear, I have all sorts of tricks that you aren't aware of. Never reveal all of your secrets to anyone. Even your best students."

Grace gave him a sideways look but said nothing. Tythas laughed, his cheer baffling Grace. He motioned for her to stay put and set off down the hill at a sprint, straight into the valley.

The beasts were a good distance out, and they had incredibly short vision. He figured he'd have a decent amount of time, maybe thirty minutes, before they reached him. That was plenty of time for him to do what he wanted to do.

As Tythas ran, he felt the cheer leaving him. The weight of everything that was happening settled onto his shoulders, and he was again reminded of how old he was. He had been down this road once before, facing insurmountable odds at the hands of Apep the Snake, perhaps the one man in the world that he truly hated. Apep had survived and endured in the most impossible of situations, and Tythas was beginning to fear that after all of the battles and the years, Apep might finally defeat him.

He watched the wall of Drones churning into the valley ahead of him. They were slow and clumsy, and every so often one would trip and fall and be trampled, obliterated by the sheer mass of the horde. Nothing would stop that army. Few would be so foolish as to try to stand against something so deeply and truly terrible.

In spite of everything, Tythas managed a smirk. He was running right at it.

Finally, he reached the spot where he'd decided to lay his trap. The broad expanse of land would be perfect for what he had planned.

He drew into himself, tapping into the deep well of power within his chest. He stretched his hands out toward the earth, and as he had done so many times before, he released his power.

Every Adept described the sensation differently; some said their skin tingled, others experienced flashes of color in their eyes. One unfortunate soul described it to Tythas as being akin to suffocating. It was a wholeheartedly individual experience.

But for Tythas, his power had always felt like a wild animal that he constantly had to restrain. Whenever he tapped into that power it was like undoing a leash and letting it leap free, his body the conduit for its awesome and breathtaking magnitude. It roared to life within him, and as he directed his hands, he harnessed that power and shaped it to his will. His entire body trembled as it rushed through him. It was so blissfully pure.

Flames leapt from his fingers, directed into the earth. But it wasn't the flickering flame that one would find at a campfire or the roaring gout that the dragons had been said to produce when they breathed it. It wasn't a cloud or a wave. Few Pyromancers could channel their power in the ways that Tythas could.

The flame came as concentrated rays, pouring out of his fingertips in straight lines and searing the ground beneath him. He carefully directed them, each drawing shapes and symbols in the dirt and infusing those symbols with his power. After a few moments of delicate adjusting, he cut off the energy and stepped back to survey his creation.

A great, blackened glyph sat in the dirt before him, glowing ever-so-faintly with red heat. It had been a long time since he had inscribed that particular glyph in anything, much less something this large. He had to put a lot of power into this one. Hopefully it would be enough to curb the numbers and give them a fighting chance.

Tythas turned back to see Grace running down the hill after him. He sighed wistfully. If he could, one day, teach the girl some patience, he could die happy and fulfilled.

"You old wretch!" she said as she reached him, staring at the glyph in awe. "You know how to inscribe, and you never taught anyone?"

Tythas chuckled. "I am not an inscriber, Grace. I just know a few tricks. In fact, this is pretty much the extent of my ability. The greater intricacies of inscribing remain a mystery to me just as they remain a mystery to every other Adept."

She sighed and shook her head. "So what does it do?" she walked close to it, and the glowing light intensified. She blinked and took a step back, and the glow faded. Crouching down, she studied it closely.

"It's a warding glyph," he said. "Sort of like the ones you find all over the castle, just… modified. Those glyphs raise a wall of solid air when they are crossed by whatever the inscriber specifies. In this case, it will go off when something dead crosses the field."

Grace eyed it with curiosity. "The glyphs in the castle are tiny, though. Why is this one so big?"

Tythas spread his hands out, motioning to the valley around them. "Those wards need only to cover doorways or hallways. At most, the threshold of a room. This ward will release a wall of fire that stretches, hopefully, the entire width of the valley. Because it's so big, it won't last nearly as long as the small wards. Maybe a minute or two. But in that minute or two, anything that crosses over the wall will be incinerated. Like I said, just a few modifications."

Grace got to her feet and grinned at him. "You're a genius, old man. Did I ever tell you that?"

Tythas chuckled dryly, shaking his head. "Let's just hope it is enough. I suggest you get ready, Grace. We have a little bit of time to rest, but don't forget that they are coming."

CHAPTER TWENTY-TWO

Wyatt sped through the air, traveling north with more haste than was probably wise. He felt Shem in his mind, silent but firm, lending great amounts of power to him to keep him fresh. Shem's constant support was the only reason he was able to do what he was doing; the cat was lending him more power than ever. Without the sword, he knew he'd never be able to fly a distance like this. He was grateful for that. The last few months had been more eventful and fast-paced than his entire life. He was starting to feel the effects, but that deep weariness brought about by constant action was being held back by the knowledge that, win or lose, this would all be over soon.

He was already working on a deadline, certainly a first for his adventures. When they were just chasing Apep, everything had seemed so open, especially when they had no plan or no real idea of where to go next. But now, the road ahead of them was perfectly, unforgivingly clear. He was terrified, but he also felt just a little bit liberated by that. His fight to find his mother and his fight to save the world from Necron had come together, leaving him with only one objective.

As the wind whipped his lengthening hair back, his eyes were firmly set on the horizon.

It was only a few hours before the main body of the Dominion's army came into view. It was, as he knew it would be, a truly awesome sight. It looked like the entire Dominion was about to descend on the Empire. Thousands marched in unison, moving out over the broad flat plains that made up the northern part of the Empire's land. Massive carts of food and supplies were pulled by horses and donkeys. Wyatt could even see huge wooden siege engines being towed by elephants. How such a huge force had managed to dodge the Empire's forces so well was a mystery, but Wyatt had a suspicion that a certain old royal adviser might've had a hand in it.

What he still couldn't figure out was Mugalo's motivation. He had slain the Emperor, but how much good had that really done him? Wyatt had a lot of trouble believing that the old man would align himself with a psychotic Necromancer bent on killing the entire world. If Mugalo had been helping Apep, why hadn't he finished the rest of them off? Why hadn't he killed Grace and Wyatt in the Archives? There were too many questions where that old snake was concerned. When all of this was settled, Wyatt was going to make it a point to find him and make him answer those questions.

As he flew overhead, he could see people in the army pointing up at him. He knew that, for as many citizens as the Dominion had, only a few were Adepts, and those were usually the leaders. With any luck, they were expecting him and wouldn't immediately try to kill him when he landed. But he hadn't exactly been that lucky lately, either.

After a bit of searching, he finally found what he sought. At the rear of their force, in almost the very center, a group of huge, magnificently armored horses carried ten equally huge and magnificent-looking riders. Around them, men carried great metal cauldrons that contained roaring fires. Each man was painted for war, and to the enemy, they could only look like vengeful, fiery spirits.

Wyatt descended directly in front of them, a strong gust slowing his fall so that he landed safely in a crouch. The horses, trained not to startle or buck, slowed and snorted at him, stamping their hooves. But they held their ground. As Wyatt straightened up, he felt hundreds of heated eyes on him. He knew he had to be careful.

From every direction, Wyatt could feel the Dominion's Pyromancers call upon their power. As if the season had suddenly shifted to the dead of summer all at once, the air temperature rose quickly. He fought back the urge to draw his sword. He had to keep calm. Any wrong move here and he'd be skewered by about twenty spears all at once. He took a deep breath but held his ground.

The Warlord sat ahead of him atop a great black horse, his gaze firm. Just behind him, the nine members of the War Council eyed him with caution. For a brief moment, the entire army seemed to hold its breath, waiting for either side to act. But as he suspected, there were a few less-restrained Adepts in the Dominion. He felt a handful of them channeling the power toward him. He gripped the hilt of his sword and prayed that his plan would work as three separate blasts of fire rolled over him.

For several moments, he held his breath, just hoping he wouldn't be cooked alive. But whatever power within him had saved him from Mubaraji was protecting him here, too. He felt his own power drinking their fire in, soaking it up and using it to energize him. Whatever fatigue that the flight here had given him vanished. The heat that he should have felt was warm, pleasant, and just a bit ticklish. He had to struggle not to squirm. But the moment was too crucial for that, so he held his ground, remaining stoic.

The flames ceased, and Wyatt was pleased to note the great surprise on the faces of his fellow councilmen. He knew that there was a possibility that his attackers had been ordered to do that in the event of his arrival. No doubt the witnesses to the blood duel would've told the Warlord how Wyatt defeated Mubaraji. Even so, they looked surprised at his survival. He saw Salif on the left flank, who looked pleased. Wyatt inclined his head.

"So," said the lead rider, the man that Wyatt knew to be the new Warlord. He was, like so many of his colleagues, a great bear of a man. Magnificently painted, an enormous axe hung from his back. "So. The outsider has come to take his place with the Dominion. Are you ready to ride with us, Aeromancer? Are you ready to destroy the Empire?"

Wyatt held his hands up. "For now, I'm just here to talk. I believe I've earned the right to address my colleagues, have I not?"

The Warlord nodded. "You certainly have, outsider. Not many men could've defeated Mubaraji in a fight like that. You do not have a great number of allies here, but I am a fair Warlord. You have earned your place, so if you have something to say, speak."

Wyatt nodded. "You've come to crush the Empire. Well, I'd like to commend you, because if you continue with your current course, you'll succeed. You've managed, probably due to the machinations of a certain traitor, to completely elude the Imperial army. You know that they're still spread out. I've seen the reports; pieces of the army are on the Dominion's border. Others guard the border to the Untamed Lands. Some patrol the seas to the south, to keep the pirates of the Scattered Coast at bay. The messages have already been sent to recall them, but those messages will be much too late. They'll return to Farillyon to find it in ruins."

The Warlord chuckled. "You have an odd way of dissuading us, outsider."

Wyatt shrugged. "Listen, if you want to go kick them while they're down, there isn't much I can do to stop you. But in the short time I spent with the Dominion, I learned how important honor is to its people. That victory that awaits you is not honorable, and it is not well fought. There are, at most, a thousand city guards and maybe a handful of Adepts left to fight you. They will do some damage, but you will win. You will win, only to lose in a much more resounding, permanent way."

The Warlord narrowed his eyes. "Explain."

"You made a loose alliance with Apep the Snake," said Wyatt, not giving the Warlord the opportunity to deny it. "He's agreed to send his own forces, an army of Drones and whatever other awful things he's dredged up, to hit Farillyon at the same time as you. Like two hammers striking either side of the same object, the capital city will be obliterated. Mubaraji suggested to me that you planned to kill Apep yourselves once his usefulness has expired." The council members were looking at each other now. Clearly, he knew a lot more than they'd anticipated.

"What you do not know is why Apep offered his help in the first place," continued Wyatt, now pacing slightly as he spoke. Restless, he brushed his hair back. "Well, I can promise you that he doesn't plan to keep you around for any longer than you plan to keep him around. And he's got more power than you do, gentlemen."

The Warlord huffed at him as a few of the councilmen laughed. "That skinny old relic doesn't have more power than the Dominion, outsider. For you to suggest it is absurd."

Wyatt rolled his eyes. "Don't be stupid. That 'skinny old relic' has aligned himself with a demigod, and the moment you underestimated him is the moment you signed away your lives. Don't you remember the last war? Apep's true intentions? Once he broke the first seal, it was only a matter of time."

Again, the members of the council looked at each other. Some of them were discussing his words under their breaths. He could tell that he was on the right track. The Warlord, however, remained stone-faced.

"Apep is breaking the seals that hold Necron at bay," he said, pointing to the north, to the Dominion's homeland. "Mount Trajnheim? I didn't do that. I tried to stop Apep from getting there. But you fools invited that Necromancer into your home and gave him the opportunity to kidnap your predecessor," he jabbed a finger at the Warlord, "and sacrifice him on the seal. He broke another seal beneath Ven, my home. He broke another atop the Mount of Light, some time ago. There is only one left, one seal keeping this world from an ugly death, and you're ready to offer it up to him on a platter. You're going to destroy the whole world by being shortsighted."

The Warlord smirked. "The seals, Necron... it's all a myth, an old story meant to keep Adepts in line. Necron is as dead as the other demigods."

Wyatt gaped at him. "Are you serious? You really, actually believe that? Do you really think that Apep would align himself with a group as powerful as the Dominion if he weren't absolutely certain that he could destroy you as soon as he no longer needed you?"

The Warlord had no answer for that. His glare was still present, but Wyatt could see that he was making an impact.

"Listen," said Wyatt with a sigh. "I'm not asking you to drop your hate for the Empire and march off to serve under them. Honestly, I think that given the choice between the two of you, I'd rather stay with you folks than them. But I promise you that this is much bigger than Dominion versus Empire. And I promise you that if you continue down this path, you'll destroy the Empire. You'll destroy yourselves, too. I swear it on my name and my power. Warlord, if you do this, everybody loses."

He and the Warlord kept their eyes locked together for what felt like hours. Wyatt did his best not to wither under the heated glare of the elder

Adept, but he was keenly aware that the large Pyromancer had probably killed more men in his lifetime than Wyatt had ever met. It was difficult to not be intimidated. But he knew what was at stake, so he held his ground.

"Perhaps there is merit to what you say," mused the Warlord, looking back to his comrades. "Are we so weak that we would align ourselves with a fiend like Apep? I'm afraid that we have been misled, my friends. If we defeat the Empire, should we not do it on our terms, not the terms of a mad Necromancer?"

There was murmured agreement and nods throughout the council members. A few of the men looked displeased, but they seemed to be going along with the group. Salif was smiling broadly at him.

The Warlord turned again to face Wyatt. "You've earned the right to ride with this Army, outsider. Mount up, if you like. We will destroy Apep and his army. We will not ride against the Empire. We will save it, and then we shall see how they feel about us once we have delivered them from death."

Wyatt shook his head. "I'm afraid that I can't, Warlord. Two of my friends flew south to meet Apep's army, and they're the only thing standing between it and the city. They'll do fine for a while, but they are going to need help eventually. They can't hold out forever."

The Warlord nodded. "Your friends are brave, Wyatt Arden, and so are you. I apologize for the mistakes we've made. You are a welcome member of this council, and we can all learn greatly from you. I hope that when this is finished, we can all find a better path."

Wyatt saluted him. "I will. But I'll help the Empire, too. Both sides need it, and both sides can learn from one another. You guys don't have to be enemies."

The Warlord chuckled. "Youth," he said wistfully. "Now go. We will ride fast and hard and defend Farillyon when we can."

"Thank you, Warlord," said Wyatt, as grateful as he had ever been in his life. "You've made the right choice."

Nearly back to the castle, Wyatt caught sight of something else as he soared through the sky. For a moment, he thought that he must've been seeing things. But as he drew closer, the grim reality of the situation came into view. A small unit of soldiers, a few hundred men at most, was riding hard and fast to the north, straight toward the main body of the Dominion's army. They bore the flags and colors of the City Guard. Wyatt realized that someone must have convinced them to ride north and meet the Dominion head on.

Wyatt noticed something else. Leading the charge was a group of about a hundred, but their colors were different. They wore black leathers and their bannermen carried the unmistakable standard of the Circle of Blades. Jag had done it. But why in the world were they here and not defending the city?

Wyatt swooped in low, landing far enough out to give them the necessary time to safely slow down. He adjusted his baldric and stood firm, eyeing the lead rider with curiosity.

The group slowed to a halt some distance away from him. He could see Jag, the lead rider, conversing with them. After a few tense moments where Jag quietly reassured the rest of the group, he and another rider broke from the force and rode forward to meet Wyatt.

"Wyatt!" yelled Jag, riding forward with a smile on his face.

As Jag rode forward, Wyatt's confusion increased. Wyatt had never seen his friend clad in so many nice things. The sheath of his sword was jeweled and decorated with silver trim. His armor was polished and expensive. Perhaps most startling, he wore a golden crown on his head. It wasn't huge or obnoxious, instead regal and imposing in its simplicity. Jag looked like a king.

"What's going on?" called Wyatt, trying to keep his alarm in check. He tore his gaze off of Jag's shiny things and looked at his friend's face.

Jag glanced back at the rest of his forces. "I mobilized the Guard, like you said. But we thought it was a better idea to send our remaining forces north, in case the Dominion betrayed you. Is that why you're flying back? Did they reject you?"

Wyatt stared at him. "No, they didn't betray or reject me… Jag, what are you talking about? This isn't what we agreed on. Why would they betray me? Who gave you that idea?"

Jag blinked, his smile faltering. He looked confused for a moment, glancing to his left. The soldier on his left was older and more gruff-looking, bearing a captain's insignia on his collar. But he didn't return Jag's look, his eyes instead fixed upon Wyatt. He looked displeased.

"We made the decision as a group," said the captain evenly, looking down on Wyatt in more than one sense. "But the Emperor made the final call."

Wyatt blinked, looking back up at the captain. "The Emperor is dead, captain. Whoever you spoke to is an imposter."

Jag raised a hand, silencing the captain. "Wyatt... after Il'Vir died, the captain found my patents of nobility. I am the new Emperor."

Wyatt's gaze slowly turned back to Jag, his expression dumbfounded. "And you made the decision for you and your men to ride north?"

The new emperor nodded, still looking unsure. "Yes, I... well, we felt that the Dominion stood a good chance of betraying their promises. That army would crush Farillyon if there was nobody standing against it. So we rode to back you up."

Wyatt was fighting the urge to pace. He felt fidgety. "And what sort of advantage do you gain by meeting them in an open field versus fighting them in the city, behind the walls?"

Jag and the captain exchanged glances again. "We are experts in combat with forces much larger than our own. We've faced scenarios like this before. That's why the Guard exists. They're the elite, and the Blades are the elite of the elite. We can defeat them."

The urge became too great. Wyatt began to pace, his hot glare fixated on Jag and his meddlesome captain.

"Well, you don't need to defeat them, because they're on your side now," said Wyatt hotly. "But fine, you're here, it's been done. What about Grace and Tythas? You've abandoned your sister and your friend to face thousands of Drones on their own?"

Jag shook his head, holding his hands out. "Of course not! We sent every Pyromancer in the city south to assist them. Backup will reach them soon. We know they didn't plan to fly too far south. That many Adepts working together should be more than enough to fight off Apep and his army."

Wyatt's breath was coming faster as he struggled to maintain his composure. "Jag... if you are here with the Guard and some Adepts, and the rest of the Adepts went south... Who is defending the castle? Who is guarding the seal?"

Jag blinked. He opened his mouth and closed it again, glancing back at the captain. The captain gave Wyatt a stern, soldierly look.

"He is your Emperor, Adept," said the captain with a stern voice. "Not only should you address him with more respect, but you should refrain from questioning his methods. Who are you to suggest he or anyone in this army has made a mistake? You are an apostate!"

That was when it broke within Wyatt. Whatever was holding him together shattered, and months of anxiety and rage flowed forth. Faster than the captain could even react, Wyatt was upon him, flying through the air to take hold of whatever strap or buckle he could find on the captain's armor. The captain let out a yelp as Wyatt hauled him off of the horse, flinging him through the air and slamming him into the dirt. Wyatt could hear the surprised breath driven from the man's lungs, but before he could even mount a defense, Wyatt was on top of him, his knees on the man's arms and his hand on the man's throat.

"If you open your mouth again," said Wyatt venomously, not aware of the darkening sky above him, "I am going to do a lot worse than humiliate you." Wyatt's eyes were a dark, volatile blue. "I don't care how many Adepts you brought with you. If you value your life, be still and be silent."

There was a commotion from the main body of the force behind them, which Wyatt had entirely forgotten about in his rage. Jag was waving his arms and shouting, motioning for them to stay put.

"Wyatt, that's enough!" yelled Jag, leaping off of his horse and gripping Wyatt's shoulders. "You're right, okay? We made a mistake. I... I don't know why I thought this was a good idea. I'm an idiot because I listened to him, but this isn't going to help! Save it for later. Save it for Apep."

Wyatt stared into the captain's eyes for a few long seconds before allowing Jag to pull him up. The captain, still taking deep, sucking breaths, also got to his feet, his eyes never leaving Wyatt. He hadn't been hurt, but his pride had been sorely wounded. Wyatt had made a new enemy.

Jag opened his mouth to speak again, but Wyatt cut him off. "The Dominion is still riding this way," he said angrily, "to defend the city you abandoned. Get back there, and when they arrive, accept their help. If any one of your men so much as suggests that they have an ulterior motive or is prepared to betray us, I will fly him out to sea and let go."

Jag nodded, the new king suddenly feeling very small in the stormy gaze of the young Aeromancer. "I'm sorry, Wyatt," he said, shaking his head as if he were groggy. "I don't know… I don't know why I thought this was a good idea. It makes no sense."

Wyatt was still eyeing the captain with distaste. "I have an idea, I think. Just remember who your real friends are the next time you decide to accept someone else's ideas. I'll never steer you wrong, Jag, at least not intentionally."

Jag clapped Wyatt on the shoulder. "Get back to the city. You'll beat us there. You're the first line of defense now, Wyatt."

Wyatt drew his sword, the ringing sound echoing through the low hills. He felt the eyes of the entire army on him. Shem's presence in his mind was alive and hungry. The weight of it all was firmly on his shoulders, but he accepted that weight. He'd use it like a weapon.

Wyatt leapt into the air, a blast of wind carrying him into the sky. Lightning boomed around him as he flew with all his strength toward the seal.

Standing several feet apart, Tythas and Grace watched as the horde descended into the valley, their unstoppable bulk having finally noticed the two soul-filled obstacles in their path. It would be only a handful of moments before the first line crossed Tythas's ward, when the fight would begin.

"Tythas!" yelled Grace, staring ahead at the seething mass of dead, the fear plain on her face. "In the interest of full disclosure, if we get through this, I want you to know that I am going to beat you senseless for ever making me think that this was a good idea!"

Tythas's dry chuckle rolled out of his mouth, which Grace found oddly comforting. Even in straits as dire as these, Tythas was able to maintain his humor. That, more than anything, she loved about her mentor. He had taught her to always maintain her sense of self. To never lose sight, to never lose hope.

"Well, to be fair, I only said it was an idea," said Tythas thoughtfully, deadpan. "Not a good one. Not by leagues."

"I hate you," she replied, smiling in spite of it all.

Tythas chuckled again. "I know Grace. Now prepare yourself. They are here!"

Tythas's ward flared to life, and Grace was momentarily dazzled by the raging torrent of fire that erupted from the center of the valley. The great wall of flames stretched the entire gap between the bluffs, and the Drones shrieked and screamed as they passed through it.

Grace had to struggle not to vomit as the smell of cooked, rotted meat crossed her nose. She covered her face up as she watched flaming, melting Drones erupt out of the wall. They reached toward Grace and Tythas, but the heat of the fire was too much. Their bodies were quickly consumed, most reduced to piles of smoldering dust and bone.

But a few did manage to push through. Occasionally, one would step through a brief gap created by another flaming Drone. Slowly, shakily, they would stumble and stagger toward Grace and Tythas. Grace was still about fifty feet from the wall, but the sight of it was still terrifying. She had once thought that the sight of a Drone reaching for her was one of the worst things she'd ever seen, but a flaming Drone reaching for her was infinitely worse.

She reached out with her hands, calling on her power. Adala's love and strength filled her as her skin began to glow with a powerful white radiance. She reached out a hand, light erupting forth and blasting apart some of the Drones who had made it through the wall.

Tythas and Grace held their ground. The two of them picked off whatever survived the flaming ward, and while she couldn't see over the wall, she was pretty sure that they were making a big impact on the numbers. If they could maintain this just a little longer...

And then the flames died. Abruptly, the wall vanished from sight and for the first time, Grace had an up-close view of the horrible truth of their predicament.

The sea of Drones stretched all the way back to the mouth of the valley, and probably beyond. They had already destroyed hundreds, yet somehow that had barely made a difference. That sight alone hit Grace like a hammer, and she found that she had to remind herself to breathe.

Tythas's arms raised up as he summoned a set of flaming rings around him that spun and surged with deadly intent. Already, he was dancing backward as the rings swirled around him. Grace realized that he was making a field to protect himself, and decided that it was probably a good idea.

She didn't have any flaming rings, but she called on Adala, saying a silent prayer to the Mother of Life and opening her heart to the Goddess. Warmth flowed through her, and she called her power in a way that she never had dared before. The air around her flared with intensity as an aura of divine light bloomed outward from her body.

The Drones reached toward her, hungry and crazed, but when they got close enough they burst into white flames. Unable to be so close to a conduit of pure divinity, they shrieked and tried to avoid her. But it was too late for many; in simply laying their dead eyes on something so pure, they were obliterated.

Grace drew her daggers as the holy aura around her began to take shape. It was still partially translucent, but anyone looking on would not have seen her as she was. Instead they would have seen Adala herself, a flaming white sword in each hand.

Tythas threw fire like the dragons of old, the flames erupting from him in every direction as he whipped his arms madly around him. The Drones surged in, but he was great and terrible in his fury. His aura glowed with hot red light as flames coated his entire body, his power surging all around him.

The sky darkened to near black as the wind came. A thunderous boom sounded through the valley as lightning arced from the clouds above them, smashing into the horde of Drones and sending them flying in pieces. Grace could see the sky begin to swirl above them ominously. Moments later, several tornados descended from the sky around them, casting Drones up into the sky and shredding them apart. The horrible, howling winds obliterated everything in their path.

But for all the might, for all the destruction they created, they were not making enough of a difference. Grace was moving through the horde like a seasoned warrior, spinning and slashing with her glowing swords as she moved into gaps left by the freshly destroyed Drones. Any Drone that came near her was either incinerated by her radiance or slashed apart by her weapons. She saw them still pouring into the valley, no end in sight, as fatigue already started to claw at her chest.

Tythas was moving too, his rings spinning and slashing at everything around him as he did his best to avoid the largest groups. He spun and threw his hands out with wild abandon, sending blasts of fire toward everything around him.

But he too grew tired. He stepped away from the Drones warily, but they were surrounding him now, pressing ever closer. One of them made it through his rings, biting down on his shoulder before bursting into flames and being incinerated by his aura. He shouted in pain and leapt into the air, the wind taking him and lifting him above the hungry creatures to safety.

Out of the corner of her eye, Grace saw her mentor rise into the sky and begin to rain fire down upon the mass of drones with deadly intent. But as he did, the tornados relented and the winds died down. He couldn't maintain all of it at once.

A line of fiery pain erupted across Grace's back and she screamed, spinning and cleaving apart the Drone that had attacked her. She saw bloody fingertips, rotted and chewed away to reveal jagged bone tips that had slashed her back.

Adrenaline was flowing now, and the pain dimmed. She continued spinning and slashing, trying to get to one of the clear spots that had been left by the tornados that Tythas had called. She cut and slashed her way through the sea of bodies, breaking into one of those circular clearings.

Tythas landed beside her. Back-to- back, the two of them rained destruction around them. But it didn't matter. They were losing the fight.

A terrible roar cut through the chaos, and the two of them turned to look toward the source. The Drones parted, and a path opened in the sea of rot to reveal a lumbering, shadowy form. It roared again and stalked forward, intent on Grace and Tythas. Flanking it were two squat spiderlike creatures, which shrieked in fury as their mandibles dripped a black, viscous fluid.

"A Shender!" shouted Tythas, sounding more worried than Grace had ever heard him. "A Shender and two Arachnas!"

"I see them!" yelled Grace, casting her hands out and sending a wave of hot light directly into the Shender's path. The blast pushed them back, but didn't stop them. Grace's forehead was coated in a sheen of sweat and she could feel her aura diminishing.

"Grace! We need to run! We can't win this!" yelled Tythas as he threw a wall of fire out in front of them, blocking the Shender and the Arachnas from sight, burning several Drones in the process.

"Run where?" she shouted back, sending orbs of light through the wall that would explode when they reached an enemy. "We're surrounded, Vance! Can you fly us out of here?"

Tythas threw more fire at the Drones around them. A huge, featureless black arm reached through the flaming wall and swept several drones aside as the Shender roared in fury.

"We wouldn't get far," he said, his voice lower. He wasn't even sure she heard him, but the reality of their situation had settled into his heart. If he tried to fly, the Shender would leap and pluck them from the sky. He didn't have enough energy for the speed needed to get them away. This was a fight that they could not win, and their backup was nowhere in sight.

"I'm sorry, Grace!" he yelled, shaking his head and throwing everything he had into the flames. "But I don't think we're going to make it out of this one!"

"Don't be sorry!" she yelled back, her swords meeting the Shender's arm as it plunged through the fire and into their circle, cleaving off great chunks of inky black stuff. "I knew what I was getting into!"

The Shender stepped through the fire as the Arachnas leapt over it, landing behind them. Grace's pure white form stood in front of the Shender's infinite darkness, and in that moment Tythas knew that they were dead.

And then everything around them erupted into flames. Pillars of fire descended from the sky in every direction, blasting everything around them into dust. Both Arachnas leapt to attack Tythas, but before they could reach him, two flaming hands caught them out of midair and cast them over the sea of Drones and out of sight. Confusion and chaos reigned all around them like never before as Tythas searched for their savior. Grace's swords connected with the Shender's fist at the same time as a blast of flames, batting it aside.

"Vance!" she yelled as she dodged another huge swing. "Was that you?" The Shender belched out a cloud of darkness in her direction, but the cloud was purified by her white aura before it could reach her, dispersing harmlessly.

"No! It was them!" He pointed toward the small group of men and women that were advancing on their position from the rear. In no time at all, they united with the other Adepts, all Pyromancers. Just as the Shender was gaining the advantage, two huge, fiery hands caught it under the arms and lifted it up into the air. It struggled and roared in anger, but before it could break free, fire erupted all around it, closing it in a great sphere. The sphere spun and compressed, and the roar was cut off as the Shender was consumed.

"Vance Tythas! Princess Il'Vir!" shouted the leader of the group, a handsome, intelligent man that Tythas recognized. "We are here to assist you!"

Tythas took the man by the arm. He was Grayson Marrek, a man who Tythas had briefly taught, several years ago. "Marrek! We need to fall back! Hold the line, but move it back!"

A confused Grace looked to Tythas, shouting over the battle. "Why are we moving back?"

Tythas released Marrek and rested a hand on her shoulder. "Even with these Adepts, we can't do this forever. We need Jag and his forces. We need to fall back to the city."

CHAPTER TWENTY-THREE

Wyatt was flying as fast as he could. His face was numb from the cold of the wind blasting across it, but that mattered little. He could just see Farillyon in the distance, its great walls and towers peeking up over the horizon. Despite his unparalleled speed, it would still be some time before he reached the city.

For a farm boy, you're awfully bossy, remarked Shem, the cat's deep voice flooding Wyatt's mind. His tone wasn't mocking, though. Maybe a little amused, but mostly he just seemed to be making an observation.

This entire world has been wrecked by people making stupid, shortsighted decisions, replied Wyatt, scanning the horizon as he did. He could just see the heights of the castle rising above the rest of the city. *Besides, Jag's captain is a fool. I've met men like him before. They're the kind of men that always tried to take advantage of my mom. He deserved it.*

Shem's chuckle reverberating in his mind was a very odd sensation. *I don't disagree. You're becoming the man you need to be, Wyatt. I'm proud of you.*

Shem was proud of him? The world really was about to end. He suppressed a laugh. *I still have to survive the rest of the day, don't I? Don't be too proud yet. We've got a long way to go before the end of this fight.*

Agreed, echoed the cat, whose presence faded again from his mind.

Wyatt considered asking the cat more, but he knew that there was no time. Like always, he had a thousand things that he wished he could ask Shem, but he never seemed to have the time. He was ready to get this finished if only so he could sleep in a real bed again.

He rose over the next hill and finally, Farillyon came fully into view. But there was a problem: it was on fire.

Wyatt's heart leapt into his throat as he saw the smoke and the flames devouring the city. He surged forward, pouring as much energy and emotion into his speed as he could. He felt Shem's power rolling through him, strengthening him and allowing him to maintain the pace. The two of them reached the city within minutes, descending into a large open square with a fountain at the center of the city. He landed gently on the polished stone tiles, drawing his sword, the blade humming hungrily in his grip.

The city hadn't been burning long, but the fire had already done a lot of damage. Buildings were starting to collapse, casting debris into the streets. Wyatt also saw bodies scattered around, no doubt the people who had refused to evacuate the city. Some were burned, others rotted, and a few were torn apart. More than just a fire had passed through Farillyon.

"And so the hero arrives," came a low, dead voice over the sound of the crackling fires. Wyatt turned and saw the shrouded, wraithlike form of Apep walking down the far street, the one leading into the castle. The ancient Necromancer was wreathed in an aura of darkness and blood. He kicked aside a body as he walked, sending it tumbling.

Wyatt lifted his sword as a nimbus of wind wrapped around him, smiling flippantly in spite of the odds. "That's me. But you aren't exactly the villain, are you? You're the lackey, the cohort. This isn't even the real fight. You're just here to stall me."

Apep took a step, and the two of them began to walk in a circle. "Youthful arrogance," remarked the decrepit Necromancer. He looked as eerie as ever, his bone-white mask hiding the upper part of his face. "I tire of you already. You have lost."

As Wyatt lunged, the old man clapped his hands. Wyatt felt a wave of dark energy roll out from the powerful Adept. He saw the bodies littering the square begin to stir, and as the energy washed over him, a feeling of fear and misery threatened to overtake him. But Wyatt was still swinging.

Apep batted the blade aside, the steel meeting his skin with a loud clang and deflecting harmlessly. Wyatt's arm tingled with the vibration as he danced away, keeping his distance from the Necromancer.

"You fight alone?" asked Apep, amused. "Where are your friends, Wyatt Arden? Where is your safety net?"

The sky above them darkened to black as thunder boomed, the sound shaking some of the dread from Wyatt's bones. "My friends are preventing your plan from working. One of your armies has already abandoned you, and the other is being held at bay by the best Adepts the Empire has to offer. You're losing, old man."

Apep laughed, the sound devoid of emotion and utterly terrifying. "You think that it matters? How cute."

Wyatt kept his distance now, still circling. The Drones that had risen up weren't advancing on him, but were moving to the far end of the square, blocking the path up to the castle.

"Where is my mother? My grandfather?" snarled Wyatt, hurling a bolt of lightning from his hand toward his enemy. But before he had even started drawing the power for it, Apep was moving, drawing something from within his robes. Wyatt's bolt of energy met a short metal rod that seemed to draw the power to it. Electricity met metal with snarling fury, but the rod absorbed all of the energy, all of the shock from the bolt. As quickly as it had leapt toward Apep, the bolt vanished.

"Your mother is helping my master to break the final seal," drawled Apep with a sneer, as if he hadn't even noticed Wyatt's attack. "Her blood will release him. Your grandfather died at your home when he foolishly attempted to destroy us all by releasing his life force in an explosion. It was a clever trick, one that I hadn't ever seen before. It caught me by surprise and nearly ruined me. But I have taken precautions against every Aspect. I fear no Adept. Any other Adept, even a great Pyromancer, would've been consumed by your grandfather's rage. But not me. Not Apep."

Wyatt's blood rose as he stared at the Necromancer. His mother was a Vitamancer. That had been their plan all along, of course. Kelsar was dead, giving his life to try to kill Apep and prevent him from carrying that plan out.

"You have fought admirably," remarked Apep, still sneering. "But your efforts are misplaced. Even with that remarkable blade in your hand, you could never have prevented this. You have already lost, just like your family is already dead."

Rage erupted within Wyatt, a rage like he had never felt before. He saw his mother's warm smile, heard Kelsar's gruff voice. They were all he had ever had, the only family he had ever known. Kelsar hadn't even been family until after it was too late. Whatever semblance of a family he'd known had been snuffed out by the scheming of Apep and Necron. He could feel his heartbeat in his whole body.

He screamed in fury and surged forward, a great gale taking him by the back and propelling him at Apep like a cannonball. Flames roared from inside of him, wreathing him in an unstoppable heat. Thunder crashed in the sky above them as a bolt of lightning met Wyatt's blade, joining with it as Wyatt swung with all his might. Whatever Apep had done to block his blade the last time would not be enough now. His hand reached up to catch it, but that mattered little to Wyatt.

Apep the Snake was obliterated by the blow, his body cut completely in half as the energy-charged blade hit him. Wyatt expected blood, but the old body of the Necromancer appeared to have no blood to give. Instead of flesh and muscle, the old man's form broke into clumps of dirt and bone. Grave dirt, said a voice somewhere deep within Wyatt.

But where Apep's body had broken, his aura lingered. As if his shadow had come to life, a great dark shape glared down at Wyatt with glowing red eyes. A blow caught Wyatt in the chest and sent him flying across the square. He managed to correct himself in midair, landing in a crouch and sliding to a stop, his chest aching as his breaths came in wheezes.

"You destroyed my body," remarked the shadow, its voice a low, cold whisper, devoid of anything human. "No matter. I'll make another, as I have done countless times before. I cannot be killed, Aeromancer. I have mastered Death."

Wyatt slowly got to his feet, using the sword for support. The humming blade poured strength and reassurance into him, and he somehow managed to calm himself, finding his heart again. Wyatt took a deep breath, his rage transforming from boiling hot to cold, calm, and unstoppable.

He raised his hand up, some instinct from within directing him, telling him it was the only way. He focused on the shadow that Apep had become as his outstretched hand closed tight in a fist. His power flowed, not a raging torrent like normal. Now it was a cool current, icy and steady.

"What are you doing?" echoed Apep's voice, sounding a little frantic. The shadow struggled to move, but Wyatt held it in an unseen grip.

"Apep the Snake," said Wyatt, his voice sounding much deeper than normal. "You have survived and existed for far too long. Although you claim to be a Necromancer, you have no respect for Adala's design. You have no respect for Death, instead trying to defy it. You defy your own nature, Apep. Everything has a time to die, and your time is long overdue."

"You're an Aeromancer!" shrieked the struggling shadow. The Drones in the square stirred, staggering toward Wyatt.

Wyatt locked his gaze on the red slits that were Apep's eyes. "I am many things, Apep," said Wyatt, Shem's voice echoing with his own, "and today I am the end of you." The strength of the sword radiated from within him as he took hold of Apep's cold, lifeless spirit, his grip unbreakable.

"I cast you out of this Life," said Wyatt and Shem simultaneously. "You will walk here no longer. You are dead; go and journey into Death and never, ever look back."

Apep screamed as his shadow flickered. It struggled and writhed as it fought against Wyatt, but it was no match for the two combined powers holding it. Wyatt's vision darkened, the world shifting and changing to a black and white hue. Great black doors materialized behind Apep, featureless and beautiful. Unlike the kind of Necromancy that Apep worked, the doors weren't twisted or vile. They were pure and powerful. The doors creaked open, and a great, dark hand reached out, taking Apep's shadowy form in its grip. Apep gave one last push, trying to break free, but he stood no chance. The hand dragged him through the doorway as the doors slammed shut.

Wyatt's vision returned to normal, and he saw that the Drones were nearly on him. But as if they had suddenly lost their focus, they all faltered, confused. Some wandered off in other directions. Others bit and clawed at each other, stumbling and falling.

Without Apep's will to drive them, they are just mindless animals, said Shem quietly.

Wyatt nodded, and he extended his dark power again. He felt the small bits of energy within them, the energy that Apep had siphoned from their souls and used to create the Drones. He let out a low breath, the icy power again calmly flowing out of him. He commanded those bits of energy to go onward and reunite with their owners.

All at once, the Drones collapsed as the broken souls left their shambling forms. With nothing left to fuel them, the bodies broke apart and rapidly decayed to dust that blew away with the wind.

Well done, said Shem. *But we aren't finished just yet, Wyatt. Necron awaits, no doubt already in the castle. You might still be able to save her, Wyatt. We have to hurry.*

Wyatt was already running. He knew that whatever was waiting for him in the castle would probably be the thing that killed him, but he had to try. He couldn't let his mother die. He couldn't let Necron win.

He ran down the long path that led up to the castle. The gates were already open, blasted apart by a great strength. The bushes along the path were smoking and burnt, much like the rest of the city. He saw more bodies, but to Wyatt's relief they stayed down. Without Apep to raise them, they remained dead and unmoving.

The castle was already in ruins. Many of the towers had collapsed, and Wyatt could see a sticky dark ichor scattered along the walls. It looked like the servants and the other patrons had done their best to defend the castle, but against Necron they would've had no chance. He saw the main entryway ahead of him, the great oaken doors splintered and broken. Although the castle at large was falling, the main hallway leading into it was still intact.

As Wyatt drew near, a great boom sounded from within the earth, and Wyatt felt a familiar surge of energy. Just as had happened at Mount Trajnheim, a great wave of fear and despair rolled over him. But he was ready for it this time, his anger and determination acting as a shield. He pushed forward, breaking through the waves of negative energy and walking slowly, resolutely toward the castle.

A wall of concussive air erupted from the broken gates, slamming into Wyatt and hurling him back the way he came. As he tumbled backward through the air, he saw the entire castle start to fall inward. The whole building looked as if it were imploding, as if a great power were drawing the walls and stones inward.

Wyatt skidded across the tiled road, drawing his limbs in tight to best avoid damage to them. He rolled and bounced for several feet before finally, mercifully, coming to a stop. He groaned and clambered to his feet.

Dust billowed out of the open doorway as the castle collapsed. That doorway somehow stood tall as the rest of the castle was destroyed. And through that broken archway, through the dust and bits of raining stone, Wyatt could see a silhouette. He felt that silhouette, too, a great and cold presence that was far worse than Apep ever could've dreamed of being. It was a void of energy and life that chilled Wyatt's blood, that made him want to lie down and die. The silhouette stepped through the smoke, seemingly without caring that the castle was coming down around it. As it stepped through the smoke and Wyatt saw its face, he knew that he had arrived too late.

Out of the smoke stepped Wyatt's mother. Her face was gaunt and wrong, carrying a cruel expression that his mother would be incapable of making. Her normally blue, pure eyes were deeply and completely black. Wyatt could just make out a strange red color on her face and the sides of her neck. But as she stepped closer, he realized that it was blood, blood that was leaking from her ears, her eyes, and her nose. The shadow she cast on the smoke and dust behind her was impossibly huge and inhuman, the true shape of the thing that had crawled inside of her.

"My son," she said, her deep, alien voice breaking Wyatt's heart. "I'm glad you're here, Wyatt. I've missed you so."

Dimly, he could feel Shem calling out to him through the haze that was building in his mind. He could feel the sword in his hand, but it didn't seem to matter. He couldn't bring himself to listen. He opened his mouth to respond, but he couldn't seem to find his voice.

Necron laughed, the sound like a knife to his soul, a sound he would never be able to forget. "You have a rare opportunity, Wyatt," said the shell of his mother, her smile vicious and animalistic. "You get to see me cast this world into darkness. Everything, from the smallest bug to the largest animal, will die. You, your allies, and even that pretty little Vitamancer that you're so enamored with. But I'll save you for the end, Wyatt. I'll let you watch as I tear their souls asunder."

Grace. Her face sprang into his mind, a shining light that penetrated the darkness. The way she smiled, the way she walked, the way she kissed... that kiss. He remembered his beating heart, the feel of her against him, her teeth biting his lip. He could see her, feel her, and taste her again. She was still alive, still out there waiting for him to return.

The haze lifted. A great force roared to life within him, and he felt as if his heart were on fire. Shem's presence bloomed to life in his mind once again, and he let the ferocious lion add to his strength. Their combined power lifted Wyatt fully out of the dark place that Necron had tried to cast him into. He let that power surge outward, and a wave of Wyatt's own energy blasted the smoke and dust back. Necron's aura of fear and despair was dispelled as the air around them cleared. He raised his sword, the tip of the blade pointed directly at Necron. At his mother.

"No matter what shape you wear," he said slowly, gripping the handle tight with shaking hands as the sword buzzed with life, "you are not my mother. She may be gone, Necron, but I am still standing in front of you."

He could still feel the rage inside of him, but it wasn't uncontrollable fury. It was focused and sharp.

His mother's eyes narrowed, but her smile remained. "Stronger than you look. I see why he chose you. Clever of him, you know. So very clever."

Wyatt's head cocked. "What are you talking about?"

Necron laughed again. "And you don't even know! What a funny place this world has become. It's almost unfortunate that I have to destroy it. Almost."

He felt Shem in his mind, urging him to attack before Necron gained the advantage. But he couldn't help but wonder if he didn't want Necron to keep talking.

Wyatt eyed his mother's shape with skepticism. "I don't think you know anything about this world, Necron. Otherwise you wouldn't want to destroy it."

"So young," remarked the demigod. "So foolish. Do you want me to tell you who he is, Wyatt Arden? Do you want to know what you hold in your hand?"

Wyatt blinked. He felt Shem's presence bristle as the cat's disposition changed. Suddenly, he was more difficult to reach.

Wyatt stared at the sword in his hand for a long moment. He'd been wondering about what Shem really was ever since he found the sword. The cat certainly had his own mysterious motivations, but he had also saved Wyatt's life on more than one occasion, as well as that of Grace and the others. Despite his evasive, mysterious personality, Shem had proven time and time again to be an invaluable ally. Whatever secrets he was holding were his own. It didn't matter what he was, it only mattered that he was helping Wyatt.

Wyatt shrugged. "A sword, obviously. With a dragon or god or some other great beast living inside of it. I don't really care, to be honest."

Necron motioned to speak again, but Wyatt was done talking. He reached out to Shem once more, and their minds touched again. The unstoppable, unending strength of the lion filled Wyatt as he ran, calling the wind behind him. Just as they had been when Apep had fallen, the two became one. The sky cracked as lightning flashed from every direction. Wyatt ran faster. He brought the sword up and swung, his muscles pulling with a superhuman force. To the untrained eye, he was just a blur.

But Necron was faster. Wyatt swung down, his sword dropping in an arc of blinding speed as the lightning struck. Necron sidestepped, dodging the blade just in time, moving faster than Wyatt could even see. The tip of Wyatt's sword crashed into the stone tiles beneath them, completely obliterating them. Wyatt's energy drained into the ground, and it was too late for him to react as Necron countered.

His mother's tiny, bony fist slammed into the side of his chest, sending him crashing across the stone ground beneath them. He felt his ribs bend and crack as the fist hit him like a hammer. He rolled and tumbled painfully before sliding into the closest building, some kind of shed or outbuilding for the gardens. He slammed painfully into the foundation, letting out a wheezing breath.

Necron let out an empty chuckle. "I'm a demigod, Wyatt. You're strong, for an Adept. Maybe even the strongest ever born, especially with that little toy in your hand. But you're not strong enough to face me."

Wyatt realized that his hands were empty. He reached and clawed for the sword, but it was nowhere near his grasp. He looked up to see Necron reaching to pick it up from the broken ground. His mother's face was smiling evilly as she bent to retrieve it.

I will distract him, echoed Shem's voice, from a great distance. *You must strike now. You can do this, Wyatt. Remember your grandfather. Remember your mother. Remember her love.*

He did remember. He remembered the way she would sing to him when he was scared. He was five, and her arms were around him, her soft melody swimming in his ears as a thunderstorm passed over their house. He was eight, and she was singing softly as she stitched a cut on his knee, helping him block out the pain. He was thirteen, and she was singing him a funny song to take his mind off of losing his first girlfriend. Her love, her voice, filled him.

He felt Shem's power flare within the sword as Necron's hand closed around the hilt. Springing to his feet, Wyatt ignored the searing pain in his ribs and dashed forward, unarmed. He felt his own power rise, felt the familiar tug at his navel as he called upon it without Shem's assistance or guidance. It was harder now, without the sword in his hand, but not impossible. It answered his call in a way that he had never experienced; not angry, fearful, or pained. It was filled with love: his love for his mother, his love for his friends, his love for a world that only he could save.

His hands glowed with lightning as he sprang, flaring out like claws. Necron looked up, surprised, as Wyatt dove at him. From the other side, Wyatt could see a great ring of golden fire hanging in the air as Shem's beastly shape materialized. The huge flaming lion roared in fury and descended on Necron from one side as Wyatt leapt at him from the other.

The two forces collided with Necron all at once, their massive power surging into the demigod. He snarled as his dark aura was suppressed by Shem's golden fire and Wyatt's hot, crackling light. Wyatt's hands burned his mother's body with their fury as Shem's fangs tore into her. For the first time, Necron was in distress. The shadow behind his mother seemed to twist and shrink as the two colossal powers punished it. Wyatt was certain that they had done it, certain that they had penetrated Necron's defenses and finally landed a hit...

"No," growled Necron, his impossibly long arms reaching out on both sides. Wyatt felt a firm, cold hand grasp him by the neck, the fingers attached to it long and alien. Before he could react, he was lifted from the ground. His mother's body grew and stretched, making her look more monstrous and horrible than ever. Necron's other arm had Shem by the scruff of his own neck, and as that hand grew huge to compensate for the large cat, Necron shed the last semblance of his mother's form. The cat struggled and roared, but his claws did nothing to the demigod. Dirt and dust went flying in every direction as Necron's power surged anew, plunging Wyatt again into a sea of fear and despair. Vaguely, he could hear the sword clattering across the ground, sent tumbling by Necron's power.

The demigod spun, his arms uncoiling and hurling Wyatt and Shem in opposite directions with impossible strength. For the third time that day, Wyatt rolled and tumbled and bounced across hard stone, every hit bleeding more of his life away from him. He felt his left arm break as he crashed into another building. His mind felt thick and sluggish, and he couldn't seem to make his body work right as he struggled to rise.

He could feel Shem reaching out to him, practically screaming in his mind to look up. Wyatt raised his eyes, finding the sparkling silver blade on the ground just a few feet ahead of him. He was distantly aware of Necron's elongated, twisted form walking in his direction. He could still feel the aura of darkness oppressing his mind.

He crawled forward, the distance of a few feet seeming like a mile to his broken body. He coughed, spitting a mouthful of blood to the side, but kept going. He had to reach the sword. He could feel the life draining out of him with every inch, but he already knew what he had to do.

"So futile," mused Necron, the dark aura settling around him like inky black robes. "You could just quit, you know. Death might seem scary, Wyatt, but the truth is that it's the most peaceful thing you'll ever know. No more pain, no more heartbreak, no more loss. Just sweet, pure oblivion."

Wyatt's right hand grasped the hilt of the sword, and he looked over at Necron with a bloody smile. "I know," he wheezed. He numbly rubbed his other hand across the blade, his broken forearm searing in pain. He felt the steel bite into his skin as he rubbed blood down the length of the blade.

"What are you doing?" asked Necron, his pace increasing as he walked toward Wyatt. Wyatt felt Shem's alarmed presence come to life in his mind.

What are you doing? echoed the cat, his voice far more concerned than Wyatt had ever heard him.

Wyatt laughed, the sound somehow punching through Necron's aura. He held the sword up with his good arm, pointing it toward the sky as best he could.

"Shem the cat," he said, focusing all of his remaining power into the sword, "I release you."

Pain erupted through Wyatt's entire body as light flared from the hilt of the blade. The light was shining from within him, too: out of his mouth, his nose, and his ears as he looked to the sky and screamed in agony. The sword lifted from his hands, floating out above them. The light from Wyatt and the shining sword sent Necron backpedaling. There was a blinding flash of light in Wyatt's eyes as he blacked out.

Tythas and his allies ascended the final hill between them and Farillyon, finally gaining a view of the city. He had known there was something wrong when a plume of smoke came into view on the horizon, but without looking he knew that they had made a mistake.

He felt a wash of energy explode out from the castle as waves of anguish and fear rolled over him. His allies felt it too: some dropped to a knee, others clutched their heads. Tythas could feel it in his very bones as the King of Death stepped into the world once more.

Tythas gripped Marrek by the arm and hauled him to his feet as Grace tended to the others. "Get it together. This is where we make our stand." Marrek swallowed and nodded, helping Grace lift the others back to their feet. They turned their backs on the burning city to appraise the horde that was on their heels.

"They've slowed," said Marrek, his voice low. "Almost as if they've lost whatever focus was driving them."

"Apep is probably dead," replied Tythas. He knew that Wyatt was in the city; he could feel that, too. "My guess would be that they're just being pulled by Necron's aura, now, rather than Apep's specific commands. That will help, but we still won't be able to stop them unless the others make it here."

Marrek blanched. "You mean… what we felt, that was…"

Tythas nodded gravely. "Yes. Necron is free of his bindings, although I can't imagine he's at full strength, having been locked up for two millennia. Wyatt Arden is fighting him, doing his very best to stop him. I'm sure you heard the stories about him."

The Pyromancer nodded. "I did. Do you think he can do it? Can he beat a demigod? Or should we go in and assist him?"

Tythas shook his head, but before he could reply he saw a group of soldiers marching around the city. It looked like they were trying to find a way in, but the gates had all been blocked by debris. If they wanted in, they'd have to scale the walls.

"Soldiers, to arms!" he shouted, sending a sparkling blast of fire into the sky to get their attention. Their lead rider saw him, and immediately rode toward the Adepts, the rest of the soldiers hot on their heels.

That lead rider was none other than Jag, clad in the armor of the Emperor. Tythas smiled a small smile. Finally, a ruler who wasn't an Adept.

"Vance!" shouted Jag as he and the other mounted soldiers reached them first. "We're here! The Dominion, they're not far behind. We'll hold the line until they can get here to back us up. How bad is it?"

Tythas gestured over the hill, where the horde was perhaps two miles back, slowly surging their way toward the defenders. "We greatly reduced the numbers, but Apep had more than I ever thought possible. We've still got a long fight against us, Jag. Prepare your men."

Jag began shouting orders out as the soldiers formed a tight formation atop the hill. The high ground would be their best defensive option, so they held the position. The Adepts spread out behind the line to offer support as they could. Grace took a horse, ready to ride the line and offer healing wherever it was needed, or to help re-energize the other Adepts. The dead slowly crawled forward as the line waited in anticipation.

Tythas felt another surge of power from the city. He looked back just in time to see a blinding flash of light that seared his eyes, forcing him to look away again.

He tried to blink the spots out of his eyes, to no avail. In his periphery, he saw Grace on her knees, holding her stomach. He knelt down, helping her up.

"Necron is here," she said, ghostly pale and looking more than a little bit sick. "And... something else. I don't know what that flash was, Tythas, but Wyatt had something to do with it."

Tythas nodded. "I know, dear one, I know. But you need to get up. We have to make our final stand here while Wyatt fights off Necron. Whatever he's doing, I firmly believe that he's got this under control. I know you're worried about him. I am, too. But we have to believe in him."

She swallowed and got to her feet with his help. She looked up at the sky, and after a moment, the aura of power around her blossomed again, the shining white light flowing around her once more.

"Then let's fight," she said, steel in her voice. "Fight and make him proud."

Necron's huge, twisted form recoiled as the gleaming, radiant sword pulsed with energy. He reeled backward, away from the pure and burning light that he knew could only come from one source. As he was now unbound, so too was the light that dwelled within a sword he had helped to forge thousands of years ago.

There was another flash, a flash that seared Necron down to his core. Hissing, he raised his arms to shield his eyes from the light, but it was burning his arms, too. He had to do something.

Necron pulled at his power, growling in fury and sending waves of darkness and negative energy toward the glowing sword. He called upon the same sealing magic that he and his siblings had used on that sword the first time around, trying to stop it and put another lock on the blade before its inhabitant could be released.

For a short time, Necron thought that he had managed it. The light began to fade, and Necron could feel the power inside of the sword begin to diminish as his power closed it off. If he could just keep it down a little bit longer...

Light flashed again, blasting Necron's feeble lock apart as it hurled the demigod backward, into the rubble of the castle. He snarled in anger and righted himself in the air, but couldn't stop himself from crashing into a half-collapsed stone wall. The wall blasted apart as he flew through it, skidding across the rubble behind it. He dug a huge, elongated hand into the stones and came to a slow, painful stop.

Where the blade had been, there now was a large sphere of glowing light. The sphere pulsed as it grew and unfurled, taking the shape of a large humanoid. Necron climbed to his feet, warily awaiting his new foe, a foe he never expected to see again.

The light finally, mercifully faded. In its place stood a huge, imposing figure. His long hair and great, wild beard made him look almost like a lion. Every inch of him was built of rippling muscle and dark, tanned skin. His bare chest was scarred and hairy. His face was wild, feral, and filled with rage. His eyes were a luminous gold, their furious glare cutting through Necron.

"Hello again, Shemdalah," said Necron warily. "Brother."

CHAPTER TWENTY-FOUR

Shem looked down at the sword in his hand, the magnificent silver blade that had been his home for so many years. Dimly, he still felt the shreds of the magic that had bound him, like a distant desire to climb back into the blade. But he was not under that power anymore.

He stretched and yawned, his bones cracking and popping as if he had been sleeping for too long. He tasted the air, even the smell of smoke and wanton destruction a welcome stimulation to his senses after centuries of nothingness. He looked up at the sky, the blood-red sun shining through the haze of the burning city. His brother had certainly done a good job of stirring things up. It would take the Empire years to recover from Necron's crimes. So much death for so little reason.

"Not even a greeting for your long-lost brother?" came Necron's distant voice. Shem had almost forgotten that he was there.

He looked up at Necron, who still held the horrible, twisted form that was an abject mockery of humanity. A low growl escaped his throat as he began to walk toward his younger brother, savoring the feel of the earth beneath his feet.

"You have fallen so far, brother," he said, his low voice deep and booming. Power surged through every inch of his body. "Have you forgotten everything that Mother tried to give to you? Everything that she taught us? She gave her life so that you might live, Necron!"

Necron spat at his feet. "Mother left us long ago, brother. She had the power to stop Wyrdax but chose not to, too soft to defy her brother.

She fled and left the fight to us. When we locked you away in that sword, she didn't stop us. And she didn't stop the others from locking me away in a piece of rock and burying me deep under the earth, hoping that the world would forget me! She has done nothing!"

Shem shook his head sadly. "You act like our situations are the same. You went insane, Necron. Even where I was, I knew what you were becoming without someone there to guide you. You killed humans, the very thing you were created to protect. You wanted to rule them, but that is not our place. That was never our place."

Necron was pacing now, centuries of anger pouring out of him like a dark miasma. In this moment, the two of them weren't demigods. They were just estranged brothers, forced to try to reconcile.

"They betrayed the both of us!" he roared, his anger and sadness evident. "None of them understood me. None of them wanted to understand me! They were too busy drawing their lines, building their castles and leaving me alone in the dark!"

Shem sighed. "You alienated yourself, Necron. And lest you forget, you helped them to put me in that sword. All six of you banded together against me. If anyone was left alone in the dark, brother, it's me. None of you could handle having me watching over you. You sealed your own fate. I would've stood with you, would've found another way. I was your only hope, but you had already burned that bridge."

Necron snorted. "And yet here you stand, fighting their fight against me."

Shem motioned to Wyatt's limp, unconscious form. "I fight their fight, Necron. As I always have and always will. That was your job, too. That is why you were given life and given the power you hold."

Necron laughed, throwing his unnaturally long arms out. "Protect them from what? The moment we threw Wyrdax and the rest of his get into the Pit, they no longer needed protecting!"

Shem nodded. "You're right. And that's when we should've stepped back. That is when we should've given up our places here and gone on to be with Mother, to sit back and watch this world flourish without us. But you and the others held on too long. You grew attached to your power and your positions. For some of you, you were attached to your followers. You thought your place to lead them. You thought that you could continue to exist here as a part of their lives, their world."

"I pointed this out, if you recall," continued Shem, the memory of that moment as fresh in his mind as it had been two thousand years ago. "I tried to tell you that you existed here not as their leaders, but as their guardians. I told all of you that the moment Wyrdax was defeated was our moment to go. But instead of heeding my warning, the six of you bound me within that sword. You couldn't just kill me, though. Maybe you feared that Wyrdax would break free of his cage and you would need me again. Maybe you just couldn't bring yourselves to kill a brother that had only ever loved all of you. I do not know, nor do I care."

The two powerful figures paced in circles around each other. Necron's expression was sullen, like a young boy who had been caught with his hand in the cookie jar.

"And without me to protect you from them, without me to help the six of you keep your harmony, you too were lost," he said, shaking his head sadly. "You disconnected yourself from your family and forced them to eliminate you. And just like it had happened between Adala and Wyrdax, just like it had happened with me, they could not bring themselves to kill you. They locked you away, buried you under stone and blood and hoped that they could forget you. They stepped across the threshold that I had been begging them to walk across not long before, leaving this world behind to go be with Adala. They fled in shame, a shame that tainted their children, shame that caused two thousand years of strife in this world. They left us behind, their two greatest mistakes."

Necron stopped with a sigh. "So now what? Do you finish the job, dear brother? Destroy me, purely and utterly, so that Necron may never again harm this place?"

Shem paused, stopping to assess his brother's distorted face. "You have done many horrible things, Necron. Destruction would be too easy for you. No, you must understand your crimes, understand what your hatred has done to you."

Necron barked out a hollow laugh. "So what, then? You'll take me captive and torture me until I repent? Sear the sin from my flesh and soul?"

For the first time in two thousand years, Shem smiled at his brother. It was an odd feeling. "No, Necron. I am not the vengeful hand of justice. I am the guardian, not the executioner. I will do nothing more than what is necessary to bring you to Mother. But I will bring you to her, Necron. We will cross the threshold together, and you will have to face her. Alone."

If it were possible, Necron would've gone pale.

Shem held out a hand. "I give you the choice, little brother. Take my hand, walk with me to see her again and repent. Or fight back, and be dragged, kicking and screaming. Either way, you will come with me."

Necron eyed Shem's huge hand for what seemed like a century. Shem was outwardly calm, but inside he was begging and pleading with his brother to take that hand. He didn't want to fight anymore. He was so tired.

Necron reached out, stepping forward. But before he reached Shem, he struck. His fingers curled and he sent a blast of dark, deathly energy into Shem. He channeled as much power as he could, enough to rot and wither an entire forest. He wasn't going to be stopped now, not this close to the goal. He'd go see his mother on his own terms, after the world she loved so much was left in ashes.

Shem recoiled, taking a step backward and shrinking down as he tried to defend himself. Necron snarled, pouring even more power into the attack. The blow should, at the very least, knock his brother down. Anyone else would be obliterated by it, but he knew not to underestimate his eldest brother.

Shem's arms crossed on his chest and then swung open, blasting Necron's energy apart. An aura of golden fire danced on his arms. "Not anymore, Necron," he said forcefully as he shredded Necron's dark miasma. He stepped forward, holding his hand out again, a hand of golden, pure light.

"No!" shouted Necron, letting loose another blast of energy as he backed away. But he was losing focus. His first blast had felt like a focused punch; this was a wild wave, easier to shrug off.

Shem batted it away with a sigh. "Have it your way, then," he said sadly, raising his hands up and calling upon his power.

He had always hoped that he would never have to do it. But Necron's choices and his unwavering desire to leave the world broken left Shem with no choice. Calling upon each Aspect, he closed his eyes as that great and terrible power surged forth from within him. He felt a rush of energy as he united all six sides of his power, bringing them to bear. He channeled them outward, toward his brother.

Necron was already running. He knew what Shem was going to do, knew the familiar feeling of magic he couldn't control or block closing in around him. The last time, it had only been five Aspects, five pieces of his mother. But now he felt his own power in what his brother was doing. All six pieces of Adala brought to bear. The power wrapped around him, forcing him to a stop as he dropped to his knees. A ring of pure golden light formed around him, flawless and unbreakable. He turned to face his brother, his eyes filled with a broken, mad rage.

"You're just like them," he said quietly, his voice as human as Shem had ever heard it. "You should be different. They betrayed you, too! They betrayed the both of us!"

Shem gave his brother a small smile, now walking toward the ring of light. "Unlike you, little brother, I have never forgotten the love that Adala tried so hard to inspire within us. I never forgot that despite the mistakes and shortcomings of my siblings, they are still my siblings, and I love them dearly. I may not always like them, but I do love them. And I forgave them, long ago, just as I have already forgiven you, Necron."

The ring of light drew in on Necron, and the twisted, inhuman form that used to be Nora Arden dissolved, leaving a great shadow behind in its place. Shem could feel Necron's eyes still on him, shapeless eyes of smoky darkness.

"Will they forgive me, too?" asked Necron quietly, the rage finally gone from his voice.

Shem reached out, his hand resting on the smoky shadow, somehow finding a solid place. "There is always forgiveness, Necron. It is perhaps the greatest gift that our Mother gave us. Your redemption will not be easy. It will hurt. Even I do not know what lies beyond the threshold of this life. But we'll go together, and when you're ready, you'll find peace once again."

The ring closed in, and with a flash and a loud bang, Necron's dark and smoky form solidified. Where the shadow had been but a moment before now stood a huge statue of roughly-cut obsidian. It was far from a perfect rendering, but it bore the general appearance of Shem's misguided younger brother. Walking up to it, Shem placed his hand on the surface. He felt his brother inside, felt the rage, the fear, and the shame that his brother had driven into his heart for so long.

He sighed, letting his hand drop and temporarily closing off the thoughts of his family. He had other things to worry about. He turned, walking over to Wyatt's limp form and crouching down. The boy was broken and bloody. Shem could feel his spirit just barely hanging on, hanging on with a strength that Shem knew only Wyatt Arden had. He rested a large, strong hand on Wyatt's shoulder and channeled his power once more.

Wyatt gasped, drawing a deep breath. He expected the breath to hurt and prepared for a wave of pain, but there was none. He blinked several times, looking around. The castle courtyard was gone, and gone with it was the smell of the smoke, the taste of blood on the air, and the pain that every inch of his body had known when he was in that place.

Instead, there was just white. Pure, endless white stretched around him in every direction. He looked down, surprised to find that even he was somehow wearing white; a sleeveless white robe, open down to the middle of his chest. It had no markings and was barely distinguishable from the white backdrop all around him. He touched the fabric; it was airy and light, but impossibly warm and comforting.

"Hello, son," came a quiet voice from behind him. Wyatt wheeled around, astonishment rolling through him as he came to face his mother.

But this time, it was not Necron's black eyes that met him. His mother was likewise dressed in white, but she was unlike anything he'd ever seen. Her whole form glowed with a warm, pure light. Her eyes were as blue as ever, but here they seemed to glow with that pure blueness. Everything about her seemed exactly as he had remembered it, but enhanced even more. She was exactly how he'd imagined Adala his whole life.

"Mom," he breathed, fighting back a choking sob as he ran forward and wrapped his arms around her, pulling her into a crushing hug. She was so warm, so soft. He missed her so much.

She embraced him tightly, not seeming to mind that he was squeezing her as hard as he could. Instead, she sang to him, her voice ringing softly in his ear. The sound made his heart hurt, but in a good way. He lost his composure, tears falling from his eyes as he clung to her with all his strength. He clutched her tightly, and for just a moment he ceased to be a warrior and was once again just a young boy afraid of the thunder.

Her soft singing filled him with strength, and he found his calm again. He shook the tears from his eyes as he pulled away from her, holding her shoulders and looking into her soft, luminescent eyes.

"Are you..." he began, his fear and confusion coming forth first. "... am I dead?"

She chuckled and shook her head, her smile warming his heart. "No, Wyatt. Nearly. That's why we're able to speak here. This place is... a sort of middle ground between your world and the next. It's a small space where they overlap, and when your side is brought close to mine, the living and the dead can sometimes reunite."

Wyatt's heart fell. "So... you really are gone, then," he said softly, not questioning it. A small part of him had already known, the first moment he'd laid eyes on her in this pure white place. But it still hurt to have her confirm it.

She still smiled at him, however, and nodded again. "Yes. But you are not. And the rest of your world is safe because of you. I'm sorry that I didn't tell you about your heritage sooner, son. I had hoped to spare you some of the chaos and pain that I felt in my youth. But I see now that you were meant for much greater things, despite my hopes."

Wyatt shook his head, looking back on how he had gotten here. "It's okay. In a way it's probably good that I was raised so far away from all of it. I was able to make my own decisions because of that."

Nora motioned for him to sit, and suddenly there was a simple wooden bench resting next to him. Wyatt shrugged and took a seat as his mother took the spot next to him.

"Your father and I were soldiers on the opposite sides of the war," she said softly, staring off into the whiteness of wherever they were. "I was a Vitamancer for the Empire, and he was a Necromancer for Apep's cause. Raised on the streets and treated horribly from a young age, your father held in his heart a deep hatred for the Empire and the Adept Council. We met far from Farillyon, in the deep wilds to the far northwest where Apep had erected his stronghold. He was captured by our forces, but I ordered his life spared."

Wyatt noticed the distant look in her eyes. "Why did you want him spared?" he asked, a little at a loss hearing her talk about his father at length.

"He knew what we were getting into," she said simply. "And we didn't. He knew where Apep's forces and traps were hiding in the deep jungle, and without that information we stood a much greater chance of dying before we ever reached our goal. I knew from the moment I laid eyes on him that he wasn't committed to the cause. There were two types of Necromancers fighting in that war: a small number who were zealously devoted to Apep and his mad quest, and a much larger number who were simply along for the ride with no other options. Your father fell into the second group; his hatred for the Empire had, in his eyes, drawn a line that he could never cross. But as the war progressed, as Apep and his lot committed atrocity after atrocity, his dedication faltered. Eventually, he was willing to tell us Apep's secrets, just to put a stop to the madness."

Wyatt gave a soft nod of understanding, just glad to be hearing so much about the two of them, about a side of his mother that he'd never known.

Nora sighed, her smile fading and wistful. "We won the war, and your father ended up on the right side in the end. But after the dust settled, the Council still wanted him dead. The new Emperor had taken control and Necromancers might as well have been lepers in his new Empire, even the ones that had been on the Empire's side. So he made the only choice he could. He ran, and I ran with him."

She sighed again, shaking her head. "We had a lot of happy memories, but we spent those years always on the run. Eventually, they caught us. Your father threw himself at them, giving me time to escape with you, newly born and fast asleep. He died to protect us. I ran to my father, even though I thought our relationship broken beyond repair. He agreed to help me and hid me there, far from the prying eyes of the Empire. And that's where you grew up, far away from magic and politics and all the other things that I wanted to shelter you from."

Wyatt smirked in spite of himself, looking off into the whiteness around them. "So much for that."

His mother laughed, her smile returning as the sweet sound echoed around them. "You have always had a way of getting where you want to go, despite how many roadblocks I put in your way. You've done more than I ever could've hoped with your life, Wyatt. And you're going to keep doing more, I think. You're my son, and your father's son, and nothing is going to stop you. I'm so proud of you, Wyatt."

He looked up at her again, somehow managing to feel small even though he was larger than her. "I'm sorry you died, Mom," he said, his voice threatening to break. "If I had gotten there sooner..."

His mother shook her head. "No, Wyatt. I was dead the moment that Apep and Necron found me. I was weak and poisoned and could do nothing to stop them. I'm just glad you weren't there when Kelsar blew up the house trying to kill them."

Wyatt sighed, thinking of his grandfather. More regrets. "I was. I made it about one step out the front door when it exploded. I rolled all the way down the hill and nearly drowned in the creek."

His mother winced.

He shook his head. "I made it, though. That's where my friends found me. Jag dragged me out of the water and Grace healed me. They gave me the means to look for you. Jag helped teach me how to fight. Tythas taught me about magic and Adepts. Grace made me laugh and made me feel better when things were looking bleak. I owe all of them so much."

She smiled at him. "I remember being young and having close friends to adventure with. Hold onto them, Wyatt. You won this fight with a lot of outside help, help you're not going to have if things get bad again. But you will have them. So hold them close."

He nodded, grinning like an idiot when his mind drifted to Grace. "I will. Yeah, I will."

She smirked at him. "I'm sorry that I didn't get the chance to meet her. But treat her right, Wyatt."

He laughed, smiling sheepishly and running a hand through his hair. "I knew that was going to come up."

She squeezed his leg. "It's about time for you to go, son. If you spend too much longer here, you won't be able to turn back. I wish I could keep you here with me, but your world still needs you. Mine... mine can wait awhile."

Wyatt sighed, looking at his mother for what he knew was going to be the last time. He felt a tightness in his chest as he tried to absorb that image one more time, hoping that he would never forget it.

"What if I'm not ready?" he asked her after a short silence. "What if... the world needs me and I don't know how to help? I don't have you to guide me anymore, Mom. What do I do if I need help?"

She grinned at him, her smile big and broad and full of love. "You are perfectly capable of being the man the world needs you to be, son. You made it this far, didn't you? But when the time comes that you think need help, just remember that you're never alone. Look to your friends. They're your family, too. Blood isn't everything."

Wyatt nodded, smiling back at her. "Thanks, Mom. I love you."

They stood and embraced again. "I love you too, son," she said quietly in his ear. Wyatt could feel her tears. "I love you and I'll always be with you. Don't you ever forget that."

He nodded, holding himself against her, no longer able to contain himself. He broke, tears flowing again as they cried and held each other tightly. But it wasn't long that it became a different kind of crying. There was despair, sure, but there was something else: a kind of unbreakable hope filled his heart as he hugged her. She was safe. He would miss her, but he would make her proud. He would live on and honor what she had given him.

He stepped back as she released him, smiling a tearful smile at his mother. In the distance, he could now hear a deep voice calling his name, a voice that pulled at his mind and his memory. Shem. The voice grew louder, and Wyatt knew that his time here was now over.

His mother waved at him, grinning and crying and laughing. He waved back as her form grew fuzzy and drew away from him. The whiteness dimmed as Wyatt's vision blurred. He blinked and rubbed his eyes for a moment before falling back into reality, back into his body.

Air filled Wyatt's lungs in a ragged rush as he gasped and opened his eyes. His whole body was on fire. He could taste dried blood in his mouth and feel it crusted onto his face and arm. He blinked several times and looked around, trying to get his bearings again and shake off his disorientation.

"Just stay calm, Wyatt," came Shem's deep and calming voice as two strong hands pressed him to the ground. "I'm almost finished. Stay still while I work."

Wyatt relaxed as a surge of warm, tingling energy flowed into him. He had felt the healing power of a Vitamancer before, but nothing like this. If Grace's power was a river, this was the sea. It was so vast and deep that he felt like it were going to swallow him whole. His whole mind was thrumming with that power. He'd never felt anything so wonderful.

And with a horrible abruptness, it was over. Wyatt blinked again and took a deep, even breath. Shem's hands released him as he sat up and looked around. They were in the wrecked and ruined castle courtyard. Wyatt could see the blasted craters and destroyed stone tiles that had been left behind by their fight. The castle was mostly rubble, only a few towers and walls left standing after the blast of the seal breaking.

"We really did the thing right, didn't we?" asked Wyatt fuzzily, rubbing his eyes as he looked around. "Farillyon is going to take months to repair."

"Years, I think," said Shem as he helped Wyatt get to his feet. "Years of building and rebuilding to get it anywhere close to its former glory. That castle was built by Petra and the first Terramancers. I don't know that anyone will ever truly be able to replicate it."

Wyatt looked Shem up and down, taking in his true form for the first time. "So that's the real you, then? What you looked like before you were put into the sword?"

Shem nodded, strolling around the courtyard and looking out over the city. The flames and smoke were dwindling, and Wyatt could feel people using magic in the city. They were putting out the fires, trying to save the buildings and the survivors that were still left standing.

"It was my siblings who put me there," said Shem, now free to tell Wyatt anything he wanted. "I am the eldest child of Adala, the first demigod. My mother instilled within me some part of each of her Aspects. She wanted me to care for them, to keep them balanced after she was gone. She wanted someone around to ensure that they would stay on the right path. She was worried that once she left, they would fight amongst themselves."

Wyatt chuckled. "That didn't exactly work out, did it?"

Shem shook his head. "Not at all. Shortly after we defeated Wyrdax, they conspired against me. They didn't want to be watched over; they wished to be left to their own devices in their own corners of the world. So in one last show of unity, they worked against me. I am more powerful than any of them individually, perhaps even two or three united. But all six was much more than I could handle. They overwhelmed me and bound me within a sword, hiding me away in the dark, hoping that the world would forget me, that I would be left alone there until they needed me again. It was a clever binding; one of two parts that would allow them to partially wake me should they need my help, without fully freeing me. Very clever."

Wyatt nodded, walking up to the great statue of Necron. He could feel the great demigod inside of it, and as his hand rested against the cold stone, he could feel Necron's anguish.

"But I knew one day that it would happen," said Shem, with a sly smile. "So I made sure that my powers would be passed on to another, when the right criteria were met. You are that person, Wyatt. When you were born, I knew, and I started paying attention to the world, something I hadn't done in a long time. When you drew near to me, I could feel you. My siblings had done a very good job of containing me, but after two thousand years, cracks were forming in their binding. I could project myself out of the sword, as a small cat. You know the rest."

Wyatt raised an eyebrow. "So why am I alive? You told me that releasing the second binding on your sword would kill me."

Shem nodded his great, shaggy head. "I had to. That was a part of my binding. The others knew that a day might come where the world would need me again. In case they weren't there to release me themselves, they made it so that the bonds could be broken by any Adept with the right amount of power. But in order to break that second binding, the Adept in question would have to think it was going to kill him. He would have to be so committed to letting me out that he would give his life and his power to do it. They made it like that to prevent the wrong people from letting me out. They were worried that if the wrong person somehow happened upon the sword, that they'd be able to control me and use me for their own ends."

"So now what?" asked Wyatt, stepping back from the statue and appraising the statue of Necron. "We defeated him and you locked him back in his statue. Do we hide him again, down in a cave or something?"

Shem walked up to stand next to Wyatt, his huge form towering over the smaller, youthful Adept. "I'm taking him to my mother," said Shem simply, his expression unreadable. "To my mother and to the rest of my siblings. I'm reuniting our family and turning control of this world over to humans once more, the way it should've been so long ago. We should've moved on long ago, but due to our own failures and mistakes, two of us were left behind. But I'm going to correct that. No more demigods to meddle in the lives of humans. You will be free to live and grow without fear of these great powers working against you."

Wyatt looked up at the yellow eyes of his tall companion. "Thank you, Shem," he said softly as he clapped a hand onto the demigod's huge arm. "You were the true hero here. Without you to guide me and save me so many times, none of this would have happened."

Shem gave him a soft smile. "You did more than you think. You've probably figured it out by now, but I'll tell you anyway just to remove any confusion. Like me, you hold power over every Aspect. Now that I'm gone and you've finally been born, there will be one Omnimancer born in every generation. You'll be the first, Wyatt. As your patron, I give you just one task: bring balance to my mother's children and instill some harmony in the six Aspects. This world is an open wound, Wyatt. Your job is to help it heal, help it find new life again."

Before Wyatt could respond, Shem held out the sword. Wyatt took it in his right hand. Not feeling Shem's presence and power flowing out of the blade was profoundly strange, but it still seemed to hold some fragment of the great demigod. The hilt hummed faintly as he gripped it. He felt attuned to it, like it were an extension of him.

"Just like I helped you to understand your powers, so will this sword help your successors," explained Shem, his deep voice echoing with power. "It still bears a small piece of my power, and will carry that forever. The blade cannot be destroyed, cannot be locked away, cannot be hidden. If an Omnimancer dies, it will appear when the next is born. If you lose it, it will find you. If another tries to wield it, it will be useless in their hands. That sword... that sword carries the power to change nations, Wyatt. Use it wisely."

"So this will teach them how to use their powers?" asked Wyatt, studying the gleaming silver.

Shem scratched his unruly beard. "In a way. It won't converse with them, but it will help attune their minds to their power. It'll help their hearts and minds find harmony. When they need help, it will give them strength to go on."

Wyatt nodded, focusing some of his own power into the sword. It hummed energetically for a just a moment, absorbing that power. "I give some of myself into this sword, as well," he said quietly as Shem watched him with interest. "As will every Omnimancer after me. To help and guide the next generation."

Shem nodded with approval. "Now you're really getting it. With that, I suppose it's time for me to take my leave. You have a long road ahead of you, Wyatt. I'm not going to be here anymore to guide you through it the next time the world is about to end, Are you ready for that?"

Wyatt felt two familiar powers coming closer to him, and he turned to look down the road leading back into the city. He saw his friends running toward him, with Grace in the lead. He saw their concern, their joy, and their grief. He smiled at them and waved, and they shouted out as they ran faster.

He turned back to Shem, smiling and nodding. "Yeah. I've got help."

Shem clapped him in the shoulder. "Good luck, Wyatt Arden. Make me proud."

Shem turned his back on Wyatt, walking toward the statue of his lost brother. He stopped for just a moment to stare up at it, one last moment in a world he'd been protecting for his entire existence. He reached out, pressing a palm onto the statue as he closed his eyes. All at once, the statue and Shem began to glow with a warm yellow light. Motes of radiance floated off of them and dissipated as that golden aura intensified.

Wyatt watched with a faint smile as his friends reached him, coming to a halt next to him. They watched in awe as Shem opened the gate to the next world, where Adala and his siblings awaited him. Love and energy flowed from that open doorway, and for just a moment Wyatt could feel his mother again. All of them stood transfixed as Shem and the statue disappeared into the golden light. After a few more moments the light faded, leaving the four of them alone in the courtyard.

Wyatt sheathed his sword and turned to look at his friends. "Hey guys," he said with his usual sheepish grin.

All three of them surged toward him, and the group embraced each other tightly. They were all laughing, all the seriousness of the situation lost in how glad they were to see one another alive. Lost in the moment, they forgot the destruction around them, forgot what they had already lost. They had each other, and that was enough.

Finally, the group broke apart, wiping tears from their eyes and looking around the broken castle courtyard. It looked like a tornado had gone through and leveled the castle.

"I realize that you fought a demigod," said Jag, looking at Wyatt and doing his best to feign displeasure, "but did you have to destroy the castle?"

Wyatt laughed. "It was like that when I got here. Promise."

Grace kicked her brother. "What, now that you're the Emperor, you suddenly miss the place?"

Jag laughed, shrugging. "Well, I have to admit it would've been nice to sit down on that throne at least once before I had it thrown out. I'm willing to bet it was pretty cushy."

Several soldiers rushed up the road, momentarily breaking up the reunion. Jag shifted his attention and his demeanor as they approached him. He saluted them with his fist and the group returned the gesture reverently.

"Sir," said the one in front, the burly captain that Wyatt had embarrassed in the field. "We've secured the city. The fires are out and the survivors are being rounded up and cared for. We've had contact with the main body of the army; they've been recalled and will be here in a few days with supplies and Adepts. Triat has sent word that they will offer whatever assistance is required. The Drone army is largely defeated, and the Dominion's forces are eliminating the remainder. We'll have the area secured within the day."

Jag nodded once. "Good. Send word to the Warlord that I'd like to meet with him. On friendly, grateful terms. Hopefully he and I can work something out for our two peoples and make some sense of this mess."

Wyatt stepped forward. "I can help with that. I'll serve as an ambassador between the parties, if you need me to. I'm a member of the War Council, after all."

Jag gripped his shoulder. "As well as one of my most trusted allies and friends. We'd be grateful for the help, Wyatt."

Wyatt smiled at his friend and nodded as he felt Grace's hand slip into his. He squeezed.

Jag turned to face Tythas as the soldiers marched off. "Mugalo's dead. Normally, I think there's some sort of voting process, but we don't have time for that right now. Vance Tythas, I hereby declare you the new High Chair of the Adept Council. Let's try to do it right, this time. Fix the mistakes of our predecessors."

Tythas scratched his goatee for a moment before giving a salute of his own. "By your command, Emperor," he said, his eyes gleaming with pride as he surveyed his student. He finally turned to look at Wyatt.

"I know you'll have your hands full with the Dominion," he said with a knowing smile, "but I want you on the Council. To help guide us in a new direction. Your voice will be important. The soldiers already revere you, and most have never even met you."

Wyatt looked down at the gleaming hilt protruding from his baldric. He felt the lightest hum, a hum that passed through his whole body, as if the sword could tell him what it was thinking.

"I'm afraid I have to decline the invitation, Vance," he said softly. "I'll be abdicating my position with the Dominion once everything is sorted out, too. My place... my place is separate. I'll help, I'll guide you, but you all have to lead each other, lead yourselves. I'm not a part of it, not in that sense."

They all blinked, looking at Wyatt in confusion. Tythas looked a little crestfallen. Wyatt lifted the sword, his stormy eyes reflected in the gleaming blade.

"I've got my own patron," he said, his smile widening. "And I've got my own mission, my own goals. If I'm going to be able to follow my true destiny, I have to stand apart from all of these entities. I'll guide you, I'll voice my opinion, but I can't commit myself to any sides."

His friends still looked confused, but Grace was smiling at him.

"I was born with all six Aspects," he continued, his hand resting on the hilt of the sword. "The thing in my sword wasn't a dragon or a demon or any other horrible monster. It was a demigod. The first, the eldest son of Adala, given all six Aspects of her power. He was created to keep his siblings from fighting amongst themselves. To keep them on the path and help them to guard mankind."

Tythas scratched his chin thoughtfully. Jag looked a little uneasy. Grace was absolutely beaming at him now.

"Shem entrusted me with the same job," he said, briefly looking into his own reflected eyes. "I'm the first of my kind, and my job is to make sure that the Dominion, the Empire, and everyone else out there in the world uses their powers for the right reasons. Not against one another, but for the good of the world. And when I die, another will be born, will take up the mantle."

Tythas grinned at him. "You're right. That's a much better idea. We'll stand with you always, Wyatt, no matter where that path takes you."

Wyatt motioned toward the castle. "We've got some rebuilding to do. And I think we should see about making contact with a certain island in the seas to the south. There are some people there that might want to come back to their families. People who deserve apologies and a chance at a new life."

The four of them walked out of the courtyard, back into the heart of the ruined city. It was going to be hard. People were going to argue, were going to disagree, were going to protest. But it didn't matter. They would endure and rebuild.

CHAPTER TWENTY-FIVE

O ver this way," called Wyatt, motioning to the line of cooks to set their food down under a large, tent-like awning. "This is where the serving area is."

The cooks hurriedly placed their collection of trays and bowls on the multitude of tables that had been placed under the tent for serving. Wyatt saw foods of all kinds; traditional Imperial dishes mingled with those found in the Dominion. He even saw some foods that he didn't recognize, and made a mental note to investigate them later. It was a lot of food for a lot of people. This was a very big day, and Wyatt was very strongly hoping it would go well.

Wyatt sensed a figure approaching behind him. He could feel a familiar mixture of fire and storm swirling within the person, and he knew without even looking that Vance Tythas was walking up to him. It could be no other. He turned, smiling at his old friend and mentor.

"Well met, Wyatt," said Tythas, returning his smile. "It's good to see you again."

The two of them embraced tightly. Save for a few quick meetings and lessons, the two of them had seen very little of each other in the last several months. Wyatt had been in the far north, helping the Dominion reorganize after losing so many people in the eruption of Mount Trajnheim. He'd also been helping Jag and the new Warlord tentatively negotiate a new kind of peace between their respective peoples, a process that was slowly but surely moving forward. Their armies had withdrawn from the contested areas and were in the process of standing down.

Tythas, meanwhile, had been on peace missions in the south, to the island on which the exiled Necromancers and their families had made their homes. Those sent to contact those people had been surprised to find that not only had the Necromancers survived on the island, but had thrived and formed a new community of their own. They numbered only about a thousand, but they had requested to remain on the island in order to make their own way. It took some convincing but eventually it was agreed that they should stay put. Wyatt reasoned that forcing them to leave their homes yet again would only damage the fragile relationship between the two sides further. Better to assist them in forming their own home rather than trying to force them into something they no longer wanted.

Today was to be the day where all of these different peoples came together for the first time. It was a happy day, where the Warlord, the Emperor, and the leader of the new community to the south would all be in attendance, as well as many of their citizens and warriors. It was a peace-making event, intended to give all of these different sides to meet on safe terms and to know those whom they had once considered enemies. If it went as well as Wyatt was hoping, all three groups would be able to exist peacefully in the future.

Wyatt released his mentor. "Good to see you, Vance. How are things? I hear that you've spent nearly a month on Porkhoya."

Tythas, his skin deeply tanned, nodded thoughtfully. "Indeed. It's an interesting place. They've created a unique sort of tribal culture. I would compare it to the Dominion, but it's not nearly so warlike. They're content to live there, to train Necromancers how to respect and revere Death. Their elders are called Watchers, and they've learned quite a bit about their powers in their time of exile. It's a harder life than the Empire, but they've managed it on their own. I certainly can't fault them for that."

Wyatt inclined his head. "The Dominion is doing well, too. Their new Warlord, Felah, has done a good job of listening to Salif and the rest of the Council. Apep's ruse seems to have greatly humbled them. They listen, and they don't want to fight anymore. They lost a lot of lives in the eruption, and they just want to rebuild and live in peace."

"So does the Empire," replied Tythas, looking out over the large open square where the gathering was being held. "Jag already looks ten years older than he did the last time I saw him. He's not interested in war or enforcing any kind of agenda. He just wants his people to be happy again. He's done a lot to encourage trade between the three entities. I've even heard that some of the neutral fringe communities have been talking about joining the Empire again. Having an Emperor who is not an Adept has done a lot to bolster confidence."

Wyatt smiled at that. About time. "Let's hope so. I'm excited to see what happens next."

Jag, dressed in simple yet elegant clothes, rushed to meet them. He wore no crown on his head. He smiled broadly and hugged his two friends.

"Good to see you both," he said. He had been Emperor for only a few months, but Wyatt could already see the change in his brash young friend. For a man in his twenties, he looked regal and authoritative. In the time since Necron's defeat, he had grown a full, well-trimmed beard. Wyatt could already see the beginnings of the lines around his eyes, lines that came with carrying so much on his shoulders. He really did look older. Wyatt certainly didn't envy him.

"Keeping busy, you two?" he asked, appraising them both with a wry smile. "I see not too much has changed, although you're looking a bit crispy, Vance."

Tythas scowled at him while Jag and Wyatt laughed.

"Too busy, I think," said Wyatt with a light smile. "Today's the closest thing I've had to a day off since we all met. I'm looking forward to things calming down a bit."

Jag motioned toward the far side of the clearing, where a large round table had been set up, as well as a platform and podium. "Agreed. I'm hoping to draft up some kind of treaty today. Everyone will be here, so it's as good a time as any. We haven't had relations this good between the Dominion and the Empire in centuries. Not to mention the islanders being here as well. I'd prefer to keep them on good terms. They've discovered a number of unique goods on that island, some of which are already fetching a large amount of coin in the Empire. It's a good start."

Tythas shrugged. "It shouldn't be an issue. They really just want to be left to themselves and left to really build their new home. If we can make sure that they have a voice in any trade sanctions that are established, we'll be doing a lot to keep the relationship strong. We did most of the work in inviting their leader, a man called Yxashi, to join the Adept Council. He's an odd fellow, wears a great goat skull on his head, but that's pretty common in their culture. He has good intentions for his people as well as ours, I quite think."

Jag rubbed his eyes. "I had a chance to talk with him, and we both got a good impression of one another, I think. He doesn't seem to be anything like Apep or any of the other Necromancers who went bad. Even the air around him is different. He's not so... I don't know. Alien, I guess. The others were cold and distant. He's not like that."

"Necromancers have a hard time interacting with people who don't understand their power," said Tythas knowingly, "but Yxashi and his people have the right attitude toward it. They always did, of course, but when they were exiled people couldn't see that. They're still human, still alive. That's the key, I think. They still embrace life."

Wyatt peered around the clearing. They had chosen the now-empty space where the Imperial Castle had once stood in Farillyon as the site for this meeting, something Jag found especially symbolic. Nearly every Terramancer in the Empire, even those not in service to the throne, had been tirelessly working to repair Farillyon since the attack. With the help of the Army and hundreds of volunteers from the Dominion, the Imperial capital was quickly on the path toward reconstruction. The castle itself was being saved for the end, but a memorial had been built on the grounds, a memorial that stood at the center of the clearing. It was a simple stone obelisk, marked with the six-pointed star of Adala, a star that symbolized unity.

Etched into the obelisk below the star were the names of those who had given their lives in the war. The names of Tyvarion Il'Vir, Nora Arden, and Rex Kelsar could be found on that list, with hundreds of others joining them. Jag had offered to put the names of the people in the Dominion who died in the eruption of Trajnheim, but the Warlord had declined. Although he greatly appreciated the sentiment, he declared that the Dominion remembered its fallen in a different way.

The rest of the courtyard had been repaired. The stones beneath their feet were polished and smooth, although Wyatt could still remember the exact spot where Necron had stood wearing his mother's skin. He would never forget it.

"Is Grace going to be here?" he asked, shaking himself out of his memories. He tried to sound as casual as possible. He hadn't seen her in months, either. Their work had pulled them apart.

Jag smirked at him. "So that's why you're looking around the courtyard so hopefully. Yes, Wyatt, my sister will be here. But it's a pretty open area, where do you plan to steal her away to?"

Wyatt gave Jag a sour look. "I'd just like to point out that while you may be the Emperor, I am not afraid to kick you."

The three of them laughed. Tythas gripped Wyatt's shoulder and pointed toward the memorial obelisk. Wyatt turned to look at it again.

Grace stood at the base of it, reading the names and the sentiments that had been etched into the stone. Wyatt couldn't see her face, but he had the strange feeling in his gut that she was smiling. He just stood and stared at her for a time, drinking her in. He felt strangely warm and fuzzy inside.

Jag nudged him. Wyatt tried to hit him, but missed.

"Just go already," snickered Jag, nudging him before wrapping an arm around his shoulder in a brotherly way. "You guys haven't talked for months. She misses you. She told me so."

Tythas also nudged him. "Me, too. I'm getting old, Wyatt, and if you two don't get together soon, I'm going to miss the good parts. So get going."

Wyatt sighed in defeat and steeled himself. He didn't know why he was so nervous. He hadn't been this nervous when he was staring Necron down. Even dying hadn't made him this nervous.

With a final, resolute nod, Wyatt pushed his leering friends off of him and walked steadily toward Grace. His heart was pounding in his chest, and his palms were sweating. Great.

He stepped up next to her, hastily trying to dry his hands off on his pants. She was smiling slightly, and her eyes weren't sad or wistful. She seemed genuinely happy, even in the face of such a stark reminder of all that they had lost. She did not, however, appear to have noticed him.

He looked up at the obelisk. "Hi," he said simply, keeping his eyes ahead and trying to keep his expression even.

She blinked and turned to look at him. Wyatt wasn't looking at her, but he could feel her surprise. She blinked again, not moving.

He glanced over at her and couldn't help himself. His face broke into a stupid grin.

She looked like she wanted to punch him and hug him at the same time, but she opted for the latter. She threw her arms around his neck and pressed tight against him, clinging to his chest. Wyatt hugged her back, gripping her under the arms and lifting her up. He spun her around happily, laughing as he did.

Finally, he set her down. She loosened, but didn't break away, her arms still around his neck. She just smiled at him, a smile that made his heart feel like it was in his face.

Neither of them said anything for a long time. They were too caught up in the moment, too lost in one another. It had been nearly six months since they had seen each other, but it had felt like ages to Wyatt. But now that he had her in his arms, could see her and smell her and touch her again, it felt like it had been no time at all. He hadn't forgotten a single inch of her.

"You're real," she breathed, still smiling at him. "I didn't... I didn't know it would be so long. If I had known, I wouldn't have taken on so much. I missed you so badly. I'm sorry, Wyatt."

He grinned at her again. "Don't be. You were needed where you went, and I was needed where I went. We're together again. That's what matters." Grace had been called to virtually every corner of the continent; the world was in dire need of trained, driven Vitamancers, and Grace was both of those things. She'd been traveling and healing as many people as she could, as well as helping to repair the small communities that had been caught up in the destruction. Her work was invaluable to restoring the Empire; while Jag worked from the heart of it, Grace worked from the edges, helping to restore and strengthen it wherever she went. She was the perfect ambassador.

Grace nodded, wiping her eyes. "You'll be here, for a little bit?"

Wyatt looked out over the courtyard. "Yeah, for a few days. Once this meeting is over I have a couple of days to myself. After that, I'm going back to the Dominion to help finalize their plans for a new capital. Once that happens, I'm going to relinquish my title and... I don't know. Go somewhere new. Find my own place."

Grace raised an eyebrow. "What do you mean?"

He shrugged. "Shem told me that I was the first Omnimancer, and that after me, one Omnimancer would always be born to help keep the rest of the Aspects in balance. It got me thinking that... well, that we should have a place to keep our knowledge. So that if I die and this next Omnimancer has no idea what he is and what his responsibilities are, he'll... well, have somewhere to go, I guess. A safe haven, where he can learn about his new powers away from the rest of the world."

Grace cocked her head. "That sounds like a wonderful idea, Wyatt. Where are you going to build it?"

Wyatt shrugged again, smiling sheepishly. "No clue. I haven't gotten that far. But that's my plan, eventually. What about you? Back to saving lives after all this is done?"

Grace smiled lightly. "No, I don't think so. Tythas asked me to join the Council. The current High Vitamancer is also the Magistrix of the Academy, and she wants to devote her time to that work. There aren't as many of us as the other Aspects, and Tythas thinks that with my youth, my power, and my diplomatic history, I'll be the best fit as a replacement."

Wyatt grinned and squeezed her shoulders. "That's great. Congratulations, Grace."

She smiled up at him. "Although I'm still not as famous as you. Everyone wants the Omnimancer to sit at their table, to offer them counsel. Have you heard the names they're calling you?"

"Unfortunately," said Wyatt with a roll of his eyes. "I just try to ignore it. My job isn't to be famous."

Grace laughed, her eyes shining. "Oh come on. I bet you call yourself Wyatt Brightblade when nobody's looking."

Wyatt snorted. "Right."

Jag and Tythas, unable to maintain their distance any longer, strolled leisurely up to the two of them. Grace finally broke her hug, but kept one arm wrapped gently around Wyatt's as she stood next to him, facing her friends. She gave his arm an affectionate squeeze.

"And so the lost lovers are reunited at last," mused Tythas in a nauseatingly philosophical tone. "Have you two come down from the clouds yet?"

Grace made a face at him. "Don't forget, old man, that I'm not afraid to hit you, even if you are my boss."

Jag and Tythas shared a look. "They're so alike it's disgusting," remarked Jag with a smirk. "Always with the violence and the threats, never any respect!"

Tythas elbowed him. "Hey, that's my line."

Behind Jag and Tythas, Wyatt noted that a large procession of people was walking into the courtyard. By their clothes, he assumed they were soldiers of the Empire, but he wasn't sure what they were doing here. He hadn't been told to expect any knights.

Jag saw Wyatt's face and turned to look for a moment before turning back. "Oh yeah. The greater body of the army returned to Farillyon, so I invited some of the higher-ups to join us. They have a say in these matters, too, and I figured that they'd be the hardest to convince of our new stance on tolerance and cooperation."

Wyatt had to agree with that. "A good plan. I suppose we should go have a word with them."

The four of them approached the group of knights and introduced themselves. As they exchanged pleasantries, Wyatt could see the other groups arriving as well. He saw many of his friends from the Dominion, including Salif, Hakim, and Yasmir. They all waved happily at him as they entered the courtyard.

Wyatt also saw representatives from Porkhoya, tall men dressed in dark robes adorned with furs and bones. They stood apart from the rest, still trying to assess their place in the collective and find a way to cautiously integrate themselves.

Tythas strode over to them, shaking their hands and welcoming every one of them. Jag and Grace and a few of the soldiers followed him, and it wasn't long before they were all talking and smiling. Wyatt could see now what Jag had been talking about earlier; they were far less cold than Apep had been. They carried themselves with a quiet kind of respect and confidence.

"So much for farming," came a voice from Wyatt's left that was both unmistakably familiar and impossibly nostalgic. He felt his knees weaken as he turned quickly to see Desmond, his best friend, standing next to him with a wry smile on his face.

Wyatt felt like he couldn't breathe, stunned by a face that he thought he would never see again. After the fight with Necron, Wyatt had searched Desmond out, only to find that his unit was one of those lost to Apep. Wyatt had searched for him, but every member of his company had been killed or had disappeared. Wyatt had carved Desmond's name onto the memorial himself. But here he was, healthy and dressed in his best military regalia.

Wyatt stepped forward and embraced his friend, still stunned and at a complete loss for words. He'd already been forced to let go of his past and his childhood; he had burned it and left it behind in Ven. Yet here was Desmond, a link to the person Wyatt had been before all of this. A reminder that life had been normal, however long ago it felt.

"How… how are you alive?" breathed Wyatt, stepping back and gripping Desmond by the shoulders. He inspected his old friend closely, but aside from a few scars and a deep tan, he looked the same as ever.

"Mostly luck," he said with a laugh. "For some reason, Apep left me behind. He didn't kill me when he killed the others. I was pretty wounded, and I crawled around the battlefield for a long time, just trying to get somewhere where I could be found. I happened upon a group of settlers that lived nearby in the neutral zone. They had come to bury the dead and scavenge useful supplies. They took me back to their town and patched me up. I only just made it back to Farillyon."

Desmond shrugged, grinning again. "Dunno. Like I said, it was luck. Blind, dumb luck. But I'm alive, so I'm okay with it. You, on the other hand, have become quite the hero, or so I hear. Wyatt Brightblade! Wyatt Godslayer! Wyatt Stormcaller!"

Wyatt winced. "Easy with the nicknames. I'd say it was mostly luck for me, too. It's a long story."

Desmond nodded, clapping him on the shoulder and squeezing. "Well, you can tell me sometime. Maybe once things calm down a little more around here. I'm told that you're one of the reasons that I'm out of a job. Pulling back the army, eh?"

Wyatt chuckled. "That's the new Emperor's directive. I may have... suggested it, but it was his call. Are you complaining? After nearly dying I would think you'd like a vacation."

Desmond's gaze drifted away, toward the horizon. "A vacation would certainly be nice, but I honestly don't know what I'm going to do."

The two of them took some time to walk around the courtyard, reminiscing about the old days. Wyatt gave him a rough overview of where his road had taken him, but he knew that he'd need a lot more time to tell Desmond the real story. Mostly he was just glad to have his best friend back in his life again.

After a time, Desmond stopped him. "Introduce me to your allies," he said with a smile. "I've heard all the stories about your brave band of heroes. It would be nice to put faces to their names."

Wyatt took Des toward the groups of people that were eating and socializing in the courtyard. First he introduced Desmond to Jag, and Wyatt saw an instantaneous respect between the two of them. They shared war stories and Jag thanked Desmond for his service. It wasn't long before another diplomat snatched Jag's attention away, and as he left, Wyatt told Desmond that Jag was the new Emperor. Desmond nearly fell over.

"You could've told me that before you introduced me," sputtered Desmond as he watched Jag leave. "Couldn't he wear a crown or something?"

Wyatt let out a small laugh. "He likes to keep it simple."

He introduced Grace next, who gave Wyatt another long hug when she came near him. Desmond eyed the two of them with a bemused smile and winked at Wyatt when she couldn't see. He grinned back.

"So you're Desmond," she said, shaking his hand. "It's nice to meet you. Wyatt told us a lot of things about you. Good things, I think, although I'm sure there's more to tell."

"And that would make you Grace," he replied with a sly, charming smile. "I've heard things about you too, but I don't think I've heard enough."

Grace looked over at Wyatt with a warm smile. "Yeah, I think we have a lot to tell you."

Wyatt returned her smile, and for a brief moment he forgot where he was.

"What about this Tythas I've heard so many stories about?" asked Desmond pointedly. "Even the other recruit soldiers have heard of him. He's a legend in the army. I want to meet the man behind the legend."

Wyatt motioned toward his mentor, who was directing the group of Watchers from Porkhoya around the courtyard, introducing them to different groups of important people. Wyatt caught Tythas's eye, motioning the old man over. He broke from his group with an apologetic bow, leaving them with some of his colleagues from the Council and walking over to Wyatt.

"Vance," began Wyatt, motioning to Desmond, "this is my friend Desmond, from Ven. We grew up together. Des, this is Vance Tythas, my friend and my teacher."

Tythas smiled as his eyes drifted to Desmond. They appraised each other for a moment. Tythas's mouth twitched, but Wyatt didn't notice. They shook hands pleasantly and engaged in some small talk.

Wyatt wasn't listening. Grace had caught his eye again, smiling at him from across the courtyard. His insides felt itchy. It was a little bit stupid how easily she could destroy his focus.

He turned back to find Desmond walking away, headed for a group of soldiers. He could see Jag heading for the tents, where a small stage and podium had been constructed. He smiled, prepared to hear a speech he knew Jag had been rehearsing for many weeks.

Tythas gripped Wyatt's arm. "After the ceremony," he said softly, his smile faded, "we should talk in private, before we have to go our separate ways."

Wyatt looked at his friend with a puzzled smile. "Yeah, Vance, that's fine. Just come and grab me whenever Jag's done."

He flashed Grace another smile and turned to watch Jag's speech, to watch the beginning of their new world.

"And so, my friends," concluded Jag, speaking loudly over the crowd and motioning toward them, "I hope that today marks the beginning of the next step in our history. I hope that today, we can move forward and build a new kind of world together, a world where everyone has a place. A world where we don't need to be at war in order to settle our differences."

The crowd applauded Jag as he stepped down from the podium. He motioned to the table that had been set up nearby, where his scribes had drawn papers for treaties of peace between the communities. Warlord Felah and Chief Watcher Yxashi both stepped forward with their assistants to join Jag and a few Imperial military commanders around the table, ready to find the common ground that they all so desperately needed.

Wyatt watched from the side, pleased to see everything going so well. He could almost feel Shem watching on approvingly. This was exactly what the cat had wanted; the children of Adala coexisting in peace and prosperity, building a world together, not separate worlds apart. The process had begun two thousand years later than his patron would've liked, but Wyatt knew that he'd be pleased that they got there in the end. Wyatt was pleased too, since his job would be easier with everyone getting along.

Jag was calling for Tythas, but the old man was conspicuously absent from the table. Wyatt looked around the crowd curiously. They were going to need the head of the Adept Council if they were going to finalize these peace treaties. Where had he gotten to?

And then he saw it. Once again, his eyes fell upon his best friend, and the breath left his lungs. Time seemed to slow down as he tried to comprehend what he was seeing. Desmond and Tythas were also apart from the crowd, far to the side of the courtyard. Tythas was rearing backward, caught off guard. But worst of all was Desmond, who Wyatt couldn't even recognize.

Great scaly wings had erupted from his back, a gleaming crimson in the afternoon sun. His eyes were a solid red, like they were made of blood. His hands were gone, replaced by razor-sharp, scaly claws. His skin darkened and hardened, taking on the same crimson sheen as his impossible wings. His bladed hands slashed at Tythas, an inhuman, monstrous grin on his face.

Wyatt was running toward them now, drawing his sword as he did, but he knew he was too late. He watched in agonizing detail as one claw raked across Tythas's chest just as the other swung in low, arcing up into his stomach. Desmond, or whatever Desmond had become, stiffened his hand as his sharp fingertips plunged into Tythas's torso, right under his ribs.

Tythas gasped and stared at Desmond in shock as Desmond's arm plunged deeper into his chest, stopping where Wyatt knew the old man's heart would be. He was off the ground, now, raised two feet into the air by the strength of that monstrous, horrible arm.

"NO!" shouted Wyatt, hurling a wild blast of lightning at the two of them. He knew that hurting Tythas was a danger, but he had no choice.

The crackling bolt arced toward the two of them, but somehow Desmond caught it with his free hand, batting it aside as if it had been nothing. His other arm held Tythas's sputtering, dying form up in the air above him as blood dripped from the old man's mouth, falling onto Desmond's twisted face.

Desmond's wings stretched out, giving a great beat of the air. Wyatt felt it against his chest as they continued to beat. With a few more flaps, Desmond dragged Tythas into the air before Wyatt could reach them.

Wyatt leapt into the sky without another thought, still too far away to do anything but shout. Desmond flew fast, even with the added burden, swooping in over the crowd. Wyatt gave it everything he had, doing his best to catch the two of them.

Just as he thought he would, Desmond finally released Tythas. He threw the Adept's body down toward the earth, toward the table where the crowd stood gaping in shock. Wyatt saw Tythas's bleeding body flying downward, saw Desmond flying away, and made his choice. He swooped in low, trying to catch Tythas's body, to stop it from smashing into the ground, but he was still too late. He missed it.

Vance's broken form crashed onto the table where Jag and the other leaders had been writing their treaty. Blood splattered all over them as the table exploded, casting wood and papers in every direction. The crowd shrieked and scrambled apart as soldiers drew their blades.

Wyatt let out a frustrated scream and surged back into the air, intending to pursue the monster until it killed him. He could hear the thing laughing, a hollow, high-pitched voice that was like nothing Wyatt had ever heard. He heard Grace over the noise of the crowd, trying to get his attention.

"Wyatt!" she shouted, crouched at Tythas's limp form. "You're the only other Vitamancer here! I need your help!"

Wyatt swore loudly, breaking off his chase and flying back to the group. He landed next to Grace and Tythas, crouching down, ready to do whatever she needed. He had no idea how to actually heal someone, so he simply placed his hands on hers and channeled his power into her.

He thought of all the good things that Tythas had done for them. He thought of a new, reinvigorated Adept Council, led by an eccentric old man. He thought of his mother, of his grandfather. He thought of Grace. He poured his love and his need into that energy, letting the light flow into Grace. He gave her everything he had.

Tythas's mouth was moving, but no words were coming out. His whole body glowed golden with the effort of their healing. His eyes seemed to search the skies for something he could not quite find. Their tears streamed onto his fallen form, but finally, his eyes stopped searching. His mouth stopped moving. All the power in the world would not have saved him from the damage that Desmond had done. Vance Tythas was dead.

Christopher Clark spent his childhood filling notebooks with tales of powerful wizards, terrible monsters, and most importantly, genuine heroes. He went to college to earn an English degree before putting his studies on hold to chase his dream of becoming a published author.